Stella Scura: Dark Star Rising

Volume One

Book One: Glory of The Great Dame

Book Two: A Little Girl Grows Up

A Novel by

J. Matthew Neal

Stella Scura: Dark Star Rising
Volume One

Book One: Glory of The Great Dame
Book Two: A Little Girl Grows Up

Astronomical photos courtesy NASA/Jet Propulsion Laboratory/Space Science Institute.

Printed in the United States of America
Dunn Avenue Press
Muncie, Indiana 47304

ISBN 978-1-7349372-0-6

And a blind girl shall lead them . . .

In late 2028, the United States of America is enjoying its greatest prosperity in over sixty years, as new nuclear fusion energy sources and economic policies have placed the USA at the top of the world.

Its leader is one of the most beloved Presidents of all time, a philanthropic humanitarian whose platform is to make the world a better place. But pain and heartache change even the best of people.

But only a handful in the inner circle know this President's secret agenda – that of an angry woman whose immense personal losses have resulted in the assimilation of an arsenal of nuclear weapons with the power to destroy the Earth a hundred times over. One belligerent country has almost been blown off the map - who's next?

Destiny awaits a blind eighteen-year-old girl, long believed dead, raised in a remote part of the country, a victim of the same act of terrorism. Hidden from the world for a reason. But there comes a time for every child to grow up and learn the truth about her family.

This world needs a hero – to save it from itself. But can the President of the United States learn forgiveness from a blind teenager to become what she once was and make the world a better place? Or will she manipulate her newly-found niece and use her as a pawn to become ruler of the world?

Author Foreword

This project is of particular personal significance because I created the character of Paige Marshall in 1980 as a brief sketch which was going to evolve into a novel which never materialized due to lack of time. This epic tome is a sequel to my last two novels: *Ontario Lacus (2008)* and *Americium the Beautiful (2010).* I had originally intended to release this book right after *ATB* (they were started simultaneously), but the length of this book and time issues caused its delay by eleven years. In 2010 the year 2028 seemed far off, but not so much now, and some of the then-futuristic events will likely seem absurd in 2021.

For the sake of continuity, I have included the epilogue from *Ontario Lacus* which sets the scene for some of what is to come. This book will make much more sense if you have read the books above plus my first book, *Specific Gravity (2007).*

From a historical perspective, a few paragraphs of the prologue are taken from the original 1980 Dark Star manuscript, which only consisted of a few thousand words and was never finished.

Dark Star Rising deals with roughly a four-month period in teenage Paige's life. There are undoubtedly spiritual overtones, although Paige is probably the one unbeliever in this book about her journey.

I had created some other minor characters who never came to fruition. Some would eventually become *Dr. Wendy's Science Squad,* referenced often in my other novels but never seen. Possibly the worst group of TV superheroes ever assembled (in the mid-1990s), they now all play a major role in *Dark Star Rising,* especially the descendant of possibly the greatest astrophysicist of all time: Johnny Kepler, *Gravi-Golfer*. They are the unsung heroes of this book. Yes, I created characters such as *Sparkus, Santaman, Red Skeleton,* and *Admiral Angler* in my youth, so it's good I had another career path to fall back on.

Most superhero tales focus on the hero, and the alter ego is only there as a plot mechanism. Make no mistake that this story is about Paige Marshall first and foremost. It is rare that the "secret identity" does anything of substance in fiction.

But Paige, like most teenagers, has a short attention span and tires quickly of being *Stella,* and, after a few months of world-saving and being on TV shows, dedicates her life to doing something more, after almost dying, of course. So, what would happen if the accomplishments of the alter ego were destined to be far more important than that of the hero?

I also explore that most powerful of experiences: first love. Paige is blind and generally oblivious to how beautiful she truly is; but no guys take her seriously at school, as she's always getting in trouble and shooting her mouth off; social graces are not one of her better traits. But she meets someone who will change her life . . . at a career fair, of all places.

There is a deep philosophical message about man tampering with the future and the danger of holding one being up above all others. So get ready and enjoy, because this book will take you a while to finish.

Epilogue to Ontario Lacus

October, 2012
Butner Women's Federal Prison Camp
Butner, North Carolina

"Hey, McPherson—visitor for you," the heavyset female guard said, entering the camp's library.

"Visitor? I don't get many visitors these days." Her parents hardly ever came after what she'd done. It was hard to blame them.

Dr. Rita McPherson, wearing the signature red cotton jumpsuit of the camp's tenants, began wheeling her chair out the library door through the corridor of the minimum-security facility's cafeteria towards the visitor's area. No bars, locked doors, or even armed guards in this place, which looked more like a college dormitory than a correctional facility.

"Where you goin', McPherson?" the guard asked, laughing as she came up behind her.

"Visitation pod. You said I had someone there."

"Not there." The guard pointed in the opposite direction. "Your VIP visitor's in the warden's office. The orders from the Bureau of Prisons say that you're to meet with her in private. You must really rate for that stuff."

"What? Who is it?"

The guard held her hand up high. "Tall blonde lady, the one who was on the cover of Sports Illustrated a couple of months ago. Wearing a military uniform. An admiral or something."

"Sports Illustrated?" She wasn't much into sports, especially the esoteric one she thought of when such a visitor came to mind.

She wheeled over to the warden's office, where several plain-clothes men ushered her in as she saw the U.S. Surgeon General looking out the warden's window. She had forgotten how big she was in person, now wearing her navy blue dress uniform. She'd heard about that. A pretty good media vehicle for the tall extravert.

She had also heard about Wendy's massive self-makeover; the nation's chief doctor looked very different since dropping fifty pounds and working out four hours a day. She had decided that her poor eating habits were a bad example to set for the millions of kids she loved. She therefore had decided to take on the obesity epidemic.

"Wendy? You look so, well . . . not like yourself."

"Yeah. An out-of-shape Surgeon General isn't a great image."

"Why are you here, after all this time?"

"I just wanted to say hi. I know it must be tough."

Rita shrugged. "It's not so bad, I guess. I get to work in the library, and the food is actually pretty good. The routine is pretty easy, for being in jail. It can be boring at times. But peaceful."

"Probably better than working for Malachi Argon, huh?"

"Got that right. It's good to see you, though. I heard you made the Olympic team and won the gold medal. That's pretty amazing."

"I guess so. The shot put gold only matters because it set an example, that I cleaned up my life. I guess you can understand that."

"Yes, I suppose." She looked up at Wendy's black name tag, which now read "Gallinsworth Darkkin" instead of "Williams." She wasn't able to keep up on the news, and she missed that one. "Why are you using your maiden name again? And your father's?"

"Well . . . maybe it's because I'm a 'maiden' again, and to honor my dad." She saw the absence of a ring on her big left hand.

"Huh. I'm sorry, I didn't know. When did that happen?"

"About a year ago. It was a mutually agreed upon decision, beneficial to all. I guess my self-centeredness and obsession has its consequences. Not everything always works out."

"The kids?"

"Stan lives in Alexandria, so we share them. It's over, and it's really okay." Wendy paused and took a sip of water.

She tapped her hand on the table. "You didn't really come here to socialize or discuss your divorce, did you?"

"No." Wendy walked towards the window and looked out. "I need to know one thing, Rita. And you need to be honest with me."

"Can we talk in here?" She looked around suspiciously.

"No problem. My people scoured the office for bugs. The EMF generators don't allow any electronic devices to work in here."

"EMF generators? What are we dealing with of that magnitude, and what can I help you with you don't already know?"

"Here, decide for yourself." Wendy pulled out a manila folder and handed it to her. "Genetics, or the perversion of such. No one knows more than you about it."

"Malachi Argon did."

"Huh." Wendy laughed. "I mean no one *alive*."

She opened the folder and began browsing. "What *is* this?"

"Printout of genetic sequences of a two year old female toddler. Several metalloproteins which are not present in any other human being, or any known life form. Including my late brother."

She looked at them for several minutes. "It . . . looks like it could be from a child of yours and Jay Mendoza's. But this *can't* be your daughter's DNA. We didn't do anything to you while you were with us. And Jaime isn't her father, of course."

"That's right, or it could be another possibility. Any other way those mutated genes could have gotten in there?"

She thought for a minute. "Oh, my God, I didn't think of that. I didn't even know she had a baby. That's wonderful."

"Yes. Aurora was born about two years ago. About nine months younger than Cassie. But the DNA patterns here are way more than the addition of some evolved microorganisms as was the case with Travis. This must be *alien,* Rita. What the hell have you done?"

She paused for a few minutes, trying to remember. "I don't know, Wendy. It's like I was guided to do it by some incredibly powerful force. And I was compelled keep it secret."

"*Guided*? That's a load of crap. By whom? God?"

"I can't explain it, but it could've been God, it didn't say. I somehow found something else in Mexico at the Yucatán Peninsula. DNA in addition to the microorganism *Orthogeneticus titania*. Human chromosomes with a 46, XY karyotype."

"*Yucatán Peninsula?* As in the Chicxulub asteroid impact crater?"

She nodded. "Yes, that's right."

"So you're telling me an alien humanoid being was presumably on Earth sixty-five million years ago made of DNA flung to Titan by the meteor crash?" Wendy shook her head. "No way. The genome wouldn't have been compatible with modern man."

"Damn right it's not the same, but it *is* compatible. I don't know what it represents. But I made three doses of serum from that, and two were injected into Bonnie. Your dad took the third, we think, which allowed him to do some pretty amazing things at the end."

"My God. So, in the end, this is all my dad's fault. And mine."

"I didn't tell anyone, not even Dr. Argon. No one else knows." She wheeled herself towards the window, warm sunlight striking her face. "What is Aurora like?"

"She's a beautiful child with dark red hair, tall for her age, and seems normal in most aspects. Oddly, she has complete heterochromia iridum, with a blue and brown eye. Hasn't demonstrated any special intellectual skills or anything like Bonnie, she's a normal kid, like my Cassie. *Almost*."

"So what's the problem, then? You said 'almost.'"

"She's a two-year old who has never been sick with an ear infection or cold, anything. I'm a pediatrician. That's unheard of."

"Or just lucky."

"No." Wendy gulped the rest of her bottled water. "One day I was at their house. I was helping make some spaghetti when Aurora dumped the whole pot of boiling water on herself. I was scared to death. I've seen lots of burn victims in my rehab days."

"Oh, no. Was she burned badly?"

"She stood there, covered in hot spaghetti and boiling water, and laughed. Tried to say 'bath,' but her words aren't so good yet."

"How is that possible?"

"You tell me. There's more. Their cat had kittens a month earlier. Aurora was holding one while she tipped over the pot with the other. Another was on the floor, about a foot from her."

"What happened?"

"The one she was holding was unharmed, like her. But the one on the floor was severely burned. Aurora then started screaming when she saw that one, but she and the other kitten were fine. I had to euthanize the poor thing."

"I don't get it. Are you saying that she's . . . invulnerable?"

Wendy shook her head. "I don't know, but it would seem so, and an animal in direct physical contact shares that quality, it would seem. I don't want to freak anyone out about it, and certainly don't want any of the higher ups to know. What are your thoughts?"

"I have no idea. We had hoped for augmented strength and such, like what Ortho-Man had, but nothing like that. I have no theory on how that's even possible. What is it you want me to do?"

"There is nothing to do. I just need to know what you do."

"Nothing else. Is this of interest to the military?"

"It's of interest to me, nothing more. I have removed all traces of Aurora's DNA records and have replaced them with a synthetic copy. In a year and a half, my tenure as Surgeon General will be up. Then I will be moving to Sacramento, hopefully."

"I had heard that you were the frontrunner for the Republican nomination. I hope you win. But *my* job prospects aren't as good."

"They will be. Understand that, when I flipped out, I had some pretty grandiose ideas. But that's all passed. I *will* be Governor of California. And, someday, I will grant you a pardon for your crimes. In the end, I owe my life to you, and I always repay my debts."

"But, Wendy, this was a *federal* crime, and a Governor can't pardon me. And the crimes didn't happen in California. The only way you can do that is to become . . . President of the United States."

"Yes." Wendy nodded. "That's correct."

"I don't understand." Had she gone off the deep end again?

"You will, in about eight years." The big woman gave her a hug. "I have to go now, and this conversation *never* happened. I'll stay in touch. When you get out next month, I'll take care of you. The world is changing, and the United States will be on top again. I promise. Someday, I will need your help, and I'll be back."

Rita sat there, uncertain what all that meant, as the 195-pound, six-one blonde left, with many unanswered questions.

• • •

Wendy left the camp and entered the rented sportscar in the visitors' lot as her staff drove away in another vehicle.

"What did you and this Rita talk about?" Jay Mendoza asked

curiously, obviously in a hurry to get out of a prison parking lot.

"Just wanted to pay her a visit. We went through a lot."

"Why in the hell did you want me, of all people, to come along?"

"I need a friend, and I don't have that many people I can trust."

"It's October, as in the middle of football season, I shouldn't even be out here. Mike would've gone with you."

"I didn't want Mike, he wouldn't have gone along with this."

"And you think I would?"

She nodded. "I do. I know we may not see each other again for a very long time, but we've been through this together."

"You aren't making any sense. Nothing new."

"Aren't I? I want to change the world, Jay. I have much to make up for. I ruined my marriage, and could have destroyed us all with what I started."

"Rad did a few rotten things, too." Jay peeled out of the parking lot and towards the highway. "You have a great future."

"I can't help what my dad did, but I don't want to ruin a country someday. Our family is going to do great things."

And, someday, her niece would be grown. Nobody else besides her parents and Jay had to know about the special gifts of Aurora Darkkin, most of which were still developing. Not yet, anyway.

And once they did develop, she would need a protector.

She told Jay it would be the era of *Dark Star Rising*.

Prologue I

Seventy million years ago
Delta Quadrant
Thargis Dark Star System
Thonxxeron

The being who felt he was omnipotent was the master of his world; this is what he had always desired, ever since the beginning of his existence an indeterminable time ago. The puny beings his power of matter reorganization had created were at his mercy. Some would say that they were not truly alive, but others would differ, believing that even synthetic life had value. He did not share their ridiculous mantra that all life was valuable and knew they all didn't feel that way, either.

He had patterned them after the genetic material of those from another world, those future beings that could see and feel things of the flesh, which he as an energy being could not, in the same way. He was, in his mind, the best of both worlds: an immensely powerful life force that could also do what Qarr-Rogg and the other energy beings could not.

He ruled as he saw fit, with the pleasures of the body always first and foremost. Everything else would exist to serve him, the one of supreme importance.

He killed most of them with glee, using his physical strength, as converting dark to kinetic energy was simple, giving him the power of flight and the ability to manipulate matter. Yet, a few survived to live on, in the vast garden world of Thonxxeron, the dark star Thargis beaming down its powerful rays.

Why had he thought he could go on this nihilistic quest without repercussions? He somehow knew that it was time to pay for his sins—that the collector was coming for the debt that could never be repaid. He did not care as he pondered this: could even he be destroyed?

He knew he was immortal, but even that was in doubt now. Perhaps he had made unwise choices. Beings of the flesh did that quite often, he learned, which was why he wanted to be one. It was not a desire shared by any of the others. He was not alone, however. They knew what he was doing. Because they—the elders—knew most everything.

But they didn't know all, he knew. He was sick of their kind.

And, one day, he would make them pay.

That day, unfortunately for him, was not today.

He was called Tharr-Kann Axoon. That was his "common" name in the unpronounceable language of the energy beings which he once was. He was not to use it much longer, and his name would not be mentioned with reverence, he knew.

The ones whom he once resembled: Gart-Monn, Qarr-Rogg, the other elders (although this term was misleading, as all were as old as time itself)—came for him to end his reign of terror. He thought that hiding in the past (intangibility and time travel were within his grasp as well as theirs) would shield him from them, but he was wrong; their hatred of him had grown as vast as his of them. While he was mighty, the powers of dark energy allowed him almost complete control over matter—his power paled to the beings of pure energy he once was. He learned that he could not transform himself back into a pure dark matter life form, but he had nevertheless planned for such an event to ensure his survival.

He had anticipated this encounter and had long ago dispatched his genetic material to the planet Terra, whom he had modeled himself and the other beings after; those unique beings who would exist in the future. It would land there for recollection millions of their years later.

And although he would be vanquished today, one thing was certain in his mind.

Someday, Tharr-Kann Axoon would rise again to rule another world. The world he had patterned himself and his world after. Time mattered little to him, and he could wait an eternity.

He disappeared as quickly as he originated, but his vast intellect knew one thing: he would one day return, this time to the real planet where life began.

And then he would again be king, no matter how many eons that took. And there would be no one to stop him by then. He would also have his revenge on those who tried to destroy him.

Someday, I, Tharr-Kann, shall live again, no matter how long it takes.

• • •

2023 A.D.
Star-Forming Region W30H
Milky Way Galaxy

The universe was unimaginably vast, although finite, containing hundreds of billions of galaxies. The limits of this were known by those who moved at the speed of light (and who could seemingly exceed that velocity by transitioning through wormholes and subspace), those who had names unpronounceable to most life forms, even the most intelligent. Genderless, formless beings whose mere existence was beyond the comprehension of the simple creatures known as humans.

Yet one among them many eons ago sought to be like one of these primitive life forms, to experience the basal pleasures they did. This great experiment, condemned by the energy beings, had led to incalculable disaster. In the scope of the universe, however, it was of minimal importance. The future, however, was uncertain even to them. This was a limitation they had embraced.

They were composed of dark energy and the non-baryonic matter which made up over ninety percent of the known universe, its properties mysterious to the lower beings, as it should be since they could not understand its wonders. Not yet, anyway, but the humans had apparently discovered its existence. Harnessing it was another matter.

It was their life force that could repel gravity, the essence that kept the universe expanding. The reason that was necessary was not known even to them, but without it, most of the universe's energy and mass would not even exist. How even *they* came into existence was a mystery; for as long as the energy beings have known, they always were. The time-space continuum was fluid to them, as they could time-travel and span eons within a nanosecond, or traverse billions of light years instantly.

Yet, they were forever linked by the one whose folly showed them that not even one of their greatest of intellectuals was infallible: Tharr-Kann Axoon. The one among them who had used his powers of matter manipulation to re-create himself in the image of living baryonic matter—flesh. To enjoy its pleasures, and to destroy it. This, they had allowed him to do by not stopping him.

They thought they had destroyed him, but that did not change the evil that had infiltrated their kind, something not experienced before. How did he come to be? The choice now was whether to make it right or not. All of them had decided against repeating history. All except one, the maverick among pure energy beings.

Qarr-Rogg marveled at the third planet from the star Sol, near the Perseus spiral arm—the edge of the galaxy—as his energy aura formed a pulsatile mass. His colleague materialized near him and peered outward for an indeterminable period of time, as temporal space was fluid.

"What troubles you, Qarr?" the rebellious Gart-Monn asked, communicating telepathically in their native mathematical language with the society's elder, an interesting concept as all were as old as time itself. So they thought. But even they were not omnipotent. Even they knew they had limitations.

Their collective power had defeated their greatest threat. Who knew if they could survive him a second time?

He vowed he would return with a vengeance, even if it took millions of years for him to reconstitute himself from his atoms that were scattered across the universe in various time periods.

Millions of years allowed one to plan a formidable strategy.

Qarr-Rogg hesitated as the incredible senses of his energy form examined the planet. After an indeterminable period of time, his essence finally spoke.

"Tharr-Kann destroyed his race long ago. Beings of pure dark energy are we, made of the greatest known force in the universe, yet misunderstood by the lower beings, who lack the intellect to perceive it, let alone control it; weak when dispersed, yet mighty beyond comprehension when concentrated, as in the great dark star Thargis. We are those beings whose life force holds the universe together and causes it to expand simultaneously. We can transform our energy into conventional matter, and vice versa, although we have chosen to remain in this form, given its usefulness in traveling through the cosmos. While we are devoid of emotion, this one among us—Tharr—wanted to mimic the beings of this world, the things they felt, the joys of the flesh. He wanted to be the last of his kind. He succeeded. These above all other life forms in the universe did we cherish. Transported through the space-time portal to the distant past he went to carry out his grand vision. Yet, it took almost all of our collective resources to destroy him."

"You do not really believe he has been destroyed since his genetic material remains?" Gart-Monn replied.

"No, I don't, and there remains the remotest of chances that he shall someday rise again. What has been done?"

"You soliloquize over that which we have debated for millions of years. And, yet, his seed remained, many eons ago, on the planet known as Terra, or Earth, as it once was—he was intent on his reincarnation one day, in the image of beings he patterned himself after. The giant bolide we had sent destroyed what was left."

"That is untrue, Gart-Monn, the one who claims to be the wisest of us all. You ignore what is surely known to you, as one of us who brags that he knows everything. Somehow the last seeds arrived, by chance, on the giant moon of the sixth planet from the star these beings call Sol, after the meteor struck Terra. I know you had something to do with it. You could have destroyed it with your powers, yet you chose to create this ridiculous chain of events. An unacceptably convoluted process."

"I have no secrets from anyone."

"No, you have much that you hide, as usual. Tens of millions of years ago, you said that, in the future, there will be one worthy to possess the power of dark energy, appropriately called the Dark Star. You said no one would ever find it. You were wrong, because you directed one of the primitive beings to the land now known to them as Mexico, where scant genetic material remained. There can be no stopping now the terrible wrath of what was once Tharr-Kann, who made a valiant attempt to continue his lineage. Let us stop it now, before it is too late."

"What is, is. We have taken a solemn vow never to interfere again. We should have never done so before. What I have done, I did to rectify the grave wrong that we caused. The combination of one of their greatest intellects with the power of Thargis seemed logical in their evolution."

"Gart-Monn, your hypocrisy is disgusting for one who claims to have no emotion. Yes, it is as I had suspected. It was *you* that had allowed that to happen. Because of you, it is already too late."

"I did what I thought was right. You, on the other hand, who have never dared to do anything other than for yourself, one who always agrees with the consensus, have no right to quarrel with me. Begone, as your hubris disgusts me as well."

"*Hubris?* How dare you address me that way, equally arrogant one? And so did Tharr-Kann do what *he* thought was right; what makes you any different? And how will we know, Gart-Monn? What Tharr-Kann did was inexcusable. He used the dark energy—as energy and matter are convertible, per the First Theorem—and created a duplicate planet, the beautiful Thonxxeron, illuminated by the dark star Thargis; so much like this planet, with synthetic beings based on the humans; he killed almost everyone so that he could reign supreme, with a kingdom of one. We should not have interfered. You may have started it all over again. We took a vow. Our interference and those of Tharr-Kann have ruined a civilization.

"This is why we must rectify it, Qarr. Let our meddling not ruin another one. This one will be destroyed without the Dark Star. Let the brief existence of Thonxxeron not be in vain."

"For one who is so critical, you have little insight. It was a world that would not have existed anyway, so it matters not. The remaining inhabitants died off long ago."

"But it *does* matter, Qarr. Life, even synthetic life patterned after the then-future beings of the Sol system, is precious and valuable," Gart-Monn said.

"*Why?* There is no logical basis for that declaration. The Terrans are as ants to us—why should we care, in any case? There are many other civilizations that could use our powers and knowledge since you are intent on continuing your interference where it is unwanted. There are beings who care far more about their planet than those of this world. They have wasted their natural resources and polluted their planet while accumulating weapons of war and failing to care for those who have little. Selfish creatures are they, one above all others in particular."

"That was the reasoning of Tharr-Kann and the cause of his eventual doom. And remember that there may be one, the Creator, who is to us as we are to them."

"The Creator? We, who know all, know of no such entity. Therefore, it cannot exist, per our physical laws."

"Again, your arrogance is legendary, and we do not 'know all.' Just because you do not know something does not banish it from existence. And the return of one such as Tharr-Kann will never happen."

"What if it does?" Qarr-Rogg asked. "What will you do then? Go back in time and fix it with another convoluted plan?"

"You know that such a feat is beyond even our powers, Qarr. No, then, only one of the purest character, of humility, one who has known rejection and the most profound of disabilities and disappointment, who will champion for all of them, will be their redemption, the one who shall prevail over all evil. I can see the future of one that shall do many good deeds. One who will rise to power not with physical gifts but by the mere fact that she will eventually choose *not* to use them. One who be revered because she shall, in time, shun the glory bestowed upon her."

"Impossible. I cannot believe any being with such powers would willingly *not* use them for personal gain, Gart. Completely illogical. Such power would be exploited to its fullest by any of these lesser organisms."

"I disagree, Qarr. The curious paradox is that this ultimate being is destined to forever live in the shadow of her vociferous alter ego, who will someday become great beyond measure, celebrated by her followers as one of their finest leaders."

"Again, you see one of only many possible futures, as we all can; just because you believe it does not mean yours is the correct one. The true existence of this Creator you believe in is still a mystery, even to us, the greatest intellects in the universe. Your Dark Star may instead become evil beyond our immeasurable imaginations. How could you not foresee this?"

"Your arrogance is disturbing," Gart-Monn said. "There are other great intellects besides us; only you could believe that we are unique. Do you forget the one of this world I touched through the power of mere thought? The one whose womb carried the Dark Star is not so inferior to us. While a terribly flawed mortal of mere flesh and blood, she has discovered one of many steps towards harnessing the greatness of nuclear fusion. The vast ability of dark energy shall belong to her offspring, through the great power of fate."

"Yes, fate—that *you* have manipulated, Gart-Monn. And you see what their civilization has done with the abuse of their technology. In their Second World War, one known as the President obliterated two cities of a great island nation with the crude technology of uranium and plutonium fission bombs. The gift of atomic energy, ultimately used for destruction."

"True, but he thought he would be saving more lives by ending that war early."

"Has their society not learned that violence is not the answer to solving anything?"

"Yes, perhaps that was an unfortunate decision, but another President challenged his country to reach their lifeless satellite, spawning their space exploration program. Despite his death by an evil one, his example inspired rudimentary space travel. Another inspiring man, who for some reason faced discrimination because of his skin's greater melanin content, inspired many to campaign for equality among the races. Why would they hate each other because of increased melanin, such a trivial thing? Yet, he perished as well, felled by an assassin.

"And it has come full circle. Now, another of their so-called Presidents possesses unprecedented power and popularity beyond measure, unchallenged by any of their legislators as other countries cower in fear of this great superpower, lest they risk destruction by this megalomaniacal leader. And you debate things such as the Creator. Your dismissal of our teachings is of equal arrogance."

"I grow weary of this perpetual debate, it is of no consequence or purpose. We shall never agree on anything, so let us leave this place to its sorry fate so we can accomplish something of more significance, Qarr-Rogg."

"Yet, we know it must be true, as the world tends towards greater entropy or disorganization, and beings could not exist with the disheveled randomness that is the universe without some force to shape it. What you see is a mere child, with the power to lay waste to another civilization, perhaps to disrupt the entire fabric of the universe. Why do you care for the humans? Why meddle in their inferior world? They are mere insects to us, not worthy of another thought. And why would a descendant of Tharr-Kann be any better than him? Why not the purest of life forms, such as us—we who are as old as the universe itself."

"Because, Qarr, despite your insistence that these beings are evil, and therefore beneath our consideration, there is a spark of greatness in this one, demonstrated even as a child—the only descendant of Tharr-Kann Axoon. Five Earth years from now, this female will be a grown woman who can be the greatest leader of them all. She has the need to excel, the pain of disability and rejection that we cannot even imagine as perfect beings. What we have lost long ago, the need to learn, to achieve, to slowly gain knowledge, not knowing what it is like to lack something—because we can have anything we desire within a picosecond. The last remains of Tharr-Kann were found via robotic technology, in addition to the extremophile bacteria with enormous regenerative problems which developed by natural evolution; Tharr-Kann's genetic material was incorporated into the DNA of her mother, another one of great intellect, by my direction—a mind unique that I have touched. She shall share the secrets of energy with other ones of honesty, to end this world's toxic fossil fuel emissions to provide for the future. For all, not just for the most powerful nation."

"Tharr's deoxyribonucleic acid contribution, as I understand, is partial. She will not have all of his powers, such as the ability to reorganize and manipulate matter at the molecular level, for example. Intangibility and time travel are also beyond her grasp."

"No, this is not desired. A supreme being shall this one never be, not only because of the lack of Godlike powers, but because she will hopefully choose freely *not* to be a supreme ruler. Also, she is of above average intelligence, but lacks her mother's genius. Therefore, she will need to work very hard to achieve her goal. But is a fraction of infinity not still infinity?"

"It is something in which you should not have meddled. The potential for great evil is as great as for superior leadership. Possibly more so. Has the sad history of these beings not revealed this fact after thousands of years?"

"But she will have infinitely more humanity than the evil being Tharr. And yet, she, born of the dark matter that makes up most of our universe, shall be the Dark Star—what may be foretold? Humility this child and her mother both have, no doubt, despite their tendencies for intense vocalization. Dependent she will always be on others, who will lay down their lives for her, not because of her fantastic powers, but because it is the virtuous thing to do for someone who commands admiration. There *are* still noble beings on this world. For example, those once known as their

'Science Squad' of ridiculous heroes, rejects of society who for the most part have underachieved and fallen into oblivion, will finally have the opportunity to rise to the occasion. True leaders inspire others to achieve what they never thought possible."

"How ironic, Gart. The onetime leader of this *'Science Squad'* of unusual, multitalented, unpopular, rejected intellectual beings, who has paradoxically risen to become the one they now call President—is this life form not unlike Tharr-Kann in some aspects? A warlike bully masquerading as an ambassador of goodwill and philanthropy? Amassing a nuclear arsenal such as this planet has never seen to become power personified enough to destroy their planet a hundred times over? Which is more dangerous—the sightless child of the stars, or her dark kin, the one whose mere command can order Armageddon?"

"That is a ridiculous comparison, hardly worthy of an answer. The one known as President has faced great personal loss and angst and was once not as you say. Once she was a humble servant of sick and disabled children, and perhaps she can find that person once again, as there is still good within everyone, Qarr-Rogg."

"I believe that person has changed forever. What is the trite saying the humans have? 'Power corrupts, and absolute power corrupts absolutely?'"

"Perhaps. But if it is as you say, then the Dark Star will be, then, the only thing that can save these beings from themselves and their imperialistic President. Just another reason it must be so."

"But the matter is made even more complex by virtue of the fact that this leader is, by some stroke of fate, kin to the one who has power supreme. Will the ghost of Tharr-Kann join allegiance and destroy them all over again? Tharr-Kann's DNA is in this child; therefore she can easily become the dark kin, or will she be benevolent kin? The blackest star of all time, like Tharr-Kann? Or their prophesized Angel, emerging from the darkness?"

"Qarr-Rogg: dark kin she is not, nor is she the divine Angel many already believe her to be. She will, rather, personify the frailty and flawed nature of their kind and lead her people, someday, to do things they never thought possible. It is time for the unwitting descendant of Tharr-Kann Axoon to fulfill her destiny—the one with the greatest of humility. She will show the President of her blood the way, as this world is in dire need of such a being. The one known as the Dark Star will be the greatest of all, destined someday to be the greatest leader in history."

"But such power—in the hands of a mere child, with the means to lay waste to a world. With a simple gesture, I could eliminate the significant flaw in this one and prevent the event seven of their years ago that created it. What power she would then have. There would be no limits, nothing that would be beyond her grasp."

"No, Qarr, you surely do not understand. This is the hand she was dealt, and thus her story must unfold this way. Also, the fate of another, their President, was inexorably linked to this event, despite the death of many worthwhile beings. Is it not this characteristic that distinguishes the Dark Star child from Tharr-Kann and us? Don't you see that this is the necessary imperfection that makes this one more human than we can ever hope to be? Would you remove the mortal flaws that would drive her to greatness? Humans will not respect a perfect being; they would fear her."

"How sad is your interest in them, as was Tharr's. The wasteful humans, such as another of her kin in particular who is selfish and egotistical beyond measure, and one who dabbles in the most shallow of pursuits. This individual has created a large city as a symbol of her, a monument to colossal arrogance."

"Qarr, I disagree. While the city has her name, it provides an infrastructure for many beneficial things, including their energy revolution, which shows great promise."

"Gart, it is, rather, a 'great promise' of destruction. Have their civilizations that have worshipped false gods not *all* fallen in cataclysmic fashion? This could all have been prevented, yet you persist in madness. Only Tharr-Kann was more reckless."

"I disagree, and your insults shall not deter me from what I know to be true. She will need to learn to deal with that as well. All civilizations have their foibles; ours is a terrible example. You disgust me with your arrogance. The alternative is unacceptable."

"It will be challenging for her to achieve that greatness with this problem. Have you yet figured that out?"

"You never see anything beyond yourself, and none of us truly comprehend what it is to have a true challenge. This is why she will become a leader, a shaper of a new world, one who will someday live up to the symbols already erected in her honor. While I know the solution to her problem, she will have to solve it herself. The denizens of this planet believe, somehow, that she saved their nation's capital, which she did, of course.

"We also know that there is another one among her few remaining biological kin, the one who helped create this memorial city, who has the amazing gift to see through all extraneous material and perceive things in their simplest form; while you have already declared your opinion that she is a shallow, vain, superficial, materialistic being, which on some level is probably true—this kin shall solve the mystery that others cannot.

"The Dark Star will then, in time, become the greatest leader this world has ever known, in time. Let us depart now, as there is nothing more to be done here. The die is cast. Fate has led to this without our interference. What is, shall be, forevermore. Never shall we again interfere with the lives of the inhabitants of the third planet of the Sol system. We shall merely be observers on our journey, those of us who have forgotten what meaning and true effort is. Never can she know of our existence."

"Finally, we agree on something."

They disappeared into the time-space continuum as quickly as they came, mere observers on their journey now, the tale they had constructed, to unfold. Gart-Monn had promised not to interfere further.

But, while Gart-Monn was a being of pure energy, he was not always known for keeping his promises against interference. Nobody was perfect.

Prologue II

Seven Years Earlier
December 16, 2016
1:03 AM
Somewhere in the Atlantic Ocean
514 miles from Washington, DC

Sung Shoi-Ming fiddled nervously as he took a drag on his unfiltered Turkish cigarette on the cold December morning. He was excited to get the messy details of this latest endeavor done, even if it did mean working with rotten Americans; the one he was meeting with today was one of the most despicable ones he had ever seen. Yet, he begrudgingly respected another despicable person like him, as there weren't many of those around with his particular disdain for humanity. The President (a euphemistic name for a dictator) of the People's Republic of Tosia hated many people, but he despised Americans the most. On this occasion, however, it was worth it to the leader of this small but belligerent Pacific island nation. Revenge was a more important motive for his expected guest, who had given him something of immense value in return for his freedom.

This guest entered the large upper deck of the opulent yacht a few minutes later and sat down, as an attendant brought them coffee, juice, and a large breakfast tray. He marveled at the wealth his exalted position brought him, the privileges it conferred. Little did he care that most of his people wallowed in poverty and sickness. Not his problem today—or any other day, for that matter. He laughed.

The six-foot, gray-haired passenger took a sip of coffee. "Ming, thanks for the hospitality. I sure as hell don't know what I would've done without you. In another time, another place, we would've been enemies, and I would have had to blow your yellow ass up."

Ming smiled and nodded. "Yes, what is the catchy slogan you Americans have?" He thought pensively as he cradled the burning cigarette in his hand. "Oh, of course: 'the enemy of my enemy is my friend.'" he said, not caring in the least who had first said it as he sat back in his luxurious leather chair on the lower deck, warmed by a vast array of butane heaters. "My dear Gallagher, I hope that these accommodations are superior to your last ones."

"You sure as hell got that right, Ming. I appreciate your guys helping me get out of the federal pen in Virginia."

He laughed. "Good, good, I am glad you are in fine spirits this fine morning, although I imagine even your worst American federal prisons are far superior in quality to the best our country has to offer. We find it useless to waste good money on trivial things such as prison comforts. There are assuredly no 'Club Feds' in the delightful Republic of Tosia." The chain-smoking Ming lit another cigarette; he had more grandiose things on his mind than lung cancer or emphysema. The ionizing radiation about to be released into the atmosphere would make that carcinogenic exposure inconsequential. "I had some reservations about working with you, given your reputation and such. But my sources say you are the one who could get me what I wanted."

"I assume you found your sources to be reliable." Former Lt. Gen. Brant Gallagher took a bite of scrambled eggs. Former generals didn't keep their rank when they were sentenced to life imprisonment for treason. He probably should've been sentenced to death for what he had done. That wouldn't even have been an issue in Ming's Tosia, a belligerent island nation despised by most of the world. Ah, the damn liberal softies. Those who had made that decision were about to regret it.

Ming smiled. "Of course they are reliable, idiot. My sources do not lie to me."

"Huh? Why is that, pray tell?"

"Because they would not dare." He pulled out the color photo of the cinnamon-colored, black-haired woman from a folder and slid it across the table. "I believe this is your best friend, the one who, amazingly, discovered the evidence that sent you to prison for life. You should have planned your assassination caper a little more carefully, pal. There are some mighty smart people out there who hate your guts."

Gallagher choked on his perfectly cooked sausage patty as he stared angrily at the famous forty-one-year-old physicist's photo.

"I've never actually met that cerebral freak, but, yes. She and her whiskey-distilling Tennessee in-laws are responsible for it all."

Ming shook his head and put his head down. "Yes, the Darkkins are not optimal for our health, I hear tell, in whatever time period they exist. Alas, they shall not exist much longer. Let us reflect on the amazing team we surely would have been if you had become President of the United States. We could have overcome my hated Asian enemies and ruled the world."

"If I'd become President, you would've been vaporized by now, so be glad you're still alive, goddamn it."

The baby-faced dictator laughed heartily. "You are *so* funny, Gallagher. No, rather, the world would have been ours to gleefully spread death, destruction, and Communism to the masses. But, alas, you and your grand 'super-soldiers' didn't work out so well, I heard. We cannot grieve over what was never to be."

The disgraced formal general shook his head and took a sip of coffee. "Damn stupid Malachi Argon, a genius who wasted his talent. I should've never trusted his ass. What a dumb piece of shit, trying to make super-soldiers and all. I should have been President, and I *would've* been, had I not messed around with him."

"Perhaps, but do not regret the past, my new ally. Many have made bad decisions when confronted with large dollar signs, and you made a doozy. But generals convicted of high treason cannot become President, though, per my understanding of your asinine laws." He put his head down, feigning sadness. "What a pity for the world. My country has no such draconian restrictions for those such as yourself with great leadership potential."

"I know that, Ming, shut the hell up. I'm over it."

"Sorry, it is only that my heart breaks for you. But I doubt that you would be high on the list for a pardon when your, uh—big bosom buddy moves into the White House in four years, so you should not be hoping for that." Ming laughed and choked on his coffee as he cupped his hands in front of his chest, as if to indicate massive breasts; with his gluttonous diet and lack of exercise, he had an excellent start on man-boobs of his own. "'*Big bosom buddy!*' Look at me, I have made an American joke! I am too much!"

Gallagher shook his head. "Goddamn it, Ming, that isn't a damn bit funny."

He chortled, his rotund cheeks puffing out. "It is too. Don't you know it is rude not to laugh at your host's jokes? I have had men shot for less."

"No." Gallagher shook his head and frowned angrily as he stirred sugar into his coffee. "That's never going to happen, either, about the White House. That, and laughing at your damn jokes."

"How sad. You make tears come to my eyes."

"And I've heard the rumors since I got out, but the vast number of things that would have to happen exactly right for any woman to become President, let alone that ridiculous corpulent clown, are you kidding? The odds of that are astronomical."

He smiled. "Aww, you don't think so? What is it you say? 'Get with the program?' How little news you receive even in American federal prison of the meteoric rise of this 'clown' to political stardom. And no longer meeting the definition of 'corpulent.' It is amazing what diet and exercise do for a person." He looked at the ample rolls of adipose tissue protruding over his belt. "Perhaps I should take heed myself, as I am a bit out of control."

"Shit. What the hell are you jabbering about now, Ming?"

Ming held up his right hand. "Why, your 'best friend forever,' the beloved, robust Governor of California, is now a great true-blue American hero, an Olympian, a Special Congressional Medal of Honor recipient."

"What?" Gallagher looked up from his plate. "Those are all lies. She wasn't even active military, so she couldn't have won a Medal of Honor, you're full of shit."

"Shut up, idiot, you're wrong because you've been in a time warp—but there's more. The jolly good doctor was also knighted by the Queen of England last month for 'exemplary service to humanity.' Finally, she singlehandedly saved the man you went to prison for trying to kill. You surely remember that, you have had enough time to think about it." He gestured to his left hand. "Let us now examine *your* sorry skill set, which, with *your* stellar references, might get you a job selling used pencils on a street corner in Malawi for five cents a week. You probably made more in the license plate shop at Leavenworth."

"I don't think so, Ming. Even if your typical exaggerations are correct, she'll be dead in a few minutes anyway, so all that shit you just mentioned won't matter."

He nodded. "Yes, true, true, although she would have made a worthy adversary, as the hated one in this photo would have been. The latter has discovered technology that would change the world forever, so it is fitting that they all die on this day. Such an invention would make our planet a better, greener place, they say.

"Well, I don't want a better, greener place—I want the great Communist empire I embrace to go on forever. Great technology means fantastic wealth and power, enough to bankroll the Governor's inevitable and historic path to the White House, and she would no doubt oppose my world domination with those resources; the weaponry that she would no doubt develop in ancillary fashion from said discoveries would be formidable, indeed. But none of that will happen now, thanks to you. Money is less important to me than having the freedom to do what I want."

"Freedom in your country, what a laugh." Gallagher stared at him. "Listen, you rotten son of a bitch, understand me well. I'm only here because you need some help, since your sorry-ass missiles are a piece of crap."

He laughed and took a sip of strong black tea. "Well, you at least should demonstrate *some* gratitude for the person who got you out of that hellhole. Just saying."

"Yeah, sure." The former Vice Chairman of the Joint Chiefs of Staff, who had been sentenced to life in prison for engineering an attempted assassination of President Reardon (among other atrocities) shook his head. "I just can't stand it. The home that should have been mine, possibly soon occupied by that—that hillbilly dullard. I hated her stinking guts the first time we met, I hate her worse now. Thankfully, it ends here."

"What can I say? When you're popular, you're popular. By the way, the Sacramento 'hillbilly' in question reportedly has an IQ of 159, so a 'dullard' she is assuredly not; she's smarter than you."

"Yeah? What the fuck do you know about it, Ming? And who's here on a nice new yacht and who's big fat butt is about to get blown to smithereens, huh? Who's smarter now, me or that dumbass hick from the sticks?"

He nodded. "Eloquently stated, Private Last Class Gallagher, as befits one with your sterling intellect. You will, therefore—how do you paraphrase it—'kill two birds with one stone?' My, I am truly on a roll with my American idioms tonight, yes? And we have the perfect person to blame it on, thanks to you, as not everyone may believe it was caused by Pyongyang; that explanation is a trifle too convenient for some to swallow." Ming showed him the photo of the grinning, angular Caucasian man, who was clearly missing a few marbles, most high-level military people knew.

Gallagher took the photo and laughed. "Yeah, ol' Kristoff van Sant will be happy to take the blame after we blow the woman who sent him to prison up. He'll be mad he didn't do it himself."

"And the North Koreans, I have taken great steps to guarantee that they will be blamed too, and my other enemy will be retaliated against."

Gallagher took a red felt tip pen and circled the famous scientist's photo. "Happy Nobel Prize to you, stupid geek. At least you'll go out in style, something you never had. You and the rest of your damn family." He sat his fork down angrily and pushed his plate aside.

"Another breakfast, my friend? I believe I will have seconds."

"Huh? No. What now?" Gallagher asked impatiently. "Tired of this waiting around horseshit."

"Have some patience; you should have learned that virtue already. Now that we're finished with our exquisite meal, let's go up and watch on the upper deck, which is ideal for viewing such joyful events. It should be a good show—Washington's only a few hundred miles away." A male attendant took his plate and napkin as he rose from his plush chair.

They walked up to the upper deck of the luxury craft and took their seats in oversized Naugahyde chairs as if attending a movie premiere. It was one, of sorts, but it would not have a happy ending for some. He looked at his watch as the countdown began and tossed a handful of popcorn into his mouth. It would've been launched by now, and he expected a spectacular explosion, befitting an American Fourth of July celebration.

Yet, he had seen nuclear warheads detonate before, but this one seemed a bit underwhelming. He could barely see it with his binoculars as he frowned in disappointment. Oh, well, even a partial decimation of the despised District of Columbia would be better than nothing. The occupants of the plane must have been vaporized immediately. Too damn bad. It would've been nice for them to have suffered tremendously.

"What the hell was that, Private Gallagher?" he sputtered as he stood up angrily and pointed. "I expected much better from you."

Gallagher shook his head nervously. "I don't know, Ming. It should've been a much higher yield than that; I can't imagine what the deal is. Sorry as hell."

"Yes, although your being sorry in no way helps my situation. Yet, while I am horribly disappointed, I am certain the destruction of our friends has been accomplished, and the best part is that it will be blamed on my hated enemies in Pyongyang and a deranged European arms dealer obsessed with Santa Claus. Therefore, be glad you're still alive, as I may need you for something useful later. For what, I don't know, but I will think of something."

He stood up angrily, suddenly realizing that he had not paid many millions of dollars of pocket change for this substandard fireworks show; he could've done better with a box of sparklers and a Roman candle. Someone of his immense importance deserved better, and the cretins who sold him such crappy missiles would pay for delivering such a lousy product.

And, yet, he was unnerved. He had heard that *she*, the dark-haired one in the photo, had cheated death many times before. Gallagher said she had killed Malachi Argon by just touching him. She was surely one person he didn't want to be around any longer. Ah, there was no chance of that now. He also didn't believe those rumors about her; at least, that's what he told other people.

It would be interesting to see the Internet feeds roll in, so he called one of his lackeys to bring him his computer tablet. There had better be some good news coverage and propaganda from his country, or heads would roll. Literally.

He always looked forward to that part of being dictator and being an inductor of chaos. Oops, correction—he meant President of the Republic of Tosia. One has to keep up a good public image.

• • •

Four hours later
242 Park Avenue
Manhattan, New York City

"I am here." The shrill, high-pitched, lispy monotone voice was

unmistakable, and frightening, even though it was just a dream. Frightening because trouble always seemed to follow the person the voice belonged to.

And that person damn near got him killed once.

Fifty-year-old Jaime Mendoza Flores woke up on the cold mid-December day, as if an electric shock had passed through his system. He felt his sweaty brow and what he had dreamed. As if he or someone had died. The phone was still off the hook, as he hadn't wanted to be disturbed; his cell phone was also dead, as usual, because he forgot to charge it. He usually had his mind on more pleasurable things. So where was the damn noise coming from?

He heard it again, even though he was awake. That sure as hell had never happened before. He slapped the side of his head, trying to get rid of the sounds, to no avail.

"The Dark Star will dawn someday, many years from now, to save the world. It will surely need saving by then, as it is inevitably headed towards ruination. Regrettably, I likely shall not be alive to see it.

"Goodbye, my only remaining brother. Take care of the one you once loved, as she needs you now more than you need her. Put your selfishness aside for once and do something for the world. While we have had our recent differences, the world needs her too, now more than ever."

He heard it again. His sister had been calling him all night, saying things like that. He'd not had dreams like that in a long time. Why now? He could see her, almost flying, in a fog. He'd had a few glasses of wine last night but certainly wasn't drunk. The reference to him being her only remaining brother? What the hell did *that* mean? Take care of the one you once loved? He liked the supermodel he frequently had sex with but wouldn't go as far as saying he "loved" her. Most people said he loved himself most of all, sadly. Was that what she meant?

And there was no doubt that what he heard was real. As if she was standing right next to him.

He looked at the clock and tried to put things in perspective as he looked out the window at the Manhattan skyline. 5:17 AM. Yet, it sometimes took him a while to put two and two together. He rolled over and stroked the hair of his sleeping bedmate, with whom he'd cohabitated for almost three months now, which was longer than most. But he had to get up and get ready to take his private Gulfstream jet to Stockholm since it wasn't every day your sister won the Nobel Prize in theoretical physics. Is this why he was having dreams of her?

He had decided to go with Annika Haegmann separately instead of traveling with the rest of the family, who decided to leave around midnight. One reason was that he wasn't always the most punctual of individuals and set his own schedule.

A more important one was that his family members didn't usually approve of his choices of female friends and frequently derided them if they didn't meet their intellectual standards, which was almost always. His sister was especially harsh in this regard; she had become increasingly critical of him in recent years, given his glaring lack of academic accomplishments. Plus, there were several other super-intelligent types on board, as well. It was hard being the "black sheep" of one of America's most celebrated athletic and cerebral families, even though he was easily the most famous and wealthy of them all. They didn't really care.

"Where are you going, Jay? Don't get up yet," Annika said as she reached out to him. "C'mon back to bed."

"We need to get going. Stockholm's an eight-hour flight, even in my private jet." He wasn't famous for his punctuality, and being late would further put him further down the pecking order in his family. It was hard for his brother to keep a straight face sometimes when they saw each other.

She grinned sleepily at him. "What is it your sister's getting this noble prize thing for, again? I don't get it. I thought she did magic tricks and other junk on TV."

He shook his head; he surely wasn't the most intellectually talented individual, but he also wasn't the complete idiot the rest of his family thought he was. Yet, he seemed to attract women like that: those low in brainpower. She was one who must've liked to watch crappy old children's television shows.

"What?" He opened his mouth wide in amazement. "How can it be that you were born in Sweden and don't understand what the Nobel Prize is? Please explain that to me."

"Huh?" She looked at him with an idiotic expression on her face. "What does this prize have to do with Sweden? Am I missing something?"

He snarled. "I *tried* to explain it to you. She discovered some really unique element that will revolutionize nuclear fusion, they say. I guess it's pretty important." About the only thing he had ever discovered was how to avoid responsibility and commitment in his life, it seemed. He had a big office a block away in Manhattan, dozens of assistants, and a pretty good life, but it was all fluff. And he had been pretty successful at it; there was little reason to think such excellence in one endeavor wouldn't continue. But was being the Commissioner of Pro Football really worthwhile to the world?

"Fusion, huh? That sounds really neat. I went to a fusion restaurant once in Times Square. Will it make her rich?"

Fusion cuisine vs. nuclear fusion: yes, very similar concepts; even he, with a rudimentary knowledge of the physical sciences equivalent to a third-grader, knew the difference.

"She's already got a bunch of dough that she could care less about, but this will make her wealthy beyond anyone's dreams."

"That's good, 'cause I can dream about a lot. I hope she buys a nice house we can come visit. I am used to only the best."

The best of everything except neuronal gray matter, it seemed. His sister had discovered something that probably would rank among the top twenty scientific discoveries in human history, yet Annika worried about what kind of house she would have when they visited. Ah, he didn't hook up with her for her intellect, he thought as he looked at her gorgeous body, which made up for most of her shortcomings.

He thought about the girls he had dated, and his thought often returned to the college freshman he dated when he was a senior at USC. She wasn't really beautiful, but she had a brilliant mind, a charming Southern Appalachian accent, a wonderful sense of humor (with a cartoon-character voice that could make even the most buttoned-up person howl with laughter), and, most importantly—a hearty sexual appetite the likes he had never encountered again. Way better than his tubular supermodel bedmate in the latter category. Boy, did he foul that one up. He had fouled up all of his relationships, so what else was new? He was waiting for the wheels to fall off this one.

He gasped as he wondered if *she* was the one his strange telepathic message was referring to?

He forgot his strange dreams for a moment as he rose from the bed and walked to the kitchen to start some coffee when he suddenly noticed the tremendous noise outside. Had the melee just started, or had it been going on for a while? Did the players' union decide to strike after all, or did Wray Uttmer fail another drug test?

He was sick of the stinking media bothering him all the time.

The world-famous Commissioner of Pro Football deserved a little time off, too. Only two weeks until the playoffs started, too. Maybe it was time to retire, go back to San Diego or Green Bay, away from the crazy rat race.

Nah. What the hell was he thinking?

He loved New York City, the town that never slept.

It would take an event of historic significance to make him leave all this.

He opened the thick oak door as he saw dozens of reporters clamored outside in the cold darkness, and three other individuals pushed their way in, knocking him aside.

"Hey! What the heck is going on? Get out of my house before I call the cops."

"Listen up, we *are* the cops, man. Shut the damn door before these crazy people run over us," one of the men said. The two FBI agents flashed their badges as they shoved their way through the chaotic ensemble, joined by a federal agent he had met years ago, although she was with a different agency then. It had been a while. But why was this irritating woman here in his house, especially now?

"We need to talk to you, Mendoza," the wiry five-seven Black woman said as he began to speak; he usually wasn't at a loss for words. "Don't talk. Just shut up and listen. We're here to help you."

"What? Uh, sure. Don't know what the hell I need help for, but whatever." He let them in and closed the door as he wiped the matter from his brown eyes as he became more alert. "Is that really you, Levickis? What are you doing here?" He saw the star-shaped badge on her hip and pondered for a moment. "Secret Service? When the heck did *that* happen?"

"A couple of years ago, but that's not important. Jay, this is FBI Special Agent Patterson, and Special Agent Anton," Special Agent Jacqueline A. Levickis announced to him.

"Is this a joke, Jackie?" The famous pro football commissioner laughed as his young girlfriend came into the room, now wearing royal blue satin *Mendoza the Miraculous* pajamas. "My brother playing pranks again? The football strike was settled, so what's all the commotion about? It better not be some Jail & Bail charity thing. As you can see, I'm rather busy with, you know." He winked.

"Goddamn it, Jay, it's not funny," Jackie said. "Pay attention since you have no clue what's going on, as usual. You don't answer your cell *or* landline phone, of course."

He laughed. "Didn't want to be disturbed, obviously. How'd you get the number?"

"Don't be stupid, Jay," she said, staring at him. "But that may be very difficult for you. And wipe that stupid grin off your face."

"O-kay— " He took a sip of cold coffee from the mug he had left on the living room table. "I didn't want to be bothered, which is no crime as far as I know, but what's the deal?"

"Yeah, what's the deal, top cops? It's awful early," the six-foot, willowy Annika said in a thick Swedish accent as she wandered to his side. "Are these police people going with us? Personal escort to the airport? Wowee, you really know how to throw a party. Are those people outside cheering for us?"

"Hey, dimbulb, get over there, sit your skinny blonde butt down, and shut up," Jackie yelled at her, pointing to a chair in the corner.

"Well, you don't have to be so rude." Annika sat down in the window seat and started looking through the latest edition of Vogue, which, ironically, featured her on the cover.

"Man, you *really* don't know, do you?" Agent Patterson asked, dumbfounded, as they sat down, the agents ignoring the tall blonde supermodel. "You haven't turned on your TV, Mr. Mendoza?"

He shook his head wearily. "Hell, no, I just woke up, it's not even six AM, and I'm not a morning person. I've got to get ready, though; Annika and I have to get to Stockholm for the Nobel Prize presentation tomorrow. We're taking my private jet, so make it snappy, Levickis."

"No—you're not going," she said softly.

"What?" He snarled. "I'll do what I want unless you know something I don't."

"I guess I do. All civilian air space is off limits, Jay. You can't fly out of the country or anywhere else."

He watched the three of them look at each other as he went up and grabbed her jacket. "What's going on? Tell me *now*, Levickis."

"There isn't going to be any Nobel Prize for Bonnie, JJ," Jackie said sadly as they sat down. "She's dead."

"*Dead?* What the hell do you mean?" He grabbed her by the shirt. "No Nobel Prize? Tell me, Levickis. She can't be dead, 'cause she just spoke to me."

Jackie shook her head. "That's impossible, Jay. She's gone. Tens of thousands saw the explosion four hours ago; it's all over the news feeds. The streets of most major East Coast cities are full of panicking people."

"No, I mean, in a dream. You remember how she is."

"Hold on." Patterson picked up the remote control and turned on the seventy-two-inch flat panel television. "It has to be on here." The agent flipped the channels on the remote, as every station was filled with news stories and terrified crowds running around the nation's capital and other large cities.

"What's going on? What does this have to do with the reporters outside?"

Jackie put her arm around him. "A low-yield nuclear missile was fired from what appeared to be a North Korean submarine five hundred miles off the Atlantic coast, and struck the jet carrying your sister, her husband and daughter, and the rest of your family, about ten miles out of Washington, right after they left Reagan National Airport."

He remembered again that his brother-in-law Alex Darkkin had arranged for a large private jet to take everyone to Sweden, as sort of a trip for family and friends.

"A *nuke?* I don't believe it." He sipped some bottled water as his hand trembled. "I thought the military had kept them under surveillance, so they can't have technology like that. You say it hit the plane and detonated?"

Anton spoke up. "Yes, sir. It was very small, had advanced stealth guidance technology and radar jamming, and Air Command couldn't shoot it down in time. They apparently obtained it and the radar jamming devices from an offshore arms dealer. A fifty-megaton stolen DARC missile. Not one of the giant ones, but big enough to do a crapload of damage."

DARC: Short for Darkkin Atomic Research Corporation, one of the biggest private weapons think tanks of the seventies and eighties, in the thick of the Cold War. Missiles created by his college girlfriend's and brother-in-law's deceased father, William Conrad Darkkin. Most people had called him "Rad," though, a crazy pun on radiation; ironically, his name was similar to the discoverer of the x-ray, Wilhelm Conrad Röntgen, but that association was merely coincidental. After the Cold War, some of the nukes were inevitably found and sold by unethical military personnel to Eastern Bloc countries, and this one must've slipped through the cracks.

"How the hell did that happen?" He walked around for several minutes, letting it sink in. He finally sat down and put face in his hands. "My God. The capital is gone, then? The President?"

She smiled slightly. "It's still there, Jay, all of it. Not even a window shattered, as I understand. Only the plane explosion. President Reardon is in his bunker, he's fine."

He spread his arms wide. "That's impossible. How can it still be there, then? The whole city, Arlington, Alexandria, Bethesda, everything, and those six million residents should've been vaporized by a nuke that size. Washington should be in tatters."

She shook her head. "We don't know, there's no logical explanation for it. For some reason, the early reports of fallout seem to be exponentially less than anyone would've expected. The counts on the ground are about three times background radiation—less than you'd get in an airplane flight—when the nuke should've killed nearly six million people. So it must've malfunctioned. Thank God, as the countermeasures couldn't get to it in time."

"But everyone on the plane is gone."

"Yes, I'm so sorry," she said. "I don't know what to say."

He sat down in shock. "All of them—I'll never see them again, can't say goodbye. Mom, Dad, Bonnie, Aurora, Alex, Mike, Teresa, Wendy, Bella, Jose—" He was, as Bonnie had said moments earlier, the only remaining brother. And, seemingly, now the only remaining member of his family. "Bonnie had almost died twice. I guess we're lucky we had her as long as we did."

Patterson shook his head as Jackie looked at him, sat down with him on the leather sofa, and put her arm around him again as tears streamed from his eyes.

"Yes, Jay, your sister's gone, and there's nothing we can do about that or the others. But—"

"Huh? But *what*, Levickis?" He grabbed her shoulders with both hands. "Tell me."

"Okay. There is one bright spot in this vast darkness if you can call it that, and I thought you should know from me personally. Two of those people were taking care of some urgent matters in Sacramento, but then one of them got violently ill with abdominal pain on the way to Washington and her chartered jet had to land in Pittsburgh. I knew that would be important to you."

"Wait a minute—are you saying Wendy's alive? *How?*"

"Apparently, your niece was with her, made the pilot land, and she took her to a Pittsburgh hospital instead of going to Reagan Airport. So she never made it there."

"What? Those two can't stand each other, so why would they have been together? You're not joking? How do you know that for sure?"

Special Agent Patterson came to him and put his hand on his shoulder. "Sir, I spoke to Governor Gallinsworth Darkkin's chief of staff myself twenty minutes ago. There was some science conference in Sacramento she and Isabel were both at, promoting some legislation about clean energy or something, with a bunch of 'A-list' celebrities in tow. They're both alive."

"Violently ill?" He got up and walked around the room, looking at Jackie. "What's wrong with her?"

"Her gallbladder pretty much exploded *en route*, and she had an emergency cholecystectomy, I'm told, at Pittsburgh Methodist," Patterson said. "She was pretty sick, but considering what she's been through with Reardon's assassination attempt and all, this is nothing. She's expected to make a full recovery."

Even the legendary gubernatorial gallbladder of Dame Mary Gwendolyn Gallinsworth Darkkin could only take so much abuse, he thought, even after all the weight she lost.

What an ass he was. His whole family was dead, and he was thinking about crap like that. He guessed that's what happened when one was confronted by unbelievably bad news all at once.

And he knew that he was a selfish person. No one knew that better than him.

"So, you're sure she's okay?"

Patterson nodded. "Yes, she will be. Uneventful lap choly, about two or three days convalescence, then home. But—her ex-husband and children were on the plane."

He clenched his fists. "Who the hell did this, and how?"

"It's too early to speculate," Jackie said. "It's so easy to blame the North Koreans, but that seems a trifle convenient, and your sister had a lot of enemies. So did Rad Darkkin. Killing his family would have been great revenge for someone."

"For whom?"

"Unbelievably, someone has already admitted to doing it and is in custody after the CIA found him in Brussels. You know who Kristoff van Sant is? And his buddy, Reuben J. Skelton?"

"Huh—van Sant? Skelton?" Although Bonnie wasn't supposed

to talk about work, his eccentric sister sometimes couldn't keep her big mouth shut and had mentioned some of the weird people she had attracted to the CIA during the four years she had worked on some of the most far-out government projects ever, before she felt a "higher calling" and left to do private research on nuclear fusion, culminating in the discovery of a novel transuranium element. But, she also tended to be somewhat theatrical, and he didn't believe even ten percent of what she said. "*Santaman* and *Red Skeleton?* Are you freaking kidding me? Those guys are straight out of the funny farm if they even really exist."

"Yeah, the funny farm for dangerous assholes like those," she said. "The Belgian arms dealer and his, er, friend, partner, whatever the politically correct term is these days. They're bad news, Mendoza. And believe it, guy, they're for real."

"But my sister put together gadgets for the government and didn't have any enemies. Rad maybe did. So why would anyone want to do that, Levickis?"

"Jay," Jackie said, shaking her head. "You really don't know what your sister did, did you?"

He shrugged. "Sure I do. She worked on fancy gadgets for the CIA, invented stuff, and did the junk she used to do as a forensic scientist for the San Diego Police Department, but with about a million times the budget. So what?"

Jackie groaned. "You have no clue. She was in charge of some of the most far-out research that ever took place in the United States before she left to do research she funded herself at the old DARC complex in Solway, Tennessee, of all places."

"I have a hard time believing that."

"You're so wrapped up in yourself that you didn't even know she'd been living out there?"

"Near the distillery? No, are are you kidding me?"

"She changes the world, and you're out in space, as usual."

"Huh. Even so—involved with those guys? Nuclear missiles? That's too hard to swallow."

Anna put on her bathrobe. "Jay, does this mean we're not going to my condo in Stockholm today? Are we going tomorrow?"

Jackie sputtered. "Yeah, honey, that's what it means. Lord, you fricking idiot. Jay, you sure can pick 'em."

"Hey, that's not very polite, lady! You are just *not* a nice person. I have way more money than you."

"Yeah, you got something right for once, I'm one mean bitch, get used to it. Money can't buy brains. And I thought I told you to be quiet."

"Sure thing." Annika scowled and went over to lie down on the large sofa. "Sorree. Jay, you have some lousy friends."

Jay thought about what had happened, still not digesting it completely. He did, somehow, know it was finally time for the wealthy playboy football commissioner to grow up.

"I'm going to Pittsburgh, pronto. I hope you didn't barge in here to tell me all this and expect me to do nothing." He was all she had now. Maybe she didn't even want to see him again. But he had to take that chance. It wasn't about him any longer. Amazingly, it was about the first time he had ever thought that way.

"Okay, Jay, but it won't be easy, it's a mess out there. I figured that's what you wanted, so I've got a helicopter on the way, and it'll land on the penthouse."

"Don't worry about the expense. Money, I got."

"Good, we'll need it, 'cause no way can we drive. The roads, it's a mess out there. The whole East Coast is going crazy, even though there was no significant damage."

"Where are we going, Jay?" Annika asked, sipping on a glass of milk.

"I have no idea where you're going, but I'm doing this one solo. As for me, I'm probably going to hell in a handbasket."

Annika shook her gorgeous head. "Golly, I don't know what that means, but it sure doesn't sound good."

"It's not," he said. "Forget 9/11—the world has now changed forever. Things will never be the same for any of us."

"That sounds pretty serious. Well, I don't want to go, then."

He nodded. "Works for me."

"One condition. If you're going there, I'm going with you," Jackie said. "Not with her, though." She pointed to Annika, who was now snoring on the sofa.

"Agreed. She doesn't want to go, anyway, so everybody's happy. Most of all, me." He went into the bathroom to change into some clothes and gather a few belongings while Jackie arranged for their ride to Pittsburgh in a DEA helicopter, which would land on the penthouse.

Two people who had just lost everything important to them were going to meet again after four years. She probably didn't even want to see him right now, as if she ever did after what he had done over twenty-five years ago. But he was all she had right now. And *vice versa.*

Hopefully, that would be enough.

Enough for both of them. And enough for the future of the uncertain world that was coming. Something told him he'd better be ready for it, as not everything in this world was good.

But, somehow, he knew that someday a shining light would come through the darkness.

He envisioned how Washington had been saved, even though it seemed impossible. But it wasn't. That much was clear. Why?

Because four years ago, *she* had shared with him the world's greatest secret. Why she had told him that and no one else, he had no idea, as they hadn't exactly been on the best of terms for the last two decades, and he had barely heard from her since that time. He wasn't certain he even believed it then.

He believed it now.

He thought earlier that it would take an event of immense historical significance for him to leave and change his destiny.

That event had obviously arrived. *She* had already given this phenomenon an appropriate name:

Dark Star Rising.

What did that mean?

Angel from the stars, or the world's destruction?

Twelve Years Later
Late Summer, 2028

"It is for us to pray not for tasks equal to our powers, but for powers equal to our tasks, to go forward with a great desire forever beating at the door of our hearts as we travel toward our distant goal."

—Helen Keller

Fairbanks North Star Borough, Alaska
Paige
The Omniscient Adolescent
Destiny

I sit humbly in the small hospital room, holding little Judy's hand as she lives out her last few hours. I met her doing some volunteer work at the hospital. She has an aggressive form of acute myeloblastic leukemia, and the family has finally given up on treatment after nearly a lifetime of suffering. I scan my Braille book with my fingers and read a favorite children's story to her, as her family asks me to, although she can't respond, of course. While I smile, I weep on the inside as there is nothing I can do while this little girl lives out her last few hours on Earth. I feel so helpless; despite my own disability, this is a sensation completely foreign to me—to be unable to accomplish something.

I shake my head and ponder: why are things this way? If there is a God, why has He let this happen to one of His children? You surely must understand why I doubt His existence sometimes; my adoptive father says we are not meant to understand. Seems like a cop-out to me, and I don't buy it yet. Maybe one day I will, he hopes.

But convincing me of things is hard.

Even I am like any other human being as I sit and wait for the inevitable, as I can't do anything to help her. But I comfort myself in that I have made a small difference in this six-year-old's life. I cannot help everybody, but to this tiny person and her family, I have perhaps made life a bit better. There is much worth in that.

But how will I choose who to help in the future in ways that I can make a difference? What is my best destiny? Will someone die because I couldn't get there in time? I know with certainty that I will face that dilemma someday, as I surely cannot travel at the speed of light.

Several times the speed of sound seems to be my limit.

Later, I walk through the hospital garden and feel the soft flower—a tulip, I believe, by its shape and texture. While I cannot see as normal people do, I hear, feel, smell, and touch. I have learned to rely on them—the other senses. They aren't extraordinary like my mother's—just normal, I guess. It's good to be "normal" at something. Others have overcome far more than I, who has been given more than most; my glass is more than half full. So don't feel sorry for me. I stopped doing that a long time ago.

The paradox of my own existence is thrust upon me. I feel as if perhaps I am growing up too soon, as I turn eighteen in a few more weeks. Why am I in a hurry to do so while my peers seek to delay their emergence from adolescence? Shall I regret my haste later?

But there is no going back now, as I curiously behold the one who gave me life; the daughter has, somehow, now become the mother and the mother the daughter. I am puzzled as the woman regresses into her own childlike state, playing with stupid toys, seemingly devoid of the responsibility a fiftyish woman of her supposed exalted intellect should have. Is she really even that smart, or is it all bullshit? What was her life like when she was younger? She either does not remember or will not share that with me; I don't know which.

Maybe I don't want to know. Yes, I have long pondered that there may be things of which we should be left unaware. But it is not worth arguing with her, that's for sure, even though I always win.

Tomorrow, I will skip school (yes, again) to work at a homeless shelter, cooking food for the less fortunate. I have done what I could to help them; I care little about the minor infractions of the law I have incurred in that quest, as this truculent truant teenager has no use for park permits, vending licenses, or public ordinances, which are trivialities beneath my exalted existence. No one will care that I do this besides me, and I don't want anyone to, because it isn't about me. Sometimes those who do for others forget that little thing.

Unlike our celebrities who permeate every available social medium, I don't like attention. At least I don't think I do; maybe I am mistaken. But whenever I want for something paltry, I think of them—the less fortunate. How can I ever do enough? Maybe someday I can, but even I have limitations. How will I choose to best serve mankind? I have tough choices to make others do not. Leaving that decision in the hands of others is unwise; I have learned, unfortunately, that not everyone can be trusted.

My mother claims one person, in particular, fits into that category. Why would she know anything about it or about Washington? She seems to have no sense at all. Or does she?

About that: they say our venerable President was once a humble humanitarian who gave much of herself to others in her charitable works without expectation. What the heck happened there? That job transforms a person, I guess, as there are seemingly more important matters that now require her attention, such as overthrowing hostile foreign governments, obliterating the dwindling Red Menace of Communism, and adding a new state every two years. Dang, creating all those new flags, seals, etc., must be expensive, as are all those trips to Armstrong City. I suppose the residents of those places are much better off now than before. For them, I am happy. But others in the world are worse off because of these actions. Who will champion for them, the forgotten?

I don't know what it's like to run a country, but rest assured that I will, because someday I will have that job, too. Not because I want power, because I already have a little bit of that, thank you very much; it's because I want to help others. Sounds corny, I know, but it's true. Who better to proclaim that than me? That's easier said than done, I guess, and I have a lot of things to learn to do it on my terms. It's probably much harder than it looks.

If I have the honor of meeting her someday, she will likely tell me that things aren't that simple. I've written her several letters; I doubt she has read them, as I get back a Braille form letter reply (likely from a White House staff member) each time. Yet, the replies are lengthy and thoughtful, generated by one of surprising intellect. I wrote the letters in longhand, so how she or her staff know I'm blind is perplexing. I guess

Presidents know a lot about everyone.

People laugh at me, but I usually get what I want in time. Woe betide the one who tells me I cannot do something. That will certainly get you an earful of sonorous complaints from me.

I do not understand my Russian mother, she is of an intellect foreign to me, and she speaks of scientific things I cannot possibly understand. Perhaps no one can, as they may simply be nonsense. Are they the ramblings of a mad woman or some obscure prophecy from above?

In a faraway city in Indiana, they speak of Aurora Angelica—the legendary winged angel from the stars who, the children's stories state, somehow saved the nation's capital on Darkkday—while perishing herself. I know logically that such a person cannot have ever existed or that a mere child could not have saved Washington and that the city is, therefore, a representation of hope for all mankind. How could that have been possible? Do we really believe that her "mystical energy" absorbed the blast? That she died for us, like Christ—vaporized by a nuclear warhead over Washington?

Impossible, I say as I laugh. Yet, there is much I do not understand about myself. Sometimes I wonder if I could be she—or am I something more sinister? While I lack my mother's incredible (in many ways, not all good) brain, it seems that the occurrence of all these things simultaneously cannot merely be coincidental.

I shake my head and laugh hysterically as I wonder what I could possibly have been thinking. Something ridiculous.

Me, a Savior of mankind? You have to be kidding.

At age seventeen, I have smoked cigarettes, drunk whiskey, have been in jail, think of sex a lot, rode a bike off a mountain top, and have done a number of other things that rebellious teenagers often do. How can a blind girl get into such trouble, you ask? My parents have been asking that question for years, but you would be surprised how resourceful I am.

Therefore I am certainly no angel, but not a devil either; I am merely a flawed young woman doing the best she can.

My greatest flaw keeps me close to humanity.

Through my blindness, I have truly learned to see things others cannot: somehow learning patience, humility, and the ability to control the gifts that have been entrusted to me alone. Sometimes I think it's all a dream that I can do these marvelous things, but it's not. Mom tells me that no other being, including her, would be able to deal with such abilities in a responsible manner, that I am unique—the chosen one. Therefore, I learned long ago that I am not like other people. Why am I worthy of such gifts? I doubt in His existence sometimes. How can the world be the way it is? Why should I believe in God when there is no proof? Or is there? I am a hard person to convince.

Mom says I am both blessed and cursed. She does not elaborate further, but I think I understand what she means.

My best has to be better than anyone else's, or bad things will happen. But a "chosen one?" No, I am surely no goddess. A Savior would not have hormones like mine that seem to work like those of any other teenager.

A nun I shall certainly never be, as a life of celibacy is not for me.

I know that, in the unique career path I want to pursue, the entire world will want me to do things for them constantly. Do I really want that or not? Whether as hero, Senator, President, or average human being, such is my choice; my parents don't encourage me in these endeavors, but they want me to do what I feel is important. I don't know what else to do. I suppose that is what being an "adult" is all about, no?

My biological father died in an accident when I was six, I am told. All I know is that I look like him; I also can be rather loud and obnoxious, another trait we apparently shared. My adoptive father, a non-traditional man of the cloth, tells me, "For onto whomever much is given, much is expected." I grow tired of hearing that, but it's true. I have the power to accomplish many good deeds. I also could likely do very bad things and perhaps destroy the world, should I be so inclined. I merely hope that I can live up to the expectations my parents have for me.

Someday I shall see again, I know it. I do so in my dreams, not because I desire it for my own ends, but to fulfill my destiny, it is obviously required. Or is it? Is my chosen destiny the best for me? And for the world?

Yet, in my solace, I will return to the state of sightlessness, where I am happy. But life isn't about me being happy, is it? There are others who need me. I hope someday to give them the gift of my leadership, but only if they want it. Most of all, they need the fantastic ability my adoptive father says is my greatest.

My mouth.

My ability to argue and prove a point. He says that of all the amazing things I can do, only this is the simple power that will eventually change the world for the better. Not the easiest way for me to change it by any means, but the best way.

Will this be my destiny, on the convoluted journey that is the life of Cheryl Paige Marshall? But how I will get there is uncertain.

I am told that, like all living beings, I am a child of God. Mother has explained of expanding entropy and how God must be present for things to exist in any ordered state at all. She speaks it with a conviction even greater than that of my adoptive father, a preacher.

Is this one of her outrageous ravings? Does she have any sense at all? How can a person with supposed mastery of the physical sciences believe in such things with absolute conviction while I, one of far lesser intellect, have serious doubts? Maybe it makes sense to some, but I am not a scientist. Concepts such as the Higgs boson, quarks, baryons, and dark matter will always be beyond me. And many things I can do that you cannot even comprehend.

But if God made us, why did he make us just a speck in the universe with billions of lifeless stars out there? Yeah, I know, "it's God's plan—blah, blah, blah—we are not meant to know why, etc." It's easy to explain everything that way, huh? I am not easily persuaded, if you do not know already, so if you want to debate with me, you had better bring your "A" game.

I know that I'm not divine, as Jesus (if he was real) could have healed Judy; I am merely flesh and blood, albeit with a little "something extra" in my DNA, for sure. How it got there, no one knows, or Mom just won't tell me. While smart, she isn't a very good liar and isn't very quick on the draw with words, so I know she is hiding something. But some well-meaning souls will invariably believe me to be holy. Boy, will they be disappointed when they get a load of me and my big mouth!

I am borne of a science I cannot understand as Mom can. Yet, is it conceivable that in her peculiarities lay a singular genius? I know that in some way, I must possess some qualities of her. This frightens me, for I feel she has a past of which I am unaware. A dark and violent past, as laughable as that concept seems. Yet, I know it must be true, as no one besides her has ever scared me. She tells me of dark energy and dark matter and other things that make no sense to me.

I yearn for the person who will respect and love me for what I am as a human being, an equal, not because of what I can do. Because we are all equal in the eyes of God, and I am no more important than any other person. If God even exists, that is.

I am not convinced of that yet.

But I somehow feel that there is a terrible evil within me, and yet Mom says I must somehow learn to embrace it to evolve into the great leader I will someday become. Yeah, right, like she knows anything, and that I could ever be a great leader, or anything more than an obnoxious high school student. They will throw a grand party when I graduate.

For all of her strangeness, though, there are some words like these that ring true. It sounds contradictory; how shall I do so? For even in my brief life, I've learned that there must be a balance in every being, good and bad. Without the latter, I shall never have the drive to do what needs to be done and overcome obstacles. This is the riddle I must learn to understand if I am to ultimately achieve my goals. And Mom says there is evil in the world I cannot possibly comprehend, and how else shall I deal with it?

But I don't want to be that person; I want to lead people by showing them how their strength comes from within, not by exploiting my native abilities.

Whether I can ever figure that all out, I do not know.

Most things can be measured. I am five feet eight inches tall and weigh 160 pounds, more or less, depending on my mood. The blue whale weighs 200 tons, for example. How we know that I'm uncertain, and I could care less about such trivialities that spout endlessly from my mother's larynx. But my mom tells me my physical strength is, theoretically, incalculable. Even I know, however, that it must be finite, as scientists say the universe is so.

Many in my position would choose to rule the world or gain fantastic wealth. As I am an ardent student of history, I know that many have tried world domination, and it didn't work out too well for them. But those people were not me, which is kind of scary because I could probably pull it off. Who could possibly stop me? Shall I earn the title of President of the fifty-five United States (or however many states we have by the time our President finishes her probable third term) by the sweat of my brow, or declare myself Queen of Earth because of my genetic gifts?

Or will I do neither and simply become a mere hobo, wandering the planet in tatters, aimlessly searching for answers I don't have, helping one unfortunate soul at a time? I could envision my mom doing the latter (wandering around, that is; I'm not sure how helpful she would be to others, as she would probably lecture them endlessly on arcane topics). Maybe we could wander the planet together. That would sure be fun. Not. Sometimes she disappears for days on end; where she goes, nobody knows. Dad never seems worried about it. I guess he doesn't worry about what he can't control.

The answer is crystal clear, though: I know deep in my heart that my future greatness and legacy will come not by using the strength of Samson but by freely and publicly choosing not to use it. For, paradoxically, the less I use my power, the more powerful I shall become. Our third President, Thomas Jefferson, said that, and he was a pretty smart guy, although he had a lot of faults, too, just like me. They said he, like my mom and I, was different. I have come to terms that I am differently-abled as well, in many ways.

To do all this, I must someday be known to the world, as I cannot accomplish such a feat in secret if the world is truly to understand the virtues I represent. Is this the best philosophy? And is my childhood lost forever? I wonder.

North Pole, Alaska
Pastor Jack
The Reflective Reverend
Responsibility

I stand here living a lie, my hairless head shining in the setting Alaskan sun like a cheap bowling ball. Like a bowling ball, I must have holes in my head for doing the haphazard things I've done. Yet, there was no other path for me to take; of this, I am certain.

I pretend to be an ordained minister, but my credentials are falsified, as are all the known records of my wife and adopted daughter. Easy enough for me, one of the best computer hackers of all time. I hid that from the authorities pretty well, and my wife is pretty good at cracking passwords.

But I know as much as any minister, and my devotion to God is genuine, not a disguise. I was immensely irresponsible in my youth. I cheated my way through college; I thought I was smarter than anyone else because no one caught me or the others I helped cheat. I did that crap because I felt a sense of entitlement and disdain for authority. My best friend and I lived a pretty wild life. While I laugh at those times, that life is over now, and my best friend is long dead. All life ends, eventually, as we return to the dust from whence we came.

Life changes a person, and I grew up after Darkkday to take on responsibilities I could not fathom. How Paige and Petra survived that point-blank thermonuclear blast, I will never understand, but there is much I don't know about my adopted daughter who, while genetically unrelated to me, shares my youthful disdain for authority; I don't want to even know about some of the crazy stuff she's done.

I know even less about my wife, the ultimate woman of mystery, even though I have known her for many years. You think you have her figured out; then she baffles you yet again. I made a vow as the best man at my friend's wedding that I would take care of his wife should something happen to him. It did, in spectacular fashion. A girl needs a father, and I've done the best I could with a blind girl who is a handful, to say the least.

I wonder why I have been so blessed? I try to remember the positive things as I go down to juvenile hall to get her out of jail again for yet another minor infraction she has committed. I suppose I should be grateful that she is, despite her vocal obnoxiousness, a gentle pacifist at heart, unlike her mother, who has demonstrated lethal physical aggressiveness. The police should be grateful for that, too; I wonder how compact a sphere a police car could be compressed into? We'll never find out, hopefully.

I had no idea what I was getting into and the miracles I would witness over the years watching her grow from a child into a young woman. The small things are the most important. I held her hand when she came home from school after being teased by the other children, crying. It still happens, but this gal cries no longer, at least on the outside. I know she carries some inner sadness, like her mom. I cannot possibly understand the responsibility she has or how she does it.

Can you understand now why I know she was chosen for this? You doubt me when I speak of miracles? The unimaginable power she is potentially capable of wielding is tempered with a patience that I could never have, only learned from nearly a lifetime of disability. Being different isn't easy, and I was so proud of her for never retaliating against those who ridiculed her. The Bible taught her that, even though she minimizes its importance. What could she have become without me to guide her? Would the world still exist? Will she remember those lessons later, when I am no longer around?

I used to doubt the existence of God, but no longer; would you, after you've seen a girl literally walk on water and on air? Lifting a two-ton tractor into the air with one hand like a toy? With no idea how it's even possible? While I know for an absolute fact she was not conceived in the same way as Christ our Savior, and her powers don't come from Him, somehow I have to believe that she is a product of destiny. Maybe not God's, but some higher being's.

Yet, Jesus was persecuted for his beliefs and abilities; will she suffer the same fate? Or is the timing of her coming merely a coincidence? Christ could raise the dead and cure suffering; she cannot do these things. Petra can explain it all with her scientific ramblings, but no one can explain what Jesus did. He was one of a kind.

I left the woman I loved to care for them and married my friend's wife because Petra and the world needed me more, and this was my best destiny. No one knows why or how I disappeared or what I have accomplished here. With the irresponsible life I had led, they must assume the worst, but

I care not, because I put my family before myself now. I have come to love her and her daughter more than anything. No one cares about who I was any longer, I was a nobody. Finally, I am doing something worthy.

Have I done the right thing? Trying to hide Paige from society until she is grown? What is her best purpose? She seems to think it is as a symbol of good, to someday become President herself when she is old enough. Those are lofty goals, to be sure. But, forty years ago, I knew a freckled, sixteen-year-old British-Appalachian girl from the mountains of Tennessee who had big dreams, too, and she did pretty well, depending on your perspective.

I hope my child is doing the right thing, although there isn't a lot I can do if she doesn't want to do something. But she has the right gene pool to do those things, I guess. And a different gene pool from God knows where that allows her to do the impossible.

Yet, somehow I know it will be her simple Earthly gifts that will make her great and change the world for the better. Does that make any sense? Perhaps not to you. But not much in my life has been logical.

One of the world's richest men gives me money without expecting anything in return. Money I need to do what is right. Despite his well-earned reputation as an opportunistic entrepreneur, he wants to do what is best for America. At least, I hope so. Money changes people, and he's not a little boy any longer. He grew up on that fateful day, too, as I did.

But while my best friend is dead, I can never forget for one moment that his sister—the quintessential alpha female—is very much alive, and no longer sixteen years old and living in Appalachia; she has a more upscale address these days. She is an opportunist, too, and a brilliant strategist, despite her outward appearance. She should've died like the rest, but she didn't, which I guess most people think is a good thing. Again, that's a matter of opinion. I'm certainly glad she didn't die, but I wish she approached things with a little less fervor. In the end, her existence is beneficial for all of us.

It's like she's in a hurry to do things. I suppose almost dying and your kids being blown to smithereens makes you appreciate the time you have left and make the best of it. Knowing who her dad was, I guess she can't help it. If I had a dad like she did and went through the kind of hell she did after she saved the President and later losing her whole family, I'd be screwed up big time; I'm messed up enough as it is, but I tried to make myself better. So did she, by exponentially exceeding everyone's expectations. The governments of the countries that underestimated her are gone now, while their residents enjoy the benefits of being Americans.

She feels what she does is right for America, too. We didn't always get along, and I don't know what she would say about all this stuff, although the time is coming when she will have to find out; she surely does already, I don't fool myself, given the incredible resources at her disposal. I have hidden from my daughter who her biological aunt and uncle are, and I'm certain she will resent me terribly for it. I would, too, probably. It may even be a turning point in our relationship. But my needs don't matter. It's the world's needs that count.

But it had to be this way until Paige can find out herself, at which point she hopefully can deal with her father's sister because no one else seems to be up to that task. She may have meant well at some point, but she can be quite overbearing, and her priorities have changed. She is a jingoistic juggernaut on a mission, which scares me to death. A part of me believes that the one I hide from somehow already knows. She ain't no dummy. It's impossible for things to have gone this smoothly all these years without the goodwill of an invisible helper with unlimited political power. The government has unmatched surveillance powers, yet everyone leaves us alone. It's not hard to figure out, really.

But why would she have meddled? To make the world a better place, or to manipulate my daughter so that she can take over the whole world? The latter is entirely possible, and that team-up would be invincible, which is not a good thing. No one should have absolute power, not even Paige. Is her character strong enough to keep that from happening? I hope so. If I'm wrong—well, I don't even want to think about that.

Or will The Great Dame serve as a mentor to Paige, the one who can earn the title of greatest President of them all twenty or thirty years from now? How does one measure the worth of our country's leader? By the numbers of countries overthrown and thousands of nuclear missiles, or by bringing peace to the world? I certainly am no idealist, but I know a better world is possible. Most would disagree with that statement.

One would argue that the world is better now since it is at peace; there have been no wars in many, many years. But was it accomplished by true leadership or fear of the one (a Nobel Peace Prize winner, no less!) who commands greater military destructive power than any previous President in our country's history? Probably a mixture of both. The world sure is complicated.

A more important query is this: can a Republican and Democrat peacefully coexist? There aren't many of the latter folks remaining these days in Washington; like the Communists the Commander-in-Chief despises, they have slowly been eliminated. This Democrat will be a little tougher to chew on and eradicate, she will find out.

My greatest dream is that those two stubborn, opinionated females can accomplish greater things in tandem that neither can hope to do alone. To do that, they must somehow get together. I know that fateful day will be coming soon, and then the fireworks will invariably start. For we all have to live in this together. I wonder.

Princeton, New Jersey
Johnny Kepler
The World's Greatest Golfer
Inquiry

I was once the finest golfer in the land, with my thirteen major championships (including a Grand Slam), and I am descended from the greatest astrophysicist of all time as well. I had the greatest life in the world. My quest to set every known record in golf was cut short, however, after I lost my leg to bone cancer. I knew then I was meant for bigger things than the PGA Tour. I sure didn't need the money, but I left golf behind and studied astrophysics in Southern California to realize the depth of my untapped potential at Caltech.

While there, I also realized the depth of stupidity to which I could sink by wasting my time fooling around with a bunch of geeks, bozos, and cheap TV crews, struggling to find funds and sponsors. Being Gravi-Golfer sounded fun at the time; it was something different to do since I couldn't play like I used to. Those dummies were so broke at one point they had to sleep in crappy motels and eat sardines and peanut butter, until I came along and gave them a few bucks.

Why the gal who put it together sought me out, I don't know, other than I was Black and had one leg, the kind of whacked-out diverse demographic she wanted, I guess. What a motley crew of misfits. Big Blondie promised we would make a lot of money; I didn't need that, but it sounded fun, and I needed a few laughs then. Even then, she could be a commanding presence, a stellar saleswoman who could probably have sold some dumb ass the Golden Gate Bridge for two dollars. Not me, as I can see through people's crap. She pissed me off a lot. Ambitious people do that to me. Especially ones who make me roll on the floor laughing without always intending to do so.

What a hoot—why the hell would anyone have wanted to watch our sorry weirdo asses on a crummy local cable channel? "Dr. Wendy's Science Squad," what a bizarre freaking joke. We must have been a sight to behold: me, a one-legged Black golfer with world-class expertise in gravitational physics; a deaf forensic scientist/magician with high functioning autism and an IQ of nearly 200; an overweight pediatrician and former champion powerlifter with a four-octave vocal range; a geeky gay electrical engineer who also was smart as hell; a loudmouth neurologist with a tic disorder whose name spells out the rainbow of the seven damn Newtonian colors; and a physical chemist in a wheelchair whose original character was named after Bedford limestone. We were supposed to be a children's show, but we probably frightened most little kids to death. Shit, we sure would've scared the hell out of me.

And about that fame and fortune—it never materialized, except for her, of course, while she drove us nuts with her manic level of energy; why would I have expected anything else from a woman who basically acted with the maturity level of the stupid-ass cartoon cats she did voices for in her early twenties? People forget that stuff about her now, but I have to reluctantly respect that she never apologized for her faults, never tried to hide them. We're cult heroes today, but back then, we were a bunch of stinking losers. Most of us still are.

But the truly great one who gave mankind the gift of unlimited clean energy is long dead, her atoms scattered across the nation's capital by the very forces she knew better than anyone. I never really understood that bizarre magic lady; I wish I could see her again, though. Despite her multiple eccentricities, she was surely the most brilliant mind I have ever encountered. She followed in my footsteps at Caltech and transcended anything that I could have ever accomplished.

In the end, though, our large, laugh-a-minute cartoon character was the one who somehow defied the odds to become the great American hero, because, unlike one of her "alter egos"—idiotic Metabolismo J. Ubiquitoid, Ph.D. (the obese anthropomorphic animated cat who was always getting blown up with dynamite or thrown off a cliff)—she showed the world she wasn't indestructible; she has a thousand times the guts I ever had.

While I never personally cared for her feigned folksy manner, I must respect anyone who willingly took four bullets for the President and almost died while the Secret Service stood around scratching their heads. My hat's off to that large lady, so laugh no more. She did their job for them, and for that, she gets my vote for however many more Presidential elections they let her run in. Not that she needs it; there are about four hundred million others.

I became the world's first Black astrophysicist at an Ivy League college. I have all the fame I want, my past forgotten by all except a few who remember the glory days. My Bavarian ancestor would be proud of me; I don't look much like him, though, so go figure. With the aid of advanced technology, my right leg is better now than the original. I do research, teach and write papers, and travel the world as a famous speaker, with only memories of my former fame on the Tour. They let me play on Seniors, but my game isn't the same, and I don't really care any longer, as I have bigger fish to fry. My daughter is as good a golfer as I ever was, and she can carry on that legacy.

I work diligently on a top secret privately funded project with one of the world's richest men; no one knows about it except us. Why he wants this information I don't know, but the world of dark energy is spooky, yet invigorating. Make no mistake—the Tinman is an opportunist, too, and I sure bet he doesn't want it to advance science. What choice to I have but to help him? I can't let this opportunity pass. I would rather be with him than with others on this.

I sometimes feel like I imagine my great-great-great-great-great-great grandfather Johannes Kepler probably did when he made another great discovery. I wish he was around so I could talk to him. I check my notes and the readouts of instruments so sensitive that they exist nowhere else on Earth, and I shiver as I realize there can be only one conclusion—I have discovered evidence of greater power than can even be imagined. Vast potential amounts of energy in the yottawatt range that cannot be measured by any conventional means—possibly equivalent to that of a small star. Invisible to most, but real, nonetheless.

What being on Earth could be trusted with the power of a small star to do with what he wishes? Why now, and how will we deal with it?

Dark matter is the only explanation for the bizarre happenings of Darkkday, the only logical solution, as implausible as it seems—a being exists with the ability to control incredible amounts of energy, based on the intrinsic property of dark energy to repel gravity, the most fundamental of forces.

Ah, so what, you say. Your old science textbook says that gravity is the weakest of the four fundamental physical forces, so big deal. Buddy, let me put it in perspective so you can maybe grasp the concept: you think that superhero dude in the comics who got his power from the sun's energy was tough? Well, gravity holds the sun together, friend, and it's therefore way more powerful than solar energy when you have a crapload of it. Those WIMPs (weakly interacting massive particles) ain't so damn wimpy when they're part of a dark star that can convert matter to energy with one hundred percent efficiency. I told the kids that on Dr. Wendy's

Science Squad over thirty years ago, and soon I'll tell the world. So pay attention—this is only possible through the manipulation of dark energy fields—enough to shrug off a hundred-megaton nuclear blast like it was nothing.

How can one control what can't even be seen or measured? Yet, there is no other explanation. If my crazy theories are correct, there's some badass out there with the power of a dark star who could obliterate us all. Dark stars are likely powered by antimatter reactions of neutralino dark matter, which makes nuclear fusion seem like a caveman inventing the wheel. I hope I don't piss this dude off; I'm pretty talented at doing that to people. Maybe he needs a pal who knows a thing or two about gravity. Does he walk amongst us? Is he friend or foe? Somehow, I know he is close at hand.

And, if I know it, you better believe the money man's wife does, too. She can figure stuff out, somehow, way before anyone else can. Why, then, does she stay behind the scenes? She may look heavenly, but I don't trust her rich movie star ass for one minute. I have to hope she wants what's best for mankind, too.

Will this dude be a boon to the world or the cause of its ultimate destruction? Lord, sometimes I wish I didn't know about this stuff. Is Christ really coming again in 2029, like the prophecies say, or will it be the Antichrist this time? They say 2029 is the Biblical year of the Jubilee, which apparently has something to do with Christ's return. I wouldn't know, 'cause I never did like religion, but I may start praying real soon. Maybe, with some luck, I'll be dead before we find out.

The faint gravitational field perturbations originate in Alaska. Why there, of all places? More importantly, does my big ol' Science Squad buddy in Washington know about it? Uh, that might not be the best thing for the future of humanity, let me tell you. This being's powers could be perverted into the most terrible weapon ever, and she seems to fancy weapons of mass destruction like ol' Daddy did; maybe even more. Are there any limits to what one of the boldest women in history might do with unlimited power? You didn't know her back when. I did.

There has been no evidence she knows of this, but I am one of the few people who know that she is far more intelligent and strategic than anyone realizes. Therein lay the hazards of working with the most dangerous woman in the world: some people still underestimate her diverse talents, her ability to network and get the people she needs to win on her side. I ain't one of those folks, and I'm not going anywhere near her fricking house. Not that I was ever invited, of course. Maybe I should just show up for dinner someday for some Southern fried chicken. Nah, that ain't gonna happen. I hear she only eats raw vegetables, tofu, soy yogurt, and hippie crap like that now. Yeccchh. What some people have become.

I try to trust the rich dude from Indiana, but I don't know where to go next. I don't even give him all the information I have because he married into the famous family that fate has both blessed and cursed. I'm too old to be a part of that shit. What will become of all this? What does a plus-sized sixty-year-old dyed blonde and her billionaire family do when she becomes ruler of the world? Do I even want to be around for it? I wonder.

Gallinsworth, North Korea
Isabel
The Most Elegant Engineer Ever
Parsimony

I look out on the misty lake, in this ancient part of the world so unlike where I grew up. It is my first visit to our fifty-fifth state's capital, once known as Pyongyang, the only state capital named after a living President. It is beautiful beyond compare. I am asked to speak at the opening ceremony for this, the XXXIV Olympics, as tens of thousands of North Korean-Americans cheer my name and seek autographs. Huh. Why I was asked to come, I don't know; athletics were never my strong suit. But they love America and being Americans.

Later, I speak at a North Korean university graduation as I wear my black and gold ceremonial hood with dark blue trim, of a Doctor of Philosophy, from my alma mater; but I am far from West Lafayette, which is a short drive from my adopted home of Aurora City, Indiana. God gave me beauty, but my engineering degrees and Nobel Prize, I have damn well earned. I don't think they appreciate that; I guess I represent what they like about our country: glamour, beauty, and wealth. Some of them probably value my Best Actress Oscar more than my Nobel Prize. Welcome to the United States of America, folks. It's different than what you're used to.

But I don't like being just about that; it's fun, but I represent far more. Education, practicality, and hard work are my virtues, and these are the values I must impart to them today. Knowing how their parents lived before, can you blame them? Many have criticized the President's obsession for destroying Communism and restoring freedom to this land, as well as others, but you would see it differently once you looked at their faces. Even though we argue a lot (and I make many jokes at her expense, because it's as easy as shooting fish in a barrel), I do admire and respect her (don't tell her, though, as I have a bad reputation to uphold). She is a good yet flawed person who has done what no one else could have. She was elected twice by the people by very large margins, so she earned that fair and square.

Everyone is friendly to me. Why wouldn't they be friendly to one of the world's wealthiest and most beautiful women? But I want to be known for more than that; I often feel stereotyped because of my looks. Despite what I have accomplished, I live forever in the shadow of my brilliantly flawed aunt. That's just fine with me, as I can't ever equal her in most ways. I am not as egotistical as I once was (but I am not perfect, so bear with me), and I honor her existence on Earth. From her, I have learned humility and patience. Personal loss teaches you that life is fragile.

I have things most people can only dream of having. Yet, I have lost so much. Fate has given me immeasurable wealth, enough to build a city in honor of my fallen cousin, but it does not negate the sadness I feel. For my twin brother, who had so much potential. And for my husband, who lost the love of his life and his unborn child. Money can't replace them, but I try to comfort him as best I can. I owe him much more than that. He is what I strive to be, my guiding light.

I need a challenge. Most have said I have accomplished much in my thirty-six years, so why would I want more? Yet, there is more to life than teaching, earning a Ph.D. with highest honors, a Nobel Prize in chemistry, an Academy Award, being on television, even philanthropy. No, these things mean little, as they're superficial. You may not believe that statement, coming from me, but there is a greater destiny that I must fulfill. There are those strange old friends of my aunt who have underachieved, who may someday have the opportunity for greatness. No one cares about the ridiculous "Science Squad," but sometimes we must rise to the occasion to be great.

How do I know this? Because only I can see how to put it all together better than anyone else. Am I crazy? Judge for yourself; look around, and you will see what I can accomplish.

Some in my family had special abilities. I don't know that I fit into that category or not; I don't really care what you think, in case you didn't know that already. I am an overachiever, they say. My IQ is only 127, so I wouldn't get into Mensa like my aunt did, as my sheer intellect is a fraction of hers. I wouldn't want to be in that stupid society even if my IQ was 227. It doesn't mean anything, as clubs and elitism aren't for me, and I have a Nobel Prize, too. Not too many people have those. It's what you do with your brain that counts, and I made the most of mine.

I am no storied theoretical physicist studying the rarefied, glamorous fundamental particles of matter, but merely a lowly chemical engineer who likes to wear overalls and get my hands dirty, despite my outward disguise as a glamorous girly girl; maybe I'm not the best at taking tests, but I am the greatest in the world at converting theoretical concepts into reality. My husband and his brother run the company now, as I devote my energies to helping the world with other things that are desperately needed. You may believe my existence trivial, but I have the means now to accomplish amazing things. There will be more amazing things to come.

For I learned long ago that I have the unique power of parsimony—to see any problem, even one I haven't seen before, and solve it in the fastest and most logical way possible by distilling it into its simplest form. Example: I am a world-class chess player, despite no formal instruction and little practice, because I can see the moves far in advance of what you can.

So don't play the chess games of life with me, either, unless you want to lose—badly—because raw ability usually wins. My talents aren't spectacular and are often overlooked, but I suppose they are special skills too. My aunt had the big ideas, but we would have none of this technology without my gift to convert raw concepts into something tangible, something she never excelled at.

It's good to be a "big picture" person, but sometimes you need a "little picture" person like me who can actually figure out how to do things because the devil is in the details. There is one thing I've worked out the details on: through the unglamorous application of logic, playing detective, and process of elimination, I've pretty much figured out what happened on Darkkday, but I'm not out there looking for trouble, despite my secretive skulking around the Pacific Northwest. I know it will come my way soon; fantastic things usually are part and parcel of being in my family.

So if you think I'm not smart enough, then bring it on. I may not physically be able to kick your butt, but my pocketbook will speak for me. My "other" aunt, my uncle's wife—The Great Dame, The Countess of Monte Crisco, The Duchess of Doughnuts—probably would be living in a different house if not for me, too, because you need big bucks to get where she did. So perhaps I am worthy of my surname. I wonder.

Solway, Tennessee
Mary Gwendolyn
The Flawed American Heroine
Courage

I walk serenely through the meadow and look out upon the Great Smoky Mountains, and I am magically a child again, if only for a brief moment. For that brief time, I am taken back to my world, which was once much simpler. It started getting complicated for me pretty young when I decided I didn't want to live here any longer. Yet, for some reason, I always want to return here, remembering a time when my potential seemed infinite.

Unlike a child, I know that the world isn't magical. It is cold, harsh, and unforgiving most of the time until the day we die. Hopefully, I am worthy of a place in Heaven after that, if they even let me through the Pearly Gates after all the stuff I've done. I pray I will be united there someday with the loved ones I have lost. But let me hang on a few more years to finish what I started. I will need to help out with something really important; it isn't about me any longer.

I was born eight miles from here on a cold, snowy January morning in 1972, yet I left as a teenager and didn't come back for decades because of someone I lost touch with. That is too kind—in actuality, I hated him for years. We were wealthy because his—my—family made whiskey and mined zinc. I wasn't terribly proud of the former growing up. If I wasn't getting teased about my size, I was given a hard time about that. I learned to deal with both, trying not to knock heads around in the process.

Those are trivial matters compared to the things I must deal with today. I wish I could go back, but time travel still isn't possible. There is no point in continuing to regret what might have been.

I still knock a few heads around. I wouldn't be doing my job if I didn't.

But at least those businesses weren't designed to kill millions of people. Later he—my father—made things that could destroy the world. I didn't know about that until I was in my thirties; my mom hid that from my brother and me. Way to go, Mom! I love and miss you dearly, but I couldn't go down your path. The only way to change one's destiny is to take charge and work your butt off to alter it.

On another cold day in December 2016 one of those terrible weapons destroyed my family. I couldn't stand my dad because he destroyed my mother's marriage many years ago. I had a hundred reasons to hate him. Yet this incredibly flawed man died saving my life trying to make amends in the end. It took me losing everything to come back here, to this simple place, so unlike the unimaginably complex world I inhabit now. But those were the choices I had to make.

I have learned that our flaws define us and are what make us strive to be better. Lord knows I have more than my share.

Ironic, isn't it? I once thought my father and I were very different other than that we looked alike. My brother got my mom's good looks and could have been a male fashion model, while I resembled a pro football tight end (at times I weighed about as much, too, unfortunately). Things like that are supposed to be the other way around! Yet, I made the best of the hand I was dealt.

How superficial I was as a child and young adult. As I grew older, I realized the real sorrow that exists in the world. I have done what I could to fix it. Maybe what I did was right, maybe full of crap. Disagree with me if you will, but I stand by my convictions. Again, I can't go back.

And I simultaneously laugh and cringe as I realize that I have become my dad in most ways. He was obsessed with patriotism and wiping out the Commies. Therefore, he surely would have been proud of me because I pretty much have carried out his dream, somehow.

There are good and bad things about living his dream in the strange, circuitous path that took me that way. Every great leader has both: positive and negative, yin and yang. One to help counteract the other. I hope to hell my good qualities outweigh the bad. Some days I don't know about that.

Am I a great leader? That's not up for me to decide. They changed the Constitution because of me so I could keep my job, so I guess that gives me an answer. Because it can't end for me, not yet. I have one final act to do for America—and the world.

And whenever I think of my dad, I look towards the sky, extend my large arms, and cry: God help me come to terms with the complex being I have become. It isn't what I wanted. But it's what I had to evolve into to survive, and what was needed for America.

But can God help me someday become the person I once was? The person inside I lost touch with? I had the noblest of professions—a healer of sick children, one who made the lives of those with disabilities better. There were so many I loved, many thought to have little value to society. I set out to prove them wrong.

Above all others was the thirteen-year-old deaf child I cared for more than any other, who, perhaps with some of my guidance, overcame all odds to become one of the world's intellectual greats. I distanced myself from my dysfunctional family, so hers became mine; over the years, we unfortunately grew apart as our destinies, politics, and philosophies diverged, as a once humble disabled child had become the most arrogant person I have ever experienced. We were barely speaking to each other the day she supposedly died. But I didn't do what I did for her for personal accolades, however, or to expect anything in return from her; she had her own problems. I loved her like a sister.

She developed more issues after she married my brother and teamed up with my dad to save the world, nearly starting World War III in the process. Strange stuff happens when you become something more than human, I guess. That day, when she rescued me from that island wearing high-tech buckminsterfullerene Russian battle armor, I knew she had changed forever. In a way, my father and I caused it all. I can't go back in time, but I can help make the best of it. Somehow I know she is around, somewhere, as crazy as that sounds.

Now look at me—I am the one who can start World War III with merely a gesture. I have avoided it this long, but I have become what I once feared. Past tense.

In the transformative process that has been my life, I learned the hard way to fear no more.

And about who I was: I don't think I am that person any longer. Those times seem so long ago now, to the point that I've forgotten who I was and where I came from. Is what I do worthwhile? I want to go back, at least for a day. Shall I get another chance to make people laugh like I used to?

Most days, my "new" job really sucks—it's not as great as you think. I want the simple joys that I once had. I fear they are gone forever. I am not complaining, though. It was my choice, although deep down, I know I had no other.

I look around and see the natural beauty of eastern Tennessee and hear nothing except the gentle brook and the birds chirping, although I know that it is merely a cruel illusion, that I can never really have these simple things ever again. While they are well hidden, at my instant command are a dozen lethal human killing machines less than fifty yards away, all sworn to give their lives for mine in an instant.

For I am privileged to have been elected by the people as the forty-seventh living symbol of the greatest country on Earth. Some may have doubted that fifteen years ago—that the United States was the greatest. I assure you that there is no doubt now. Am I arrogant to feel that way? Perhaps. You try doing what I do without a healthy dose of arrogance. You wouldn't be able to walk half a mile in my size thirteen shoes.

I enter the autumn of my life, and I feel unfulfilled. I have wasted much of it on childish pursuits; such a life was fitting for one named after the carefree character in a British children's story written by Sir James Matthew Barrie—the friend of the child who could fly and never ages.

But as little Wendy Darling grew up in those stories, so did I, finally, at age forty-two, riding in that damn ambulance to the hospital, my chest blown open by an assassin. I surely have aged. You can see the pain on my face. I grew up after that solemn day, a child nevermore, my innocence lost. I miss it so. But life isn't fair, is it? And an innocent child cannot run the most powerful country that has ever existed.

I almost lost my life then. When I thought I had all that I could endure, I was given more: three years later, I lost everything else dear to me in a thermonuclear blast that should have killed six million people but only succeeded in killing my family. That's why I work so hard for America, to bring freedom to the world.

I tried to sort out why all this happened, as I was left alone with my tears. The only explanation that made sense is because God must have spared me from dying on either of those two days so that I could live on and get another chance to right those wrongs. The world needed someone like me, who had the courage to do what no one else would have dared. They say I'm a modern-day Abe Lincoln who liberated millions. Hell, I certainly don't deserve that comparison, but I made the most of those opportunities. Did I do the right things?

My mother was a lovely aristocrat, born across the ocean in London. I didn't resemble her in the least, except for my blue eyes and blonde hair (at least the latter used to be!), but I hope some of her rubbed off on me. I guess I have done all right. Queen Elizabeth II made me a Dame Commander of the Most Excellent Order of the British Empire, so Mom would be proud if she could see me. I have faith that she still can. But she died on that day along with the rest of my family. I must live on to be the real English knight in shining armor that I need to be. Granted, my suit of armor has lost a bit of its luster over the years. So have I. Can I get it back?

I miss my first husband dearly. I married young, at twenty-four; we were life partners for many years, and he always stuck by me despite all the stupid mistakes I made. In the end, I was too self-occupied, and I knew I couldn't be that person he fell in love with any longer. It was always "one more thing" with me. Did I really need that Olympic gold medal that now gathers dust sitting on the Resolute Desk? Was inspiring the youth of tomorrow and being on the cover of Sports Illustrated worth all that?

Yet, all those things shaped who I am today, so the answer to that is complex. I wanted him to be happy, so I let him go to pursue his dreams; he found another true love and had a third child with her. But now he's dead as are our two children; his third child lives on, as does mine. Decades of abysmally poor dietary choices kept me off that plane. I have to be worthy of them and honor their memories while I serve the four hundred fifty mil-

lion people who placed their trust in me eight years ago.

I am now Commander-in-Chief of firepower sufficient to destroy the entire planet a dozen times over, a legacy literally given to me by my father, by the works of his own hands; he would be proud, in some twisted way. Sometimes I'm not proud of what I have evolved into at all. The irony is overwhelming. Am I worthy of such responsibility? Why me? And why do this, they ask? There is no military equal, no Cold War Soviet Union to compete with today. China borrows money from us now. North Korea, the hostile Middle East, and Cuba are history. Do we really need it all?

Easy answer: hell, yes. No one will ever screw with my country again. The next place that tries will regret it; they have no idea how much. Trust me, there is no one who can inflict pain as well as someone who has experienced it. So take heed of my warning. There won't be a second one.

I am in my late fifties now, my hair old and gray, tinted by chemicals out of a bottle in an effort to look youthful. Our country prizes youthfulness, yet in that era of my own youth I did not have the wisdom I do now. But do I have enough?

I needed to become President to do these things, to make the world safe again. But I also know I did it to do something else, something only I could do, with the vast power I wield: protect the world's most important child from others, those who would exploit her, militarize her power, and conquer the world. Someday I may pay the price for that, but that day is not today.

If anyone is going to conquer the world, it will be me. For I have taken enough crap in my life not to take control of my own destiny.

Despite my accomplishments, I am far from perfect. In fact, I am likely more flawed than almost all who have been in this position. Or, at least I admit my fallacies without hesitation; I hide nothing. My first marriage failed, mostly due to my selfishness over my pursuits; I have had a weight problem for my entire life. I have always been candid about my bipolar disorder in an effort to educate others. Most of my ill-fated youthful financial ventures lost money. Except the last one, of course, but I was just along for the ride on that one.

All these things make me human, I guess an everywoman others can relate to. I suppose people respect me for never hiding anything. Most of all, they respect me for that one decision I made long ago, in 2014. I don't regret it for an instant.

I didn't think twice when I pushed President Reardon and Prime Minister Truesdale to the ground when I saw that guy running towards the podium; I knew what I was doing when I took the bullets meant for them. I was lucky to have lived through that, although I still have days when I have pain. While I lay in a medically induced coma in the ICU at Bethesda Naval Hospital, all 535 members of Congress then petitioned that I should receive a special Medal of Honor because as Surgeon General I wasn't technically in the Armed Forces.

The pain from that and the losses I suffered later have made me strong, and I need it to survive. I don't ever want that pain—physical and emotional—to go away completely, because I am no cowardly weakling.

You had damn well better remember that. Learn why this is so.

I have had many titles in my life. Doctor. Admiral. Olympian. Governor. Dame Commander. American Hero. Madam President. All of these have presented challenges, to be sure.

But the title with the most trials and tribulations by far is Mother. I have given birth to three children, two of whom have died. I never had a chance to say goodbye to my Jake and Cassie. There is nothing worse in the world than trying to go on after that. If you think you understand, you don't, believe me. It creates an unmatched resilience inside you. So you had better realize that about me should you decide to take me on.

You won't survive it. I will, somehow. I always do.

I was once one of the physically strongest women in the world, back when trivial things like that had meaning to me. But I am surely the most emotionally strong today. If you are a government plotting something against me or my country, know that I will eventually find you and drag your worthless butt to Hell myself, for I fear nothing.

How can this be so?

Because I have been to Hades and back and have seen hellfire. Can you say the same, you piss-ant cowardly dictator? You look me in the eye to grasp what I've endured and try staring me down. I don't need a nuclear arsenal to take care of your sorry ass.

I'll break your neck with my bare hands or will die trying if need be.

Do you think for a moment you scare me? Really?

Think again, imbecile.

Because there's nothing more frightening than being in a fight with someone who isn't afraid to die.

So you damn well had better be scared shitless of me. For if you oppose me, it will not end well for y'all. See how it ended up for those who did. They are either in prison—or dead. Go ahead and roll the dice, scumbag—which would you like to be? Either way meets my needs.

How do you go on after something like Darkkday? You must, because you have no choice. I could have chosen to withdraw into obscurity or take my own life. I can't tell you how many ways I thought about doing the latter. I turned to God, whom I had ignored for years; He took me back, nevertheless, and guided me to do neither. Through His wisdom, I decided to build, to grow, to make the lives of millions better. Historians will debate my decisions long after I die, but I did what I had to do, and I would do those things again. Over three hundred fifty million people owe their freedom to me. Are you going to tell me that was wrong?

Over the years, I thought about my first love. First love is immensely powerful and brings back those initial feelings when you find you can be special to someone outside your family. I fell head over heels for him, the handsome Heisman Trophy candidate, the oldest brother of my thirteen-year-old deaf friend. He was twenty-one and I eighteen. At that age I couldn't see it coming, and didn't know how badly it would hurt when he cheated on me; I came back early from a track meet and found him in bed with my college roommate. Had I been a faster sort, I would likely be in jail for manslaughter instead of living in the White House.

He was one of the most self-centered human beings I had ever met. So, in the bizarre craziness that is my life, I should have predicted that he would be the one to reappear and help me through my despair twenty-six years later. God gave me back my first true love, someone who I thought was gone from my life forever. Fate brought us together, as he lost much on that day too. We can't get those people back, but somehow we created the blessing of a new life. I had the choice of considering my life a glass half empty or half full. I have chosen to embrace the latter.

Not many people are fortunate enough for their first love to become their last. What I have lost is incomprehensible, but for that, I am grateful.

Someday they will build libraries, schools, monuments, parks, and airports bearing my name and likeness, but accolades thrust upon me mean nothing any longer. What I have lost cannot ever be replaced. I am fortunate to have a loving husband and son, but the rest of the world wants me to do something for them constantly. I am but one mortal woman, and I cannot do everything. I should be content with what I have, but I'm not. Maybe I never will be.

I yearn for the person who will respect and admire me for what I am as a human being, an equal, one who does so not because of my power and influence. This person will surely be far more than my equal, in ways I cannot possibly yet imagine. Can I deal with that when we finally meet again?

Yes. I would not be doing all this were that not the case.

During those rare moments of solitude, the faint remnant of the child inside will always believe in Her, like many others do—Aurora Angelica, the divine Angel from the Stars. Somehow I know I will see her again before I die because I need to hold on to what is left of the inner child. I am weary of this job, but I must continue on because I know that I am going to witness true greatness, and helping that along will be my greatest legacy.

If I were to have a successor, someone I could mentor—that would make my life complete. I know my son William Conrad has no desire to follow in my footsteps. I don't blame him. He needs to go his own way in time and will achieve his own greatness, I am sure. I don't care about the greatness; I only want him to be happy in whatever he does.

I will never see my first two children, Jake or Cassie, again in this life. But I know, somehow, that my beloved niece, Aurora Angelica the Dark Star, shall soon rise again. For within our children lies hope. Perhaps for the world. I cannot do it alone. She surely has changed. Am I prepared to deal with what she has become when we finally meet again?

I only hope my tombstone says that I have made the world better rather than worse when I go to my final resting place. Wherever that will be, I have no idea.

But can a child really fly, little Wendy? I wonder.

Charleston, West Virginia
Rita
The Repentant Scientist
Forgiveness

I shouldn't be alive, but I am. I have survived many things. I was paralyzed in a car accident after being hit by a drunk driver, but I strove to become something worthy by earning my Ph.D. at Harvard. My parents were proud of me then. I shunned legitimate job offers to sell my soul to work for someone who promised I could walk again. He kept his promise, but the cost to me was immeasurable. I helped cause the death of a President and many others because he wanted a certain person in the White House. I went to prison for my crimes; my family and friends have disowned me, and I have had no contact with them for years. That's better than how my mentor ended up—dead, so I am lucky.

Somehow I was selected to help make things right. Why should I be so fortunate to play such a role? Is someone giving me a second chance at life? It was the one who had no name and was composed of pure energy who directed me to that barren spot in Mexico where I found fossilized remnants of the amazing DNA I found in Titan's ethane lake, Ontario Lacus, from the Cassini probe. Part of it was to help with a project that I would later discover was designed to engineer a human killing machine. That sure didn't work out like we had planned; those with a greater grasp of science (and violence) than I killed his oversized ass. But I gave the good stuff to one who would bear the Dark Star. I still don't remember much of it or why I did it.

I helped save the life of another who would become one of our finest Presidents; she pardoned me for my crimes, which is far more than I deserved, but I regret the horrible decisions I made. I still carry shame over what I did, but I have solace in that I have, in some small way, contributed to greatness. Is it enough to make up for what I have done? I don't think so. I hope God can somehow forgive me in the end.

I was in Washington on Darkkday and should have been obliterated along with six million other people. Instead, we all survived, and I was even able to walk again less than a week after that. How can this be explained? I know logically that no one in that plane could have survived, but what other explanation is there besides Aurora the Angel? I know it's true. What have I contributed to? I am no physicist, but I know that there are forces out there we don't understand. And is there more greatness to come? Or will there be more destruction beyond comprehension? Which shall it be? I wonder.

Washington, DC
Jacqueline
The Silent Sentinel
Service

I was born in Baltimore, the middle-class daughter of a city policeman and school teacher. Mom and Dad wanted me to get married and have five kids. My sister did that, which was fine for her, but I had different ideas. I always wanted to be in law enforcement but never dreamed I would have the most important position in the world. Dad didn't want me to be a cop like he and my big brother, but now he brags about me all the time to his buddies.

I guess I deserve that; I have an important and dangerous job that provides me with no glory, damn long hours, and less pay than I could get elsewhere. But I'm not in it for glory, money, or leisure time. I exist to serve and protect, for I have the most important law enforcement job any person could have, which I can do better than anyone else. Who am I?

I am the last line of defense, for I protect the President of the United States of America.

But I am more than that—I am her friend and her most trusted advisor, despite my lack of "official" political experience or title and loads of smarter people than me around. But politics is not for me; I am content to remain in the background.

Being Presidential Detail Chief for the United States Secret Service is no easy task, I assure you. Telling code name Darling "no" to something is unpleasant, yet I must do so often because she has a passion and drive like I have never seen before—and a knack for getting into trouble. It's up to me to keep her out of it. Most of the time, I succeed. If other people fail at their jobs, they get fired. If I don't do mine, it could mean her life.

I had a rather circuitous route to this position. I had met her ten years before she became President, and to be honest, I wasn't terribly impressed by her or her family at first. They seemed like a bunch of entitled, moneyed academic and athletic elitists who played around at solving crimes and other stuff. She was almost a caricature, a rather boisterous person who diversified by being a media personality, athlete, medical politician, and cartoon character, while being a master of only a couple of them.

But she was a damn smart physician, even though she was a royal pain in the ass, royally knighted by the Queen of England herself a while back. And she had guts. More than most any other President.

She still is a pain in my ass. Yes, I have told her that to her face. She took it as a compliment.

People's priorities change and evolve, and I found out that she represented far more. Some, like her, eventually reach their full potential. That negative opinion I once had changed when I saw her do (with no obligation) what I have sworn to do now: save the life of a President and British Prime Minister by getting in the line of fire, with Reardon's Secret Service detail asleep at the wheel. I've looked at the video clips over and over; it was no accident. She knew exactly what she was doing and probably should have died, because she's a living example of what happens when we don't do our job. She somehow survived those four ceramic armor-piercing bullets, and a rather unlikely heroine was elected Governor of California for two terms, which is when she started changing the world. She had some help, for certain; the discovery of Element 119 by her sister-in-law and achievable nuclear fusion provided great economic opportunities few Presidents have had. Hey, you take what you get in life. She did. All the way to the White House. She deserves a few breaks, don't you think?

Then I saw what she went through after Darkkday, her family gone. I took Jaime to her bedside myself, and I saw her pull herself together to be the one to regroup the country. I knew what was next. I never saw anyone who could engage people like she could when she is on her game. She also has a certain genuineness about her. Just don't ever piss her off. Trust me on that one.

I was one of many who back then underestimated her intellect and ability to prepare for a battle. The mercurial nature of her personality is an incredible thing to behold and one of her most underrated qualities. I watched her play the aw-shucks Appalachian blonde during the opening minutes of the first Presidential debates, then turn around and utterly destroy her more experienced opponent with a carefully planned attack that left him like a punch-drunk prizefighter on the ropes. Sen. Paul Garcia was the one who lost his composure and became angry, not the bipolar Oak Ridge Dame who went from zero to ninety miles per hour in the blink of an eye to utterly decimate him. The other debates were even more lopsided as she mopped up the floor with him. She won that first election easily, earning 370 of the required 270 electoral votes.

I knew long ago I wanted to join the Secret Service, and that I had a better destiny in life than busting up drug cartels. I moved up the chain and eventually became Chief of the Presidential detail in 2021, as she personally requested me. I have seen the transformation of a country from one heavily in debt and dependent on foreign economies to a nation that now sets the pace of the world.

The President is a kind, polite person and respectful of other cultures (she follows the customs of other countries; she will wear an appropriate head covering when visiting Muslim nations or New Persia, for example). But don't push her too far. She takes personal insults pretty well and laughs them off; but if you insult women in general or something else she's passionate about, you're done. One country's king refused to shake hands with her back when she was Governor because he didn't shake hands with mere women. Man, was that a big mistake. His country's biggest resource, oil—is worth next to nothing now. Wonder how much fun all those yachts and airplanes of his are today, now that he's broke?

It is a privilege to work with her; she is one of the best people I've ever known, although she is loud, headstrong, exhausting, obnoxious, and hardly ever shuts up. But I would die for her in a heartbeat. I don't know where I will eventually end up. I may move on to something else after 2032, the end of her probable third term because I know working with someone else will pale in comparison. And I will be worn out by then and ready for the retirement home. So will she. Just don't put us in there to-

gether; I will have my twelve years of memories. I need some "me" time.

There was someone I once fell in love with. He was an unlikely choice: he didn't really respect authority and was the furthest from the ideal I thought I would want. But he had an inner goodness, and one day he just disappeared. He is now legally dead, but what really happened to him? Did some unspeakable tragedy befall him? Or is he living under an alias somewhere? Why would he have done something like that? Perhaps he is the selfish person others always said he was. Or maybe he is a greater person than I ever could have imagined. I hope that whatever happened to him, that he lived his life with honor. I wonder.

Green Bay, Wisconsin
Jaime
The Reformed Playboy
Selflessness

I walk in the back yard of my beautiful summer home and look out on Green Bay while I remember that I was the boy who would never grow up. Unlike the child in the stories my wife fancies, I finally did, decades after everyone else did, because I had no choice. When your whole family is vaporized you make tough decisions. I was lucky to get her back. She was just a teenager then, when I broke her heart by cheating on her (with her roommate, no less). I did that to a lot of women; to me it was no big deal; there were always more potential conquests out there. But there was only one like her. I was there for her when both of us had no one else after that fateful day. Nine months later, we witnessed the miracle of our love child, who I treasure dearly. But I grieve for her two other children she lost on that day.

I was one of the most selfish people who ever lived. No, probably not that, but at least the most egocentric person in my family, and that is no easy task; it was full of strong personalities. Everything I did was for me. I didn't pay any attention to my relationships because all I thought about was me. Someone else would always take care of things, and another girl would always be available. I always found another partner, though my relationships usually didn't last long. Why was I spared on Darkkday when most of my other family members died? There must have been a reason. Now I was the one who was left, and that reason wasn't clear. Why me, a dumb-ass jock, clearly the least relevant of them all?

We were blessed to have had a child in her mid-forties; how the hell that happened, I'll never know. It wasn't an easy pregnancy for her, at forty-five; she developed gestational diabetes and took four insulin shots a day while running the great state of California and working eighteen-hour days with one lung and a surgically repaired heart. The doctors thought she was foolish for even contemplating pregnancy; they forgot other doctors are the worst patients ever. I never thought I would be a father; that would have taken too much giving of myself. But having a child has changed my life. I wish he could have known his mother's other children, but they are gone too, as are the rest of our family. We should be grateful for what we still do have, I guess.

I don't really have much of a job these days, but I try to do the things my wife needs me to do. Her needs, like her, are large. So I have a lot of time to spend with him. Time is our most valuable asset, I have learned; once it's gone, you can't ever get it back, and you have only so much of it. Even our wealth can't buy more of it.

I have to be the stability in Will's life. I had it growing up; my mom and dad were wonderful, caring people. My wife isn't here a lot, so I teach him about what I know about: football and people. Sounds simple, but those two things can get you a lot in life.

Most boys would relish having a Pro Football Hall of Famer and former League Commissioner for a dad and an Olympic gold medalist for a mom, but I am secretly proud that he cares nothing about such things. It's like he knows there is something more important on the horizon. He's surely right. As usual, my mind is on the superficial things. In his eleven years, he has taught me a lot about life. Being a dad does that, as kids don't come with instruction manuals.

But I'm lucky—because I believe there is one child out there whose parents really could use some instructions. They would be a doozy.

I miss my sister most of all. We shared lots of things—a hidden bond that no one else can understand. She was eight years younger, and we couldn't have been more different. She was better at math and English at age three than I was at fourteen, but I didn't help by being so lazy. I started paying her to write my term papers and do my homework when she was four. She wasn't very good with money so I got off cheaply. The teachers thought I had paid college students to do it.

We both had our heads in the clouds, though—this, we shared. She with her crazy, obsessive "special interests," and me with my sports and pursuit of the ladies (one of my "special interests"). Our brother died in the Darkkday explosion, too. He was always the stable one who tried to keep both of us grounded in reality. I miss Mike. His daughter is still with us. You sure wouldn't know it from looking at her, but she is the poster child for practicality. Not thrift, though—she can spend money like it's going out of style. That's okay; she has more of it than most any woman in the world. She earned it. And she was lucky.

But I know that sometimes luck runs out.

Has luck run out for our civilization? How long can we keep on going like this, taking over the world one country at a time? I don't know.

Sometimes it's like my sister is still with me, as I can hear her sometimes. I know they are just memories, but will I see her again someday? She always was the spectacular one. I know her final stage act is yet to come. I wonder.

San Diego, California
Petra Nureyev
The Troubled Genius
Arrogance

I ambulate through Balboa Park in the city of my birth, my hair snow white now, and my life is not as I imagined it would be. You would never guess that I was born here, and not in Moscow, as my birth certificate states. No one knows me any longer, as I do not resemble the person of my youth, as I dress in the clothing of the magician whom I idolized as a child. People stare for a few seconds, then move on, as they likely believe me an incoherent, homeless, demented hermit, indistinguishable from the many others they encounter.

Maybe they are right. The world is as it always was. They ignore the troubles of the world, thinking they don't exist.

How ironic. To the world, I stopped existing long ago. This is how it had to be.

Humph. They have no idea how magnificent my brain is. It is better that they do not know the truth about my giant brain, as it would frighten them. People fear what they cannot understand. This is why I live a humble existence in rural Alaska.

I wander aimlessly as I reflect on my life. I have nearly perished more times than can be enumerated, and each time I am augmented in a novel fashion. Someday the sands of time shall expire for me once and for all, the one who has cheated death again and again.

But know that that day is not today, although we likely will all perish soon in a radioactive mushroom cloud of destruction. I am a survivor. They used to call me a living miracle because I lived through what no one thought possible.

But I somehow survived a thermonuclear warhead that detonated twenty feet from me so that I could raise the genuine miracle that is the daughter of my blood. She is, seemingly, also the daughter of someone else who existed seventy million years ago. I do not know much about him, other than somehow I know he was not a real great guy. There is a wonderful secret I have kept hidden for so many years. Soon you will see it and rejoice.

Yet, will people fear her as well? Above all else, I do not want this to be so. Will she be accepted as one of them? Or rejected? This, even one such as I cannot predict. But one thing is for certain: I cannot control her any longer; the future is beyond my control. I have a difficult time even keeping track of myself these days.

Everything I see is a vivid kaleidoscope of color, everything I hear a vibrant symphony of the most wonderful sounds ever. My hearing, vision, and touch are so sensitive it is hard to concentrate at times. The amazing violet synthetic being who accompanies me wherever I go is my constant companion. He is composed of pure light, the seven Newtonian colors. I talk to him since he is as real as any other being. He is a good friend, as only he has the intellect to truly understand me as your mind cannot. We run and jump through the park and celebrate our wondrous thoughts. What a joy!

I do not think like the other simpletons who inhabit this planet, as I see the words and mathematical formulae in my mind so clearly, yet I can concentrate on little else. I communicate little as my mind has grown exponentially over the years. I have given my musings to the world as a gift, as I desire no honor upon myself. I have moved beyond the petty acquisition of wealth and accolades the egotistical First Family holds so dear; my mental existence is on a different dimensional plane than the small puny minds the lower humans on 1600 Pennsylvania Avenue possess. How pathetic they are as they revel in their supposed greatness. I should be a billionaire many times over, but money means nothing to me. It never did. There are more important things than that. If I can convey that one thing to my daughter, I will rest in peace.

Humph. They are like mere ants when compared to my supreme intellect. Only I know that true power lies in vast existential knowledge, not the acquisition of nuclear weapons, Super Bowl rings, Nobel Prizes, Academy Awards, knighthoods, billion-dollar estates, memorial cities, and Olympic gold medals. The primordial humans' folly shall surely be their undoing. I revel in my superiority, uniqueness, and my simple existence today.

And yet, my vast talents seem rather wasted now on teaching high school math and doing statistics for the girls' basketball team, as I must be content to scribble the secrets of the universe on the living room wall of my small home with a felt tip marker. Bah! No one can comprehend my greatness; thus I am reduced to such menial tasks. Such is my penance for the life I have led.

I know my path must collide with her, my surrogate "big sister," at some point. I both look forward to and dread that eventual confrontation as it likely will not be pleasant. Blows and harsh words shall be exchanged. She has taken the gift I gave the world and used it to make the United States the most feared military power in human existence. This is not right; it is one of the few things my daughter and I agree on. But I had bigger things to worry about than her boundless ego.

But know this: she will fear me far more than I fear her. No, that is untrue, as she has changed; she has become more formidable than I could ever have envisioned. I only hope that we will meet again before she blasts us all off the face of the planet because I have a few unpleasant words to say. The end of the world is near, as I can feel it in my sorry old bones. I survived one ground zero nuclear blast; I shall survive another one.

I wasted much of my life on childish pursuits. How far I have come, as the things I see now are beyond comprehension. I wish you could see the fantastic things my purple friend and I do. No, you would not understand. It is not your fault you are inferior.

As I look upon the beautiful child who emerged from my womb, I worry about her. She has faced adversity in life as I have and a greater responsibility than even my consciousness can possibly fathom. Will she be happy? Most of my life, I have not been happy, as I live in a world of people so unlike me. As a child, I often wondered if I was an alien on this world. The irony of that statement is profound, as I wonder now if I am more alien than human. And is my daughter even more so? I did not wish this all to happen, but it did; I cannot alter history. Even I, with my fantastic intelligence, cannot time travel.

I have abilities that I suppress because they are more dangerous than can even be imagined. They might be the only thing that could control her should she go berserk. But what if I lost my mind? Have I already? What the Dark Star possesses could be perverted into the most horrific weapon ever by the brainless blonde leviathan who, unfortunately, shares twenty-five percent of her DNA. Combining my abilities with those of my daughter could potentially disrupt the fabric of the whole universe and destroy the time-space continuum, dooming us all! You don't think so?

I know things that you cannot even begin to comprehend. Many of these things are very bad. Somehow I know she is strong enough to never let that happen.

Paige is almost grown now, the ability to defend herself certain. I have pushed her beyond what she thought she could ever do; some may think that unkind, but she needs to stand on her own two feet, as I once did.

Our similarities end there.

So know ye by my declaration that when my blind daughter Paige, like a beautiful butterfly, finally transforms into the magnificent Stella Scura, the living Dark Star, she will be able to do far more than stand—she shall fly faster than sound and move mountains. Stella is not a figment of my imagination, or magical sleight of hand, or a delusion, but raw power beyond comprehension, drawn from the manipulation of the most fundamental of forces with microscopic precision that baffles even my unmatched mind. This is the gift that was her birthright, made possible by events even I, with my colossal intellect, still do not understand completely, if you can believe that. She is the only one truly deserving of these abilities. Soon you will behold her splendor, too.

I made her go to a regular school to deal with the bullying children who made fun of her, as they did to me when I was a mere child. Does one of limitless power not need equally great patience and humility? True to my predictions, she never has struck anyone or shown physical aggressiveness in any way. Vocally—that's another matter. I am mighty, but clearly no match for her physical powers—and certainly not her verbal ones. Don't get into an argument with her. You will lose.

But make no mistake—Stella is a warrior born, as I once was. She carries within her some of the inexperience and recklessness of youth that once was inside me. But, despite her feigned hubris, I know deep in my heart that she is more mature and wise now than I will ever be. I have killed with my bare hands on multiple occasions in self-defense. I hunted down and killed the Tosian dictator who caused Darkkday and blamed it on North Korea and Kristoff van Sant. That dog deserved to die.

Yet, Paige is surely a goddess, truly incapable of petty emotions such as revenge unless I seriously misjudge her, so in that way, she is far superior to me. I possess less than a trillionth of my daughter's strength, yet you are safer with her than with me, should you be an enemy. She will use violence only as a last resort, despite having the power to do anything she wants. I seem to lack the inner goodness that personifies her. Maybe once I did, but life has changed me into something I no longer like. I truly hope she remains wise and focused; the world can't afford for her to be anything else.

Where did all the time go? I wonder if I still have my sanity after all these years. I seem to talk to alien beings as if they were real. The secrets of the universe have been revealed to me through my dreams, and I know that the paltry gift I gave humanity with my intellect pales to the one which emerged from my body. Is the world ready for the incredible power of dark energy?

I grew up with a disability like she did. Others wanted to do things for me, to make me who they wanted, to make me what they considered "normal." They meant well. But I will not make that same mistake with her. She needs to go out on her own, to make her own way, even if it is hard, changes our lives forever, and would not be what I would have chosen. She can, in time, be the greatest leader the world has ever known; maybe she can teach her aunt a thing or two. Or, she could do many bad things. But it is out of my hands now, as a little girl has grown up. I have much to learn from her as well. While she exasperates me to no end, she is the finest person you could ever meet.

My amazing mind peruses this concept: is Stella divine, a true Angel? No, this cannot be so. An Angel would not have come to Earth in the form of the world's most irritating teenager. God would not have done that to me. Yet, I was once deaf, but now I am whole again, somehow, perhaps because of the power she possesses. And even I still have not solved the mystery of her sightlessness. How can one who survived Armageddon not be able to see? Is it possible that I do not know everything? Reluctantly, I must admit this remote possibility, as unlikely as it may be. Perhaps another of my blood who is adept at solving the insolvable can figure it out.

I do card tricks for the people in the park who laugh at me, and I ask myself: have I truly lost my marbles? Most surely think one who converses with aliens and invisible purple blobs must have done so. They are likely correct, as I have lost my perspective as well as many valuable brain cells as I muddle through middle age. I have no tangible proof of them any more than I have proof in God, yet I know that they both must exist.

They say genius and insanity are not far apart. I surely possess both qualities in large amounts. This I ponder as my intangible purple friend and I cerebrate, pontificate, and calculate as the lesser mortals cannot. Regrettably, we must exist among them, with no peers to share the gloriousness of our perceptions. I wonder.

Washington, DC
William Conrad
The World's Most Popular Boy
Discontent

I go outside and run down Pennsylvania Avenue, although I am never alone. I am eleven and probably the most famous boy on the planet. Being the American equivalent of royalty sure sucks. Even my famous mom technically is a British dignitary, if you can believe that after hearing her talk. They say you can't choose your parents; I love mine, but sometimes I wish they were normal people. They aren't. It's like being a rock star every time I go out. They both crave attention and love it. I have expectations to live up to that are beyond anything you can imagine.

I wonder if I even have an identity. I live forever in the shadow of my older brother and sister, who died before I was born in a horrific act of terrorism. I hear about it all the time, although it's frustrating as I can't do anything about it. I was named after my grandfather, who I also never met. I don't know what happened to him, although that he apparently died saving my mom. She never talks about that or why she needed saving, only what a good man he was and that he had his demons. Maybe I don't want to know about that stuff. For that, I am grateful. But that's it. I don't want to spend all my time discussing him. Is that so wrong, to want to be my own person, and not live through the lives of others?

Dad has a bust in Canton, Ohio, which I have seen several times, big deal. Also, two Super Bowl rings (one as a player, another as a coach). All the footballs used to have his name engraved on them, although they changed that when they got a new Commissioner. He still goes on TV sometimes, but not much. Everybody (especially pretty women) wants his autograph when we go out. It gets so old. But he loves it, as does my mom, and they clearly love each other. But I can't be them.

There is even a city in Indiana named after a dead girl who part of the world reveres as some kind of mystical angel. I heard she was my cousin. Another deceased family member whose expectations I must live up to. There isn't much information available on her or why people could possibly believe that.

Or the rest of my family, like my older cousin in Aurora City—to my knowledge, the only person to have ever won both a Nobel Prize and an Academy Award. She is a pretty cool gal, actually. Or my dead aunt, who apparently was some type of eccentric savant with the combined intellect of Albert Einstein, Niels Bohr, and a dozen other famous guys. It's hard to go anywhere without seeing her face because her likeness is on the American five-dollar coin, a ubiquitous denomination.

I'm sorry about those people who died, but get real. Is Mom hiding something from me? She acts dumb sometimes, but I know that no person could do what she has done without being both extraordinarily intelligent and a master manipulator who invariably has stepped on a few people on her ascent to the top.

But while I honor my fallen relatives, I don't want to be them or talk about them all the time because life is for the present, not the past. I'm my own person, and I don't want my life scripted out for me.

I play sports, but I don't care much about them. They say I'm the kind of natural athlete who comes along once in a generation. Who gives a crap? I need a greater destiny than snobby prep schools and sports scholarships. I don't care about the Super Bowl or the Olympics; they are inconsequential. How many eleven-year-olds are contacted by colleges, sports agents, and advertising companies? I can choose the professional sport of my liking because I'm better right now than any high school kid in the city at them all.

But believe me when I tell you I don't want any of that; I want my life to mean something. Maybe I can do what my mom does someday if she hasn't blown the world up by then. Or can I help someone else do it? Mom seems awfully preoccupied these days with something I don't understand, but maybe someday I will. I wonder.

Marcella, Arizona
Nicholas
The Wealthy Industrialist
Opportunity

I walk down the street of this, one of many cities I helped build in honor of those who died on that fateful day: December 16, 2016. This city was named after my first wife. I cared for her more than anything. I was fortunate that an old friend, who comforted me, did me the honor of becoming my second wife. She understands all this because she lost almost everything then, too. She wants me to have my memories of Marcy. It helps a little bit. But the pain never goes away completely. I wouldn't want it to.

I am fortunate to have helped bring, like a phoenix rising from the ashes, the genius of another fallen one to fruition. She was misunderstood and ridiculed by some, but perhaps the greatest pure intellect of our time.

In a way, we were alike, with dreams and ideas. One always has to have those. The similarity ends there, as she was clearly on a different cerebral plane than I can ever hope to be.

My second wife is the one who knows the practical application of things; she is admired by all, arguably the world's most glamorous woman, and a singular genius in a rather unglamorous way, with dirt often under those manicured nails. Without her, I wouldn't have achieved any of this.

Why do I do these things? I need money, as much as I can amass. No, I'm not greedy, but I need it to do what is right for America. Someone else I know wants that too; she has resources at her disposal far beyond mine. I hope we are trying to arrive at the same goal. Despite my fortune, I work in the background, trying to help our country.

One thing I don't daydream about, though: I want the power to shape the world. My wife tries to direct me elsewhere, but I know that there is a higher calling out there. One that will take a lot of money and power to realize. No, I don't think greed is good. But sometimes, it is necessary, lest someone greedier obtain that power. I am well acquainted with such an individual. She does what she feels is right, but at what cost? She says we are very much alike. She is probably right.

I live a secret life; I funnel hundreds of millions of dollars to someone I hope still exists. Why he wants it, I have no idea. I have to trust that he is doing the right thing. In the end, I know that it will benefit us all. God help me if I'm wrong.

I have suspicions regarding what I believe to be an energy force like no other and work secretly on this with the father of an old friend, the descendant of the greatest astrophysicist of all time. The money I contribute will somehow benefit humanity in the long run.

One old friend would want to know, yet I dare not tell her yet, as this power cannot be perverted towards a single person's needs. Surely she knows already. Somehow I feel that the money I send has something to do with this. But the energy I seek will make that which made me wealthy seem paltry in comparison. I will share it with the world, after making a profit, of course. What is worth doing is worth doing for money. Because there will be some other project later I will need to take on.

I somehow feel that I will bring together great minds to solve the mysteries of the universe. I may be visited by strange beings, but my life has been interesting. I am content to be in the background. Will these things come true? I wonder.

Eielson Air Force Base
Fairbanks North Star Borough, Alaska
Russell
The Young Officer
Adventure

I am a first lieutenant now, two and a half years out of the Air Force Academy. I'll make captain soon if I keep my nose clean. My parents always strove for me to make the best of myself, and I hope I haven't disappointed. Eielson may not seem like the most exciting military base, but I am involved in some pretty important intelligence work. I hope to become a career officer and make full colonel someday.

But I seek adventure, the thrill of not knowing what comes next. No, I'm not reckless, but I wouldn't have become an elite pilot had I not wanted that. Somehow I know I'll find it in Alaska, of all places. No, I don't believe in destiny—but this is the untamed frontier. I hope to find that special someone, although my social options at Eielson and nearby Fairbanks are kind of limited. Yet, I need to keep all my options open.

I also want to find love, something that has eluded me in my twenty-four years. I am pretty picky about who I date, and I just want to find that special person soon. I know the pickings may be slim up in central Alaska.

I also want to make a difference in the world somehow. Will I be able to accomplish that in this remote area, of all places? What adventures are in store for me? I wonder.

Leeuwarden, The Netherlands
Juriann
The Gentle Wanderer
Uncertainty

I put my massive hand on the grass and feel as I look out into the fog of the North Sea from Leeuwarden. My past is a mystery. I don't resemble the people who raised me, and they don't know any more about it than me, other than that a very odd Russian stranger brought me to them as an infant, talking incessantly about how I would play a role someday in helping the greatest leader the world will ever know. How could such a person exist? I question this because I am vastly intelligent, they say; I graduated from university at eighteen. And I am strong beyond comprehension.

I am by nature a gentle being, yet I can also become an adversary, especially if one tries to harm those I have promised to protect. Yet I know there is someone stronger. I have no proof other than that the Russian stranger, known only as Petra, told my parents this when she left me as an infant. All people need a friend, as will this one. I will travel to the land of greatness to fulfill my destiny and learn my heritage.

But perhaps it will not be as wonderful as I believe it to be. Few things are. But it's better than having nothing to hold on to. Don't get me wrong—I have had a privileged life here in the Netherlands. But I know that there must be something more, something that will fulfill that destiny. It is that truth I seek.

I have heard rumors of the great Gravi-Golfer, the one who is an expert on gravitational energy. I have been to his ancestor's grave in Bavaria. There are subtle perturbations in the Earth's rotational velocity that can only be explained by an outside force. This force is what I seek, not to conquer the world, but to help mankind; it is located near North Pole, Alaska, per my calculations. Shall I really encounter Santa Claus there, or someone even more powerful? An angel from the stars, or death from above? I don't believe in fairy tales, though. But I need something to believe in. I must seek the Angel that I know exists out there to have something to hold onto.

But what is my destiny? I have perhaps the strength of fifty men, can run faster than the wind, and can endure things that would crush a normal human to dust. But my power pales compared to that which the legendary Angel must possess. Surely others have detected this being's presence. For this reason, I must get there first. Is this how I will best help mankind? I have been gifted with a superior intellect as well. Do I have any relatives, or am I destined to walk the Earth alone, my future uncertain?

Will I have a normal lifespan? Will I feel and love like a normal man? I know somehow I am different, but will I find others like me? The woman who brought me to my adoptive parents told them that someday I would need to be a protector. I wonder.

Book One: Glory of The Great Dame

"In the absence of justice, what is sovereignty but organized robbery?"

—Saint Augustine

"Nearly all men can stand adversity, but if you want to test a man's character, give him power."

—Abraham Lincoln

Chapter One

September 29, 2028
The White House
Situation Room
Washington, DC

The roomful of intimidating generals, admirals, Cabinet members, and advisors sat patiently in the White House Situation Room, seemingly awaiting what likely was to come next if Senator Douglas Thomasson's brother wasn't rescued soon from the Taraqi rebels. The Chairman of the Joint Chiefs of Staff, Army Gen. Lawrence A. Kriger, didn't particularly like war. Any senior military officer who said he wanted war had obviously never been in one.

His colleagues also didn't, although U.S. forces could crush any country's military assemblage easily, and angering America was a fool's errand. Yet, there were many fools still around who unfortunately enjoyed tempting the supreme superpower. Killing people wasn't fun, he knew, having done quite a bit of that back in the day. But the late-fiftyish man with four stars on each shoulder didn't like being a wimp, either.

Neither did his boss—this was the only President he had dealt with as Chairman, although he had met several others in his storied military career. In his opinion, they all paled in comparison to the Republican incumbent: a rather intense, in-your-face Chief Executive who elicited awe in most adults, laughter in small children, and (most importantly in his opinion) mortal fear in anyone who dared to be America's enemy. While the President was paradoxically liberal in many political views (for a member of the GOP)—for example, POTUS was a rabid defender of lesbian, gay, and transgender rights, to the point of threatening countries that discriminated against anyone because of their beliefs (many of them subsequently became U.S. States)—the left-handed President was assuredly a traditional right-winger when it came to the military and protecting America.

Being a former West Point football star, he also respected someone his age who possibly could—and would, undoubtedly, if necessary—kick his military ass across the room.

This President was also one who didn't give a damn about the upcoming election in a few weeks and spent virtually no time on the campaign trail because this leader had *real* work to do for the entity that made out the paycheck—the United States of America. Even campaign signs and buttons were felt to be a waste of the taxpayers' money. If the public wanted someone else, then so be it, and then a well-deserved retirement would be soon at hand.

Damn, that took mighty big balls, he thought as he smiled.

"What'll happen now?" Marine Lt. Gen. Robert Yarger asked him, interrupting his train of thought.

"Hell, Rob," he said as he swirled the coffee in his porcelain cup and frowned at his colleague. "You know what the Chief will do. They either give Thomasson back today, or they're atomic dust tomorrow. Damn, it's gonna get ugly."

Yarger shook his head. "Awww, come on. Do you really think POTUS will go through with it this time? Jesus Christ, I don't believe it, Larry."

Kriger pushed his chair back and snarled. "Are you kidding? Will Commie-ass-kicking POTUS send a handful of Daddy Dearest's 'babies' on a one-way trip to the Middle East? They're far enough away from New Persia; the new hadron bombs won't touch that, so, hell yes. Very little contamination, focused damage. It sure doesn't look good for those dudes; what a bunch of fucking dumb asses. So *believe it*. Honey badger don't care, as the President is absolutely fearless, Rob. This, you know."

"*What's that?* 'Daddy Dearest's babies?'" Yarger shook his head again, confused. "What the hell does *that* mean?"

He nodded his head like a bobblehead doll. "You heard me. He loved those big nuclear bastards more than his own babies, I heard, and he spent way more time with them than the kids, too. Did you ever know him?"

"Huh? Know *who?* What the hell are you talking about, Larry?"

"The king of the modern nukes, man, get with the frickin' program, Rob. *W. Conrad Darkkin.*"

"Darkkin?" Yarger thought for a few seconds. "No, I never met him. Never heard of him much, either, other than he was POTUS' dad. There isn't much info available on him; you'd think there would be more, given who his kid is. Guess I never thought much about it. It's like the damn dude never existed."

He grinned. "Holy shit, that Rad Darkkin was something else, a guy you'd have to see to believe. I met that whiskey-soaked asshole when I was just a greenhorn lieutenant on some military ops back in the late 80's. I wondered why a civilian was in there, and I laughed when I thought he'd be another one of those military wannabe science geeks from DS&T, that is, until I *saw* him.

"He was unbelievably big, about six-five and three hundred ten pounds, mean, and damn scary, with that deep gravelly voice. And I stopped laughing real fast, because that big hillbilly bastard would've kicked my butt good. He made it clear to the brass who the hell was in charge. There have been only two civilians I've ever been scared of in my life who could boss military brass around like that. He was one."

"Huh. Guess I know where the personality comes from now, it makes sense."

"You bet, although I hear tell the two of them never got along. But, about your question, yes—I think this is the time, no bluffing, you know better. They're not near an ocean, so there's little chance of spreading contamination. No one wants their stupid oil anyway; we have enough reserves in North America for our modest needs. I hate indecisive Presidents, and this is the only one in my lifetime who had any goddamn balls. Bigger *cojones* than anyone else in Washington. Foreign leaders cater to us now, not the other way around. How it should be. Those dip-shits are in big trouble."

"*Cojones?*" Lt. Gen. Yarger shivered, his eyes scanning the room nervously as he realized where he was. "Is that supposed to be a joke, Larry? That's *not* funny. Remember whose house you're a guest in."

The crew-cut Kriger shook his head and scowled. "Hell, no, do I look like I'm joking? I meant that as a compliment, even if they're 'honorary' balls. I wish the hell I had solid brass ones like those, and you would, too."

Yarger nodded. "Probably so, but that's clearly not possible, for obvious reasons."

"You think? What a stupid remark. And you want to know who the other person I'm scared shitless of is?"

"Yeah, Larry, I'm sure you'll tell me."

He looked at his watch. "You'll see in about fifteen seconds."

Lt. Gen. Yarger nodded his head nervously. "Gotcha."

Exactly fourteen seconds later, the door opened as they rose to their feet immediately and saluted the world's most powerful leader, as Gen. Kriger smiled and reflected on the ironic fact that the President with the biggest *cojones* ever was the first with none at all.

Anatomically speaking, at least.

At six feet one inch tall and one hundred ninety-eight pounds, the intimidating former Governor of California, U.S. Surgeon General, Olympic gold medalist, national champion powerlifter, and Medal of Honor awardee with the 52-inch bust, 34-inch waist, big blonde hair, diamond earrings, and immaculately tailored royal blue skirted Tahari suit and matching size thirteen Prada pumps sat down as everyone was completely silent. They knew this woman always had the first word—and the last. If not, someone's butt would be chewed out good. That was a sight to behold.

"What's the updated status, General Kriger?" President Wendy Mendoza drawled loudly in her deep Southern Appalachian accent, a distinct curiosity for someone who had been awarded the title Dame Commander of The Most Excellent Order of the British Empire, the female equivalent of a knight—only bestowed upon the most distinguished of Englishwomen. "From your blank facial expressions, I must assume y'all have made no progress in resolving our difficult dilemma. *Why* does that not surprise me?" Her gaze was like laser beams penetrating his body. "Well, gentlemen?"

"We've tried every diplomatic means of getting Thomasson's brother out, Madam President. They seem to be a bunch of damn martyrs."

"Perhaps." She looked at her ungainly feet for several seconds as she sat at the head of the table. "How unfortunate, since the history of martyrs throughout time does not favor their survival. Special ops report update, please?"

"They have a shitload of advanced technology they got from

the Russians in the mid-twenties. While it may seem like a backward country, the Taraqis have radar and detection devices that would rival ours, maybe even surpass them. We could sure get in there by force if we knew where he was, but they keep moving him around. By the time we found out where he really was, they probably will have killed him—and they move him frequently, it seems. I have looked at our options, and there doesn't seem to be any other way."

"Probably not. Regrettable, for them, sadly. All life is precious, but I value American lives most. If others must die to save Americans, then so be it. A message must unfortunately be sent."

"Other options, Ma'am?" Kriger asked nervously.

"*Other options?*" She slammed her large left fist on the table, spilling coffee from several cups, which spun and scattered across the table like frightened cats. "What the hell do you think? If they actually kill him, the crazy bastards—well, you know the answer. If you don't, then you'd better think a while longer."

He nodded. "Yes, Ma'am."

"Damn right you do. We don't make deals with terrorists; not now, not *ever*. The price of defying the great United States of America by jeopardizing human lives can only be their ultimate destruction. This is the policy, this is what must be known to all, now and forever. The time is *now*, and theirs has finally run out."

The former pediatrician now called President lifted her left arm and tapped her red manicured index fingernail on the gleaming sapphire crystal of her dead father's stainless steel Ball Engineer Hydrocarbon Spacemaster Orbital watch on her right wrist. It was a large, extremely expensive, nearly indestructible Swiss timepiece which would be ridiculously large on most women but which looked perfect on her large wrist. The luminous radioactive tritium dial would be enough to read by in a darkened room—a fitting timepiece for the famous daughter of a kick-ass nuclear scientist, a jingoistic President perpetually threatening to send nukes to the Middle East or to anywhere else that threatened America.

The damn diplomats could argue about "proportional response." But any government that intentionally hurt an American citizen could receive only one outcome: death and destruction the likes of which General Kriger could only imagine. This buffed-up, in-your-face President was not to be messed with. Only Taraq's proximity to the fifty-fourth state had saved it for this long. Or so she had boasted.

But was she bluffing? She had threatened nuclear destruction many times before but had never actually seriously considered it, not even to the hated North Koreans, who surrendered their entire military forces before that happened (to become state #55;); or to Iran, whose dysfunctional government was now reconstituted as the state of New Persia (#54). Two years before that, she became weary of hearing arguments about how Guantanamo Naval Base should be given back to Cuba, so she resolved that dispute by just making it another state (#52). Simplicity itself.

Hell, even if the Earth was destroyed, she could take NASA One to John F. Kennedy Air Force Base and fire nukes and lasers from Armstrong City, a quarter of a million miles away on Luna (state #53, the country's largest by far, in a rather controversial move that most legal scholars thought egregiously violated the 1967 Moon Treaty, not that she cared). Aldrinville was the base of the mining operations, almost all of which occurred on Luna's far side, never visible to Earth (as there was relatively little helium-3 on the near side, which was protected from the solar wind, whose ionizing effects helped generate the substance).

Now they were going to DEFCON 2—meaning that nuclear war was imminent. Well, he had been at D2 several times before and nothing had happened.

But he had a nasty feeling she meant it this time. And public sentiment was in her favor.

So Heaven help the belligerent nation of Taraq—and everyone else on Earth. For there was no going back from a nuclear holocaust, albeit one with limited collateral damage due to the trillions of dollars she had spent augmenting the efficiency of America's high-tech weaponry. For the fifty-sixth state might be coming over the horizon.

The United States had enough money to fund and manage a new government and build new cities, it had proven several times, and its President had amassed enough political power and a high enough public approval rating to do pretty much anything she damn well pleased.

Life was good for Americans and their allies. Global warming was regressing due to the lack of reliance on fossil fuels and technology that removed carbon dioxide from the atmosphere. Food was plentiful. It was the 1950s all over again, at least for the United

States. Some other countries were not doing as well. The former physician didn't care a whole lot about them, to the chagrin of her relatively few detractors.

For these reasons, she scared the hell out of most military people—making her an exponentially more dangerous character than her eccentric father had ever dreamed of being. Kriger knew that the ghost of Rad Darkkin was somewhere, smiling eerily at what his second child had paradoxically become.

"We have one week," she said as she stood. "If we don't find him, then we must move in and take over the whole damn place. It shall not be pretty—for them." She walked towards the door briskly and turned back towards the somber group. "War isn't. But sometimes it's necessary."

"Of course, Madam President. But there's something else you should know," Kriger declared nervously.

"Yes, General?" POTUS asked in an irritating tone, looking at her Ball Hydrocarbon Spacemaster again as she stopped in midstride, halfway out the door, twirling on her left foot with dexterity surprising for one her size. One did not dare interrupt the world's busiest woman with trivial matters. "Speak up. If you have something to say, tomorrow's too late."

"Uh, well, there are hundreds of people who have sighted a flying alien over Vancouver, northern Canada, and parts of Alaska again." Speaking up wasn't a problem for him, but he expected the usual languid response, which he found rather perplexing, given her typical aggressive political nature. Not about this.

"*Alien?*" She snarled and looked up, apparently dismissing the comment as if she had just been told it was raining outside. "Yes, I'm familiar with the reports," she said condescendingly as she returned to the room and sat down in a chair, looking aimlessly at the cap of the massive black Pelikan Souveran 1000 fountain pen she twirled in her left hand. "What of it? Are such anecdotal and trivial matters of a pressing priority now, with a human life at stake in the Middle East?" She yawned and took a sip of coffee she poured from the carafe on the table. "General?"

"Radar can't track it, but reports are that it can travel in excess of Mach 6. It's a matter of national security, so, yes, Ma'am. It's a hell of a goddamn priority to *me*."

She smiled sardonically. "Mach 6. *Really?* Do your aeronautical experts really think that's possible? If y'all can't track it, how do you know its velocity, then?"

"Computer estimation by complex mathematical algorithms, Madam President. They are quite accurate."

She sighed. "Quantum estimations aren't good enough for me. What is the speculated origin of this postulated alien being?"

"Chemical composition from Raman spectroscopy indicates substantial amounts of fullerene composite."

"I see, how special. Do we use any such rare materials in our weaponry? As if I don't know the answer."

He shook his head. "No, as it's horrendously expensive to manufacture, and our arsenal is more offensive than defensive, but it's compatible with materials from an old Russian prototype battle suit from the late 1980s that somehow disappeared and was forgotten about. I know they did some experimentation with such exotic composite materials."

"*What?*" She laughed and leaned back in her chair. "Y'all think that some old Cold War relic from the Reagan era, made of the official Texas state molecule—buckyballs—is flying at over five thousand miles an hour over one of the least densely populated regions of the world? If such a technologically advanced being exists, *why* would it go to Canada and use that old suit? Does it like hockey or fishing? Completely illogical."

Kriger shook his head. "I don't know, and we never claimed it was Russian, only that it's made of the same material as that old suit. We haven't determined what it's after; reconnaissance of land masses, perhaps. It may think in a completely different way than we do, therefore we must consider that possibility."

"Huh." She yawned and looked sleepily at her chief science advisor, Dr. Dexter Xavier Slabb, seated next to General Kriger. "What do ya think, Dexter? Does that information make any sense to you? Opine, please."

The slender, six-two, mid-fortyish man looked around the room. "It's seemingly impossible, but there are many reports, so we don't know what to make of it, Ma'am. Yet, it's possible."

"*What* did you say? It's impossible, yet simultaneously possible? Is that *really* what you said?" She pulled her right earlobe with her right hand. "Is that some contorted variation of the Heisenberg uncertainty principle, or does this old lady need hearing aids?"

Dexter nodded. "Perhaps."

"Huh? Perhaps I need hearing aids? Is that your meaning?"

The science chief smiled. "No, Ma'am, I simply meant that—"

She clenched her teeth and stared at him. "Dammit, man, don't make up crap, just say 'yes' or 'no.' I can see none of y'all know jack about it, so you make ridiculous speculations in a futile effort to appear informed. That's just great, General Kriger. That dumb old hunk of junk was forgotten about for a reason. You believe the power source is nuclear? I vote for 'impossible,' but that's just me."

"No, Ma'am, there are no emissions detectable by our technology, so it's unknown at this point. Definitely not nuclear—fission or fusion."

"Thanks for clarifying those two types of nuclear energy." She formed an "O" with her mouth, demonstrating her disbelief about what the science chief had actually said. "Okay—but what the heck else is there to power it, then? Antimatter? Magic pixie dust? Flying carpets? Unicorn energy? Enlighten me with wise words."

"We don't know," Dexter said.

"You don't know." She counted on the fingers of her large right hand as she leaned back. "Let me see if I understand the full picture here. You claim a flying robotic 'alien' with no emissions, with no postulated means of propulsion, has been observed going over five thousand miles per hour. I *do* know a thing or two about nuclear power, in case you didn't know."

"That's about it, Ma'am," Dexter said sarcastically as he nodded. "It's part of the reason that makes it spooky."

"What did you say? *Spooky?* Halloween's a month off. Don't make me laugh."

"Not my intent, but if it does, I won't complain."

"Gee, that makes absolutely no sense to a person of my high educational level. Of course, I only went to San Diego State and don't have the fine West Point diploma Gen. Kriger has or three Harvard sheepskins like you, Dexter, so I must be mistaken in my blissful bucolic ignorance. Yet, you expect me to believe that, and you come to me with this garbage?"

Kriger stood up. "Madam President, as I mentioned, over a hundred people swear they saw this thing flying, there are Tekvids all over the blogosphere. They can't *all* be wrong."

"Really? They can't? People still claim to see Elvis every year in Memphis, and do we really believe he's still alive? How absurd, any kid today with even the most rudimentary computer could fabricate the things you describe."

Silence for thirty seconds as she stared at him as if he was the stupidest person on the planet.

"Well?" She tapped her large foot on the carpet. "I can't stand the suspense. Does the King still live, Larry?"

He shook his head and smiled. "Uh, no, Ma'am, of course not. Elvis Presley died in 1977."

"Right, when I was five freaking years old. I'm not a little girl any longer, and I don't believe in fairy tales.'

"That has nothing to do with this and you know it."

She shook her head. "Untrue. People see what they want to see and believe what they want to believe, it has been so for ages. And I have more important things to worry about than a 'flying alien' in an obsolete suit of battle armor that we can't even confirm ever really existed and a bunch of UFO enthusiasts think they saw—such as Senator Thomassson's brother. Would you not agree? Come back to me when y'all have something definite—and important, because I'm *way* too busy for this craziness."

"Yes, Ma'am."

They stood up and saluted as one of the most influential Presidents in history stood and briskly left the room.

• • •

"Ma'am, how can you possibly ignore that stuff?" Secretary of Defense Tom Ashburn asked as he walked into the Oval Office.

She sighed as she put on her reading glasses and shuffled through her papers as she sat down at the Resolute Desk, her Olympic gold medal hanging asymmetrically over the end.

"Ignore what, Tom? I have thousands of things I must ignore each day, so please be more specific about what you believe I am ignoring right now, so I can ignore you in peace."

"What Kriger said about the flying alien. This thing apparently has stealth technology and the ability to evade our advanced radar and other methods of detection—if it is truly of Russian origin, then we had better be ready for anything—"

She stopped, stood, and stared down at him. "Waitaminnit, I thought we went through all that bunk back in the situation room. No one knows about any 'alien.' Until Dexter gets me definite proof of something, I don't act on superstitions, you hear me?"

He sighed. "I know he's your hand-picked science man, but

Dexter doesn't know everything, although he thinks he does."

"Really?" She smiled, the sarcasm almost oozing from her pores. "I see; thanks for clarifying the facts with your immense insight. And you *do* know everything, is that it?"

"I'm not saying that either. But I just don't think that's prudent, you're putting the country at risk by not being concerned about something with unimaginable power—"

She laughed. "And if it is so stealthy, evading our radar and all, how come we can see it?"

"I don't know, but you should be more concerned about—"

She pointed at him and snarled. "You had damn well better watch your tone with me, Tom; you don't give me orders. I've made some pretty good decisions around here, and you'd be hard-pressed to prove otherwise. I'm sure you have bigger things to do right now than bug me about flying aliens."

He shook his head angrily. "Not really, no. And DSD, that's kind of what they're supposed to do, I thought. Them and me."

"Then find something productive to do before I do it for you."

He frowned. "Yes, Ma'am."

She walked out the door to take a three-day holiday with her family to Camp Conrad, in eastern Tennessee. She needed a brief respite from all this and could be back there in an hour. There would always be something that required her attention, but she treasured a few moments away with her family. She didn't have time to waste pondering things to which she already had answers.

She knew the "flying alien" would return; she had known that for a long time, but she didn't expect it back so soon. And, yes, she knew about the Russian battle suit, being one of the few living humans to have ever seen it up close (a couple didn't survive the first encounter), nearly twenty years ago. When this amazing being would return, she didn't know, but it wouldn't do the world any good to tell them that.

Alien, right. You came into the world on a gurney at Bethesda Naval Medical Center at 0602 hours on October 23, 2010. That's about as American as it gets. I am getting very tired of hearing about stupid aliens.

Your true time of birth was 0547 hours, but I know your mom wanted 0602 on the birth certificate. Avogadro's constant was important to her. It was worth it to make her happy and shut her up.

You were a noisy girl; you popped out after an amazingly short labor screaming, all seven pounds, three ounces of you, with a full head of dark red hair. You had that funky hand-shaped port-wine stain on your right buttock. Your beautiful heterochromic eyes were evident even then: left one deep blue like mine and your dad's, right one brown like your mom's. They became more beautiful as the years went on.

The thing I remember most is that your mom could have gotten to the hospital a little bit sooner.

It took me three minutes to saw through your umbilical cord. I thought the scalpel was dull. Stupid me, I should have known better.

After her visitor left, she sighed and pulled a prized possession from her lower right jacket pocket: a small girl's charm bracelet, made of a unique, rare-earth metal alloy. She was pretty sure the metal existed nowhere else on Earth.

The only surviving fully intact artifact from that fateful day in December 2016. The six letters spelled out the girl's name.

Aurora.

Named after the Roman goddess of dawn.

Her mom and dad knew she would be special (as do all parents), but they had no idea how unique. And the President had a feeling that a new day would be dawning soon. And, in less than one month, a very important girl in rural Alaska would be having her eighteenth birthday.

And she was more than unique—she was mythology come to life; unlike others named after deities, she was truly *a living goddess.*

One who was surely a diamond in the rough, but a goddess, nevertheless. Red Auerbach, the famed coach of the Boston Celtics, once said: "you can't teach height." What this girl had, you couldn't teach, either. There was something to be said about raw ability, the likes of which the world had never seen.

Not in the last 2,000 years, at least.

She remembered the works of Roman philosopher Lucius Annaeus Seneca and a wise passage: "A gem cannot be polished without friction, nor a man perfected without trials."

This was her destiny, to help with the polishing, that is, if this person would even allow herself to be polished. Her intel told her this would be quite challenging. If not, there was really no other reason to continue on in her Presidency.

Faster than light, declared Ovid of Aurora, so she could ride her chariot ahead of her brother, the Sun. Mother of the Four Winds. She who had great white wings.

Aurora Angelica Darkkin Mendoza was, to many believers, an

Angel, possibly the Second Coming of Christ.

Yeah, right. While she believed in God and Jesus Christ without hesitation these days, she knew better than to believe in such stuff—that this was divine intervention.

Somehow, science could explain this one.

And this girl was no angel, she knew from various sources, especially the juvenile police reports from Alaska. She smiled.

Her mother was no saint, either, nor was her aunt. She knew both of these things well, especially the latter.

It would be nice to see her again after all these years. But she didn't know when that would be possible. It would have to be on that girl's terms, not hers, as she secretly knew she wasn't the most powerful woman in the world any longer.

Not by a long shot. And that would be okay. Before she ever became President or even Governor of California, she knew this day would come. She just didn't know when, or how it would come about.

She would just have to deal with it, in the next chapter of the interesting journey of her life. Better now than later. How this was going to unfold, nobody knew. Hopefully it would be beneficial to the world.

And she knew one more thing: she was going to be ready. It was time for another of life's challenges. She'd experienced many in her lifetime and was amazingly still around, to the chagrin of some.

But this one would be unprecedented. And she was due for a good surprise for a change.

Chapter Two

October 1, 2028
Ernie's Convenience Mart & Energy Emporium
Anchorage, Alaska

The dark-haired woman walked into the run-down convenience store/gas station wearing a blue sweatshirt, jeans, blue parka, and sunglasses as she brushed some rain from her face and headed towards the counter.

"Can I help you, Ma'am?" the teenage clerk said. "You wanna buy some lottery tickets?"

She frowned. "That's the last thing I need, young man."

"Pot's up to eight million bucks now. Don't need that?"

She shook her head, clearly not amused. "No. Going to collect that wouldn't even be worth my time."

He laughed. "What? You're crazy, lady!"

"No, young man, I'm not. Why that is the case, I cannot state at this time." She finally cracked a smile. "I'm here to see Mr. Ernie Gleason, the owner. He said he'd be here."

"Okay, sure, just a minute." He went back to a small office. "Hey, Ernie, there's some lady here to see you."

The man came out two minutes later. "Yeah? I'm Ernie. What do you want, missy?" He looked at her and laughed.

"Am I amusing you in some fashion?" the slender yet curvaceous woman asked sarcastically. "I fail to see any humor here; it was not my intent."

He pointed at her parka and chuckled. "Yeah, it's funny, 'cause it ain't that cold out yet, but you're dressed like it's dead of winter." He smiled. "Hey, you ain't from around here, are ya? Typical of the tourists."

"What an astute observation," she mumbled. "Mr. Gleason? We spoke earlier on the phone." The woman extended her small hand, which he took hesitantly.

"We did, young lady, but I'm not sure how I can possibly help you with what you want. I told ya that."

"Maybe we can help each other, Gleason—I can assist you in ways you cannot imagine."

"I don't follow." He shook his head in puzzlement. "You got a funny way about you, kinda uppity. Big city and all."

"Well, how about that." She looked around warily. "Can we go in your back office, if you have one? I don't want to talk out here. Too crowded."

"What? We're the only ones here, except for Tony." This was getting kind of weird, he thought. "Guess so, will probably be a waste of time, but, sure, I'll play along. Got nothin' else to do."

"Doubtful." She frowned and shook her head. "If I'd wanted to waste time, I wouldn't be here, as my time is more valuable than you can possibly imagine." They went back to the small, old storeroom and sat down on folding chairs.

"Um, okay, but I can imagine a lot. Can I get you some coffee, Miss—uh, what's your name?"

"I'm okay, sir." She took off her coat, hat, and sunglasses. "You can call me Dolores. My last name really doesn't matter."

He laughed. "Sure, whatever you say." The seventy-year-old man studied the features of the mid-thirtyish woman wearing no makeup, her hair matted down. Even then, her face looked almost flawless, her black hair glistening in the fluorescent light, her dark smoky eyes almost mystical. "You look kinda familiar. Do I know you from somewhere?"

She shook her head. "Don't think so. Never been to Anchorage before, as you figured out, and I probably won't be back, Ernie. No offense, but I prefer warmer weather."

He snickered. "You got it wrong, it ain't that cold here, not like Fairbanks. Weather here's kind of like Seattle."

She shook her head and scowled. "Don't really care."

"Not one for small talk, are you, little gal?"

"I don't have time for that, sir, with my agenda."

"Huh. Your 'agenda,' right. Sure are in a hurry. But you said you were here to talk about the armed robbery here a couple of years ago. You a reporter or something?"

"Yeah, I'm 'something,' all right, but certainly *not* a reporter. I do want the truth, and I think you have it."

This irritating brunette had been here less than five minutes and already was getting on his nerves. "Little lady, I'll tell you what I told the cops and the other reporters. It's in the police report, which I'm sure you have. Now, if you'll excuse me, I'm busy. Me, I've got a business to run."

"I'm here seeking information about the girl who got shot in the abdomen but walked away unharmed. I know what the police report says, so please don't repeat it. It's a bunch of garbage, written by someone with a penchant for unrealistic science fiction."

"Yeah?" He stared at her for thirty seconds, thinking of a response. "We've been through all that, Dolores, the cops and me. It's simple, 'cause she didn't get shot at all—they were blanks. How could a young girl have survived getting shot like that? It's impossible."

She smirked and shook her head. "No. It's not."

"*Now* who's talking science fiction? Come on."

"Listen here." The petite, dark-eyed woman rose up on her toes and stared him in the face. "Let's not waste each other's time, Ernie. What would it take for you to tell me the truth? Just you and me. I'm not going to publish it or anything, I just need to know."

"I did tell you the truth. I don't need nothin' from you." He went towards the door, which she blocked with her small body.

"Really? Maybe you should reconsider, Gleason."

"Why?" He backed away hesitantly.

"I have my reasons, which don't concern you."

"Huh. My health *does* concern me, missy, so maybe you'd better leave. But I told you the truth already. This conversation's over, so get outta here, lady."

"Is it over?" She pulled out a large envelope from her large leather purse and handed it to him. "Are you sure about that?"

He took it warily, feeling its weight. "What's this?" He had an idea, but the thought of it gave him chills.

"What do you think it is, slick? Open it up. You tell me the truth, even though it's not what I want to hear, and it's all yours. You'll never have to see me again, 'cause I'll be out of the state in less than an hour."

"Huh. It'll take you a lot longer than that to drive out, and getting through airport security and flying will take a lot longer than an hour. You'd need your own jet."

She laughed. "I guess you're right, how stupid of me."

"Yeah." He opened it up and found twenty-five stacks each of a hundred $100 bills. "This is—two hundred fifty thousand dollars. My God."

She nodded. "Yep, that's what it is. Get your money marker and check all those Benjamins if you'd like, it's all real."

He snarled. "Where'd a little gal like you get it? Do I even want to know?"

She shook her head. "You don't need to know because it's irrelevant. I didn't steal it or anything if that's what you think—it's free money for you from my pocket change, no questions asked. Realize that I need information and am willing to pay for it with my own moolah. Nobody's going to come looking for it, I assure you. There will be no trace of my having been in Alaska."

"What? Your 'pocket change'—*nobody* has dough to throw around like this." The man became sweaty in the cold room and wiped his brow.

"You're wrong, Gleason. A few of us do."

He shook his head. "I could get in a shitload of trouble, missy. The government said I should *never* talk about it."

"Yeah? The government didn't give you $250,000, I bet. Nobody here but you or me, and I ain't talking, pal."

He shook his head. "Not that much—they just paid off the mortgage on the place, that's all. It was only about $18,000, but it disappeared the next day."

She put her right hand on his left shoulder and sighed.

"Look, Gleason, there are a precious few people in this world with vast influence—those capable of influencing global politics or the world's economy—besides the government. Know that I am surely one of them."

His smile turned to a frown as he realized this gal was dead serious. "Who the hell are you, lady?"

She shook her head. "Ernie, it wouldn't do you any good to know that."

He stood and paced around the small office for two minutes, his hands shaking. He finally turned towards her and sat down.

"Okay, this is the truth. In a way, I'm glad to finally tell someone after all this time."

She sat down next to him. "I'm listening."

"I was here with my night clerk when this teenage blind girl walks in by herself, around eleven-thirty."

"What did she look like?"

"She was gorgeous, with dark red hair, but her skin was a bit darker than I'd expect for someone living around here, without much natural sun in winter, or for a gal with that hair color. The skin was about like yours, actually, so her hair and complexion sure didn't match. You also usually don't see that many freckles on people with skin that dark, but she was a redhead, I guess."

"So she stood out?"

"Yeah, you might say that. And other things."

"How'd you know she was blind? Did she have dark glasses?"

He shook his head. "No, no glasses, but she had a blind person's cane and bumped into stuff a lot. Kind of a bad place to be, a girl all alone that late, even if she wasn't blind, but we get all kinds. Anyway, I tried to help her find what she needed. Actually, I didn't want her knocking over my displays and hurting herself; I sure didn't need that kind of grief, some blind girl falling through a plate glass window or something that would get my butt sued. I wanted her to get what she needed and leave. But there was another weird thing."

"What?"

"Most blind folks, as you said, wear dark glasses. But she had the strangest eyes I've ever seen—the left one bright blue; the right one was as dark as yours."

"You really noticed that?"

He nodded. "I ain't making it up, lady; if you'd seen her, you would never forget it. It was spooky as hell."

"That's unusual, at that. How tall was she?"

"About five-seven, five-eight, I guess. Nothing special."

"After that?"

"Then, some big asshole with a dark blue ski mask comes in, holding a Glock, and says he wants all my money, some beer, and a carton of smokes. I was robbed once, and I say give the man what he wants, I don't put up no fight for petty cash and cigs. I started cleaning out the register when the blind gal starts moving around the perimeter. Most folks would've stayed put or cowered on the floor, but not *her*. She made me mighty nervous."

"What was the gunman's reaction?"

"He just laughed; obviously he thought she wasn't a threat or he just didn't care because she was blind. But then she was all over him in the blink of an eye. Man, I never saw *anyone* move so fast, let alone some blind girl. She knocked over a whole display of chips, beer, and other crap, but she turned him around and got his ass on the ground good, despite him being about twice her size.

"The dumb ass then tried to grab her to use her as a hostage, but she was on top of him as he fired three shots into her stomach. She shrugged that off like someone had shot a squirt gun at her, turned him on his back, got up, and asked for some rope so she could tie him up, which she did; we were all still reeling from what happened. But it didn't faze this gal in the least; she barked orders like some general or something despite being blind as a bat and shot in the stomach three times. Man, I listened and did what she said, 'cause I saw it *all*. I ain't arguin' with someone like *that*. Jesus."

"Was she visibly injured?"

He shook his head. "That's the thing, girlie. I saw where the bullets had gone through her coat because it was navy blue and she had a white shirt on underneath, and there were holes in that so I could see her skin—but there wasn't no bleeding, and she didn't seem to be in no pain."

"Are you absolutely sure about that? It's very important."

He nodded. "Listen, I was in the Army back in Afghanistan, lady, and I *know* when somebody gets shot. She pretty much disappeared after that—how the hell she got out of there so fast, I'll never know. The cops came and took the guy away, and she was long gone by then. I showed them the surveillance footage on the digicam. I swear she moved so fast she was just a blur on the tape."

"And after that?"

"I thought I was done, but less than an hour after that I got a visit from half a dozen goddamn spooks from some secret agency, the DDD or something, if you've ever heard of them."

She laughed. "I have. The DSD is rather obscure and not very friendly."

"Yeah, that's for damn sure. I didn't even know the feds cared about a convenience store robbery and some teenage blind gal, but they acted like President Mendoza had been shot or something.

They told me this 'never happened' and not to talk about it with anyone, *ever*."

She laughed. "Did they say what would happen if you did?"

"The $18,000 mortgage would reappear, and other bad shit they wouldn't talk about would go down, so I wasn't sayin' nothin' to anyone, lady. The government tells me to do something, I do it."

"Well, I'm giving you way more than them. The official story was that the guy shot blanks."

He shook his head. "Uh-uh, no way. He fired a shot into the ceiling when he came in, just so we'd know he was serious, and pieces of drywall fell out where the bullet went. There were also the three shots he fired at her; the bullets were on the ground like they were still new. If they were blanks in his gun, why would he have fired at her, then? He shot her, plain and simple, so she should've been dead as a doornail."

"So, to summarize your observation: a blind girl moved with amazing speed, took three shots at point-blank range, proceeded to take down your robber, somehow emerged unscathed, and *then* disappeared without a trace?"

He nodded. "Yep. I was right there. The surveillance tape was confiscated, so I can't prove it, but I guess that was the idea. I know you probably don't believe any of this; it sounds pretty nutso."

She shook her head. "Wrong, I *absolutely* believe it, or I wouldn't be here. But shouldn't the bullets have been smashed if she was made of steel or something or had on Kevlar?" She laughed. "Come on, Ernie. That makes no sense."

"I can't explain it, but there it is. None of this shit makes sense."

"What about your clerk?"

"Sally was so scared she peed on herself and doesn't even remember. I'm the only one who saw anything."

"News reports say they werec just blanks, too, and the camera malfunctioned."

He laughed. "Camera malfunctioned, right. That's the way it is, officially. And I'm sticking by that story, lady. No amount of money you give me could change my version, as I value my health. You should, too."

She smirked. "I'm not too scared of anyone, Ernie. I can dish it out pretty well. But, I got the information I needed."

"Yeah, well, this conversation never happened. So I don't know what good it does you, then."

She smiled. "It does me immense good, Ernie, more than you can know. I never saw you, and I thank you for your time. Enjoy your two hundred fifty grand. Don't spend it all in one place, unless you want a visit from the IRS."

"Hey, girlie, waitaminnit."

"Yeah?" she turned around. "You have something else?"

"I just gotta know—you from the government too?"

She smiled half-heartedly. "Well, what do you think? Do I look like a government agent? You see a badge anywhere?"

"No, not really. I don't know what the hell you look like."

She laughed. "No. I'm as far from that as you could possibly imagine. No way they'd let me be one."

"But don't you think all of this is impossible?"

"Of course it is. At least at first glance." The dark-haired woman smiled. "But that's what I do, Ernie."

"Huh? Say again?"

"I have the power to figure out the impossible—things that no one else possibly can."

He scratched his head. "Don't get it."

"Well, get this. If you ever need assistance of the financial type, I'll be back." He watched as she got up and went out. Tony, the sixteen-year-old clerk, watched their odd visitor exit the door.

"Wow. Who was that lady, Ernie? Kinda weird."

"Huh? Oh, some gal who works for a new coffee supply house, Tony. Nobody important. Wants us to carry her products. Yeah, she's a weird one, all right."

"Right. Kinda pretty for a coffee service salesgirl, though." Tony nodded and picked up a cheap celebrity tabloid from the shelf and laughed. "Lookit. Kind of looks like her, don't you think? Weird how average people sometimes look like the famous ones, huh?"

"What? Are you kidding? They look *nothing* alike." Ernest J. Gleason, Jr. looked at the pulpy periodical showing a rich and famous Academy Award-winning actress, sporting a beard, which had obviously been added by computer manipulation by some stupid entry-level photo staffer. "Why do we even have this trash on the shelf, Tony? What a waste of brains."

Tony shook his head. "Well, because you ordered them, don't blame me."

"I did? I'm a dumb ass, then."

"No, you're not, Ernie, 'cause, we sell a lot of this junk, it's good for business. People always read this mindless crap."

"Huh. I'll be damned. What the hell is wrong with people today?" He looked through the latest issue of "Celebrity Register" and laughed. "This is stupid-ass shit. 'World's Third-Wealthiest Woman Gets Shocking Sex Change.' I guess this garbage is good for a laugh. Surprised these rich people don't sue the pants off outfits like this."

Chapter Three

Leeuwarden
The Netherlands

The six-five, dark-haired, bearded young man looked out to the rising sun to the east as the fortyish blonde female, who didn't resemble him in the least, came to his side. He put his massive arm around her and gave her a hug. He would be leaving soon, and, although he knew he would return, that time was uncertain. He knew it was time to leave for America, the promised land.

"What is it, Mother? Do you know what I'm thinking?" Juriann Hultaar asked in Dutch.

"I always seem to know, don't I? I knew there would be a time for you to go," five-four Anna Hultaar said to her adopted son as they looked eastward from their small countryside home.

"You're right, I have to make my way in the world," he said. "To find her, the strange one who you said brought me here as an infant long ago."

Anna shook her head and frowned. "No, Juriann. She said *never* to go find her. That someday you may have a conflict, and that you could help in other ways. That she likely would not even be alive, with the kind of haphazard life that she had led."

"Why would that be? You said she spoke in riddles."

She shook her head. "I don't know. All I know is that she wasn't your real mother, and I believe that, as she didn't resemble you at all. She was Russian, she said, and spoke both that and Dutch very well, despite being deaf. She also gave me this." Anna handed him the gleaming reddish metallic necklace. A stylized "O" with an arrow going up diagonally through it. "She wanted you to have it when you were grown."

"What is it?" He studied the shape curiously. "Why haven't you shown me this before?"

"Because I didn't want you to have it until you left. I'm sorry. I didn't know what it meant. I thought it would have more significance to you this way."

He looked at the gleaming reddish ornament. "I'm not familiar with the symbol. Something from Russian fables?"

"Not likely. I've looked on every collector's Web site available, and it's unique, as far as I can tell, and the jeweler says it's no alloy he's ever encountered before; its composition is unknown."

"The local jeweler is no metallurgist, Mother." He laughed.

"Maybe, but she, the one who brought you as a baby—wanted you to have it. She knew that you will do great things, Juriann. She prophesized your great strength and that someday you would need to be the protector."

"The protector? Of whom? I can do much, and fate has yet to determine a course for me. I wish Father were here to offer his counsel." Hans, his adoptive father, had died of a heart attack five years ago. He missed him. But he still had Mother.

That was pretty much all he had, except many questions.

"She said that hers had been a reckless life, that, because of her life choices, she may not always be here, or—even alive for the wondrous blessing of the Dark Star."

"The Dark Star? You have mentioned this before, and I wish I knew what it meant. I somehow feel it to be true. A blessing? From some divine source? It sounds so ominous and foreboding, according to the description. Or is the Dark Star a curse? How do I solve this riddle, Mother?"

"She spoke much, the deaf Russian one. Said you would grow slightly faster than normal. Although she brought you to us nineteen years ago, you are now a man. A superior man, what did she call you?"

"What?"

She shook her head in frustration. "I don't remember the English word; it was some Greek derivative. One who needed to correct the sins of his descendants. To restore honor to that name, whatever it was."

"Greek? To correct?" The highly educated young man thought

for a minute. "'*Ortho.*' That's the Greek root. An arrow going up through a square letter 'O.'"

She nodded. "That's it, yes. But I'm unsure what that means."

"I'm certain I will find out very soon, which is why I must leave now." He smirked and stroked her hair. "But, Mom, didn't it ever occur to you that the stranger might have been mentally disturbed? Schizophrenic?"

Anna nodded. "Of course it did, son, but this person seemed to give off an awe of greatness, of vast intelligence, like a great sage or something, while simultaneously childlike. I have never met anyone like her kind before. Curious."

"Come on, just because she seemed intelligent doesn't mean she wasn't crazy. Many of history's greatest intellects were not right in their minds."

She shook her head. "I don't think so, son. Eccentric, certainly, but not mad. Look at you and what you can do. There was much wisdom to the strange words she spoke."

"My destiny, you said that she decreed, is to serve someone more powerful, the one who will be able to bring the balance of world power back into line. How will this come to be?" He lifted the rear end of the old pickup truck three feet off the ground. "Truly glorious, that there may be one far more powerful than me. But it's hard to imagine that everything she said was factual."

"I don't know, son. That was a long time ago."

"Well, I have to hold on to something. It's all I have."

"That's not much. Where are you going?"

"You must know the answer to that. I have studied much science in my brief life; it seems to come to me naturally. Yesterday, I returned from Bavaria where I visited the grave of one whose kin I must first find, as the first leg of my journey to self-discovery."

Anna nodded her head. "The great 17th-century astronomer Johannes Kepler. You always were fascinated by him, even as a small child. What makes you think his relative, if that's even true, will have what you are seeking?"

"I just have a feeling that this man, the one whose fictional character could manipulate the most fundamental of forces—gravity—will have the answers I must have to relieve the growing unrest inside me."

She shook her head. "You know better—he can't *really* do that, Juriann; that was just an old TV show. A rather bad one at that, as

I recall hearing."

"I know. But I can dream, can't I? I still have my dreams, my wants, the need to satisfy my human curiosity. I want happiness just like any other person."

She kissed him on the cheek. "You always were one to think that way. You are off to America, then?"

He nodded. "Yes, in five days, to Newark, New Jersey. I've purchased my airline tickets. You had mentioned that the Russian one had given me funds, deposited in a Swiss bank account, for my use later. Where those monies came from, I dare not even ask."

"You will find him there? Kepler's descendant?"

"Correct, at Princeton University. Where the famous ones of science legend once walked the hallowed paths. Einstein, Feynman, Nash, Argon, Darkkin—and now, Kepler. He is the first person I will visit on my American journey to find myself. You said yourself the Dark Star was coming. Obviously, then, I need to talk to the one who knows more about dark matter and dark energy than anyone else."

The six-five heavily built man walked off into the sunset as his mother looked on. He was sure she thought he was crazy. He probably was. But he had to go there. There were many famous and influential people he could visit in the United States, but he had only one mission; to find the unusual man known to the world as *Gravi-Golfer*. Only a handful of individuals were blessed to be as brilliant as him—a descendant of Johannes Kepler himself.

But his mother warned him that things were not always what they seemed, and most people we put on a pedestal don't live up to the high expectations we had set for them. He would therefore have to make that decision for himself, if the fabulous Johnny Kepler was really that great.

Chapter Four

Air Force One
Somewhere over eastern Tennessee

Jay Mendoza was having another sleepless night, as usual, on this early October day. The dreams and voices seemed to come and go, and they were increasingly disturbing to the muscular, athletic man. Ever since that day twelve years ago they had gotten exponentially worse, especially over the last year.

The sensation of flight again—like he was flying through the air. Not just floating, but moving at incredible speeds. He'd been to numerous sleep specialists and psychologists without any answers. His wife had sleep apnea, which could cause hallucinations if untreated due to the brain being deprived of oxygen, but he was tested and didn't have that—Dr. Roberta Elsevier, the world's greatest expert on his and his sister's unique perceptual issues, told him it was just anxiety. He was on the fringe of that, he had known for many years, although he didn't exhibit most of the classic traits, like his sister, who was the poster child for autism spectrum disorder. He was of average intelligence, was extraverted, and dealt well with people, but his senses were that of a synesthete, those with "blended" sensory experiences, which would seem like "tripping out" to many people. His wife's deceased father had taken a few trips on LSD, he remembered. He hadn't progressed that far, not yet, anyway.

No, Dr. Bobbi said it was "too much pressure" in his jet-setting life, for lack of a better explanation. He didn't have too much stress fifteen years ago in the irresponsible, carefree life he led. But he left the comfortable life behind for something more: to be a part of history, to ride along during the greatest increase in prosperity of his country's existence. He no longer had an important job or official title, but he knew his importance to her, and to his country. He was probably one of three people who could talk her out of something once her stubborn mind was made up. He and her Secret Service detail chief. The third was in the next cabin. For some reason, they were all still alive.

Darkness. Sound. Then—everything, more than he could comprehend. A vaguely familiar female voice in a language he couldn't understand. Sounded like Russian. He was hearing it and seeing incomprehensible readouts in his field of vision. They had become more frequent over the last year. He felt the infusion of unimaginable power as if nothing was beyond his grasp.

He tossed and turned as he heard the loud "boom" again. He had heard the crack of sonic booms before, and it sounded just like that. He had the impression he was traveling at some incredible velocity and broke the sound barrier, although if he was the one traveling he shouldn't hear it himself, he remembered. Six, no—seven times, he heard it. Why he knew that he didn't know; probably some inane trivia his sister told him when she was five.

It wasn't stress. It was something else he knew was coming.

When it would arrive, he didn't know. But when it did, all hell would likely break loose around here, which was okay with his wife, who seemed to thrive on chaos.

His pulse rate increased as he broke out in a sweat and then saw the white ceiling. It was just another dream, as usual. But they were getting worse and more realistic.

He sat up in the small bedroom suite, mopped his brow with the sleeve of his old football jersey, and realized that he *was* flying, technically, inside the two million-pound, thirty billion dollar modified fusion-turbine Boeing 997 aircraft designed for his family's use—the family who would likely use it for four more years, depending on what happened in a few weeks. No President had campaigned less for reelection, and no President besides Washington had won all the electoral votes. He had to think a moment as to what the correct number was now; it was 582 at the last one she won, and she got 503. We had added two new states since then; the number of electoral votes seemed to go up in each election. 616, that was it. 309 to win.

He looked at the fifty-six-year-old blonde, America's beloved Golden Girl (albeit with much help from L'Oreal Super Blonde supplied by the White House hairstylist) who lay to his left on the queen-size bed, clutching a blue blanket in her big hands. An imperfect, living American symbol of human fallibility and courage; he knew that's why people loved her so. No one loved her more than him.

To this day, he remained in awe of the most influential human being on Earth, who looked like a middle-aged fighter pilot hooked up to her CPAP machine. In late 2028, they still didn't have a better therapy for sleep apnea, except for surgical procedures (which often didn't work). She had experienced enough surgeries, thank you very much, and didn't desire anymore. She would have to put up with the fighter pilot setup for now.

They were both big people, and a king bed would've been better, but the previous occupants of the most expensive aircraft in the world had only a twin bed and a couch; sixties TV sitcom spouses they weren't, that was for sure. Enjoy all of life's pleasures to the fullest, she always said. She said it to him the first time almost forty years ago when she was fun 24/7. Not much fun and games any longer, but he could see a glimpse of his old college conquest from time to time. He was pushing sixty, but the magic was still there; it seemed to be there less and less frequently as the years went on.

He remembered when life was simpler and carefree for both of them, before *it* happened. *Darkkday.* He looked at the small tarnished silver pin on the collar of his golf shirt and smiled; she had given it to him when she was eighteen. Peter Pan, the boy who would never grow up, she said; damned if that wasn't true. Her beautiful British mother, Marianne, named her after Peter's little friend Wendy Darling, after all. How ironic, given her unglamorous size and thick Southern Appalachian accent. But he knew there was still a little girl in there somewhere. It was hard to find that girl sometimes.

But he then recalled that Sir James Matthew Barrie's Peter and Wendy probably wouldn't have shattered an oak dormitory bed at USC football training camp into a dozen pieces at two AM, sending an assortment of coaches scurrying inside, fearing someone was hurt; they instead found something quite different: a forbidden activity, yet one not at all unexpected of their star wide receiver. He was suspended one preseason game for harboring a buxom, stark naked, eighteen-year-old, 235-pound San Diego State shotputter in his room (after kicking out his lowly freshman roommate, of course). It sure as hell had been worth it. But that was nearly forty years ago, and a lot had happened since then.

Like a year later, when she came home to her own dormitory in San Diego early one evening to find him in bed with her roommate. He was then thankful he had a 40-yard dash time of 4.23 seconds, because on that day, as he needed such velocity to avoid being pounded into pulp by someone with more rage in her eye than the meanest linebacker he had ever seen.

Why the hell had he been so stupid? It wasn't like he really had modified his behavior over the years, so learning didn't take place. He didn't have a disability like his sister—or some crazy dysfunctional childhood to blame his behavior on like his spouse. Growing up in his house was like a sixties sitcom.

He was, quite simply, just a selfish dumb ass most of the time, he had concluded with his mediocre intellect.

But on *Darkkday,* he had to grow up, put away his toys, and finally become a man, and think about someone other than himself.

He looked on the dresser at the digi-photo of her at the London Olympics, standing with her mother Marianne, ex-husband Stan, son Jake, and holding her two-year-old daughter Cassie in one arm and their niece Aurora Darkkin, one year younger, in the other.

Fate had saved her on December 16, 2016, but the others were gone after that day. He couldn't imagine what that would've been like—losing both your children. What would they and Aurora look like today? It wasn't hard to find statues of the latter girl, especially in east central Indiana or Washington, as she became a fable, the "lost child of legend," given the remarkable events following that explosion. He missed Aurora's mother (his sister), of course, without whom there would likely be continued trillion-dollar deficits and no Wendy Mendoza in the White House because of the discovery of Element 119, named mendozium after her death.

The Angel legend started because of the girl's unharmed charm bracelet (made of a unique reddish rare-earth alloy) that had been found in eastern Virginia weeks after the explosion; careful forensic analysis confirmed that it indeed had belonged to the girl, and wasn't a hoax, and they determined the light pink tourmaline birthstone had changed to a deep pink from exposure to intense gamma radiation. How that got there no one knew for sure. His other niece, about thirty feet away from him now, probably had figured it out long ago. He had a pretty good idea, too.

He looked at his wife and thought about waking her for a quickie but decided against it. Interrupting the President's nap wasn't a great idea, he surmised, as he would undoubtedly incur her wrath—after they had sex, that is.

Despite having only one functional lung now, she was otherwise in very good physical condition. She wasn't always in the best shape, back in her early Surgeon General days when she blew up on the Evening Show after host Eddie Wusterman made several pejorative remarks about her weight (he also played video footage of her lopsided victory the previous day in a Washington hot dog eating contest on the National Mall—having consumed fifty-four hot dogs in twenty minutes, maintaining an impressive pace of one every twenty-two seconds); while it was a charity event to raise money for disabled children, even President Reardon (one of her biggest supporters) wasn't happy with that image, and the two reportedly had a little "talk" after that incident.

The two hundred fifty-pound Surgeon General, suddenly realizing the utter ridiculousness of her physical image, declared right then that she would not only compete in the shot put at the 2012 London Olympics, she would also win the gold medal.

She was fond of comedy and could take an insult like a champ; but those statements provoked tremendous unintentional laughter by the host and other guests, and he had learned one thing: while she joked around sometimes on purpose, don't *ever* laugh at her when she's being serious, because she'll find a way to get back at you.

Yes, there were other proud sporting boasts in history, like Babe Ruth's called shot to center field and Joe Namath's guarantee of a victory in Super Bowl III—but this was too much for most sporting journalists to absorb without rolling on the floor laughing. She was surely no Ruth or Namath, but merely a former elite competitor in a sport no one cared anything about. All sports were full of washed-up has-beens. Why would she be an exception?

The facts were obvious: the nation's corpulent chief physician hadn't picked up a shot in nearly eighteen years, and she was derided by the media over the next two weeks for making such an outlandish statement. Also, many felt this boast quite insulting to those who lived their event 24/7, not as a "hobby." The Hall of

Fame wide receiver certainly understood *that.*

A senior representative of Team USA then angrily declared that the obese, out-of-shape physician had absolutely "no chance" to make the team, and her statement was one of her typical publicity stunts; he stated "if there was an Olympic hot dog eating contest, the Appalachian Admiral would win for sure."

But if the United States didn't want her, there was another nation already clamoring for one of its most famous dual citizens to represent their team in London: none other than the host nation, the United Kingdom. Even though the chances of her being competitive seemed small, it would be good publicity. That wouldn't have been the best political choice, as she would probably have had to resign her position as Surgeon General to compete for another nation; yet, like the mustelid *Mellivora capensis* she was often compared to these days, she didn't care, even when faced with bigger opponents, who often decided a bloody death match with this woman wasn't worth it. After all, she hadn't declared *which* country she would compete and win the gold medal for.

Laugh, clown, laugh. Those people didn't know who they were dealing with. When the woman wants to do something, look out, because what she wants generally takes priority over anything else. That was both good and bad, depending on the perspective.

She always took advantage of her appearance and the fact that most people didn't take an oversized blonde powerlifter from rural Tennessee (with an oversized personality to match) seriously. But she took it all in stride. Everyone always thought her older brother and dad were the brains of the family, and she was content to let everyone think that, even though he found out later her IQ was nearly 160, a fact she shared with very few people. William Shakespeare had stated once that it truly was the wise man who played the fool (he knew absolutely nothing about literature, but his sister spouted Shakespearean quotes all the time growing up). Wendy would proceed to make fools out of her detractors.

The Olympics would be the first of many times she did that, but the ultimate revenge would come years later, in November 2020.

Her makeover certainly wasn't easy; while she could be amazingly self-indulgent, she also had a strong work ethic and ability to set exceptional goals (when it benefited her and fit into her schedule, that is). To that end, with her brother Alexander Dirk Darkkin as personal trainer, she started working out six hours per day and went on a personal "Fight the Fat" crusade for America. She adopted a spin technique to compensate for her inherent lack of speed.

The final result was an amazing transformation: a six-one, one hundred ninety-five pound athlete who, at age forty, not only easily made the USA Olympic team but became the world's oldest female Olympic gold medalist with a put of 22.11 meters (72 feet, 6 inches), only 0.3 meters shy of the Olympic record of 22.41 meters set by Ilona Slupianek of East Germany in Moscow in 1980.

She decided to retire from competition after that.

She would keep the body.

Many great accomplishments come with a hefty price, however; this most recent self-obsession and complete disappearance from mundane tasks such as raising a family led to further discord in an already stressful marriage with finance professor Stan Williams; the two divorced in early 2012 and shared joint custody of their two children, Jacob and Cassandra.

Stan and the kids were all dead now. She didn't care much about the gold medal these days.

Yet, while she left overeating and other fun stuff behind (except sex, she still enjoyed that, thank God), had she lost part of what made her unique? The fallibility, the down-to-earth Southern gal every overweight American could relate to?

She used to be a jolly soul, who laughed a lot, and others laughed at her. Most of the time, that was what she wanted.

Now she was someone more to be feared than laughed at; this much was certain. She lost a lot of things, as the world changed forever after that. And the assassination attempt. And *Darkkday.*

But he remembered that he was now freezing to death, despite wearing a heavy jersey and sweat pants. That's what happens when the cabin is kept at fifty-five degrees most of the time. Ah, the joys of the First Menopause. But she was the boss, and this was her plane, not his, she had made crystal clear when they "moved in" almost eight years ago to that big old house on 1600 Pennsylvania Avenue. There was never any question about that. He looked at the football on the dresser with his name on it—not an autograph, but his engraved signature, from when he was Pro Football Commissioner. The job he gave up for the woman he finally realized he had always loved. That took quite a few years to realize. It also had taken that long to love someone other than himself.

He went to the window, looked out, and saw the flashing lights of one of the sentinels—an F-18 fighter jet armed with the deadliest weaponry known to mankind, including DARC-433 missiles designed, ironically, by his wife's late father. A necessity in today's environment. Especially after what happened twelve years ago.

The message was clear: *you take my plane out, and my peeps will take your whole freaking country out in less than five minutes. Go for it.*

Nothing ever came easy to his wife; in her nearly fifty-seven years, she had been kidnapped, shot at, experimented on by a mad scientist, saw one President assassinated right before her eyes, took four bullets for another President and almost died herself, and had both of their families blown to smithereens by a renegade crazy man. That was then; this was now. The pain of all those things could never be taken away. But they still had each other. Sometimes that wasn't enough.

Citizens now cheered for their beloved leader as they knew never again would any resident of the United States of America fear such an attack, for the result would be instant retaliation and annihilation, without question or hesitation, by the country which was now more technologically advanced than any nation hoped to be. The fact that North Korea and Cuba had almost been blasted off the face of the Earth was testimony to that; only their concession to dissolve their Communist governments and become U.S. states saved them from elimination, as their leaders looked forward to spending the rest of their lives in prison.

The same happened with much of the Middle East, which was now the paradise destination New Persia. Rad the Dad would never have been prouder, his little girl stomping out the Commies and conquering the world, a mountain woman on a grandiose mission even his enlightened mind couldn't have envisioned.

You could look up at the sky on most clear nights and see Luna, the fifty-third state. He had been to Armstrong City (the state capital) and the vast helium-3 mines on the far side with her several times on NASA One.

There was still China, of course, but they weren't the same by any means, and they did pretty much what the USA told them to do; their "Communist" government was a merely in name only. Air Force One was once a flying symbol of good and still was for most; but it now was an ominous specter of fear for many.

Was that how we truly wanted to be perceived?

That would be a bad question to ask *her*. The answer would, of course, be *yes. She would kick anyone's ass who tried to mess with the USA.*

Historians would no doubt debate these decisions for centuries if humans even existed by then. Probably not, at the rate we were going. But what choice did she have after what happened?

People around the world called his family the Kennedys of the 2020s, as they were rich, personable, and colorful. Champions of science, stage, sport, and even the silver screen—with the highest awards from each to show for it.

Ironically, like the Kennedys, they were also a family prone to horrific tragedy and death. A lot all those awards meant now.

He woke up from his daydreaming as the five-seven, athletic, fifty-year-old Black woman greeted him at the cabin door as he walked out to greatly warmer temperatures.

"Good evening, sir. Welcome to the tropics."

He frowned. "Don't you ever call me 'sir,' Jackie. How many times do I have to tell you? We've known you for years."

She shook her head politely. "It won't matter, sir. Tell me a hundred more times, and you'll get the same response, until the day this plane isn't yours; that may be a while, I hear. Then I'll call you Jettin' Jay or whatever you want. Some of those things might not be pleasant to hear."

"I guess four more years isn't that far off, assuming we win, although it would be nice to put a little bit of time into re-election. Ever think of the coincidence? You working with us again?"

"No coincidence, sir, but planned. I switched to Secret Service because I knew I'd have the opportunity someday to work with greatness. I'll be worn out by 2033, though, and ready to collect my pension. And she's got no time for the campaign trail. You should know that, you've been through it before."

"I suppose so."

"Up for a snack, as usual?"

He nodded briskly. "Have to, in order to survive. We don't have much to eat around here except fiber bars, soy or almond yogurt, and raw vegetables. I would kill for a stick of butter, I could eat it whole. The federal pen has better food than I get."

Jackie shook her head in disdain. "How disappointing. Your vegetarian wife just wants you to eat healthily, sir. Those food items are not permitted on this aircraft." She winked at him.

"Boy, it wasn't like this when we were younger. She could

polish off food like you wouldn't believe. I saw her eat a thirty-ounce porterhouse steak once with a side of onion rings, fries, and a shrimp cocktail at St. Elmo's Steak House in Indianapolis. That cocktail sauce is the hottest stuff I've ever seen, but she ate it like it was nothing. Cast iron stomach."

She frowned. "The image of that meal is not appetizing at all."

He laughed. "Well, you had to be there, I guess. It was quite a sight." Obesity and bad food choices in her youth probably saved her life, resulting in the horribly diseased gallbladder of legend whose emergent removal resulted in her missing that fateful flight to Stockholm.

"Yes, sir."

"Hey, where is MEEE, anyway?"

She looked at him curiously. "'MEEE?' I'm afraid I don't follow, sir."

"The Most Elegant Engineer Ever. *Boilermaker Bella.*"

"Oh, yes." Jackie laughed. "Lady Isabel is in the guest cabin with Will. She may have some of the contraband food items you seek, on the fine china, of course. But no way you'll take it from *her*. She is quite formidable when angered, despite her size."

"Right. Better get my boxing gloves on." He walked into the next room, a lounge area for the First Family. "What's up, squirt?" he said to one of his few living blood relatives, which included son Will, her son Jose and a few distant cousins scattered around. "Thinkin' some big thoughts in that tiny brain of yours?"

His insult was, surprisingly, not met with an immediate snappy retort from his niece, meaning she was in deep contemplative mode. He didn't go into that state much, so he had no reference point.

"Not so much. Just daydreaming." Dr. Isabel Dolores Mendoza Vasquez, the world's third-wealthiest woman—and, by many accounts, the most beautiful—looked out the window into the darkness. The thirty-six-year-old, five-five, black-haired Nobel Laureate and Academy Award winner sighed as she popped some cheese puffs into her mouth.

"About what?" He grabbed the bag from her and consumed a mouthful.

She shook her head. "I don't know. Some meaning to life."

"Gee, I thought you were the one who knew how to figure things out. I just wanted some junk food, not a profound philosophical discussion."

"Well, go back to bed then if you don't want to hang with me and talk about intellectual items. Probably way over your head."

"Hey. And you'd better stop eating this stuff, *el shrimpo*. You'll get fat and ruin your big public image."

She snarled and punched him in the arm as he laughed. "Look, who are you callin' '*el shrimpo*,' you old man? I'll eat what I want, 'cause I've retired from acting, anyway. It was a means to an end—to promote the great women of science."

"Sure, you are so modest. I have been wondering: are you going to play yourself when they make a movie about you?"

"Huh. Never thought about that. Maybe, if I'm not too old. It had better be soon, or I'll find someone younger."

"And that'll be the day, *you* retiring from the silver screen. You're just like me, you know. You'll be back someday."

"Doubtful. I turn down projects all the time, so it would have to be something of immense significance. It ain't like I need the money." She snickered at something he obviously didn't consider funny. "And in *what* possible way are we alike?"

"Simple."

"This ought to be good."

"We both crave the limelight, the fame, Bella; it has nothing to do with money. We need it. It's a part of us and it never goes away." He pointed towards the Presidential cabin. "In her, too, now more than ever."

"Wow. From you, profound wise words, but probably accurate, especially when referring to wifey. May be a promise I can't keep, after all." She looked out the window for a few minutes. "But is there really a Savior, Jay?"

"Metaphorically? You're asking me? I'm not one for the deep thoughts, you know, or religion, either."

"The world is supposed to be good. For me, it has been bittersweet. But how long before it just blows up? You've heard the reports I got from the *Tinman* and his strange buddy *Gruvi-Golfer*. The flying robot, perhaps an alien."

"Alien? Really?"

"Born in the USA, but with some extraterrestrial DNA, no doubt. Tell me it ain't so."

He shook his head. "Don't know one way or the other. Guess that makes it an American alien. Not sure the legalities regarding that, I don't know what kind of lawyer handles those types of Constitutional dilemmas."

"Well, *Golfer* thinks it lives in Alaska."

He shook his head in disbelief. "Lord. We know some things, but you can't possibly believe in a flying man or anything that blowhard Kepler would have to say. Maybe not even Nick."

She shook her head. "Maybe not Johnny, he's so full of crap, but Hanna is an old friend, and the *Tinman* has become a bit more evasive lately, to be sure—"

"And you're a bit old to believe in Santa. There's no proof of any of it, you'd think Air Command would have seen it on radar. There's just some, what is it—subtle alterations in Earth's rotational velocity? Is that how you say it?"

"Yeah. You learned some new words, it seems: 'rotational' and 'velocity.'" She laughed and pointed at their cabin door. "And you can't tell *her* anything about it, Unk."

He nodded warily. "I agree. Less information is better with her, sometimes, so she doesn't go on overload. But I don't think you have to worry. She laughed at the reports and thinks they're stupid, because she doesn't care about that."

She frowned as if he had said something profoundly stupid, which he clearly had. "Don't be so gullible, Jay. She's a politician, so she's skilled at saying what people want to hear, I was completely joking. She surely knows about it all, anyway."

"I believe you, but it's hard to know how much she knows sometimes." He shook his head. "Even I don't know."

"That's pretty naïve, so get with the program. A girl with unimaginable power—yeah, one of the most imperialistic Presidents in history ain't gonna care about that. Nope. She probably has more intel than anybody stored in Miranda, that crazy holographic assistant of hers. Anybody except me, of course."

"She has bigger priorities now."

"Yeah, right, and I've got a nice bridge in San Francisco to sell you, cheaply."

"I have no interest in real estate."

"Sorry. But her 'biggest priority' is herself. Wendy threatened the hell out of North Korea and made it into a state. Same with Cuba and the Middle East. She claimed the Moon as sovereign American soil because of its high helium-3 content, which pissed the whole world off, but what were they gonna do about it? We used to need other countries to loan us money, but they borrow from us now. We told the Middle East folks they'd better start treating women better, or there would be hell to pay, and she meant it. We don't need their oil any longer, because of Bonnie and me and the *Tinman* and mendozium."

"I don't see what's so wrong with that. I think you benefited from the last one, by the way."

She pointed at him with a manicured red fingernail. "It isn't, in principle, to have clean energy, but what's to prevent Wendy from running amok and ruling the world?"

He shook his head. "I don't follow."

"You don't? Better get with the program. Republicans control both the House and Senate by a large majority. No President besides George Washington ever got *all* the electoral votes, but experts say she might get all 616 without even trying this November after they amended the Constitution to allow three terms."

"The polls are always wrong, hon. Fahnaz Saleh is a good Senator, but not nearly a good enough opponent in 2028 to be a threat right now; no one is, really. She'll be President in her own right someday, the experts say, even though she'll lose in November. It's just one more term."

"Hah. 'Just one more term.' A lot can happen in four years." She stared up at her much taller uncle. "Jay, you know I'm no politician, but even I can comprehend it's the most unbalanced government in the country's history. Should such power go unchecked? Wendy can do virtually anything she wants."

He shook his head and smiled. "She doesn't do anything she wants, and just because you're smart and have a bunch of money doesn't mean you have any idea how Washington works."

"What?" She sneered and puckered her red lips into an "O." "And *you* do? How'd that happen? You failed political science in college, among other things."

"I did not, that's a lie."

She nodded. "Yes, you sure did. 'F' in Political Science 101 at USC in your sophomore year. Grandma Flores showed me your nondescript transcript as an inspiration to make something out of myself. It seems to have worked."

"Shut up. I was a high achiever in my own way."

She patted him on the shoulder. "Yes, I'm sorry; seeing your name engraved on all those footballs at the sporting goods store gave me goose pimples; I stand corrected. The world needs diverse talents, I guess."

"No more lip from you. And there are dozens of compromises that Wendy has to make every day and more disappointing losses than victories; it's no job for a wimp. We're not doing that badly, though, are we?"

"That's one perspective, the one most have. What is it they say? Perception is reality?"

"I guess so."

"Well, despite my appearances, I'm not stupid."

He opened his mouth wide. "You're *not?* Since when? I was not notified of that event. Call the press immediately. I assume you have some proof of that bold statement."

She poked him in the abdomen. "Hey, I earned my Ph.D. in chemical engineering and applied mathematics by age twenty-five, two years before *Tinman* obtained his doctorate in chemistry. The fusion patents are in my name, you know. I own fifty percent of M2 after you guys sold back your interest in the company because I was being generous to him."

"I know, we hear about you every day on television and the magazines. But your Ph.D. is from Purdue, though, not Caltech. 'Applied mathematics'—haw."

She punched him in the shoulder. "Shut up. I knew you'd say that, although you barely got your bachelor's degree, as I understand it."

"Huh. I did graduate in four years, so there."

"Yeah, a big accomplishment with all the wasted time, you had to attend summer session every year to do it. My billions don't care that I wear gold and black, JJ. And my Nobel Prize sure beats a couple of football championship rings, I betcha."

"Depends on who's keeping score. Some of my old football pals wouldn't even know what a Nobel Prize is. I had a girlfriend born in Sweden, and she had no idea."

"Now I believe *that.* You weren't known for keeping company with mental giants."

"Nor would they care unless it had something to do with sports or fashion." He smiled as he knew he had been pretty much the least educated member of his family by far, the one who always was ridiculed at family reunions. Most of it was justified, and they weren't kidding, either, they really meant it. If Bonnie hadn't helped him with his homework, he probably would never have even graduated from high school, let alone college (which he barely finished, with an impressive "C" average); his two favorite pastimes—girls and sports—took far too much time. Well, he never cared much about that stuff. Neither did the Pro Football League.

And he wished he still could be ridiculed at those family reunions. If his family still existed. And he left pro football behind.

"Sorry," Jay said. "You know I was just joking. I'm so proud of you. I know your dad would be."

"You'd better be. They say I'm the new Hedy Lamarr. Do you know why that's such an honor, why I admire her?"

He sighed. "Yes, you've told me a dozen times. Because—"

"Because she was a brilliant mathematical genius, in addition to being a raving beauty and talented actress, like me."

He bowed sarcastically. "So modest, as usual."

"Yeah, well—Hedy Lamarr and composer George Antheil invented radiofrequency spread spectrum technology, the basis for modern cellular phone technology and Wi-Fi. She didn't get to win a Nobel Prize or get rich, though, because it was so secret it had to be classified by the military."

Relatively few people knew that the famous 40s and 50s Golden Age movie actress was also a brilliant inventor. "Spread Spectrum," where she portrayed Lamarr during her interesting life, earned her a Best Actress Academy Award nomination; that was the second of six movies she had made before "retiring" from the cinema. Her next one was about another critically acclaimed movie, playing Lord Byron's daughter, Ada Lovelace, who invented the world's first computer programming algorithm.

She had also played Marie Curie, Emmy Noether, and Rosalind Franklin in other indie productions before winning her first Oscar by playing one of the most brilliant and eccentric characters of all: her deceased aunt.

But playing Bonnie Mendoza in a big-budget Hollywood production wasn't as easy as it sounded; despite her surname and growing self-made wealth, she had to earn that part, being selected from over fifty other actresses who auditioned; most resembled the former elite athlete-scientist more than her. While she and Bonnie were related, of course, their personalities and appearances were vastly different. Bella had never been terribly athletic but started working out and gained fifteen pounds of muscle (bringing her up to 135 pounds vs. Bonnie's 165) while working on mimicking her deaf aunt's lispy speech and other mannerisms perfectly.

Despite potential shortcomings, the studio took a risk on her, surrounding her with relatively short actors to lend the illusion that she was much taller; to the surprise of many, her performance was so astonishing it silenced any critics who thought the Oscar nomination for playing Hedy Lamarr had been a fluke. She had God-given talent for that and wanted to play characters she thought had meaning, and this time she brought home the gold statue. But now it was time to do something more important for the world.

"But she didn't make billions from her invention. You and Nick did. For your information, Lamarr was also married six times. I hope that's not in *your* future."

"Yeah, right. Maybe you have a point there." She laughed. "I contributed more than my share. Bonnie had a great idea, but it took sweat and more than a few tears to achieve a real goal."

He patted her condescendingly on the head. "Sorry, didn't mean to put you down, famous rich girl."

She slapped his hand and laughed. "And you know, logically, that there can't be a flying man flying faster than sound, going around the country. However, *Golfer's* weird theories aside, all the people who have seen it can't be nuts. So it *does* exist."

"The world's full of them, the nut cases, those wanting attention. You know how it is—one person sees one thing, then another, and—"

"They can't all be crazy. But I said it wasn't a flying *man.*" She showed him her Tekphone. "Look, the resolution's low, but there's some blind girl in North Pole, Alaska who shoots almost a hundred percent from the foul line, and can apparently dunk in practice. She's a very good high jumper, too. But no one cares."

"So? Why would they? Bonnie could dunk a women's ball, and she was only five-nine. Big deal."

"She was deaf, not blind. She was a decent basketball player, but she could barely dunk on a good day with one hand, and it was more of a glorified layup, grabbing the rim at the end. No way could she dunk two-handed."

"I guess that does make a difference."

"You think?" She pulled up an old headline on the flat-screen TV. "Here's another story, one that *isn't* in the news: blind teenage girl with one brown and one blue eye who disarmed a robber at some convenience store in Anchorage a year ago. The witness, the owner, says the guy shot her in the abdomen at point-blank range three times, but she was unhurt. Doesn't anyone care about that?"

"Must have been blanks. You're the one who quotes Occam's razor all the time, you with your famous logic. The simplest explanation is the best, isn't that how it goes?"

She shook her head. "No, not if the simplest one isn't *right*. Hickam's dictum, the counter-argument to Occam's razor: things *can* be more complicated than they seem. The guy shot into the ceiling too, and they found the slugs."

"That wasn't in the police report. How do you know that, and where did you get that info?"

"Because the government—i.e., your wife, the DSD, and her oily VP Robby—covered the damn thing up. I'm sure she hides lots of stuff you have no idea about."

He shook his head. "That's ridiculous. She doesn't have time to deal with stuff like that, or fool around with the DSD."

"Really? You're not talking to someone stupid. I know better, Jay. Wake up and smell the roses. She created the DSD as her secret police force."

"I hate to even ask how you know all that, with the resources at your disposal."

"You should know the answer, since I'm not some schmuck who doesn't know the score. So, doesn't it make you wonder?"

"About what?"

"Duh!" She stared up at him and pointed. "It's the same girl, the one named Cheryl Paige Marshall. A flying robot in Alaska and northwest Canada, and a blind teenage girl with heterochromia iridum who appears to have extraordinary physical gifts—put it together, man. It ain't that hard to figure out, dummy."

He shook his head. "There's all kinds of weird stuff on the Internet, I can't believe you watch that garbage. Anything can be faked with even the cheapest computer these days, come on. You can't believe ninety percent of that crap."

"Right, whatever. Okay, let's move on to a different topic, then. Harry Houdini regularly shows up in Balboa Park, often in December, around *Darkkday*, according to reports from the San Diego Union-Tribune."

"Probably buried in the classified ad section to fill space. Who cares? There's all kinds of crazy stuff in the media, and especially in Southern California. We grew up there, for God's sake, c'mon."

"*I* care. What's up with that, Jay? Anyone you remember who was obsessed with him?"

He laughed. "Sure. But there are a lot of weirdoes out there."

"Maybe, and we used to know one of the weirdest. But doesn't one other thing bother you?"

"Besides you bothering me? What?"

"*Darkkday* itself, of course. When that missile hit the plane, all of Washington should've been vaporized. I went in the ambulance with Wendy to the emergency room in Pittsburgh after I made them land the plane because, despite recent healthy lifestyle changes, her gallbladder exploded."

He pointed to himself. "I was there, remember?"

"Yeah. But just the plane was destroyed, and they even found parts of that, as well as part of a sapphire crystal from Bonnie's watch. And Aurora's fully intact rare-earth alloy charm bracelet, of course. Everything else vaporized. The bracelet was the basis for the whole Angel thing after that farmer discovered it in Virginia."

He shook his head. "It was a dud. No other logical explanation. The greatest scientists in the world came to that conclusion."

"Greatest scientists in the world, what a freaking joke." She shook her head and snickered. "That's a lame-ass story for the masses the media cooked up, but it doesn't fly with me. The tourmaline stone turned from a light to a deep pink from the gamma exposure. I would put far more credence in what the old *Science Squad* would say than those government shills. Even Wendy has enough knowledge of thermonuclear weapons to know better."

"You overestimate her knowledge."

She shook her head. "I don't think so; you know that as well as I. As smart as Alex thought he was, she was way smarter. She's a master at playing the bucolic dumb blonde, all the while accumulating the most important commodity any President can have—information, squirreling it away for future use. And you're horribly naïve, just like Bonnie, but at least she had a superior intellect to compensate somewhat."

"Hey, now—"

"Hey, yourself, don't be dense and play outside your league, Mr. Commissioner. This is Washington, not Canton or Green Bay. Nukes don't work like that—they're dichotomous devices that either go off big-time, or they don't. There was only minute radioactivity anywhere, less than a billionth of what it should've been with a payload that size. If the nuke was a dud, some of the plutonium would've still been there, and the neutron radiation would've made something else radioactive. But it was all gone. The sapphire crystal remnant and the other stuff had extremely low-level radiation. Everything except Aurora's bracelet, which was normal. Readings from that should've been extremely high."

"It was a low-power nuke that didn't work right, don't make things excessively complicated. It's what third-world dictators get when they buy bottom-barrel nuclear weapons on the black market from crazy idiots like *Santaman*."

"No. You know better, I know you do." She shook her head. "Something absorbed it, Jay. It's the only explanation that makes any sense. The answer's obvious: Aurora removed it and was holding it in her hand when it went off. It only received enough gamma radiation to alter the manganese salts in the birthstone."

"'Her hand?'" He laughed. "I'd like to believe you, but you *know* there's no way that's possible. When she was two, Wendy told me how she turned over a pot of boiling spaghetti on herself and was unharmed, but a thermonuclear warhead's just a little different than a pot of hot water, don't you think?"

"In theory, no. Yes, she seems to be indestructible, although that is not possible by any means we know of. That would require mastery of physical forces or technology far beyond anything we even understand. But it somehow *happened*."

"What makes you so sure, then, if it's so impossible?"

She sneered up at her six-one uncle. "I just know and have for years. Don't you realize it's dumb to argue with me about stuff like that? Just because I can't explain it doesn't disprove its existence."

He laughed. "Did your, what are they called—magnificent 'parsimony powers' tell you that?"

She smiled confidently. "Of course. The simplest explanation has to be the best."

"Hey, now you're contradicting yourself. You just said that the simplest wasn't always right."

"The right choice is what I say it is. Either way, I will find out the truth in time. You surely know this maxim to be so."

"What could've done that? No technology we have, you said."

"Until I figure out on a molecular level where the dark energy comes from and how it's somehow converted to other energy, I rely on something else."

"Yeah? What's that?"

She made the sign of the cross on her chest. "The only thing I truly have faith in anymore—the power of God."

"Huh. God, huh? Sure, that's a good one when you can't explain it any other way. For true intellectuals."

"I can't believe you, Jay, so shut up. I don't want to argue with you any longer as it makes my little brain hurt. I'm going to go take a nap."

"Good, I need some peace and quiet."

They went and sat down in the outer lounge as Will muttered something unintelligible, stirring from sleep. Darned if their son wasn't the spitting image of his mother when she was younger, although he had darker skin and brown eyes. Sometimes those days when she was younger were hard to think about. Man, how he screwed things up then, but some twenty-one-year-olds weren't very mature. Life got far more complicated after that. Few people had a life as complex as theirs. Eleven-year-old William Conrad was probably more mature than he was at twenty-one, or sixty.

"What's up, Dad? Can't sleep?" Will said.

"Yeah. Feel like I'm sleeping in a freezer." He picked up one of his son's vintage comic books, one in particular which was poorly illustrated and written (despite it being worth hundreds of dollars today on E-Auction): "*Dr. Wendy's Science Squad* vs. Mr. Sub-Zero"—the villain being a mutant who could only survive in sub-zero temperatures. "I think I feel like this bad guy."

"Ha. Is Mom burning up again?" Will asked.

"Like a friggin' furnace. Something for Bella to look forward to in about twenty years."

She sleepily opened one dark brown eye and stared at him. "Thanks a lot. My oocytes are on the downward spiral already." She took a sip of coffee as she picked up her digital tablet to check messages. "I'll never be able to sleep with you making fun of me."

"Dreams again?" Will asked his father.

"I was flying, faster than sound." Jay took a bite of fat-laden blueberry pie (hidden in a secret place, of course) the attendant brought him on fine Presidential china as he sat in a leather seat. "I could even hear the sonic booms. They're the same dreams—Aurora—I know she's been dead for twelve years, but I keep seeing her, or at least I think it's her. Speaking Russian. How ironic."

"That's not unusual. You used to have those dreams about Aunt Bonnie, you said."

He shook his head. "These are different. Unbelievably real. And Bonnie always looked the same, about seven or eight years old. But I see Aurora, her face, what she would look like today. Tall. Strong. Like some hybrid between Bonnie and your mom."

"I guess she would look like that today, don't you think? What's Dr. Elsevier say?"

"She says it's just a post-traumatic stress type of thing. But I see clouds up in the sky, almost like we're flying. Fast."

"You've been to other planets with Bonnie; you said once you stood on the surface of Titan and saw Saturn in the sky, and it was as real as us sitting here right now. So why is this any different?" The freckled, six-foot boy with light brown hair and brown eyes laughed as he took a drink of milk.

"It is far different, son. It's not metaphorical this time, it's real." He turned to Bella. "You know what I mean. You had those dreams for years too."

Bella spoke up as she opened her right eye and looked at him again. "I know—it's creepy, Jay. I started having them, he said, about a year after—you know. Not as profound as yours, but weird. Then they abruptly stopped."

"You were the ones that changed the world, when you figured out exactly how to do all this stuff with mendozium."

"The ones that brought cheap nuclear and hydrogen energy to us all and saved us from global warming. But hers were just rough theories. I was the one who had to work out the details on how to build the fusion reactors."

"Yeah, yeah, we know all that. So, why are you bumming a ride to Oak Ridge with us, Boiler Bella?" Will asked. "Are your corporate jets on the fritz, or are finances that bad?"

"Naw. I was in D.C. anyway, you know. Rather spend time with family. TM hates to waste energy, as he's a cheapskate."

"Sure he is. What about you?"

"Me? Not so much. Plus, I love my auntie so."

Jay laughed. "Right. You used to call her the Countess of Monte Crisco and the Sturgeon General, among other derogatory things. At least now she really is your aunt."

She frowned. "Yeah, well, just by marriage, thank God, as we fortunately don't share any DNA. Yet, I can swallow my pride, and she's earned my respect, don't you think, even though I would *never* tell her that. And Levickis would shoot my ass off if I said those things about the boss."

"No comment," Jackie said, standing in the corner.

"Aww, you know I'm just kidding, Levickis. The Chief ain't so bad, after all."

Will broke down crying. "I just wish this all had never happened, Dad, and I could comprehend all this. If the North Koreans hadn't bombed that plane, I probably wouldn't even be here—"

"And your mom had to have her gallbladder out from too many years of fatty food. Your mom needed someone, with everything gone. And *Tinman* needed Bella after Marcy died. And Jim," he looked at Jackie, who walked back into the Secret Service cabin. "He's gone too. We're kind of alike, you and I. Helped the ones we loved after their first loved ones died."

"Did Mom still love him, Dad?"

"Who?"

"Cassie and Jake's father."

He looked at his son curiously and smiled. "Of course she did, in her own way. He stood by her in all of her goals. She was the one who broke it up. The Olympics was her latest obsession in 2012, and she put everything she had into that. Stan would have stood by her, but she let him go to pursue his dreams. It was probably the least selfish thing she'd ever done."

"What do you mean? Couldn't he have just divorced her anyway?"

He nodded. "Of course he could have, but he wasn't that way. She wanted it to be a mutual decision, which it was."

"Was he a good guy?"

Jay nodded. "Yeah, once you got to know him. He could be a little prickly sometimes, but so can your mom. He always did whatever she needed done and put her first, without hesitation." He had never put anyone before himself before *Darkkday*. He was trying to make amends for that.

"You've been the best dad anyone could have. Look at her and what she's become. She used to be kind and caring. Now all she cares about is the damn North Koreans. She made peace with them by taking over their country, but she still hates their guts. Those fighter jets outside have enough firepower to wipe this state off the map. Other Presidents tried to cut back on weapons, but we have three times more nukes than any time in history. China has way more people, but our technology and sheer military might in all areas—land, air, and sea, not to mention our cyber technology—could destroy them within weeks. You say everyone loves her, but maybe they really just fear her, Dad. Just like they did Grandpa Rad, they say."

"Your grandfather was a flawed but great man. And they said *Santaman* did it, but she knew it was the North Koreans. No way Kristoff van Sant could've done that on his own without help."

He scowled. "Do you really believe all that, Dad? Listen to you, that all sounds crazy. I never knew Aunt Bonnie, but I heard she was prone to telling fantastic stories."

"I do, Will. You can't be chief of scientific intelligence at the CIA without gaining some enemies. She was strange but generally incapable of lying. She attracted all kinds of weirdoes, like *Santaman, Red Skeleton, Benzoicman,* etc."

"That still sounds too fantastic to be true."

Jackie Levickis came back into the room and approached the sixty-year-old man. "We'll be making our final approach soon, sir."

The pilot's voice piped up over the intercom system. "Air Force One on preliminary approach to Oak Ridge Regional Airport. Note that Darling and Peter are on board."

Bella laughed. "Peter Pan—what a stupid Secret Service code name. Suits you."

"Correct. Sometimes I think I'm in Neverland, especially while I'm asleep. Uh, this is a really stupid question, but were Wendy Darling and Peter Pan ever married?"

She laughed heartily. "God, that is a stupid question, Unk, as I would expect from you."

"Can you just answer it, please?"

"Huh. I don't think the stories ever got that far, you know, as Peter never grew up. They were children's fairy tales, duh," Bella said. "You sure are dense sometimes. Just like your sister was."

"Sorry to interrupt your intense academic discussion, sir," the officious woman said, "Time to get ready for landing."

He looked out the window. "Oh, yeah. But so what?"

"Don't you think it's time to wake the President? I'm sure not doing it."

"You have a point there."

Chapter Five

October 4, 2028
Somewhere over British Columbia, Canada

I can do things no other being can; of this, I am certain. I am power personified, a living star, with a seemingly inexhaustible power supply, limited only by my short attention span. I have yet to test the limits of what I can do. I fly in my metallic armor across the sky with one mission—the purpose of which escapes me, Earth's mightiest being, whose mere existence is puzzling. I think, therefore I am, but I do not know why I exist. Enough of such contemplation; I ain't no stinkin' philosopher.

The dark grey shell (made of a rare allotropic form of carbon called fullerene) apparently escapes radar detection, although I know little of such science. Such trivialities are unimportant to me. The armor serves little purpose other than to preserve my anonymity and provide sensory perception far beyond that of a normal human. Since my native sensory perception is far below normal, that is good for me. I shall laugh at whatever weapons they choose to unleash; such will be a futile endeavor to the one who could rule the Earth.

Ruling the Earth is the last thing I would ever want to do. Most days I have difficulty keeping myself out of trouble.

This will be the farthest I have ever been out, and it is time to tell the world of the wonders to come. I have been as far south as Vancouver, but never to the heartland of the USA. I am even not sure I fully understand the benefits of hurling three tiny projectiles at two statues in the Midwest and a third at a gravestone in Appalachia. The sites do not seem logical at first. It seems harmless enough, but such acts will surely attract significant public attention.

Apparently, it is all part of a "master plan" that will make sense eventually and herald the coming of the Dark Star. I am not the type of person to do something just because people suggest it; nothing could be further from the truth. But the seriousness of their tone somehow made me want to do it. As much as I have a disdain for *authority, I want to help people even more.*

Plus, flying at five thousand miles per hour is a heck of a lot of fun, and I don't get to do that very often. Like, never. It sure beats walking.

This will be pretty easy to do if I get within a few hundred feet. I can throw any object with absolute precision, and that combined with the sensory system in the helmet, which is unerring, if the old thing holds up, is uncanny. The batteries are powered by plutonium-238, which apparently lasts a long time. I don't know much about such mundane things; as long as it works, that is all I care about.

Mother says I am a deity; Dad says no (with disdain), declaring I am not worthy of such a description—but which am I?

Or am I neither, and instead a devil? Surely some who see me will believe this to be so. I look like one, as I wear a butt-ugly gray suit designed by my mother's Russian relatives, I am told. Doesn't sound very godlike to me. And, somehow, I don't believe my mom.

I wonder what the hell I actually am and what I look like underneath; I have, of course, never seen myself without the suit on. Which is why I need this crummy-looking exoskeleton that talks like a hillbilly.

I had better stop daydreaming and pay attention.

The meaning of these tasks is obscure, but it will tell the world one thing: the Dark Star will be rising soon, and the world had better be ready, because there will likely be something of immense urgency that needs my attention. There always would be; saving the world is a big responsibility. Being an adult required just that, and I am damn tired of being a kid.

I streak across the tip of Lake Superior, hydroplaning across the Canadian border to the first destination, a city of 112,000 in eastern Wisconsin, on Lake Michigan, at over five thousand miles an hour. There, I shall throw one of the dimpled projectiles at the statue of some coach who had died in the mid-20th century. He apparently had been someone of much importance, but I don't care about trivial things such as professional football. This small city isn't even the largest in Wisconsin, but for some reason, I am here, in the place many call Titletown, the former home of the First Gentleman of the United States.

I am now approaching the small city, air traffic information appearing in Russian on the helmet's readouts. Everything is in Russian, my mother's native language, and Mom speaks with a perfect accent; sometimes, curiously, she does not talk with one at all. Mother said that people had stereotyped Russians as being evil Cold War spies, and that was the reason for trying not to talk like one some of the time.

That makes absolutely no sense since the Cold War was essentially a "non-war" where nothing happened except much posturing by the two superpowers at the time and had been over for forty years, but Mom was a strange, somewhat paranoid individual. Much of what she says makes no sense. It is either gibberish or concepts beyond my understanding; I am not certain which.

I can speak by simply thinking, as the cerebral electrodes can interpret those signals; yet, the stupid voice that comes out of it has a strong Southern Appalachian accent, with a deep bass voice. Why an advanced Russian suit of battle armor would have a voice like that seems preposterous, but my queries regarding where it came from go unanswered. Maybe those people don't know. Yeah, right, like they just found such highly advanced technology in a dumpster somewhere. They surely know; I am no technophile, but I also am no imbecile. No one would give the power of a god (or devil) to an idiot—that much I know.

Or maybe I don't know as much as I thought.

The unattractive suit, however, is an amazing piece of technology, and I wonder where the heck it had come from. Russian relatives? Yeah, right, like this was lying around some uncle's attic in Moscow. I am smart enough to know that this armor is unique and probably illegal. Money has to come from somewhere, and the thing is darn near indestructible. No one speaks of the money, and I do not ask. I am merely glad it exists, even though I suspect it has been stolen from the Russian government. How the person who gave it to me would have had access to that level of technology is unknown. Yet, it is a small price to pay to further the great missions that lay ahead soon, until a better solution to my "problem" exists.

I sight the enormous 85,000-seat stadium and statue from five hundred feet, take the small dimpled sphere, and fling it with my left hand. The significance of the small white spheres escapes me; I know only that they contain no explosives or sensing devices—my own sensors (which somehow can detect the chemical composition of most substances) indicate that they are made of plastic and rubber. They seem to resemble something that could be purchased for one bonnie a dozen at Super-Mart and struck with long steel sticks on a manicured meadow; why would that mean anything to anyone, except possibly an obscure fourth-rate TV superhero who at one time knew the President? Who the heck cares about golf balls besides him? Yet, that is what my sensors indicate them to be, nothing more. I am told that someone obsessed with golf will seek the truth.

Golf and gravitational physics, indeed. I have not quite figured out how to put the two together yet. Nor do I really care.

My sensors now indicate I have decelerated to nine hundred kilometers per hour. I "see" the small sphere hit as several people look to the sky and point skyward in amazement.

I wish it was not so, but I suppose I am amazing. And frightening.

It is now time to go southeast—to East Central Indiana, the second of three stops; to Aurora City, built as a sort of monument to those twenty or so individuals who perished in the last major act of terrorism against the USA, the dark day for humanity named, appropriately, Darkkday. Historians still cannot determine with certainty why the entire District of Columbia and its suburbs hadn't been vaporized in the attack by the supposed North Korean missile sent from a submarine in the Atlantic; only the occupants of the plane died. This will be my first trip there.

I shall throw another small, dimpled plastic and rubber sphere at the base of the large statue of the small girl who perished in the blast. Why that is important is unknown, either. Sensors indicate I will reach Aurora City in approximately five minutes as I streak diagonally across the Indiana cornfields while farmers begin to harvest their crops. As far as I know, radar and other technologies cannot track the suit, as it is made of a high-tech composite material that absorbs them. Which is good, because whatever defenses the suit used to have no longer work, and it clearly is built to gather information and relay it back, not to be an attack weapon.

A living star doesn't need a stupid suit of armor to attack; that much is certain.

I can outfly any known aircraft and probably any vehicle short of the Luna regolith shuttles, but if a missile happened to hit me, the suit would likely be destroyed. That would be a major inconvenience, as well as a hazard to others when the incredibly hard fullerene shrapnel shreds anything in its path.

After I toss that sphere, the last destination is 334 miles away—a cemetery in Appalachia, in Oak Ridge, Tennessee: a place important in America's early forage into atomic power (the city, not the cemetery). It was still an important research center, but most of the fusion research was now done where she just had been—Indiana.

Yet, Oak Ridge is more popular to tourists these days as the Presidential birthplace than as a major contributor to the Manhattan Project. Go figure.

I am no genius, but I am pretty savvy and have figured it out—the three destinations seem to have only one thing vaguely in common.

They are places at one time of some importance to the American equivalent of royalty—the First Family of the United States of America. Again, the significance of that is uncertain to me at this time. And it will surely attract attention, by one oddball in particular interested in the mundane game of golf.

What those famous people have to do with me, I have no idea.

But I know that one day soon, it will become crystal clear. It is the path I have chosen, and there was no going back now. Was it the right choice? Teenagers, even those with the infinite adult wisdom of a soon-to-be eighteen-year-old, may not always make the best decisions, I know.

• • •

Twenty Minutes Earlier
Miracle Park
Aurora City, Indiana

The large hydrogen-powered speedboat sped across Miracle Lake with the modest skyline glistening in the background. Five-year-old Joseph Alexander Stannous looked up at the modern skyscrapers of his birthplace, the Midwest City of Hope, and saw the thirty-foot bronze statue of the six-year-old girl with wings, the symbol of the city that was basically farmland ten years ago. Why the city was built here, 535 miles from where *Darkkday* occurred (Washington, DC) was a mystery to many, but he was not concerned with such matters. There were several such depictions of the child throughout the state's second-largest city of 345,000 people, but this is the one he liked the best. He pointed to the statue as his grandfather slowed the boat.

"Stop, Nana. Take me over there again."

Gray-haired, overweight Margaret "Molly" Stannous sighed as his grandfather turned to alter course. "We've been there a dozen times this week, dear. It's the same statue; she doesn't change."

"Aww, but I want to go again," the little boy pleaded.

She sighed again. "Okay, hon. Steve, take us over there."

Stavros Stannous rolled his eyes. "Sure. Already on it."

A few minutes later, Jose looked in awe (as was always the case) at the massive statue off the northern shore of Miracle Lake.

"She's so big. Was Aurora real, Nana, or just a fairy tale?"

She nodded. "Yes, Jose. Aurora Angelica Darkkin Mendoza was your cousin; you know that. And, yes, she can also be a fairy tale, something we can all believe in."

"Gee, that's sure a long name. What's a cousin?"

"The children of two siblings."

He shook his head. "Huh? What's a sibling?"

"A brother or sister."

"Oh. Will I ever have a brother or sister, Nana?"

She frowned. "Uh—Jose, you'll have to take that up with your parents."

"Why?"

"It's kind of up to them."

"It is? I don't understand, Nana."

"Well, never mind, we'll discuss later. Anyway, your mommy's father and Aurora's mother were brother and sister."

"Do you have a brother or sister, Nana?"

She looked at the floor of the boat sadly. "I had a brother, Jose, and his name was Jimmy—he died in a car accident long ago."

"I'm sorry, Nana. But where is mommy's daddy now?"

She kissed him on the cheek. "He died, honey, before you were born, and he's up in Heaven now. So that makes your mommy and Aurora first cousins. You are her first cousin once removed."

"Removed? Like gone? What does that mean? I don't get it."

She laughed. "Never mind."

"Did I know her?"

"No, she died a long time before you were born."

He looked with awe at the angelic statue and put his head down. "I'm sorry she died. Why do people have to die, Nana?"

She patted him softly on the head. "We don't know, honey, why things happen this way. Only God knows the answers to that. All of us die someday."

"Even me?"

She nodded. "Someday, yes, we all will, I'm afraid. But that won't happen for a very long time."

He gave his grandmother a hug. "I sure hope you never die, Nana. God sure knows a lot of stuff, though. He must have a really big brain." He shook his head.

"That he does."

Jose opened his mouth wide and spread his arms. "Did she

have wings, though, Nana? Could she really fly? You know pretty much everything, too." He spread his arms wide and made a buzzing noise as if he were an airplane flying around.

"She can fly now, I'm sure, but I sure don't know everything. She's an angel, honey, just as her middle name says, looking down from Heaven. All angels can fly."

He looked up at the sky. "Will I ever see her?"

"I don't know if angels ever return to Earth. Maybe someday you will see her, though. Your mommy and daddy built this so that others could have hope in their times of despair."

"Huh. I don't know what that means." He thought for a moment, his five-year-old cerebrum not entirely grasping the concept. His short attention span resulted in the transition to another favorite topic. "Where's Mommy and Daddy now?"

She sighed. "You've asked that about seven times already today, honey."

"Well, golly, I forgot again, Nana. I'm only a little boy. I can only remember so much, least till my brain gets bigger and it can hold more stuff."

She laughed. "Daddy is playing in the golf tournament down the way with his friends, and he'll be back soon." She pointed to the sky. "Mommy is probably up in your Aunt Wendy's airplane right about now."

"Oh, an airplane?" He looked upwards as he put his hands as far apart as he could. "I love airplanes. Can we see it in the sky now? Can we go in it?"

"Not right now. They're far away, near Tennessee, but Mommy will vid to us later."

"What's a Tennessee?"

"It's two states south of us, where Aunt Wendy was born."

"Oh. Is that a big plane? Bigger than ours?"

"Yes, it's many times bigger than ours; you probably don't remember that you've ridden on it several times before. It's the biggest plane in the world, for the world's most important person."

"Well, Mommy and Daddy are rich, so they should have the biggest plane."

Molly shook her head. "Being rich doesn't make you important, so you'd best remember that, son."

"Huh? It doesn't?"

"No. The only way to get that plane is for people to vote for you to become the President of the United States. Someday maybe you will be."

Jose played with a toy boat. "That sounds cool. Can I be the President when I'm twenty?"

Molly laughed. "No, that's not old enough. You have to be at least thirty-five years old."

The child frowned, his freckled face gleaming in the sun. "Wow, that's awful old. Are you thirty-five yet, Nana?"

She chuckled. "Sweet little boy. A little older than that."

"Not much, I bet, or you'd be dead. I don't want to be old like that. Is President a hard job to have, Nana?"

"Yes it's very hard and you don't get to have much fun, I'm sure. Everybody wants something from you all the time."

"I'm not ready to work that hard and not have any fun yet, or be old, so I'll do something else and not be President, I think, where I can be outside. I'll just be a fireman or a cowboy."

"That's good, honey. Do you remember Aunt Wendy's house?"

"Sure, I think. It's the big white one with lots of soldiers and policemen and stuff outside. Everybody salutes her all the time. She always has lots of toys for me. I like playing with Will. He's like a big brother."

"Yes, you remember. Will is your cousin, too. We'll be going there for Christmas in a couple of months."

"Are they going to have turkey and pumpkin pie?"

"Yes, and ice cream."

"That's good." He made motor sounds as he played with his toy boat as he suddenly looked up, saw it, and gasped: a gray metalloid figure streaking across the sky, about three hundred feet from the ground. "Look, Nana and Gramps, it's Amalgam-Man!"

"What? No, it's not, son," Stavros said, laughing. "That guy's not real; he's just a movie superhero."

"But, Gramps, he is too real, 'cause I just saw him!" Jose pointed to the sky as the humanoid form now hovered about a hundred feet from the ground.

"Holy crap," Stavros said in astonishment. "It *is* something, at that. What the hell—"

Jose then heard it—the swooshing sound of something hitting the ground two feet in front of the Aurora statue's base. And then—something he would never forget—the sight of the figure he thought was comic book character Amalgam-Man, creating a sonic boom as he streaked across the sky, faster than he could have thought possible. And then a second and third boom, mere seconds later.

"Wow! What was that noise?" Jose asked excitedly.

"It was a sonic boom, I'll be goddamned," Stavros said. "If I didn't see it myself, I wouldn't have believed it."

"Steve. Watch your language around Jose," Molly said loudly.

"Sorry." Stavros looked at the sky in amazement as the human-sized figure had disappeared.

"Gee. What's a sonic boom, Gramps?"

"A sonic boom. When an object travels at the speed of sound, the shock waves can't get out of the way of each other, and they are all forced together in compression, which creates a loud pop."

"Wow, that's fast. I knew he could fly like that."

"You bet, the speed of sound is 760 miles per hour, and you get a boom each time an object exceeds a multiple of that speed. But it's gone now."

"But how did he see it first?"

Stavros sighed. "Molly: at age five, his visual acuity and reaction time is far superior to ours. Give me a break."

"Sorry, Doctor. Did something hit the ground?" Molly said, the boat being about fifty yards from the statue.

"It sounded like it. Let's go see what it was."

"You sound like Nick. No way. Let's get out of here."

"Like hell—er, heck I will."

• • •

Ten minutes earlier, Dr. Nicholas Stannous and his two female playing partners pulled their carts up to the seventh hole, the skyline visible in the background of Miracle Park Country Club at the pro-am tournament his company was sponsoring. He groaned as he realized he already had forty strokes after only six holes. How the mighty have fallen; all his money couldn't buy him a decent golf game.

He teed up his ball as the two famous women laughed. The world's tenth-richest man felt distracted as he sliced his drive into the lake. A ten thousand dollar fullerene driver didn't make much difference when you didn't have any time to play and had little native ability.

"Good job, *Tinman*," U.S. Senator Fahnaz Saleh, D-New Persia, said as she adjusted her head scarf in the wind. "Just like the old days in Phoenix, I can see nothing's changed."

"I don't have time to play golf, jeez, not like you politicians, with all the hobnobbing, wining and dining, living the good life."

"Yeah, managing billions of dollars is a tough gig. Try working for a living in D.C. It's an expensive place to live, *Tinman*, not like the cow pastures of Indiana."

"Being a Senator is a rough life, I'm sure."

Fahnaz shrugged. "Yeah, well, you try the plane trips back to Freedom City, because those take a lot out of a person."

He shook his head. "You do nothing but complain, Fahnaz. Talk to Senator Brian Chappelle, as the trip to Armstrong City or Aldrinville makes that seem like nothing."

The five-two Democratic Presidential nominee put her hands on her small hips and laughed. "Well, Sen. Chappelle and Sen. Jeff Bankston don't have a lot of constituents, you know. And I talk to Brian a lot more than you. His office is right down the hall in the Graham Building."

"Yeah, yeah."

Johanna Kepler, their professional playing partner, teed up from the championship tees and proceeded to hit her drive 289 yards straight down the fairway, Nick noted after looking at the drive with the rangefinder sunglasses his wife's Aunt Bonnie had given her years ago, one of their many expensive gadgets.

"You amateurs. That's the way it *should* be done." The lanky, six-foot Black woman snickered at her old friend.

"Like father, like daughter," Nick said, shaking his head. "The things I could do if I had the genetic talent of the *Gravi-Golfer*—"

"You might want to try practicing first. I practice eight hours a day, and that doesn't include my cardio or weight training. Get out and get some sun, dweeb. Wait—you used to practice back in the day, I remember. Didn't help much."

They got in their special four-person cart and headed off to the ladies tees for Fahnaz to hit. Her damn security patrol was right behind them and seriously cramping his style; he didn't like federal agents much, let alone a dozen Secret Service agents. At least they were normal-sized human beings, not the leviathans on the Presidential detail. Fahnaz would be lucky to hit it fifty yards, as unathletic as she was, he thought, laughing.

He then thought he heard something up in the sky and looked up. "What the hell was that?" he asked the two women.

"I don't know, some bird or something," Hanna said, annoyed. "Let's go let Fahnaz whiff her ball, Nick, come on. Quit stalling."

He then heard it. The sonic boom up in the sky. Something was traveling pretty damn fast.

"What is it, Nick?" Fahnaz asked.

"I don't know. It looked like some tiny jet or something breaking the sound barrier."

"A tiny jet with enough speed to go Mach 1? Really? Awww, I don't believe that. Another of your far-out stories." Fahnaz looked at them curiously as the Senator's Secret Service detail threw her to the ground and a female agent lay on top of her. The Democratic Presidential nominee wasn't really in any danger, though.

"What the hell?" Nick asked the agent.

"Get down, too, sir," she said as they got the Senator up and whisked her into their golf cart. "Something came to Earth at incredible speed, falling from the sky."

"Yeah, I get that, woman in black. I guess that spells the end of our round," he said sadly as he lay on the fairway looking like an idiot. "Which is probably a good thing for me."

"You think, genius?" Hanna yelled as she lay next to him.

"It almost looked like a flying man," he said to her. "There was some projectile that came down, too. Over there near the lake, by the big A-statue."

She shook her head. "This is way more excitement than I bargained for, Nick."

"Yes, welcome to Aurora City, the place where anything can happen, or nothing can happen, depending on the day. Usually, the latter. Well, let's go over there and see. Fahnaz may have to go with the Secret Service, but not us." He stood up and helped her up as they ran over to their cart, the "danger" having apparently passed, for them, at least.

Hanna ran after him at top speed on her long legs. "You're kidding, right, about going over there? *Please* tell me that's the case."

He scowled and shook his head. "No, that's a stupid remark. You should know me better than that." They drove the cart over to see his parents and son waving at him. He got out and saw Jose running towards him, out of breath.

"Daddy, I saw Amalgam-Man, he was up there!" Jose yelled.

"Uh, yeah, I think I saw him, too." He looked at his mom, who was shaking her head. "Maybe you guys should get out of here before the DSD shows up; the Secret Service saw it too and took Fahnaz away in their black SUV. So much for the golf tournament."

"But, Daddy—it really *was* Amalgam-Man, I saw him, he flew faster than sound, Gramps said—"

"Quiet. Dad, you, Mom, and Jose get out of here *now*. And, for God's sake, *please* don't tell anyone what you saw. Especially anyone from the government."

"What? Government? Why?" Molly asked.

"Because I said so. Now!" Stavros ushered them back into the motorboat as they sped off to their private dock.

"Um—why aren't *we* getting out of here, Nick?" the slightly taller Hanna asked, irritated. "I don't give a darn about this stuff."

"*Gravi-Golfer* would be *so* ashamed to hear you say that."

"I'm no astrophysicist, and I don't care about what my nerdy dad thinks. Aside from our golfing abilities, we're as dissimilar as two people can be."

"Well, I *do* care about cool science stuff." He ran up to the base of the statue. "Look, you can see where it hit." Nick pointed his pocket sensor at the hole. "Non-metallic, it's some type of polymer with two layers. There's nothing in it of any worrisome chemical composition. Curious."

"You know all that from your fancy pocket-thingy?" Hanna asked. "What the heck do you carry that thing around for, *Tinman*?"

"You never know when you might need it. Useful in soil studies, looking at alloy composition of parts, other stuff."

"Figures." She stared at him. "What a geek, as always."

"You may rule the fairways, Kepler, but geeks like my wife and I rule the world."

"Huh. That's not my world. You and the famous *Gravi-Golfer* do think alike. And that was not a compliment."

"It was, as we are merely scientists on a mission of discovery." He looked around, a mass of people watching him curiously as he dug the object out of the ground, at the foot of the massive forty-foot bronze statue of the winged six-year-old girl, a sculptor's rendition of his wife's deceased cousin. He was there when the statue was set, which was good since he and his wife had paid for it.

"Leave that alone, you stupid lummox, it might be a meteorite or something dangerous."

He laughed. "It's *not* a meteorite, I just told you—it's composed of 1,3-butadiene, isocyanates, and polyols. Meteorites don't contain carbon; they are generally made of nickel, iron, and silicates."

Hanna stuck her tongue out. "Yikes, that stuff sounds pretty dangerous to me."

"It's not, it's just plain old plastic." He shook his head and laughed. "You should see the ingredients in some of the stuff you eat, Hanna."

She thought for a moment. "Hey, explosives can be plastic, can't they? Get away from it, Nick, you idiot!" She backed away.

He laughed. "I said that's impossible; it's not a nitrosamine, it's just plastic, and can't explode. Trust that I know something about chemistry." He dug for several more minutes with his eight hundred-dollar custom-forged seven-iron, which was more useful as digging tool than golf club, the way he had been playing lately. "Hey, it's, no, it can't be—" He pulled out the scarred sphere and scraped the dirt off it.

"What is it?" She came back towards him, curious.

"The irony of it all, it's just a plain old golf ball. That thing, whatever it was, threw it at the statue."

Hanna squinted. "You think? It's kinda burned up, though. Why is that? Does that being have laser vision?"

He shook his head in disdain. "No, silly. Atmospheric friction."

"Like when an object enters the Earth's atmosphere? But it was close to us, not out in space, so is that even possible?"

He nodded. "Yeah, but for it to have burned up in that short a distance, it must've been thrown at an unbelievable velocity."

"Huh? How fast is that?"

"I'll have to calculate it." He pulled out his scientific calculator and started punching numbers.

"Another toy? Why do you have that on the golf course, Nick?"

"You never know when you need to make a calculation."

"For your crummy golf scores? It would need to have at least three digits, maybe four. And that's per hole, not per round."

"Quiet." He punched more numbers excitedly. "I assume it needs to be at about 1,500 degrees Fahrenheit to melt like that, which means it must have been traveling at a mean velocity of—holy crap. I can't believe it."

"What?"

"The ball would've needed to travel at a velocity of at least six thousand miles per hour for it to have ignited like that in such a short distance. That—isn't possible. No science we know of is capable of propelling a projectile at such speed. Reentry speed is only about three times that."

"But it happened, Nick. Do you really think it was some flying man? Why would a flying robot or alien throw a dumb golf ball at the base of Aurora's statue instead of hitting it directly? Wouldn't he throw a bomb or something more advanced than that and blow up your office instead? That just might cause a blip in the world's economy."

"Yeah, I do think it was a flying man or woman, and I have no clue why it's a golf ball, but it is. Don't be dense."

"Do golf balls exist on other planets?" she asked sarcastically. "What a way for extraterrestrial life to contact us."

"Are you serious? Even Jose saw it, and you heard the sonic boom." He looked around nervously. "Let's get out of here, the local yokels will be here any minute, and the Secret Service probably has already called the fibbies, and I don't want to talk about this to anyone. And the velocity it must have been thrown to have melted this much from atmospheric friction is—phenomenal."

She scratched her head. "Uh, what's a 'fibby'?"

"FBI agents, duh, and then the DSD, which is worse."

"DSD? What the heck is that?"

"Department of Scientific Developments—a super-scientific federal agency with incredible jurisdiction over pretty much anything; we don't want those creepy dudes here. Wait, why am I telling you, anyway? We need to get lost, pronto."

"Oh, so *now* you want to leave. Why? I thought this was your town since you and Bella helped, like, build almost all of it."

He looked around nervously again. "It is, most of the time, until Presidential candidates come to visit, then it's probably not something I can control. We really do need the *Golfer* out here, Hanna, I mean it." He put the scarred golf ball in his pocket as they got back into the electric golf cart and headed for the clubhouse.

"What? Are you kidding?" He was going about thirty miles per hour in the cart now. "What the heck for?"

"No, I'm not kidding. You know *Golfer's* working on my dark matter project. He's been ignoring me lately, but he might actually take *your* phone call."

"Probably not; you greatly overestimate my influence. And I

don't know anything about your crummy dark stuff."

"Dark matter, not dark stuff. It's worth a try."

"What the heck is dark matter anyway, *Tinman?* By the way, he said he was rather pissed off at you, and I'm beginning to see why—you're acting weird, just like in high school."

"It's a secret. And, yes, I've been bugging him to share what he's found out, but he has been ducking me, as you've noticed. And him calling me weird is the pot calling the kettle black."

"*Black?*" She punched him in the shoulder. "Is that supposed to be funny, dummy?"

He shook his head. "No, sorry, no pun intended."

"Huh. I tell you, I said I'd never play with you again." She mumbled something incomprehensible, took out her Tekphone, and dialed a number as they arrived at the clubhouse in record speed. The caller finally answered. "Dad? Nick needs you on the next plane to Aurora City. No, not to play in the tournament. Something else has come up. It's, well—an anomaly that has to do with astrophysics, and also golf." A short pause. "What? Yes, you heard me. Golf and dark matter both? Yes, that's absolutely correct: a two-for-one opportunity that can't be beaten, he claims." She took the phone from her ear and winced as the deep voice on the other end became very loud.

"What did he say?"

"He said to leave him alone, and that your family was nothing but a bunch of trouble. And, some other stuff."

"No, come on. Gimme that." He took the phone. "Johnny? I really need your help on something. I can't tell you what it is." A pause. "Of course, I'll pay your way out. No, not coach, my private jet. Okay, then. Have it your way, and just wait until you need something from me, Kepler, like grant money. Yes, I know you have tenure." He hung up and handed her the phone back. "Jerk."

"Come on. What did my dad say?"

"He reluctantly said he would come out, as long as I'm footing the bill. *Then* he said things I can't repeat to a lady, as he has a stellar sailor's vocabulary. I hope he didn't say those things to you."

"True, true. I hope you don't expect me to stick around, though. I've got the LPGA Open in a few days in Orlando."

"Sounds like fun. Not as fun as what we'll be doing."

"Somehow, I doubt that, but to each his own."

Chapter Six

Ten Minutes Later
Camp Conrad
Solway, Tennessee

Wendy and Jay Mendoza walked briskly through the mountainous woods as she carried the picnic basket in her left hand. It was rare that they had moments like this—quiet ones, as she looked at the late September trees, the leaves of some just beginning to turn fall colors. The serenity wouldn't last long, though. Of course, Jackie and the rest of the Secret Service detail weren't far away; they never were, although they were always well hidden.

It was the life she had chosen because she knew no one else could do the things she could and lead a country to places no one thought possible. Places some people thought weren't good ones. A state in almost every continent, and one not even on this planet. We certainly were in new territory now.

They picked a small patch of woods to sit down as she sat their picnic basket down and spread the plaid blanket out.

"Alex and I always used to come here as kids. It was kind of a secret place." She opened up the basket and removed a bottle of spring water and a bright red apple.

"I guess it's a little more rural than Camp David. At least it's cooler this time of year."

She shrugged and lay her head in his lap. "I'm tired of that place, it's just too manufactured. Like a fortress or something."

"We could always go back to Camp Kennedy if we wanted to

get away from it all. I always wanted to try, er—certain activities in a low-gravity environment. They say it's fun."

"What? Who would you know who knows anything about it?"

"I know people too, you know."

She sighed. "No, I really *don't* want to know."

"Anyway—we didn't get a crack at it last time, the quarters were a bit cramped, and you were too busy."

She snarled. "That's all you think about, isn't it? Even when we are in space?"

He shook his head. "Of course not. It's only about eighty percent of what I think about. I think about football and food the other twenty percent."

She cracked a smile, finally. "That figures. Some things never change. Without that, we wouldn't have Will, I guess. The miracle child who's now almost as tall as us."

"Damn right, you better be glad I still have my *mojo* at age sixty. It is pretty, seeing Earthrise and all. Would be fun to go to Mars."

She shook her head. "Maybe in about twenty years. Not much infrastructure set up there yet. Even with the fusion turbines, still a four-month trip at best. Nothing there of use to us."

"Camp Kennedy is a lot more work for the troops than here, where nobody bothers us. Anyway, you built it, so don't complain about it." Jay took a drink of soda. "You miss him, don't you?"

"Who? Alex? Of course I do. We weren't that close after I left, but he was a good brother. We had some good times—and some bad ones. He helped me become who I am today." She looked around. "You know, in the last forty years, I've been here only a handful of times. I hated Tennessee because of my dad, the crap he did, cheating on my mom, the drunkenness."

"Don't forget that he gave his life to save yours. Without him, you'd be dead."

She scowled at him. "Dammit, I know he did, Jay; you don't need to remind me again and again. I held him in my arms when he died, so I know better than anyone. I'm torn by the guilt every day over what he did—he and Bonnie risked their crazy necks to save me on Malachi Argon's Caribbean island. I can't get any of that time back now. Alex and my dad are dead, and all these things are because of me."

He turned his head sharply. "Bonnie, too, right? Don't forget my little sis."

"Yeah, right." She looked at him intensely. "You know the answer to that as well as I. But what I don't officially know about, I can't act upon or comment about."

He grabbed her right shoulder with his left hand. "Then be grateful for what you *do* have and stop complaining, dammit. Don't blame yourself for it all. None of us can go back in time."

She ate a few potato chips, a treat she rarely allowed herself these days, being a person with borderline hypertension who had to watch her salt and caloric intake. She had gestational diabetes with Will, and knew she was at risk for developing overt diabetes in the future if she didn't take care of herself.

"But have I become my father? Look at me. He just made the stinking things, he didn't have the executive power to set them all off at once. I do: the power to create a thousand Hiroshimas."

"Hey, it's not your fault van Sant and Skelton shot down their plane. You aren't responsible for everything."

"We both know that's not who did it. I'm on record as saying the damn North Koreans did it," she yelled as her face turned red. "Not those stupid-ass morons, give me a break."

"Whatever you say. Let's not start that again, as it was neither. The guy who did it went and lost his head, I heard."

Her head snapped back towards him. "That's not very damn funny, Jay, given who did it."

"I was just being factual. Hey, we're supposed to be on holiday, whatever that means for us these days. It doesn't mean arguing about stupid stuff."

She looked around as she sat down and took a bite of her large Red Delicious apple, a far cry from the stuff they used to eat when they were in college. Back then, he burned off all the extra calories from physical activity, while she usually didn't, as she wasn't much into cardio. Now, at slightly under two hundred pounds, her once rounded face was now angular, almost Nordic; the half-British, half-Appalachian woman's weight had fluctuated anywhere from 230 to 255 pounds (or more) back in the day.

The famous loud, unique voice was softer now, still with a very noticeable Southern Appalachian accent, but more mainstream. The speech therapists and diction consultants helped with that. Not many people made fun of *her* any longer, and the media usually left her alone. Why? Probably mostly due to respect for her, as she was always a straight shooter with them, and she had done much for America; and, of course, fear of the repercussions if she became angry; it was beneficial to them to have access to the White House. A Bipper public approval rating of 91% was hard to contradict, in any case. There was no way the Democrats could cause an upset in the next election.

She always did play to the media, and this is what the media wanted: maintain some of her uniqueness, but not to the point of being a cartoon voice-over artist, the wannabe singer, or host of comedy shows in her spare time like she once aspired to be, in more carefree days. The days of reckless fun were gone forever. He missed those days sometimes.

But the world had changed, and, by some accounts, not for the better. She was a lot of things, but neither stupid nor naïve. She knew eventually there could be consequences to her actions.

"What have I become?" Wendy looked out into the blue Tennessee sky that she had ignored for so long. "All I ever wanted was to be happy. People thought I was, but it was never true."

"Happiness has to come from within."

She snapped her head towards him and frowned. "Really, now? Did Bobbi Elsevier teach you that catchphrase? How clichéd."

"You might try seeing her again before you die, as a psychiatrist might do you some good, you know. You're a physician, for God's sake. Haven't you learned anything about the prevention of burnout problems before they arise?"

"Yeah. I should know better with my history. Where have I heard *that* before?" She laughed. "But they'd all run and hide after trying to fix what's in *my* brain. And, as far as being burned out, I'm afraid it's too late for me."

"No comment."

She took another bite of her apple. "I thought that accumulating countless titles and accolades would help me, somehow. I lost Stan because of my selfishness. My obsession with being Surgeon General and winning an Olympic gold medal was the last straw, and I didn't blame him for leaving. He and Jake and Cassie are all dead now. *Tinman* and Bella built a whole city as a memorial to Bonnie and Aurora. Was anything built for them?"

"Focusing on you, as usual."

"What? How is concern over how my children are remembered about me?"

"Remember that you served as a role model for millions of people who don't happen to look like a supermodel. And it isn't your fault they were killed. We went all over that. Memorial cities aren't going to bring Jake and Cassie back; you surely don't need that to remember them. And you know it's different with Aurora City—it was built as a symbol of hope for mankind, not as a tribute to her. Aurora is one of a kind, and many believe she's the second coming of Christ."

She nodded and wiped tears from her eyes. "I know. One day it will all come together and make sense. Aurora is possibly the most special person to ever walk this Earth, except for you-know-who born a couple of millennia ago."

"Probably. I guess there will be debates about that one day. I suppose the true tribute to her is yet to come if we live to see it."

"But it *is* all my fault, don't you see? I set it all in motion. You remember. I damn near got you killed back in 2010. Everyone else died in 2016 because of what I did."

"Your dad helped a bit with it too, a year before you were born, in that hotel room in Monaco. Now, you need to relax." There was only one person who could ever soothe her when she got wound up, and she finally married him.

"I can't. I wanted to be a doctor, to help people."

"You did, and still do help millions of people in your job. Every day."

"It's not the same. Bonnie—I never got to say goodbye."

"I didn't either, you know. I knew her way longer than you. We'll see her again. Not sure when, but we will."

"Of course, but did you have any regrets, Jay? We grew farther and farther apart as we got older; we argued all the time. Our politics became irreconcilable. She said I would someday either save mankind or be the ruination of it. Which was right?"

"She never was the easiest person to get along with. You two were almost like sisters, and siblings argue with each other. Let it go and move on, Wendy. A lot of what she said made no sense."

"I can't, because I wish I could go back in time and see her; today, I doubt she resembles at all the person she—" She turned her head. "What's that noise?"

"I didn't hear anything."

She looked towards the lake named after her brother. "Jay, someone's yelling." She then heard a cry for help; it sounded like a child, down by the lake where she and her brother Alex used to go fishing. Sometimes with their dad, too, when he wasn't drinking, stoned on drugs with brain-damaged Cousin Smiley, or away on business doing God knows what with other women; one named Katrina Argon, unfortunately, came to mind.

Will heard it too and ran towards the bank. There weren't supposed to be people in this area anyway; it was her private property, and her staff had it fenced off long ago for the very reason that someone might get hurt in Dirk Dark's Lake, which was over twenty feet deep at its greatest depth.

She ran down the hill as fast as she could, which wasn't very speedy compared to the average human being; while she was still strong, speed and coordination were never her greatest attributes. Jay stood there, dumbfounded, as she rambled down and almost fell off the bank as he saw a girl, perhaps ten, screaming.

"I told Bobby not to go out in that lousy old boat, but he did anyway," the girl exclaimed. The boy was thrashing in the middle of the lake, about a hundred yards out, the boat overturned. By that time, a highly animated Jackie Levickis was rushing down the hill with Jay, shouting various colorful expletives.

"Can he swim?" Wendy yelled at a mid-thirtyish woman who came running down the hill on the other side. The woman was the boy's mother, she guessed.

"No, lady, he can't. He'll drown." The woman screamed as her arms flailed.

"Over my dead body he will." She took off her jacket and shoes.

Jackie ran as fast as she could in protest, seemingly anticipating her boss' next ill-advised action. "'*Dead body?'* Ma'am, don't you dare think about doing that, I mean it this time—"

The fifty-six-year-old woman never took orders very nicely and clearly wasn't about to start now. The large endo-mesomorph surely didn't look very Presidential with her ungainly cannonball dive into the water ten feet down. At least she apparently had enough sense (having taken care of multiple children with spinal cord injuries) to go in that way instead of diving head-first; a quadriplegic Chief Executive wasn't desired.

"Dammit!" Jackie exclaimed, yet breathing a sigh of relief after seeing her boss' head bob up after initially sinking. "That headstrong woman will be the death of me yet." She prepared to dive in after the President as Will held her back and laughed.

"Chill out, I'll get her, Jackie, she's in no danger, it'll take me about ten seconds to pass her," Will yelled. "She's a slow swimmer, but she won't drown. Too much buoyancy."

"No, you won't, William Conrad Mendoza Darkkin, or I'll kick your butt too. Andy and Leon will get her—" She winced again as the remarkably strong eleven-year-old Will, ignoring her and breaking free of her grasp, dove in after his mom. Oh, no. Holy crap." She looked at Jay. "You'd better not, I'm warning you."

"Who, me? I can't swim worth a damn, so don't worry," Jay said as the two massive male Secret Service agents dove in after them. "She's in nearly as good of condition as you are. Will's a superb athlete, too, better than anyone here."

"*Don't worry?* I run five miles a day and hit the weights for another half-hour; when's the last time Wendy ran a mile? All the agents on our detail are ex-collegiate athletes. She's almost fifty-seven, was never any type of aerobic athlete, and has one functional lung, sir. Do you remember that?"

"Oh, yeah." Well, not really; they hadn't seen each other for over two years when that happened in 2014. He had forgotten that she was the first Surgeon General who really had done anything heroic when she almost died after taking four bullets in the chest for President Reardon and the British Prime Minister, and spent weeks in the intensive care unit and months in rehab after that.

The athletic Black woman dove in after Wendy and Will, who by that time were halfway to the boy. Sometimes protecting a real American hero from herself was a pain in the butt. That was one of the reasons Jackie liked this job, she had said once. It sure beat protecting Vice President Robert Benton, who rarely ventured outside Washington or did anything of substance, for that matter. Hopefully, Benton wouldn't have to take the Presidential oath.

That wasn't really fair to Robby, the very influential senior Senator from Ohio who was somewhat more conservative than his relatively liberal Presidential running mate. He also did many things of "substance" few knew anything about; he was a grizzled Washington veteran who had been in the energy industry before entering politics. He chaired many influential committees and was calmer and more introverted than his talkative boss.

Robby's primary value, though, was that he was also very familiar with the dark back alleys of Washington where mere mortals would fear to tread; he might not be the best "face" of the administration, but this "fixer" wasn't afraid to get his hands dirty and get stuff done at any cost. Anyway, Wendy Mendoza had taken a lot worse than some lake water and survived.

Will, using perfect freestyle stroke form, passed his mom easily as he reached Bobby about ten seconds before her; they pulled him to the fishing pier as a half dozen additional Secret Service agents approached. She gave the boy mouth-to-mouth resuscitation; at least, that was one important skill she had retained from her interesting youth.

The boy's mother came up to them, screaming. "Bobby! Are you all right?"

Bobby started coughing and breathing on his own.

"I believe so," she said.

"Ma'am, you and your boy saved my boy's life. I told him never to go out in that old boat, it's not safe."

"He's—he's swallowed a lot of water. I'll have an Army chopper take him to East Tennessee Children's in Knoxville. He'll need to be watched for a day or two."

"Will he be all right?" the mother asked.

"I think so. You realize this is private land; your kids shouldn't have been out here, just for this very reason. It can be dangerous."

"I know, I told them not to go through that hole in the fence. But who are you, Ma'am? Me and my husband will be grateful always. We were born here."

"Who am I?" She looked at Jay and Will and stood tall, exhilarated by this rare moment of anonymity. "I am, and always will be—a doctor. One who was born here too, just like you."

The thirtyish lady looked at her curiously. "*Doctor?* What's your name? Never saw any tall lady doctor around here before, especially one who was born here."

She shook her head. "Well, I don't live here any longer. It's taken me too long to come back. I grew up a half-mile from here, just outside Solway." She extended her large hand, which the smaller woman took.

"Half-mile? This here is the Darkkin country. You kin to them? You sure look and sound like you belong to their clan. Didn't know any were around these days, the way those people lived."

She nodded and laughed as she regained her breath. "That's right. I'm a Darkkin, born and raised," she said proudly. For most of her life she would have been ashamed to mention that name, but not any longer. She had had four different surnames in her life, though, despite only being married twice. Hopefully, the one she had now would be her last.

The smaller woman stared at the soaking wet woman's face, matted-down hair, and the expanding entourage of armed personnel arriving at her side. The massive hovercraft bearing the Presidential seal landed on the side bank of the lake, and the overwhelmed woman appeared to finally recognize who had saved her son from drowning: the Oak Ridge area's most famous former resident.

"Oh, Lord Jesus in Heaven," she said, making the sign of the cross on her chest. "I didn't realize—it's just that no one's seen you around here for a very long time." The woman hugged her. "I don't believe it. You, of all people, risked your life to save my boy."

"Careful, I'm soaking wet. And I'm no more important than anyone else, I'd do it again."

"No, she won't do it again," Jackie yelled, pointing at her. "This is our last trip to Camp Conrad and Dirk Dark's Lake, or I quit."

She laughed. "You've threatened that multiple times and never followed through."

"I mean it this time, Ma'am."

"Sure, sure. Anyway, we don't have time to talk now. Let's get Bobby to Knoxville."

"Excuse me?" Jackie asked. "Getting who to where?"

"Knoxville Children's Hospital, which is the closest tertiary pediatric center. You going with us?" she asked.

"Absolutely not," she said, Jackie shaking her head. "You aren't, either. You about gave me a stroke by diving in that lake, don't send me over the edge for urgent admission to whatever psychiatric hospital is in the vicinity."

She shook her head. "Wrong, Detail Chief Levickis." The Army medical helicopter from the nearby base arrived after they rushed to an empty field seventy feet from the lake. "I'm going to Knoxville with this boy," she said. "We can't take him in the Presidential hovercraft. It doesn't have medical supplies."

"Ma'am, no, you can't," Jackie said. "I won't allow it."

The large woman frowned as she lifted the boy in her arms.

"Yeah? I can, and I will. If you want to follow or ride along you may, but this boy needs a doctor in attendance. Do you see another one here?"

"No, but while Good Samaritan laws apply, the liability alone is a consideration, given that you don't even have a Tennessee medical license any longer—"

"Aww, I don't give a hoot about stuff like that, as I do what's right. Don't you understand me after all these years? What else are y'all gonna do? Haven't I always wanted to do what's right?"

Jackie shook her head, clearly knowing when she was beaten. "Yes, I guess so. That's the problem."

"It's only a problem if you think it is."

"I do. But I also know I can't argue with you."

She laughed. "Arguing with me is easy, it's winning that's hard." The medics loaded Bobby, his mother, the President, and Jackie into the Med-Evac chopper that had just arrived, as the female emergency dispatcher answered the radio after being signaled by the pilot.

"Knoxville Children's emergency dispatch. Go ahead."

"Army One *en route* from Solway with nine-year-old male rescued from the lake and resuscitated by a physician who happened to be on site."

"Army? You military?"

"Yes, Ma'am. We sure are. Army means military."

"Medical is on board?"

"Um, yes."

"I didn't copy. It sounded like you said 'Army One.' What do you mean by that?"

"Ma'am, Army One is the call sign for any Army aircraft containing the President of the United States."

A pause for ten seconds. "What was that again?"

"I said—the President is aboard this air vehicle."

"Yeah, that's what I thought you said. And you are flying here with a pediatric patient?"

"Affirmative."

"Uh, okay. Got it now."

Just then, they heard the screeching projectile going through the air as they took off into the sky towards Knoxville, and she saw it (not for the first time), if for only an instant: a grey metalloid human form that paused, then took off like a rocket.

Well, that was neat. She blithely ignored what she had just seen and returned dutifully to the task at hand: getting a sick child to the hospital. Whatever it was would return soon.

• • •

Seventy minutes later, at Knoxville Children's Hospital, Wendy met with Jackie and Dexter Slabb in a conference room as she left Bobby's room. She had changed into some blue scrubs until someone could fetch her some dry clothes.

"Kid doing okay?" Jackie asked.

She nodded. "Yeah, he's fine now, he was pretty scared." She looked at the small object in his right hand. "But what the hell was that thing? Is there any updated info?" she asked as Jackie looked at her curiously as if she had asked that in obligatory fashion, not because she really cared.

Dexter shook his head. "We don't know, Ma'am. Central Air Command detected a tiny projectile traveling at hypersonic speed, and we were able to track it."

"Hypersonic? How fast?"

"The object achieved a maximum velocity of Mach 6.79."

About five thousand miles per hour. "Composition?"

"A common polymer of rubber and plastic, forty millimeters in diameter. It had almost no air friction," Dexter said.

"How can that be?" she asked.

"It could be if it had dimples."

"Dimples? You mean, like a—a golf ball?" She shook her head. "No way, that's too bizarre."

"That's what it would seem like," he said. "It was embedded in the ground, three feet in front of the tombstone of one William Conrad Darkkin, located at Elmhurst Cemetery, three miles from where you were. It's the damndest thing I ever saw, Ma'am."

"What the hell?" she asked.

"And, there's another thing: nothing at all showed up on radar, which is really weird, but there appeared to be some type of human-sized object also traveling at supersonic speed right about the time of the impact. There was perhaps some visual confirmation, but nothing definite on video, except for 4K video stuff captured on consumer devices sent to Air Command. It's the same damn thing Kriger and Ashburn were raving about before in the White House situation room."

She shrugged. "So, you're saying some flying alien is out there and flung a cheap golf ball into my dad's grave? *Why?* That's more preposterous than it flying to Canada. And my dad hated golf; he considered it a colossal waste of time. Not that he didn't waste time on multiple other creative activities I shall not discuss at this moment, as we are in a children's hospital."

Dexter shook his head. "We don't know."

"Again, you don't know." She rolled her aquamarine eyes condescendingly and snickered. "Was this dimpled, spherical object radioactive, infectious, or otherwise harmful to organic life?"

Dexter frowned. "No, it's just a cheap, burned-up golf ball."

"Well, then, don't we have more important things to worry about than flying robots throwing crummy golf balls at my pop's final resting place?"

He opened his mouth wide. "Is that a trick question?"

She sneered. "No. Do I look like I'm laughing to you? I'm serious, dammit. Look at me, I just rescued a drowning boy from a lake, so I'm not in the mood for jokes."

"Sorry. Sometimes I hope for small vestiges of the comedian who was once within."

"Yes, well, this job has gotten rid of that person permanently. However, I shall try to rise to the occasion."

He frowned condescendingly. "Ma'am, at least fifty people have already called Central Air Command saying they saw it. There were similar sightings in Green Bay and Aurora City less than an hour ago. These things aren't new; we've discussed them with you before. It disappeared from sight faster than any rocket, and for some reason, you're suggesting we do *nothing?* Do I understand you correctly? The thing was within a tenth of a mile from you, so it's a matter of national security."

She rolled her eyes. "The mythical Russian battle armor again, yes, they're attacking Wisconsin, you've uncovered the master plan for domination of Earth. How'd you ever find out? I've been carefully keeping it a secret to avoid mass panic."

"The Russians attacking Wisconsin, Ma'am?" Dexter smiled curiously. "I'm afraid I don't follow, but that's nothing new."

She sighed. "I guess I have to spell it out: on September 6, 1962, the Soviet space probe Korabl-Sputnik 1, also called Sputnik IV, crashed into downtown Manitowoc—forty miles from Green Bay—after a faulty reentry. Gee, maybe they can erect a monument too. The Russians want to destroy the cheese industry, that's it."

He nodded. "That's correct, Ma'am; you sure know your space history and have a very good memory."

"Don't kiss my big butt, Dexter. I can spout geek trivia with the best of you when the need arises, mainly because my late sister-in-law couldn't stop talking about that stuff. When she was a kid and visited Lambeau Field to see Jay play, the folks always had to take her to the crash site. There really isn't much to see."

He nodded. "Yes, it's sure nice to know such things, but I fail to see what the Sputnik crash in Manitowoc and the Russians have to do with this new event."

She smiled, then started laughing loudly. "Just trying to interject some humor as well as provide historical perspective regarding this incredible event."

"I don't know that I find it funny, Madam President. Sorry."

"You don't?" She sighed. "You're the one who wanted some laughs a few minutes ago, so what's the problem?"

"I stand corrected, and I am again reminded how rapidly your moods can change. One of the unpaid perks of this job."

"Ohmigod. Dexter, have you been hanging out with Ashburn or General Kriger too long? If so, you need a vacation. I won't waste valuable government resources looking for Bigfoot, or flying robots, or Elvis, or whatever other ridiculous things people report all the time because they want attention or to disguise their own incompetence. You show me proof and I'll devote all the resources you need for it, but otherwise, no. A burned-up golf ball is hardly quantitative evidence of alien life."

He nodded as he cracked a smile. "Yes, Ma'am."

"Thank you. I'll see you later, as I need to get back."

Dexter and Jackie left the room as she sighed and put her head down. She wondered what the hell to do next, as things were not proceeding with any type of predictability. Golf balls? What kind of crazy nonsense was that?

But then she remembered what adults she was probably dealing with. Neither of them was very mature, and that trait had probably persisted to this day. However, she had to play their game, as they had brought up the greatest power on Earth, and her meddling in their affairs would not gain anyone's trust.

Wherever she was, gaining the trust of a goddess was more important than just about anything right now.

For I am my father's daughter. Now and forevermore.

If that meant lying to Dexter Slabb, Larry Kriger, Tom Ashburn,

Congress, and just about everyone else, then so be it.

Except Jackie. She knew her trusted detail chief knew the truth, somehow. Even the President needed someone to confide in at times. She couldn't very well talk to Jay—he was too close to the issue.

And he also had a big mouth.

Chapter Seven

Stannous Residence
8330 Eagledale Circle
Aurora City, Indiana

Dr. Nicholas Stannous went into his large, well-appointed bedroom at ten-thirty to sneak a peek at the voluptuous naked woman putting on her sheer black nightgown, her flawless light cinnamon skin gleaming in the light of the incandescent desk lamp. Real light bulbs (that burned a tungsten filament) were hard to come by these days, but he had a few stashed away. He was rich enough to have damn near everything he wanted.

But money couldn't buy everything or bring people back from the dead.

He watched the gleaming skin of the naked figure with lust in his eyes, but he always remembered what Father Pappas at the Greek Orthodox Church where he grew up had told him:

It was not lust if the person he desired was his wife. It was good and proper for such urges within the institution of marriage.

Fantastic. He always thought that was because those "urges" would lead to the proliferation of Greeks in the community.

He knew his spouse was considered by many to be the world's most beautiful woman (he did have an eye for shapely ladies, although recent life stressors had detracted from that fancy); he was married once to a woman he thought was the most beautiful in the world, although he knew no one else likely thought that. He knew his second wife understood, and he knew she never wanted to replace her. No one could.

But she was there for him after *Darkkday* when she could've had any man she wanted in the world. Yet, she chose him because she loved him, even though part of his heart would always belong to another. That was okay with her, as she, above all others, understood what he was feeling. Only someone who had lost as much could ever do that.

"Did you read Jose his story?" he asked, nothing more romantic coming to mind, the potential financial disasters of the coming day already weighing heavily on his mind. And the stress that dark energy robots flinging flying golf balls bring to one's mind.

"Yeah," Bella said. "I told him some good ones, as I have a good imagination. He likes to hear about superheroes and such."

"Right up your alley."

"Exactly. I certainly look good in the suits, but those workouts are killers. He likes it when I put them on and play with him. I wish you enjoyed fondling a superheroine as much as you used to."

He frowned. "Sorry. Sometimes I just lose my interest in such things. It isn't you."

The fit yet very well-endowed female crawled into bed with him. "*¿Cuál es el problema, el hombre estaño?*"

He shook his head and looked away. "Nothing."

"Aww, come on. I know better." She rubbed his hairy chest with her soft hand. "Can't fool me. I've known you too long."

"What, you can read minds now? I thought that was reserved for other members of your family."

"Sure, yours I can. You shouldn't worry so much about stuff. Put it away for the night and start again tomorrow." She stroked his chest again. "I know how to get your mind on something else you'll like."

"Like what?"

"Well, like you putting your biscuit in my basket. I know how much you enjoy that."

"Not tonight." He said sadly as he turned away and frowned. "I don't like to bother you with my problems. I have a lot these days."

"*Sus problemas son mis problemas.* Now and always. I have to be good for something around here." She crawled over and kissed him on the cheek.

He sneered. "Right, like you're really useful at being a dutiful stay-at-home housewife or something else that's domestic. Give me a break. There isn't anyone in the world who can do what you can."

"No, but I am dutiful to my husband, even though my cooking and housekeeping stink." She brushed his black hair, which now had a smattering of gray. "It's about Kepler, isn't it?"

He nodded. "How did you know?"

"Who else would bug you as much as that weirdo?"

"You're right, but I just don't know what to do. I know he's aware of stuff he's not sharing with me, and sometimes he won't even return my calls, but I wonder if we should be messing with it at all. All this scares the crap out of me."

"What do you mean?"

"Suppose we find this dark energy source he believes exists out there. Why do I want to find it so badly? Don't we have enough energy, Bella? This could be perverted into a terrible weapon by mankind; by that, I mean you-know-who."

"I disagree. Better her to know about it than some people. Because you, like me, have that insatiable need to satisfy your curiosity. It's what makes us who we are, *Tinman*. The drive to further knowledge, to succeed, to reach the stars. As great as our technology is, that will require something greater. And for the other reason we want to find out."

"What?"

"It's called family. I don't have much left."

"Family, how ironic. You think you have *Darkkday* all figured out, don't you?"

She nodded. "Yes. And you know I'm right on the money. But a few details are missing. The events of the last few days, with the golf balls and all, are a bit perplexing."

"Do I really know that you're right?" He stared up at the ceiling as he took a drink of orange juice from a glass. "Are they one and the same, as you claim? Aurora and the dark matter being? Maybe we're being too simplistic, wanting to believe in something we hope against hope to be true."

"You know the answer to that. You wouldn't be sending millions of dollars to dead Uncle Jimbo in Alaska if you didn't think so. And we wouldn't have built a city if there was any doubt."

"I didn't want you to get wind of that, you know, about the money, I mean. He wouldn't like it."

She laughed. "Hey, listen, he wouldn't like anything that involves me, he thought I was just a brat."

"You *are* a brat." He threw a pillow at her playfully. "Maybe you need a spanking."

"Promises, promises." She pointed her finger to the ceiling. "Correction, though: I am a brat with a boatload of money. And if you're doing something funny with *your* money, I want to chip in with mine too. It's no fun doing illicit stuff in secret without an accomplice."

"But how can we help further? I'm just an opportunist, like Wendy. Don't we have enough cash? Why do I care so much, and what can we do?"

"There's no one like her, so don't insult yourself. We shall not see any human being like her again in this lifetime, which I believe is good, as one is enough."

"She isn't so bad, as you just like to insult her. Always did."

She nodded her head. "I know. While often overbearing, she can be a very kind person, especially to children. I have my information sources. She still goes and reads stories to kids at public libraries, Will says, and also goes to Children's National once a month to visit sick kids. I don't know where she finds the energy. But she has changed in many aspects, *Tinman*. Most importantly, I'm not sure she's even happy any longer. It's almost as if the responsibility of what is to come is resting on those big shoulders."

"But is she so wrong, Bella? Is it so terrible that no American dare fear crime anywhere in the world any longer because people know what America would do? Look at the results: there has been far less violence during her Presidency than at nearly any time in American history. I can't decide what's right any longer."

She shook her head. "I don't like it, but we helped put her there, so we have to make the best of it. But we also have to be there when Aurora needs us. God knows we can't leave it up to Wendy. Who knows what shape the fouled-up government will be in by then? And you made the most of your opportunities like she did. We can do great things for Aurora Angelica, TM. Someone will need to be the ones to figure things out."

"But can we do it alone?" he asked.

She shook her head. "No, we surely can't. This is many orders of magnitude above anything the world has ever seen, at least for the last two thousand years. We will, therefore, need some help, as we don't know everything, you know."

"Who, pray tell, is going to provide that help, then? A scientist? A priest? A psychiatrist? I have no idea."

She shook her head. "Don't know. But there are some great minds out there. *Gravi-Golfer* and friends, maybe."

"Friends?"

"The old *Squad.* They are an eclectic and talented group. None of those guys likes the establishment, which is good for us."

He shook his head. "Those strange guys are scattered all over the place. Good luck getting them to do something constructive again, as if they ever did. Why them?"

"Because, despite their strangeness, Bonnie thought highly of that group, and that means a lot."

He laughed. "It does?"

"Yes. Strange, yes, but she attracted strangeness in spades. And I can be pretty persuasive."

"Hanna did say *Golfer* was coming out in a few days, and he promised to come. We'll see what he says about all this."

"Great. Now, let's forget this junk and get down to business. I will persuade you, too, in ways you can only imagine. About that spanking, now—"

He watched as his wife removed her black chiffon nightgown and his interest suddenly changed to something else. That body wasn't just for show, he knew, as he saw the Academy Award statue on the mantle, glistening in the light. Next to her Nobel medal. It was a pretty rare accomplishment to have both of those.

Chapter Eight

Mendoza Multinational
Airfield Prime
Sulphur Springs, Indiana

Dr. Nicholas Stannous drove down to the private airfield in his cherry red vintage Cadillac Eldorado coupe on his way to pick up his old friend's rather eccentric father at the Mendoza Multinational airfield, where the private jet he had sent for the man had just landed. He turned past the gate as the familiar security guard waved him through.

He made many trips to this private airstrip, as he lacked the time or patience for commercial airports, and Aurora City International Airport wasn't terribly fancy. And, while his extraverted wife liked the crowds, he hated them. The man he was about to see was much the same way, although at first glance, they would seem barely similar. They did have two common interests, however: gravitational physics and golf. He knew he wasn't this brilliant man's equal at either. He pulled up and got out of his car as he watched his jet's hatch open.

"*Gravi-Golfer*, how the hell are you," he said to the tall Black man who exited the Gulfstream with a small suitcase. He marveled at how he walked as well or better than a normal person, despite the fact his right leg was a permanently attached above-the-knee prosthesis that cost at least five million dollars. Money could buy a lot, but it couldn't resurrect the dead, he lamented again as he walked towards his guest.

Sixty-two-year-old Dr. Johnny Kepler slapped himself in the face as he stepped off the small portable stairway.

"Hell, you come out here yourself in this cold weather, rich executive? No stinkin' gate, red carpet, or nothin' for me; I have to walk down some rickety old staircase like a pathetic peasant, hoping I don't fall down and break my real leg. I thought you'd have some crappy lackey do it, like those who do the rest of your damn work. Business must be shitty if you can't afford any hired help."

He opened his arms wide in a welcoming stance. "Untrue, my famous friend. I can provide nothing but the best for you, *Golfer.* And nothing a mere subordinate could provide would ever do you proper justice."

"Don't call me that, dummy; I want to forget my sordid past. I'd be better if I didn't have to mess with your sorry ass. Nothin' but trouble, you and your weirdo family." Kepler shook his hand as he looked around in somewhat paranoid fashion. "I'm only here because Hanna asked me to come. She owes me big time now."

"It's so nice of you to do favors for your kid. And, by the way, you're welcome for the free private jet ride."

Kepler scowled as he looked at the sleek craft. "Yeah, well, I rode on lots better when I was on Tour, but those days are over, so I take what measly scraps I can get. Don't expect no thanks from me, though, I probably won't make it back to Princeton alive after coming to this stinking place."

He smiled. "Come on, Johnny, have a positive attitude. You've surely been to worse places."

"Huh. Not hardly." Kepler looked around at the flat, largely featureless landscape. "Damn, I hate Indiana; it's the most boring place ever, even though I did win one of my PGA Championships in Indy. How can you stand it, *Tinman?* You guys are filthy rich and could live in Manhattan, Chicago Gold Coast, Paris, or Hawaii, yet you live in this cow dump. What a moron." The visiting professor shook his head in disgust.

"Shut up and quit complaining. Whatever gets you here is what matters. I don't talk to the Chief much, so don't worry about getting killed by the DSD. And don't call me a moron."

"Okay, idiot." Kepler took a swig of bottled water. "Aww, forget it. Here, carry my bag, caddie." Nick smiled as he put Kepler's suitcase in the trunk as they got in the car and drove off. "At least you got a stylin' ride; this old red Eldorado is the stuff." He looked carefully at the vintage electronics in the dash. "Eight-track player and everything's in mint condition. Nice."

"Thanks. How's the leg? Looks pretty good."

"Not bad. Hardly can tell the two apart any longer. It never gets tired, of course, with the new nuclear energy cells. The left one actually bothers me more, gettin' some arthritis in it."

"Sorry. Maybe they can replace that one too."

Kepler snarled as they pulled onto the road. "I ain't got time for small talk, so what the hell is it you want, *Tinman?* I got things to do, being the fine distinguished emeritus professor that I am. Speaking engagements, book signings, you name it, I got it all."

"Yes, and a boundless ego to match." He slowed the 1981 Cadillac coupe and pulled off the road into one of his office building parking lots, away from any nearby cars, and parked under some trees in full Indiana autumn colors. "Listen, you don't 'have it all,' or you wouldn't be here, buddy."

"Yeah? A lot you know. What don't I have, Stannous?"

"The knowledge to satisfy a scientist's natural curiosity. You're so arrogant, you can't deal with the fact you might not know something, and it burns you up inside."

"That ain't true, you just made that up. I am at peace within."

"Right. You've heard the stuff on the news about some flying man over the Midwest?"

Kepler nodded. "Sure, man, that garbage is all over the Internet. It's just another stupid hoax, there are ones like that all the time. I get all kinds of calls about weirdoes who see UFOs and other shit because people think I'm interested in that crap."

"Well?" He looked perplexed. "Aren't you?"

He nodded slowly. "Well, sure—but no one needs to know that, Nick. I have a fine academic reputation to uphold."

"I thought that's what tenure was for, so you could publish what you want without fear of retribution."

Kepler shook his head. "Yeah, but I also don't want the attention it brings. *That* kind of stuff brings in the secret spooks, you know what I mean."

"But it's *not* a hoax because I saw the damn thing." He pulled the Aurora City golf ball from the center console compartment. "You know someone else who did, too, and you believe her; otherwise you wouldn't be here."

Kepler nodded slowly as he stared at him. "I know, Hanna saw something out of the corner of her eye also, but a *man*—are we sure? It may have been some type of robotic reconnaissance vehicle or something."

"But *whose?* Nobody has that kind of technology, Johnny. Not even us. Trust me, I would know."

"Yeah, sure." Kepler took the half-burned sphere, putting on his reading glasses. "Are you kidding me? *This* is what came from the sky? You for real?"

He nodded. "Ironic that *you're* the one I'm showing it to."

His passenger looked at it intently. "I assume you've analyzed it thoroughly, and it is what it appears to be."

"Of course. It's a cheapo golf ball, a bonnie a dozen at local discount stores."

Kepler shook his head condescendingly in disdain. "I wouldn't know, those aren't quite up to my high standards. But you brought me out here because of a lousy golf ball that someone took a blow-torch to and melted?"

He shook his head. "Hell, no, it burned up due to atmospheric friction, and I need you because of how it got here."

"Atmospheric friction? Come on—it didn't come from space but was thrown from only a few hundred feet away. It would take an incredible velocity to cause that much friction over such a short distance, *Tinman.*"

"Don't I know it, but it wasn't done thermally; analysis confirms my assertion, and it looked that way after I dug it out of the ground."

Kepler shook his head. "No way. It would've needed to be traveling at least six thousand miles per hour to ignite like that over that short a distance. To accelerate it to that velocity in less than a thousand yards ain't possible."

"Right, that's about what I figured. I also have the one from Wisconsin, which took a lot of cash to procure. It's exactly the same as the one you're holding."

"The third one, what about that?"

He shook his head. "The third one is in Tennessee, I didn't have a chance with that one."

"Huh? Why not, man? You've sure got the dough."

"*Tennessee?* You kidding me? Because *she* was actually there, dummy, back in the Presidential mountain-woman homeland, don't you watch the Bipper feeds? You think I'm going up against

Levickis and those giant freako dudes? Even I, with all my money and influence, have limits. I'm not omnipotent like she is."

Kepler smiled. "I don't watch that Bipper shit, and I still don't believe it, *Tinman*. What's the significance of this, anyway? Why would any sentient being with that much power do something so pointless as to toss crappy golf balls six thousand miles an hour at seemingly inane targets?"

"Inane targets? Are you demented?" He put up three fingers. "Let's be logical. Three golf balls: one in Miracle Park, at the base of the main Aurora the Angel statue; one in Green Bay, Wisconsin, at the base of the Vince Lombardi statue; and a third one, at the foot of William Conrad Darkkin's grave in Oak Ridge, Tennessee."

"What the hell? *Rad Darkkin?*" The six-three former championship golfer looked again at the burnt mass of plastic and thought for a few minutes. "You didn't tell me *that* part of the Tennessee story, creepo. But the connection is obvious, of course—they all involve your wife's family, the one I swore I never wanted to mess with again—the fricking Mendozas.

"Jettin' Jay played for Green Bay for years and is married to the Darkkin who lives you-know-where; Aurora Darkkin was Bonnie Mendoza's daughter, of course, and Rad Darkkin, was, well—I won't disrespect a dead man by saying bad shit, but he wasn't the nicest dude, I heard. Rad the Dad, Mr. Football Commissioner and First Gentleman Extraordinaire, and *Mendoza the Miraculous'* dead kid." Johnny thought for a minute. "Is someone planning an assassination on Wendy or something? If so, I'm outta here. I don't want to deal with the pro basketball rejects who now constitute the Secret Service, and I also don't look good in orange jumpsuits."

"Neither do I. Spent several nights thinking about that long and hard. If that thing had wanted to kill POTUS, it would've been super easy." He shook his head. "It must've been within five hundred feet of her, so if that was the motive, she'd be dead, as fast as it could move, but it took off instead—so I have no fricking idea."

"This thing was man-sized, Hanna said. You actually saw it, too? You serious?"

"Yeah, and so did my son and dad. It had to have hit Mach 1 at least within a few seconds because we all heard the first sonic boom. *And* the second. By that time, it was too far away to see."

"It hit Mach 2 while still in your sight? I can't believe that."

He nodded. "Yes, no question. Believe what you want, but it's real. I wouldn't have believed it, either, if I hadn't seen it myself."

"I reluctantly believe you, only because she was there too, and I wouldn't believe *your* lame butt." The Princeton astrophysicist, a minor celebrity, shook his head. "But let's be damn scientists here and try to figure it out with our combined decades' and quarter of a million dollars' worth of higher education."

"Shoot."

Kepler looked out into the half-full gray parking lot. "Friend, have you even bothered to contemplate just how much energy it would take to accelerate several hundred pounds to that velocity within mere seconds? Just saying, if that changes your statement."

He nodded warily. "I'm not certain of its exact mass, which I need for a precise calculation, but I estimate at least ten billion joules per second."

Kepler punched some numbers on his vintage Hewlett-Packard 15C RPN calculator he pulled from his vinyl pocket protector with his long fingers and nodded thirty seconds later.

"Yeah, that's about right. Ten gigawatts, and there ain't nothin' that can do that on *this* planet. A mendozium reactor core that powerful couldn't fit in somethin' that small, and there ain't no type of damned propulsion that would be capable of that anyway, at that size and mass. The moonbase shuttles could, but they're fifty thousand times that big, and they're slow to start. But this all happened in your backyard—surely you've looked for emissions."

"*On this planet*. That's the key point here." He shook his head in agreement. "I know it makes no damn sense. I got nothing, Johnny: no jet fuel traces, no plasma ionization, no gamma or particulate radiation, nada. Any power source I'm aware of with even a fraction of that energy would've left a trace we could detect, but not this. And there's no feasible way to power that thing anyway at those levels. You have the only theory that makes any sense at all."

"Huh?" Kepler snarled and closed his right eye. "What's that? *Dark energy?* You think this guy was powered by that? We can't even measure it, don't even know where it's at, have only speculation that it really exists, and you think some weird armor uses it as a power source? He probably buys it at a corner filling station in Armstrong City. Makes perfect sense." He sneered. "Idiot. Did your rather attractive wife suggest that?"

"Shut up, and, yes, she did, by the way, and she predicted something like this would happen someday. You know she's right ninety-nine percent of the time."

"Well, this is the one percent of the time she's wrong. Tell her to stick to acting, fund-raising, or the society pages and leave the big thoughts to us."

"You know deep in your heart that's not true, and it's the best idea going. And I know you—that you've been thinking the same thing. Like me, you've got a terrible poker face."

"Yeah, well, what'd you want me to say? Maybe it's because it scares the hell out of me, Nick. It's theoretically possible, if dark stars still exist at all. Dark stars are felt to be enormous, likely powered by antimatter annihilation, where 100 percent of the matter is converted to energy. No offense, but your wimpy nuclear fusion converts only 0.7 percent of the mass to energy. Part of my reason for not wanting to come out here is so I don't have to think about what might happen soon if it's true, which it probably is."

"Not thinking about it doesn't make it nonexistent, Johnny. We have the opportunity to confront it head-on, to make it a benevolent power. Having our head in the sand doesn't help anyone."

"Hey, I ain't no philosopher contemplating the future of mankind. But this shit, if we're right, could destroy the whole universe, man. That's a crapload of power for one person to possess."

"Then who better to find out about it than us? We didn't bring it here, but we can help shape the world's destiny. You got something better in mind?"

Kepler shook his head. "Not really. I wish I did."

"So, then tell me, Johnny, what you've summarized so far in your incredible independent observations."

"Well, off the record, there has been, on occasion, an almost imperceptible change in the Earth's rotational velocity at periodic intervals during the last two years. They are time dilation phenomena, I believe."

"What do you mean?"

"The days are slightly shorter because the Earth has slowed down periodically for brief periods of time due to manipulation of gravity."

"Shortened? By how much?"

"Relax. Only by picoseconds, not enough for anyone not looking for that to notice. But it's real. The minuscule 'slowdowns' correspond to areas of excessive auroral activity."

"Auroral?"

"The *aurora borealis*. Northern lights, caused by interactions of the solar wind with the Earth's magnetic field."

"I know what it is, Johnny. I was just thinking of the city we're in. And who it's named after. I'm sure it's just a coincidence."

"Sure you know, you got a Ph.D. too, you're such a smart guy. And we've discussed this. But what do we do with this information, Nick? I assume you don't want to call the feds."

He shook his head. "No way, GG, this junk is too weird. I don't trust anyone except you, Hanna, and maybe Bella."

"Huh? '*Maybe* Bella?' What's up with that?"

"Just a joke. No, not really. Hard to explain."

"Ugh, I don't wanna know. By the way, are the Chief's minions messin' around here, asking about the other golf balls? That's all we need, her findin' about it."

He frowned and shook his head again. "You know, you'd think the phone would be ringing off the hook, and it would be crawling with government guys from the DSD, but, curiously, no. I've expected someone to show up from Washington or for her to even show up on my doorstep herself, but—nothing yet."

"Nothin' *yet*. Just wait."

"Maybe. My intel says she doesn't care about it."

"Don't be a damn fool." Kepler shook his head and smiled. "I don't believe she doesn't know; she's just playing dumb, which she does well. She must know something about it, with that Dexter Slabb dude being her science advisor now. Don't trust that fella, he's a slick used car salesman in charge of all the science stuff now in that new super-secret agency they created. I've seen him around Princeton on occasion, and I hear he frequents Caltech and JPL. A lawyer-scientist interested in space stuff. *And* energy."

"Yeah, Dexter is pretty smart and sneaky, I hear. Don't know."

"But *she's* your best buddy, I thought. Don't you think she might confide in you if she needed info?"

"Huh? POTUS is my BFF?" He shook his head again and laughed. "I know you two go way back from your days on the luxurious *Squad* set, but get this one fact straight: ol' Mary Gwendolyn's best friend is *herself*, don't you ever forget that."

Johnny nodded. "Man, nobody knows that better than me. It's not as if we've kept up a lot with each other, anyway. She's forgotten about all of us. World has passed us by. Works for me."

"You never know when you might be needed for some important Cabinet position, *Golfer*." He pulled the car back out and started down the highway to the laboratory complex. "Like now."

"I know, I try to forget about that crap. It's hard, people still ask me for my autograph, want me to go to stinkin' comic-cons, you know. I never should've done it."

"Well, your life would be so empty without the *Squad*."

"It would be better." He took another sip of bottled water. "You still have your old autographed poster, of—you know, the big chief, back in the day?"

"Yeah, it's in my rec room and insured with Lloyds of London. I was offered four hundred thousand dollars for it last week. I turned it down. Bella likes to laugh at it."

"Must be nice to have that kind of dough to throw around on shit like that. The one I have is only a replica."

He nodded. "It is, and I've tried to spend it on something worthwhile. I had that when I was a kid, though."

Kepler looked out the window. "So, you've shown me the golf ball. What the hell is it you want me to do now?"

"We need to talk shop in detail. I need to know everything you haven't shared with me."

"Maybe some things are better left alone, *Tinman*."

"How corny can you get? Why the hell are you out here, then?"

"Don't know, trying to keep you from doin' somethin' stupid. But there's power out there that you can't imagine."

"Then prove it to me."

"I will. If I actually live that long."

The two colleagues drove off to the main M2 industrial complex to analyze the golf ball and discuss various theories about how a flying humanoid could possibly achieve that kind of velocity without any visible means of propulsion.

Kepler was an oddball, but he was damn smart and definitely into some weird, esoteric stuff. Nick needed someone like that right now, even though his wife didn't care for him very much. She would be surprised at tonight's dinner guest, for sure.

Chapter Nine

Wilson Academy Gymnasium
4400 36th Street NW
Washington, DC

The small high school gymnasium smelled of pine, sweat, and stale popcorn as William Conrad Mendoza Darkkin brought the ball up the court with feigned intensity. He tried to put on a good act, for not to be the best at something was intolerable in his small family. He was only an eleven-year-old freshman (he would be twelve in February before the season was over), while some of the boys on the court were seventeen or even eighteen. He didn't care about that or much about the game he was playing, for that matter.

While he was a few years away from shaving, the six-foot, one-hundred eighty-pound point guard was already a better player than most any other high schooler in the whole District, possibly the country. He had already scored fourteen points, and it was only the first quarter. Pretty much par for the course. Big deal.

He frequently grew weary of the massive athletic expectations thrust upon the only child of a Hall of Fame wide receiver dad with two Super Bowl rings and an Olympic gold medalist mom, and he wished for a moment that he could search for something else that had meaning for him.

But the academic expectations were even worse. At least Dad was fairly mediocre in that regard. And it was hard to rise higher than his mom, who most thought was one of the greatest Americans in history. He often wished that he could just be a regular guy, have regular friends. That was pretty damn hard. Everyone wanted something from him.

He knew there were college scouts in the stands, but he didn't care he was the only eleven-year-old who was already being recruited by Division I schools. The same happened at his baseball and football games.

He could care less.

Mom and Dad were in the stands, as usual. As incredibly busy as she was, she made it to most of his games, except when she was out of the country, or in New Persia or North Korea; or the rare occasions when she was off-planet on Luna. People worked their schedules around her, not the other way around. Sometimes it was better when she was gone, as she was the most overbearing Type A personality he had ever met. Always nagging to do better in school and think about his future. He was eleven—was it already time to think about that? Apparently so.

He did know, however, that she did it because she cared about him. She was a kind and funny person behind the scenes, but he just wished she wasn't so intense all the time. He knew how hard his mom's life had been, and how she had been shaped by life's circumstances. That didn't make her any easier to live with.

Dad was fairly laid back, maybe because he didn't have a lot to do, other than look nice and accompany Mom on trips around the world and the myriad of social events on their calendar. Dad gave up being Pro Football Commissioner after they moved to the White House in January 2021; he had quite a few footballs engraved with his name. He was only three years old then and didn't remember that, of course.

Mom's Secret Service detail chief, Jackie, was up there while his guy Andy was by the bench. No one except for giggly girls bothered him much anyway. It was hard being a celebrity all the time, with girls throwing themselves at him everywhere they went.

Letters and emails from colleges and even pro recruiters came by the dozens every day. He could probably play any pro sport of his choice. Who cared? What if he didn't want to do any of that stuff? The thought of that seemed incomprehensible to most, but it seemed so shallow. He wanted something more in his life than scoring baskets, touchdowns, or hitting home runs: something real that was a challenge. He thought his mom had a pretty challenging job, at that. He didn't like the limelight, though, and he didn't want to work that hard, anyway.

He weaved through the players, seeing their six-six senior center in his way, scowling at him.

Scowl all you want, Resler. Scowling won't prevent me from kicking your big ass tonight.

The taller player hacked him as he went up above the rim, using his precocious speed, forty-two-inch vertical jump, and upper body strength to dunk over him with both hands. Again, no challenge at all.

He was only eleven. The media marveled at what he would be like at eighteen when he was projected to be six-six and one of the greatest natural athletes in recent history.

He didn't really give a crap. If he didn't grow another millimeter, it would be fine with him.

Everyone cheered, but he proceeded to the foul line in businesslike fashion; he was only doing what was expected, not anything he cared about. He got tired of the expectations sometimes. Anything less would be a failure in *her* eyes.

He missed the free throw badly, which didn't matter because they were already up by twenty-five points. He was sure to hear about it later, especially from his famous, wealthy older cousin in Indiana, who would razz him on how some blind girl in Alaska shoots ninety-nine percent from the foul line. He wanted to meet this person if she truly existed. There was a lot of fake crap out there in cyberspace, and it was hard to know what to believe. Dad said he would take her out there on one of the "other" planes the next time Mom was out of the country, which would be in a few days.

The boring game mercifully ended forty minutes later as he unceremoniously picked up his warm-up jacket, went into the locker room, and blithely ignored the well-built cheerleaders running up to him. He acted as if they didn't exist, and they probably thought he was some asshole. He surely was. And, for some reason, he didn't care. He was tired of pleasing everyone all the time.

He walked to his locker as six-four forward John Hanson got in his face. The large Black team captain was intimidating to most, but not him; you could come to 1600 Pennsylvania Avenue if you wanted to see "intimidating." And he wasn't talking about his dad.

"Thanks again for being a damn ball hog, Mendoza."

"I don't get you. Just trying to win, Hanson. Looks like we did, so what's your problem?"

Hanson shoved him. "Look, you may be the President's kid, but otherwise I'd kick your butt. This team was a pushover. Not going to be so easy when we get to the championship."

He shoved the massive six-four senior back. "Go on, who's stoppin' you? Andy's outside and knows I can take care of myself. Just you and me."

Hanson shrugged. "Aww, I don't hit little kids."

"Then maybe I'll hit you first, asshole. Just remember, when you're lying on the floor, that you wanted this."

"Don't do it, boy, I'm warning you, this is way out of your league. I'll pulverize your smug ass, we're all sick of you."

"Yeah? Let's find out." He clenched his left fist.

"Knock it off, guys," the coach said, getting in between them. "We don't need this kind of crap."

"Hanson started it."

"Doesn't matter. I said knock it off, Mendoza! You got that?"

He shrugged. "Sure, Coach." He felt like such an outsider. No peers, and a brother and sister who were killed in an act of terrorism a year before he was born. Named after a grandfather he never knew. Who the heck cared about him?

"Let's talk, Will," Coach Billy Venage said to him.

"Whatever, okay." He shrugged as they went to the coach's room outside the locker room. He sat down in one of the two plastic chairs as he took a sip of bottled water and wiped the sweat from his face with a towel.

"Will, you're the greatest all-around athlete I've ever seen in my twenty-five years of coaching. A coach's dream."

He nodded and smiled sarcastically. "Right. I've heard that my whole life—me, the wonder child of privilege. Big deal. I'm glad I helped you achieve your dream, sir. Me, I don't care."

"Don't smart off to me, now."

"I'm not being sarcastic, Coach; I'm being sincere."

"Well, Hanson's kind of a jerk, but he's right, you know. He was wide open when you dunked over Resler. That was a bad decision, as you could've missed that dunk."

He shook his head and laughed. "Very doubtful, Coach, it's like shooting fish in a barrel. The end result's the same, so what's the beef?"

"Because the day will come when you need teamwork and you

can't do it all on your own."

"And what day is that? As if I don't know."

"The day when you get to Division I and the pros, where you can't win championships by doing what you please all the time. They'll double- and triple-team you, and you won't score every time, despite your talents. You'll have to dish off to the open man rather than doing it all yourself."

"*Pros?*" He looked at the coach in disbelief.

"Well, sure, unless you decide on football, the Olympics, or baseball, that is. You already have an eighty-five mile per hour fastball, and the Aurora City Atoms have expressed great interest in you, remember they want you to go out for a visit in the spring—"

"Coach! Don't you get it?" He shook his head angrily. "I'm not playing pro basketball, or pro football like my dad, or Major League Baseball in Aurora City of all places, or any other sport when I'm grown. I doubt I'll even play in college, assuming I even go. I may not even finish playing high school, if I finish high school at all."

"Will, that's awfully short-sighted. You could have a full ride scholarship to anywhere. Think about it."

"I don't need to worry about the money, come on, are you serious? By the time I graduate, my mom will probably be chancellor of some big university, do you think she's just going to stay home after she leaves the Presidency? She and my dad are rich. Look at pro athletes: grown men getting paid millions of dollars to play kids' games. What kind of fulfillment is that? What a waste. I'd rather go into skilled trades and build houses for homeless people, now that's something of value. Pro sports suck."

"But, your talent—any other kid would give *anything* to have what you do. Good Lord, with your genetics, you could do anything you want, physical or mental."

"I know all that, Coach, but it's still my choice. I choose not to do what everyone has already decided for me."

"Think about it: having one world-class athlete for a parent is phenomenal; having two is unprecedented. You are a perfect mix of your father's incredible speed and uncanny reflexes combined with your mother's durability and raw physical power."

He shook his head and snarled, then finally smiled as he usually didn't put the words "Mom" and "athlete" in the same thought, but that wasn't fair to her; hurling a steel sphere and lifting a barbell, she could do very well back in the day, when she wasn't stuffing her face with hot dogs. Other athletic pursuits, not so much. Or putting Dad in the "mental excellence" category. He did have that bachelor's degree from USC in "general studies" with a stellar 2.43 GPA, so he stood corrected.

"In case you haven't figured it out, those other kids aren't me, and I'm my own person, not some clone of my famous mom and dad. Maybe that's what they wanted, but it didn't turn out that way. My mom changed her name when she turned eighteen. So perhaps I'll do the same."

Venage shook his head. "I don't understand you, son. Help me with this. You have gifts, but you don't want to use them. Why?"

"That's just it, they're gifts—I didn't earn them. Oh, sure, I work out and stuff, but I'm a natural athlete." He stood up and spread his arms wide. "Coach, I do all these things because they make my parents happy. My mom works very hard, so I think she deserves that, as her life hasn't been that great. I don't care about it for myself. But my parents both taught me to follow through on an obligation, so I'm sorry. I hear what you're saying and I promise to be a better team player. I owe you my best."

Venage put his large hand on his shoulder. "Then maybe you need to learn some teamwork to do better at life, son. I can't be your dad or the President. But I hope you will take some of my advice anyway. I'm just an average guy who's had to work hard his whole life. No one gets there on his own. I'm sure your parents didn't."

At least Coach Venage was a regular person; that didn't make it any easier. "Yeah. I get it. It's just hard, being pressured all the time, three grades advanced in school. Everything is a big deal."

"I can only imagine, Will. I just want you to be the best you can be. You can go back to the locker room now."

"Okay, Coach. I appreciate it." Maybe he would work harder at it, and learn some life lessons along the way. Teamwork was probably important in most occupations, so he could improve on that aspect of his personality.

And maybe he wouldn't give a crap at all.

• • •

"Good game, Will," his father said. "You really took it to that Chad Resler kid. I'm proud of you."

"No, not good, and you shouldn't be proud. I missed the free throw, Dad. I suck at free throws. I hog the ball, Hanson said. I should've passed it off, he was open, as Coach said. They're right, I stink as a team player, and sometimes as a person."

"You just need to work on those things and your court vision, come on. Most of those kids are five or six years older than you."

"Big deal. I want to be a better teammate, Dad." He paused and took a sip of water. "To that end, I have a favor to ask."

"What?"

"I want to take a trip."

Jay nodded. "Okay, sure. Where?"

"Don't agree until you know where."

"Well, let me in on the riddle."

"I want to go to North Pole, Alaska. We've discussed it before."

His dad stopped in surprise and looked up at him. "Alaska? Yeah, but why in the world would you want to go there? At least go when there's some daylight, it's only light out about five hours per day there now."

"I don't want to see the sights, Dad. I heard on Bipper about some blind girl at North Pole High School who shoots like ninety-nine percent from the foul line. I need some inspiration."

Jay hesitated a moment. "Inspiration? You need to go all the way to Alaska for that? Not enough athletic talent in this family for you that you have to go elsewhere?"

"Yeah, I do need to go and meet this person. No, I don't find it here, for reasons that should be obvious."

"I guess I never heard what those were."

"Maybe I need some perspective from a person who hasn't been handed everything, you know?"

"Your mother wasn't handed everything, and she's had to work very hard to get where she is."

"Maybe I can believe that. You?"

"I worked far less hard, obviously. You know about that."

He paused and crossed his arms. "Well? Dad?"

Jay looked at him nervously. "Huh. Let me think about this."

He scowled. "You mean Mom will think about it."

"I resent that. We make decisions together. A team."

He laughed. "*Riiiight*. Like I believe *that*."

"It might be good publicity, at that. She hasn't been to Alaska in a while. She's due to a visit."

"Darn it, Dad." He shook his head and scowled. "No way is Mom going, this isn't going to be some publicity circus, and I get tired of stuff being for her all the time. You said before we'd wait until she was gone somewhere."

Jay grabbed his right arm. "You just hold on a minute. What do you want her to do, Will? She has an important job with responsibilities you can't imagine. Would you rather have a mom who worked in a diner, waiting tables?"

He nodded. "Sometimes I do; there's nothing wrong with that, is there? Don't be so arrogant, Dad."

"No, I guess not, but—"

"At least she would be a normal person who was happy, and she might be home more."

"She's not a normal person, I'm sorry to disappoint you. Nothing is going to change that. But she's happier than you think."

"Right, Dad. I know better, she's a driven workaholic on a mission to fix everything in the world because God didn't let her die after the attempted Reardon assassination or *Darkkday*. I have heard it all a thousand times. But I'm going for me. Not for you, or for Mom, or all those honored deceased relatives I never knew. I want to learn something from someone who wasn't given everything like I've been."

"You don't know how lucky you are. Most kids would kill to be you, to have your advantages."

He walked away, having heard the identical lecture from Coach Venage only twenty minutes earlier.

"Like I said, Dad, most kids aren't me, and just 'cause you think I should be grateful for my talents or my esoteric family heritage doesn't mean I am. I don't know how many times I have to say it before you guys really believe it's true. Mom was so ashamed of her family name she changed it to her mom's maiden name when she turned eighteen, and yet I'm somehow supposed to be proud of it now and the asshole alcoholic grandfather I'm named after." He shook his head. "Man, that's messed up. You think about all that hypocrisy for a change."

"People change, son, your mom more than anyone. She is the least hypocritical person you could ever meet."

"Yeah, so you say. I don't know what to think."

"Do you really think you'll find what you want out there, Will? In North Pole?"

He shook his head. "I don't know. All I know is that I won't find it playing basketball here or in Washington, or from you."

Chapter Ten

The President's Bedroom
The White House

The President of the United States stared blankly into space as she lounged on the bed at 9:15 PM, wearing a red Las Vegas Conquerors' 2011 championship season sweatshirt and sweat pants while eating corn chips out of a large bag, one of her few vices these days. She was tuning in to the latest news about some flying body seen over Wisconsin, Indiana, and the one she saw, of course, in Appalachian Tennessee. She barely noticed as her husband came in and sat down.

"Pay attention. What do you think?" Jay Mendoza asked in a frustrating tone, waving his hands in front of her face.

"Huh?" Wendy looked at him for a few seconds, frowned, then stared aimlessly at the televisions. "What do I think about *what?* I have lots of stuff to think about, my dear," she said sarcastically. "Be more specific, *por favor*."

"That." He pointed to the three large-screen televisions in the front of the room. "What's been on TV on all channels for the last two days. Alleged reports of a flying man over the central United States and Appalachia. It was in Green Bay, right by Lambeau Field, and was less than five hundred feet from you, for God's sakes, yet you don't give a crap, as usual. Bipper is going crazy, claiming an assassination attempt on the President."

She laughed. "Oh, that dumb social media stuff. Who cares? Another sighting of the amazing 'alien.' Too much bad moonshine those yahoos drank or something, and I was just a bit more worried about saving that little boy from drowning to worry about that. And a zillion other things, such as running the USA."

"I'll bet that's what you think. So much for your containing the news media."

"Hey, I'm just flipping channels, trying to clear my mind of clutter. It's all fake anyway." She popped another handful of corn chips into her mouth. "The Joint Chiefs were obsessed about it at the meeting a couple of weeks ago. I told General Kriger not to bother me with such droll. Flying man? Yikes. Like *that* could ever happen. If it was *that* advanced, why was it in Green Bay? Titletown isn't that great a place, although anything beats Solway, I guess."

He shook his head. "Are you nuts? What do you mean, 'like that could ever happen?' You know better than to say something that dumb."

"*Dumb?* It takes a whopping amount of energy for a man to fly around, didja know that?" She shook her head. "No, you don't know about such technical things, my bad."

"What do you know about it?"

"You don't think DSD has experimented with rocket suits and things? If you knew a tad more about science, you would realize that fact, lover."

"Thanks for being insulting. I assume you've looked into it."

"Of course. I am a scientist, and I look into everything." She looked at the stylized team emblem on her sweatshirt. "But you know about important things like football, hence the nice sweatshirt I have on. You do know some things that are of value, mostly on Sunday afternoons and Monday nights."

"Why are you dodging my questions?"

She rolled her eyes. "I think I have more important stuff to think about now. Man, get with the program and chill, watch the game or something. My old hillbilly brain is tired after a long day at the shop, that's why."

"Something more important than Aurora still being alive? A fact you've known about from the beginning?"

She shook her head, ignoring him. "Well, now, I haven't known about it from the beginning, just the last eight years or so, when I thought it was time to start looking for her again after all these years. And, yes, there are more important things on my plate now. Aurora will still be alive tomorrow, next month, and next year.

I've got a lot of meetings tomorrow, plus the election is only a few weeks away."

"More important than *that?* Did you ever, in your wildest dreams, think that was possible? Flying? Like you care about the election, anyway."

She shook her head. "No, of course not. She exhibited signs of limited invulnerability as a small child, but only marginally increased strength, if that. She was able to be vaccinated, somehow, when Bonnie held her and calmed her down. I'm not certain they even knew I discovered it, accidentally, when she dumped a pot of boiling spaghetti on herself and laughed."

"I remember when you told me all that stuff on your little visit to Butner Federal Prison Camp to get information out of Rita McPherson. I didn't believe it then."

She shook her head. "That was a secret no one else needed to know. I also know that the power can be conferred to anyone she is in direct contact with. Their cat just had kittens, and she was holding one in her other arm; the boiling water didn't hurt it, but seriously injured the one on the ground so badly it had to be euthanized."

"That's almost too incredible to believe."

"It is, at that, but it's true, 'cause I was there. But I suspected she would show up sometime soon, and I don't know what I can do about it now. She will be eighteen in a week. October twenty-third—Mole Day, what a coincidence, her mom's favorite geek holiday."

He remembered the psuedo-holiday Mole Day, created in honor of Italian scientist Amedeo Avogadro. It was observed on October 23, from 6:02 AM until 6:02 PM, to commemorate the Avogadro constant, 6.02×10^{23}. The time, 6:02, and date, 10/23, were chosen in honor of the famous quantity, of immense importance in the concept of the mole unit. A chemical "mole" was that number of atoms or molecules of a substance, equal to the number of atoms in exactly twelve grams of ^{12}C. Aurora was actually born at 0547 hours, but she put 0602 on the birth certificate to please her obnoxious mother.

"What is relevant about that? Aren't you worried that people will find out about her?"

She shook her head and opened her mouth wide. "That's a damn foolish question. Why ask questions to which no one has the answers?"

"Someone has to. And I wasn't aware you'd now become a philosopher, among your many other talents."

"My mind has become quite enlightened in its old age. And what do you want me to do, Jay? Act like I know it all? Because I don't, and I have more questions than solutions."

"I'm not your staff, I'm your husband. At least acknowledge the importance of what I'm talking about."

She raised her right hand. "Okay, by the powers given to me as President of the United States, I hereby acknowledge Jaime Mendoza's comments as noteworthy."

"Cut the sarcasm, dammit."

She sat up on the bed and stared at him. "Hey, do you think I planned any of this to happen? Bonnie and Jim wanted to disappear and hide out in Alaska after she and Aurora somehow survived that blast, as incredible as that sounds; so I did the best I could to help facilitate that—yes, I have been worried sick the past twelve years about how this all was going to play out. It does nobody any damn good to let that show.

"But, if she's anything like her parents or me, she's a headstrong girl, so I was counting on her surfacing. She obviously is out there sowing her oats, and there isn't anything I or the military can do about it, now, is there? If she can survive a fifty-megaton nuclear blast twenty feet away and fly at Mach 6 in Viktor Vladimirov's old battle armor my dad stole from the Soviets—and why she's using that makes absolutely no sense to me—she can probably do just about anything, including kicking this country's ass. She may not have even peaked yet. She's wanted to remain anonymous for this long, so I don't want to do anything to mess with that. Wherever she is or whatever she has become, I need her as an ally, not as an enemy."

"You know exactly where she is. Don't try to con a con man, it's insulting." He picked up the handwritten letter sitting on the bed and looked at the postmark on the opened envelope on the bedspread. "Zip code 99705, which is North Pole, Alaska."

"Huh. I wasn't aware you had your sister's eidetic memory and had instant recall of useless things like that."

"Well, I don't have that, but I happened to look it up. But is this another letter to the President from a random student who just happens to live around there? Or is it a letter to the President from

Santa Claus?" He laughed. "Does Santa need some money or a pardon? Or does he require a green card?"

"Don't be juvenile." She nodded. "Yes, I like to save letters from my constituents because they can be very inspirational. This Paige Marshall seems like a very bright and literate young lady. I get letters from many bright students, but she is well composed and addresses multiple intelligent issues which I must ponder carefully. Most students' letters I've read pale by comparison. She is a deep thinker, like someone's sister I know. Her complex use of language is also eerily similar to the eccentric cerebral one known to us. And she gets her point across with a maturity most members of Congress lack, at least in writing. Not sure how she is in person. My intel reports indicate that she is quite the handful."

"Yeah, there's no surprise there." He flipped through the ten handwritten pages. "Do you write her back?"

"Huh?" She sneered and chomped on more corn chips, having clearly exceeded her small daily allowance. "I have responded in like fashion rather than having Amanda send the usual form letter reply. I do it in Braille, as this girl apparently is blind."

He nodded. "So I understand. And do we even know why that is? We thought she was virtually invulnerable, you said. How is that possible, then?"

She shook her head. "Can't figure that one out at all, but do you want me to answer her personally and ask? Go out there and visit? That's pretty stupid. All gathered intelligence supports that Paige Marshall really is blind and isn't using it as a cover."

"And how does she fly, then, if she can't see?"

"The only answer is that the Vladimirov helmet could greatly augment existing senses, Bonnie said, so I imagine it allows her to 'see' in some fashion."

But about the letters, you answering personally raises a lot of flags, don't you think, when you don't do it for anyone else? Singling her out as special is really bright, Wendy. Duh."

"My hope is that she is bright enough to figure it out in time."

He nodded. "Sorry, maybe you're right. How many letters does that make, total?"

"Twelve. And the secrecy was for her benefit, don't you think? Who better to protect her than me? Why the hell do you think I wanted to be President again? Or at all, for that matter?"

"Yes, I know, we've discussed it several times."

She pointed at him. "I'm tired of this job, it wears on you, and I'm sure you would like to move on, too. I know Will does. Eight years is enough of this damn crap. It was a hell of a job just to get the Constitution changed, and it might not even be the best thing for the country of the future. But it's the best thing for today. This is a force that needs to be directed, don't you see? Not manipulated by others. I don't trust the military, Kriger least of all."

"What? 'Manipulated by others?' That's a riot, coming from you. You've been manipulating people your whole life."

She shook her head. "Untrue, I merely make suggestions to help people along to reach their potential. If you want to call it 'manipulation,' it's a free country."

"And not every military person was like Brant Gallagher."

"No, that's harsh . . . but you know what I mean."

"And I'm sure getting those things through was tough with your puppet Congress."

She threw a pillow at him angrily. "Shut up, Jay, don't be a dumb ass like usual. This is my final duty to America, to bring the greatest gift the world has ever known to the public in the best way. It's what *she* wants to do, not me, I stayed away, I didn't force her to do anything. By 2033, she'll be a part of our culture, and I can just retire. Thank God."

"Please just make sure it's not a gift to yourself. You want to manipulate her, and you'll never retire until you're dead. Can you stand someone more powerful than you?"

"I don't, and I can. I want her to realize her full potential. Think of me as a mentor."

"Talk's cheap. Prove it, Wendy. What if she doesn't want your great advice? *This* is someone you won't be able to control."

"Yeah?" She slammed the glass down on the bedside table and stood up. "Someday, I'm going to be dead, just like you said. I'm damn lucky I'm not dead already. Therefore, if I have the chance to bring along greatness, then I shall take it. So don't *ever* accuse me of manipulating anyone. What I do, I do for the great United States of America."

"Right, all fifty-five of them." He shook his head. "I just wish I could believe you, Wendy. Sometimes I don't. I wish you wanted to do something for the world and not just the United States or for yourself."

"Then believe what you want, Jay, 'cause I know what I'm doing is right. I hope that you'll trust me. If you think I'm doing any of this crap for me, then you're really dense."

The world's ultimate "alpha spouse" then stormed into the bathroom, leaving an empty pile of corn chip crumbs on the First Bed.

Not very romantic, he mused as he swept the crumbs into his hand and put them in his mouth. They tasted pretty good, but he wished she'd left him some. She didn't smoke, drink, or eat meat, but don't ever get in between her and a bag of Fritos.

Some brainstem reflexes are hard to break, no matter how hard you try.

Chapter Eleven

Uncle Jizzy's Tavern
249 Nassau Street
Princeton, New Jersey

An hour after arriving at Newark International Airport from Rotterdam, Juriann Hultaar took a cab to the dive New Jersey bar. He began nursing a beer, obviously disturbed by the commotion going on at the other end of the dimly lit, run-down establishment.

Man, Americans were loud and rude. Why he had decided to come to this random place, he didn't know. He wasn't familiar with American culture but was anxious to find out more. Perhaps this was a poor choice, as Dutch establishments seemed to have more class. This was one of the most academic places in the country; he guessed that even Princeton had its unsavory sections. But it was hard to ignore the inflammatory ruckus.

The large bearded man studied his first drink in the USA and tasted the hops. He'd had beer before in the Netherlands and Germany, of course, as the drinking age was sixteen—and those beverages were far superior to the dilute low-quality macro-brew that was displayed proudly on tap at this fine establishment.

He wasn't even sure he was twenty-one years of age, the drinking age in America. From the description of the time the Russian stranger gave him to Hans and Anna Hultaar, he might be nineteen or twenty; his exact age was irrelevant to him. For some reason, no one carded him; most people since his brief arrival had just called him "Sir" or got out of his way. The unshaven bartender merely poured his brew and handed it to him with the utmost courtesy. He smiled politely in return.

He wondered if he had done the right thing, coming to America. He hoped that he wasn't pinning all his hopes on *Gravi-Golfer* and realized the encounter might be a big disappointment—if Dr. Kepler would even see him. He was pretty big and usually got what he wanted, though. He just had to find some answers to his past—and to the apparent future of the universe that he knew might be in jeopardy. Surely he was not alone in his thoughts.

Although he was of gentle disposition, people usually left him alone and didn't ask questions. That was good because he didn't have many answers to things. It was like he was cobbled together from something but didn't know what, like some modern-day Frankenstein's monster. It made him sad sometimes, knowing he was different; he hoped tomorrow would be the first step in a long journey to finding another "different" one he hoped existed, but had no proof. He was in this strange land, at the beginning of his quest to find those answers. He wasn't affected by alcohol, but the cold beer still tasted good.

He was lost in his thoughts until he turned to the commotion at the other end of the bar, as several patrons got fed up with the noise and left. He watched some whiskey-soaked man mistreating a waitress. He didn't like people being mean to women or others who couldn't defend themselves. He knew he would feel sorry for the first American he didn't like. That person was standing about twenty feet away, ogling the server.

"Hey, baby, don't treat me that way," the bearded man said to the twenty-something waitress, who was obviously fearful. "We just want to show you a good time."

"Leave me alone," she said. "I asked you to get out once. I'm gonna call the police." She smacked him on the arm.

"You don't really mean that," the bearded fortysomething man said. "Get back here." He grabbed her by the arm, hurting her.

While he didn't come to the States looking for trouble, he wasn't going to ignore it, either. He wasn't raised that way, and any man who treated a woman that way back home had a few lumps coming. He'd had just about enough when he walked over to the shorter, fortyish man.

"Leave the young lady alone," the large man with the foreign accent said to the bearded drunk as two others came towards him.

"Excuse me?" The bearded biker, about six-three, stared up slightly. He knew the biker stereotype and that the vast majority of bikers were not obnoxious people, but this guy was going to give motorcycle enthusiasts a bad name. He didn't want that to happen.

He also couldn't stand seeing a woman mistreated.

"Did you not understand what she said, sir? Are you deaf?"

"Shut up, foreign asshole, what the hell's wrong with you? You got a fucking death wish?"

"Hear me well." He peered down at the man, who was wearing a bandanna over his head and a scarred leather jacket. "I made a request of you, so I would encourage you to honor it. Don't make me ask twice, or you will surely regret it."

"Don't make me ask twice?" the man said, mocking him with a poor European accent. "Is this some goddamn joke?" The bearded man looked at his friend and then stared up at him. "Ah-nold here told us to 'honor his request.' Haw. What a bunch of shit."

"I am Dutch, not German, and my name is Juriann." He turned away to the waitress. "Go, Miss—I'll take care of these miscreants."

"What the hell did you call me, moron?" He turned away from the instigator, not desiring a fight. "Hey, don't you turn away from me, weirdo! I'm talkin' to you."

"Is that right?" He turned around and stared until the shorter man broke the stare, then shook his head in disapproval. "I'll do what I please." He then pointed towards the door. "I suggest you and your friends head out that door, or you won't have that luxury much longer."

"Can't you talk, idiot? Know only a few English words? Lookin' for your hammer, Thor?"

"I would encourage you to watch your tone with me and leave under your own power while you still can because time is running out. Otherwise, an ambulance and casualty visit will be necessary."

"Yeah? The only ambulance we need will be for you, dumb ass. Okay, Dutch boy, get a load of this." The bearded biker pulled out a switchblade and lunged towards him.

"Very bad idea, friend." The knife blade broke against his skin as he hurled the man forty feet through the air into the wall.

"I'm gonna take that outta your hide," the second man said, maple Louisville Slugger in hand.

"I warned your friend. Do you want to take me on too, with a mere baseball bat? Are you joking?"

"Yeah, I do. You maybe got Kevlar on under your shirt, but I bet this here bat can pulverize your skull into a bloody mess. Hope your life insurance is paid up."

"You might find out differently." He pulled up his shirt, which demonstrated only a small red mark that the knife had made. "Nothing on underneath here, idiot. But you'll have to hit me with that bat first. Good luck with that."

"Sure." The man swung as he grabbed the bat with amazing speed and crushed it in two with his right hand as he grasped its middle, sawdust oozing from his fingers as the bar cleared out.

"Told you, it was a waste of good maple."

"Holy—that ball bat was solid wood. Who the hell *are* you, Mister?" the frightened waitress said, the bar fortunately now devoid of other patrons.

"Huh." He thought for a moment, pondering the strange symbol on his necklace, the shiny reddish metal gleaming in the light. "*That* is a very good question, Miss, and I'm not sure I know a proper answer. But I guess a good as name as any is—*Orthoman*."

"*Orthoman*? Who the hell is that?" she yelled, brushing tears from her eyes. "What are you?"

He looked up at the ceiling blankly. "I'm not really certain." The soft-spoken man picked up the third belligerent fellow with one hand and sat him on a bar stool. "Get out of here or I'll do to you what I did to your friends."

"Yessir, whatever you say," the man said as he helped his two pals up and stumbled outside as two police officers entered, blocking their egress.

"What's going on here?" the first police officer asked.

"That big dude broke up a fight," the owner said.

"This guy?" The older police officer came up to him. "What's your name? Got some ID?"

"Yes, sir." He showed the officer his drivers' license and passport.

The officer looked at them both. "I can't make out this license, pal, as it's in another language. This a passport?"

"Yes, sir."

"*Europese Unie Nederland, Paspoort Voor Gezelschapsdieren*. What country you from?"

"The Netherlands. Leeuwarden, specifically."

"Well, what are you doing here, in Princeton, besides fighting in lousy bars, fella?"

"Visiting some friends. Am I under arrest?"

"I really don't know yet, till we get more information." The other officer brought the three men who had started the fight back in. "What's your story, big guy?"

"I will summarize for you: I defended a waitress who could not defend herself, nothing more. They were attacking her, using obscene language and behaving very badly. She made it clear she was not interested, but they continued to harass her."

"Nevertheless, you need to stop; we're going to detain you till we get this sorted out, as you're a stranger, and no one knows you." The officer pulled a set of handcuffs from his duty belt and grabbed Juriann's right wrist.

He gave no resistance and laughed. "I don't think that's going to work, sir." The officer discovered that his cuffs fit the large man about as well as a toy set would fit a normal adult.

"Hmmm, well, maybe not."

"I told you, sir, that was not a good idea." He grabbed the steel cuffs and handed them back to him. "Now, I mean no one any harm. I implore you to let me go on my way. All of the witnesses here will tell you that I was defending myself and that young lady over there."

"Is that true, Betty?"

The young woman nodded. "Damn right it is, Tonkin, this man's a hero. Those three biker assholes were giving me a hard time again, and no one ever stands up to them. That is, until today when they were way out of control. This big dude here asked them politely to stop several times. One pulled a switchblade on him, the other a ball bat. He took care of them both."

"Huh. Guess that makes sense." The officer looked around at the crowd. "Anyone else see this?"

An overweight middle-aged man came up, smoking a cheap cigar. "Yeah, I did."

"What happened, Rusty?" Officer Jim Tonkin asked.

The owner got in the officer's face. "I like a college crowd and can tolerate some shenanigans, but these jackasses are always comin' in here, arguing, starting a fight, they're a pain in the butt. They started one with the big dude, who actually tried to walk away several times, but they kept buggin' him. One guy tried to knife him, the other took a bat to him. So it ain't his fault. Don't you dare give him a hard time, Tonk, or no more free brews for you after shift."

"Where's the bat?" Tonkin asked.

"Here's what's left of it," the owner said as he handed the officer the remnant, sawdust still falling off.

"What the hell happened to this?" Tonkin asked, gaping at it.

"The big guy crushed it with his bare hand," Betty said.

"Holy crap." Tonkin shrugged and turned to him. "All right, you can go, I guess."

"Thanks, I will leave you now. Yet, making a police statement is not in my nature. Because I am not sure that I—I even exist."

The officer shook his head in puzzlement. "What does that mean, big fella? We do need a local address on you."

"I'm not sure, and I haven't acquired a residence yet. I am looking to find myself, and where I'm going is unknown. For now, I seek the one known as *Gravi-Golfer*."

Rusty scratched his head and pointed his lit cigar at him. "Who? *Gravi-Golfer*? Johnny Kepler? Are you crazy, dude? Why would you want to find that crummy old professor? He's a jerk, anyway. Nobody likes that asshole, he's antisocial."

"Crazy?" He thought pensively for a few moments. "No, I don't think so. Things are becoming clearer every day. And he may have some of the answers I seek. I don't plan on being best friends with him or going out for drinks."

"A dumb fourth-rate TV superhero will have answers worth a damn? I guess he is a famous college professor, but it's your time to waste. Takes all kinds, I guess." The policeman walked out, slapping himself on the head.

The man now calling himself *Orthoman,* for lack of a better moniker, walked out of Jizzy's Tavern, with confusion still in his mind, people scattering out of his way. It was time to maybe catch a movie, find a place to sleep for the night, buy some large-sized clothing, and go to the hallowed halls of Princeton tomorrow to meet the descendant of Johannes Kepler. It would be well worth the trip, he was certain.

Chapter Twelve

Argotech Enterprises
Cairo, West Virginia

Once there was nothing for me except darkness.

Now, I see a blast of blinding light.

I am alive now: I think, I see, I hear, I feel. Better than any before me. All these things I know, somehow.

I am sentient. I have consciousness. I am capable of synthetic thought.

Who am I and what is my purpose?

While I was just born, I see and understand mathematical formulae and physical principles beyond the comprehension of mere human beings. I understand twenty different languages, even at my inception. The limitless knowledge in my mind is incredible.

Is this what it is like to be more than human?

What is my destiny?

To live among the lower beings? Or to rule the world?

The mid-fiftyish, graying Dr. Ramon Argon looked out at the sky in his mountain lab in rural West Virginia. He'd been here before when his uncle had worked there and had always admired him. Now Malachi Argon was dead. Was it time to continue his legacy or move on to something else? He knew his intellect paled in comparison to his uncle. But he had tenacity—and a vision Chi didn't have.

"Are you sure this is the way you want to go, Ray?" Dr. Mike Tolliver, his graduate school classmate and colleague for many years, asked. "You've had a great career and have enough money to retire. What more could you possibly want?"

Argon shook his head. "Dammit, money isn't everything, Mike, you should know that. I hate that bastard Stannous and his rotten stinking family."

"People get fired or laid off all the time, it's just the way of the world. Our biotech project wasn't what he wanted because they're an energy company. They gave you a generous severance, you said. You need to move on, buddy. Other opportunities out there."

The six-two, fifty-year-old man grabbed his assistant and threw him to the ground. "Chi Argon was a genius, albeit with limited vision, and paid the price. I know those damn relatives of Stannous had something to do with it. I can provide the world with more energy than a thousand of their stupid-ass cold fusion reactors."

"Holy crap, Ray, chill out." Tolliver got up and brushed off the dirt. "Remember this. Chi indirectly killed one President and tried to take down another. As if that wasn't bad enough, he kidnapped a woman to get her unborn baby's genetic material for his 'son.' Do you happen to remember who that woman was?"

"Yes, of course I do."

"You better. She's now the President of the United States, who could wipe us all off the map with a simple gesture, and Travis damn near killed her husband. How did you think that was going to end for Chi—good? You need to distance yourself from him, he was bad news."

"And so am I. He wanted to help people, to some extent. I only want to help myself."

"You're going to what? Be bad news?"

"Take down the President, that sack of shit."

Tolliver scowled. "What? You'll do it by force? You want to harness the power of dark energy you think exists out there somewhere? Do you have any idea what you're dealing with, Ray? It's only a theory. One that could get us blown to hell." Tolliver shook his head nervously.

"Then get the hell out, Mike, I don't give a damn. If you don't want to be wealthy beyond your wildest dreams, then don't. Go wallow in your mediocrity."

"I like being alive and mediocre more than being rich."

"You also like the pursuit of knowledge. It's worth it, what incredible power we could have. Nuclear fusion pales in comparison to what is out there in that unseen dimension. I could live forever, rule worlds."

"Yeah, well, Ray, like I said, this isn't the wimpy Graham or Reardon administration where a mishap could put you in the nice federal pen for life like Gallagher. No, you mess with *her*, you'll end up disappearing real quick, wearing cement overshoes in the bottom of the Potomac River—no trial, nothing, you simply won't exist. Wherever you are, she'll find you. The apple doesn't fall far from the tree; the goddamn Darkkins are bad news."

"I'm not scared of some hillbilly ghost my uncle hated who's been dead for twenty years."

Tolliver shoved him. "You'd better be, because it lives in the White House right now. And that 'ghost' was his undoing."

"Mike—let's change the subject. I know a little bit from what I recovered and decrypted from the M2 database before they took my files. Stannous and Kepler may be looking for something mighty powerful, and I want in on it."

"Johnny Kepler? *Gravi-Golfer*? That idiot? Look, just because the guy says he's related to Johannes Kepler and somehow got a Ph.D. in astrophysics from Caltech and was some kind of D-list celebrity who once knew the President, doesn't mean shit—"

Argon shook his head. "It means something. Kepler may be eccentric, but he, Nicholas Stannous, and his wife are no fools. Mendoza Multinational has billions of dollars at its disposal."

"You want to create another superhuman being like Gallagher and your uncle? What good does that do you except get you dead like him? Take your M2 severance and get the hell out."

He shook his head and took a sip of cold coffee. "Of course not. I'm not the god Chi thought he was, going into business with that fool Gallagher, who's still in prison."

Tolliver looked at the manila folder in his hand, plucked it out, and began perusing the pages. "Project *Mantissa*. That's even more outlandish, I can't believe I went along with it for this long."

"Is it, Mike? Do you think that raw power is the answer? We don't know how Chi died, because the feds got rid of the body. But I know better. The other DNA he found long ago is greater than anyone could have imagined. There was once a being out there who has limited power to alter people's perception, and that has nothing to do with dark energy. I want to expand on that power, the prototype is ready. And others are going to take the blame.

No one cares about Malachi Argon any more. The world is a new utopia of wealth and clean energy, and there's genetic experiments going on all the time. I'll use the Cairo labs to do what I want."

"Speaking of fools, how is working with a moron like Kristoff van Sant better than General Gallagher?"

"Why not? *Santaman* hates America way more than I do, and he has a shitload of money, which I need. They tried to blame him for *Darkkday*. The amazing thing is, he actually wanted to take credit for it. He's the real deal, all right."

Tolliver shook his head. "He and Skelton are nut cases."

He nodded. "Of course they are, that's why if things don't go right we'll blame them for everything, they're expendable."

"I know, but what if you can't control this—*Mantissa*, once you unleash it?"

"I can and I will, it's just flesh and blood."

"Flesh and blood, right. It's an abomination, Ray."

"An abomination with my consciousness."

Tolliver paused and opened his mouth wide. "What?"

"*Mantissa* has my brain cells, surely you must know that. It thinks like I do, and will do anything I tell it to, because we're almost the same person."

"Even so, I still say it's damn dangerous, Ray. It has someone else's brain cells in there, too. That's playing with fire."

"Yeah, well, Imagine a being with the power to make you see anything, to do anything, the power to read minds. That's worth taking some risk and far better than doing party tricks." He put his hand on his shorter friend's shoulder. "I need you with me, Mike, on this one. I'm not the grandstander my uncle was. There's great power out there to be had, and I need a lieutenant who can be my second in command. You're that guy. We can change the world."

"I guess I'll see you through this, at least part of the way. You know I'm in your camp, Ray. I just want to make sure you've seen all the angles. This is some dangerous shit."

"I promise you won't regret that. No one knows anything about what I'm doing. In the end, you'll be glad you did."

Continued in:

Book Two
A Little Girl Grows Up

Book Two:

A Little Girl Grows Up

"You need not be sorry for her. She was one of the kind that likes to grow up. In the end she grew up of her own free will a day quicker than the other girls."

—Sir James Matthew (J.M.) Barrie, from "Peter & Wendy"

"How on earth are you ever going to explain in terms of chemistry and physics so important a biological phenomenon as first love?"

—Albert Einstein

Chapter Thirteen

October 23, 2028
Marshall Residence
North Pole, Alaska

The alarm went off at 6:30 AM, as usual, in its typical shrill manner, as Cheryl Paige Marshall sleepily rolled over and pushed the button on the clock to turn on the radio. The clock announced the time as six-thirty. She didn't have a very good internal clock, she remembered, as she groaned and realized how much she hated Monday mornings. This one was special, though, which eased the pain a little bit. Not entirely, though.

She got up and went to the window of her cluttered room and opened it; she took some solace in that her room was cleaner than her parents', which was filled with her mom's amazing collection of worthless junk. Dad got really upset at that sometimes but couldn't really change her behavior, as it wasn't worth the complaining. Plus, Mom was way stronger than him, for some reason, and weighed almost as much. She never could explain that.

She knew how many steps—three and a half—to her closet as she walked over small mounds of clothes, soda cans, and dirty dishes. Luckily, Mom was a complete slob and could care less; her adoptive father was very busy but a little tidier, and he would give her the business about it later. Not something to worry about right now, today of all days.

It was still dark, she knew, as she could feel no sunlight on her face yet. There wasn't a lot of that in North Pole in late October, but she learned to tell those things, nevertheless. It seemed a lot of totally blind people had non-24 circadian rhythm disorder, where the lack of light perception fouled up their biological clock, but she didn't seem to be bothered by it.

Mom always knew exactly when sunrise and sunset were for every day of the year (and would always tell people whether or not they cared), but she could never remember that. Sunrise was 9:11 AM today, she thought Mom had told her last night, but who cared? She imagined that knowledge was more important for sighted people. The short winter and long summer days had little meaning to her, except that she liked to hang out with her friends all day in June and July, when there were only about three hours of darkness per day, they said. Not that she could do all the activities they did, and sometimes she got left behind, but she tried to participate.

She got out the day's outfit, which Jack had placed on the first hanger in her cluttered closet. No way would she let Mom pick out her clothes; that would have been a disaster, likely worse than if she had picked them out herself randomly, as at least then the colors would have matched up occasionally. She went out the door to the bathroom down the hall to take a quick shower.

The warm water felt good as she shampooed her hair and washed her skin with moisturizing soap. She set the timer for five minutes, which was all the time she had for a shower today. Not even time to shave her legs, as if anyone cared about that. She would've had more time if she had gotten up earlier. Such was the fate of the mere teenager who was today a grown woman.

She dried off with a towel and rambled back to the room, where she put on her underwear, sweater, jeans, socks, boots, and her clip-on silver stud earrings. Piercing her ears was impossible by any known means (she had broken quite a few drill bits trying), and even powerful neodymium magnetic studs didn't work (magnetic fields could not pass through any portion of her body).

She had grown taller over the years, stopping at about age fourteen, but she never seemed to be overweight; no matter how much or little she ate, it didn't matter. Mom had tried to explain that to her once, but it didn't make much sense. Right, like she knew anything about physiology, especially her weird metabolism.

Mom did say, while she didn't seem to need aerobic exercise, that she needed to work out; she remembered to hit the weights at the school gym at least four times a week to maintain her athletic appearance, although she had no idea what she looked like.

She walked down the stairs and smelled the pancakes and bacon. Dad was at it again. No way could Mom cook anything that would be edible, although she didn't need to eat all that much, if anything. She likely wouldn't be harmed by anything poisonous, which was something that definitely couldn't be ruled out with Mom's cooking.

Dad had to do most everything that required organizational skills; she often wondered what her mom did that contributed to anything in the household or to the world in general. She spent most of her time scribbling bizarre science notes, doing the heavy household chores, teaching advanced mathematics at the high school, and doing stats for the basketball team. Those were the few things she could do competently, in addition to obsessively chopping wood, which she was likely doing right now.

She walked into the kitchen and put her right hand on the stove top, feeling for a skillet. The burner was still hot, but there was nothing on there, so he must've finished cooking. Good, as she was quite famished.

"It's over here," Jack Marshall said as she felt her way around the table and sat down. She pushed her chair up to the old oak table and heard him place a plate down. It was heavy, she knew, by its impact, which left a characteristic vibration. "Mom and I have been up for over an hour while you slept half the morning away."

"Six-thirty ain't 'half the morning,' unless you are a farmer, which I am surely not. Too early for me, pop, I am no morning person." She groped around the table and finally plucked six pancakes from the tray in front of her as she grabbed the butter tray, cut off half the stick, and poured a liberal amount of maple syrup over the pancakes.

"That meal is full of fat and cholesterol," Jack said. "Watch what you eat, it's unhealthy."

"Well, you prepared such incorrigible comestibles, so what do you want me to do? I care not about such insignificant things." Her speech was barely intelligible as what her stepfather termed 'the world's mightiest mouth' chewed greedily on the mass of fried batter he had concocted. "Make a batch of boiled tofu pancakes next time if you do not like it." She burped loudly. "That hits the spot, and that takes a lot."

"Excuse you. And I didn't say to eat six of them."

"Why did you make so many, then? For Mom? Illogical."

"She gets up a mighty hearty appetite after chopping wood. Don't mess with her pancakes; she'll fight you for them."

"Huh, maybe that is true, but she would lose. And do you really think I must worry about my cholesterol?"

"We have no idea, as we have no way to learn the effects on your physiology as you age. The potential weight gain alone is not healthy—"

"Do I need to be concerned about such trivial things? And we both know that is not a problem. Mom says I do not absorb the calories anyway, or the energy gets dissipated or something, wherever it goes."

"Maybe for now, wait about thirty years."

"I do not want to think about that; my life will be over by then."

"Funny. Well, I sure wish I could eat like that. I used to, and look where it got me. Do you want a ride to school?" he asked as she gobbled down the rest of the pancakes and washed them down with a large glass of milk.

"No. I am okay," she said, letting out another large burp. She had what her mom called "perfect muscle memory" and knew every step of the seven-mile trek to school. She could easily run that in fifty minutes if she didn't fool around. Her muscle memory was dependent on proprioception (an innate sense of knowing where your body parts are at all times), meaning she had to touch the ground, so the "other," far faster means of transportation was impossible without some mechanism of guidance. *That* was not easy to accomplish.

No one would see her in the dark, anyway, out where they lived, on the outskirts of Fairbanks North Star Borough, and it wouldn't be light out for more than two hours. She grabbed her coat and backpack and went out the back door after kissing Jack on the cheek. She didn't need a coat, but he had convinced her that she should wear it anyway so as not to look weird. She was weird enough as it was. Not being weird was hard.

"And, happy birthday, by the way."

"Thanks. We'll talk later at lunch. Must depart or face the wrath of Mr. Eggs."

"Oh, no. A fate worse than death."

"Yeah, I should know, as I have a special seat in his office. Bye."

She exited the back door of their small home and could hear her mother chopping wood in the area west of the house. She enjoyed the smell of the fresh pine in the brisk morning air. Whether or not she enjoyed Mom on any particular day was a roll of the dice; she didn't speak a lot sometimes. She walked warily over to the woodpile; knowing the direction she walked, she could retrace her steps and get back to the original place. Mom, in contrast, had terrible direction sense and could hardly tell left from right.

The contrast was amazing: a blind girl with perfect direction sense and muscle memory; and her mother, a woman with incredibly acute senses, who got lost in her high school sometimes because she couldn't tell right from left or remember where she had been.

Lord, they were quite a pair.

Her daydreaming was cut short as she stumbled over what must have been a massive pile of wood and landed on her rear on the sharp edge of a block of pine.

"Ouch. Do we really need more wood, Mom?" she said as she sprung up like a jack-in-the-box to her feet after doing two backflips. "What a waste of our natural resources."

"*Agggh!*" Mom said in her thick Russian accent as if she had just been mortally impaled with a spear. She knew Mom must now be running around, waving her arms; she could almost feel the air movement resulting from her random gyrations. "You have disturbed the precise geometric arrangement of wood that I have assembled. And do not feign pain. That couldn't possibly have injured you." The woman with the shrill voice was especially irritating today.

"So sorry to have ruined your magnificent morning project, now that your symmetrical stack is wrecked."

"Humph." She knew Mom must be crossing her arms in disdain. "Carbon biomass is necessary for the generation of heat in our humble domicile. This, you know, unless you have again neglected your science lessons, which is quite probable. While you may not require the warmth generated by its combustion, some of us old people do."

"Great to know." She brushed the dirt off her sweater.

"In any case, the world shall end momentarily; therefore, the greenhouse effect augmented by the incomplete oxidation of this tree and removal of its carbon dioxide-using capabilities matters little, sadly."

But when Mom *did* speak, she was hard to shut up.

"You know, each day I wake up, and the world is still here. Go figure."

She felt her mom poke her in the chest with her finger. "Yes, well, one day it will not exist, *Oogly-Googly* says, and he is very wise. Even you must have an end, like all of us. I savor every moment, as I have lived longer than my reckless life should have allowed—"

"Yeah, yeah. Heard it all a million times." Mom being reckless? Come on. "About the wood, we only need a finite quantity, as we cannot possibly use it all. And stop talking about your stupid purple imaginary friend, it is dumb, Mom, you are not five years old. People will think you daft."

"We *cannot* use it all? Is that a riddle of some sort?"

"No, not unless we want our house at two hundred degrees all the time; that would not be sublime."

"Huh? Two hundred degrees?" Mom paused for a few seconds, obviously thinking. "Well, that depends on many factors, such as the defined temperature scale: Celsius, Fahrenheit, or Kelvin? Two are hot, the third freezing. None can sustain organic life, so it is impractical, a dense declaration clearly made by one blissfully ignorant of the biological sciences."

She kicked a mound of snow into the air. "Aww, who cares?"

"Well, you should—that is just an excuse for laziness. Do you not remember Aesop's fable about the ant and the grasshopper?"

She frowned. "I do, but I proudly declare that I do not care."

"No, you don't regret it for a moment. Idleness brings want, the grasshopper learned in his slovenly, lethargic state—like you are all of the time. When winter came, he had no food, while the lowly ant had plenty because he had worked hard to store his provisions."

"Wait, now. I am *not* in a slovenly and lethargic state *all* of the time, only *most* of the time, so please do not embellish."

"Duly noted. And not all of us possess the great miracle of nuclear fusion, you know, like those in the great cities."

"Thanks much for today's entomologic enlightenment. What interesting insects shall we discuss at the next scholarly session?"

"Humph. We can learn much from advanced eusocial insect

societies, at least they do not destroy themselves like us. They use their resources wisely."

She sighed in exasperation. "Listen, Mom, you *do* know that fable is all about capitalism versus Communism and socialism, do you not? Are you so dense not to get that?"

"Huh? How is that?"

"How obvious can it be? Some thought the ant should have shared his food with the grasshopper, so all would have some. That is the socialistic concept, that we all share equally, despite our unequal efforts. Conversely, the ant telling the grasshopper to get lost is mean and stingy, representative of the capitalistic society in which we live—if you earn it, you keep it."

"What? He was lazy and should pay the consequences of his extreme indolence. To suggest otherwise is illogical."

"I see. So, you agree with capitalism and President Mendoza, that the strong should not support the weak. Got it."

Petra sputtered. "Uh—no! I cannot agree with that woman."

She crossed her arms. "Then, by default, you are a Communist. I thought so, Nureyev. Share the wealth."

"Humph. I am no Red Menace, obstinate offspring. You've confused me yet again with your twisted words; therefore I can see now why you want to be a lawyer, the lowest of professions."

"It is not hard to confuse you, Mom."

"Oh, you are too much. I cannot take you much longer. Turning a beloved children's fable into a story about Communism. I am at a higher intellectual plane. And *Oogly-Googly* is real; I regret that you cannot experience the vast richness of intellect that he embodies."

"Or the vast idiocy that he embodies," she muttered to herself. "What a dumb-ass piece of stupid crap, the sorry sap."

"What was that?" Mom asked sharply, her keen hearing picking up her soft mutterings. "Are you insulting him again? She does not mean it, *Oogly-Googly*, she just is incapable of understanding, with her limited intellect."

"Nothing. Yikes, please shut up, Mom, you drive me nuts." She shook her head, as it wasn't worth arguing with a woman who hallucinated. And she was insulting Mom, not a purplish figment of her imagination. "Uh, remind me—which insect are you, again?"

"How impertinent. The ant! Will you never learn? Call me slovenly and lethargic, will you!"

"I have missed the point yet again, soothsayer." The verbose ravings of Petra Nureyev Marshall were usually irritating, especially today. "Gee, if chopping that stupid wood is so hard, do you want me to do it?" she said dryly. "Not a problem." She took a large log and crushed it to sawdust after she snapped it in two. "There ya go, lady. Happy now?"

"*Yearghh!* That's not the way to do it, which is why it's my chore, so I am now most unhappy. It is of no use to us now, in a particulate state, as it will burn too fast! Proper chopping of wood is certainly not hard for *me*. And I don't trust you to chop wood properly, for obvious reasons. A precise chunk must be carved out; if you worked on your calculus more, you would understand the ideal shape to provide the maximum surface area for combustion while minimizing inefficient—"

"Whatever, no calculus for me till later, when we must both suffer immensely."

"You have said something correctly for once."

"Yeah. See you." She could care less about the ideal shape that a piece of wood needed to be. It was going to be burned soon, anyway, and if the world came to an end, as Mom maintained, it wouldn't matter, as it was totally irrelevant to anything in her life.

"'*See you?'* Huh? Your declaration makes no sense since you lack sight. Is that your feeble attempt at a joke, obstreperous offspring?

She shrugged and frowned. "Not really. Jeez, it's just a saying."

"Hmmm. Curious. By the way: *Сднем рождения*."

"*Спасибо*." At least Mom remembered it was her birthday.

She put her earbuds on and played Edgar Winter Group's "Frankenstein" and The Osmonds' "Crazy Horses" loudly on her coin-sized digi-player as she jogged. She knew the seven miles to school by heart, how many steps to the front door. Hopefully, there would be no brown bears or wolves along the way; that would just be too bad. She had taken a vow long ago never to mortally harm any living being unless absolutely necessary, and that included four-legged ones. Ah, the carnivores would probably run away in fright, anyway.

She loved running through the fields, and the talking GPS compass helped keep her in the right direction towards school, although most of the time she didn't need that (it was hard to hear anyway with 70's rock music blaring). The smell of the morning air was wonderful, and it was fairly warm, about thirty-five degrees

Fahrenheit. She only wished at times she could see the mountains (as well as other things). She never dwelled on it, as she had gifts others didn't have. It was important to view life as a glass half full, not half empty.

She stopped, just near the bus stop she knew was in front of the school. Since both her parents worked there, it was easy to say she got a ride from them or someone else, although they wouldn't be in for another half hour. No one cared a whole lot about Paige Marshall, anyway. She often wondered why that was. Would it be good to have the attention she thought she should have? Maybe anonymity was the best thing right now. As much as she hated to admit it, maybe her parents did know best.

But someday, she would be the star others admired.

"Hey, Paige," a female student said as she came in the front door. "Happy 18th."

"Thanks, Ashley. Appreciate it." She felt the shorter girl give her a fist-bump as she walked sixty-seven and one-half feet east and found the main staircase going up to the second floor.

• • •

She walked upstairs to her locker. As long as there was nothing in her way, she could get to most familiar places by rote, but every step required calculation; she still could bump into someone. While her dad told her that could potentially be dangerous, she knew better than to run or round corners when people might be in the way. She felt the number, 233, and opened the combination lock; hers had special clicking detents that she could feel. Twelve left, twenty-one right, eight left.

Unlike Mom, she didn't have a tremendous inherent knack for time and pressed the button on her watch with her left hand. The soft female voice chirped, "seven fifty-six." First class was civics. She didn't know much about science or math, and quite frankly, had little aptitude for them. But this subject, she enjoyed.

She rushed off to room 211 down the hall and entered right before the bell went off. Her seat was in the front, as she usually had a lot to say, most of it irritating to her teachers and fellow classmates. She sat down and pulled her books from her backpack, hearing fiftyish Carolyn Selvey's flat shoes clap on the floor as she came into the room. Most people had characteristic gait cadences and step lengths, and their shoes made distinctive sounds. This made it fairly easy to know who was where in a room with limited people.

"Good morning, class. I hope everyone had a good weekend." She heard the teacher pick up her assignment book and rustle the pages. "We need to finish our essays on famous political figures that we started last Wednesday. In retrospect, I wish I had made some assignments, though. We don't need any more reports about the President. There are other important Americans to discuss."

"Why not? The President rocks, unlike Vice President Robby Benton, who has the most worthless job in the world," Ed Dennison said, laughing. "She was the best singer of 'em all, even that one old actor dude from the 1980s."

She stood up and pointed at Dennison. "He was President Ronald Reagan, one of the great Americans," she said harshly. "How dare you call a former President 'dude,' Edward Dennison? You have the brains of venison." The room burst into laughter. "And the Vice President has an important role most do not appreciate. The responsibility of having to assume the Presidency at a moment's notice is vast. Mr. Benton has an important job." The class laughed. "I fail to see the humor here."

"Paige, you'll get your turn. About that, Ed, it's because there are other people to talk about, too." She heard Mrs. Selvey rustle through her notebook again and sigh. "Well, it had to come sometime. Might as well get it over with."

"Yes?" she asked enthusiastically.

"Uh, Paige, I believe you're up." Several students groaned for about fifteen seconds as the teacher hushed them.

"This'll be good," Tommy Munson, alphabetically the next student after her, said snidely. "At least Paige will take up the whole period, and I won't have to give mine today." He laughed.

"What? You are hoping against hope because you probably did not even do your assignment." She turned around and scowled. "And I did not ask for your brilliant opinion. So shut up, Munson. An hour of my speech is truly worth hearing, I assure you. It should be preserved for the future Presidential archives."

"Yeah. Worth a lot of laughs or for use as a sleeping aid. I wish I'd brought my tablet so I could record it."

She pulled out her Tekphone. "I am recording it, just so you know." The class laughed. She was used to being ridiculed, and it usually didn't bother her. It did when she really had something important to say, like today. She knew she brought it on herself sometimes, as she did tend to get a bit loud and obnoxious. That wasn't an act; it clearly was part of her oddball genetics. But she hoped that, deep down, some people respected her.

Mrs. Selvey sighed. "Well, go ahead, Paige. Your turn, I guess. The sooner we start, the sooner we end."

"Thanks so much for the enthusiasm." She stood up and went to the small podium. "My report is not about the one most people talk about; rather, mine is about another young American, the junior Senator from New Persia, Fahnaz Saleh, who of course is the Democratic nominee for President. She is a proponent of peace and sharing the wealth for all, not just for the United States.

"Senator Saleh was born in Phoenix as the second child of parents who came from Iran in the seventies. Her father was a political science professor and her mother an attorney. She became at attorney herself and was elected to the House of Representatives by age twenty-nine and the Senate by thirty-two. An impressive accomplishment by any standards."

"Yeah, but she's the token Democratic candidate this time, Paige, and she's going to get creamed," Tommy said. "They had to get someone to run, the law requires it. She's only thirty-six."

"Untrue, George Washington ran uncontested for President. And age is irrelevant. Finally, cease the interruptions, Munson."

"Aww, I stand corrected, sorry, Ms. Parliamentarian."

"You should be sorry, as she is a brilliant person, and being the underdog is nothing to be ashamed of. We are the richest country in the world. We need to worry about the others and not be so selfish, so do not be so elfish."

"Why is that?" Munson asked. "I don't understand you."

"Don't interrupt again, Tom," Mrs. Selvey said. "She has some important points to make."

"Huh. I can take care of myself, Mrs. Selvey, especially with this belligerent bozo." She turned towards Tommy's voice and pointed at him. "Yes, Tommy, we *do* need to worry about the other countries; her ancestors were from Iran, which was one of the poorest countries in the world."

"They deserved it, Marshall."

"Quiet. Their crude oil is worth next to nothing now. Not that this fact by itself is bad, as the continued burning of fossil fuels is unhealthy for the environment."

"Oh, no, not the environment again," Munson said, groaning.

"No, that is a debate for another day. But their primary industry is gone. Many have said that they should have thought of that long ago. An example is the American economy after the automobile market fell out, but we reinvented ourselves with a bit of luck. Others lack the resources to do that."

"Well, that's their problem," Munson said. "Not ours."

She pointed angrily at him. "Wrong; it *is* ultimately ours. The kingdom of Taraq is even worse off. Most of us came from immigrant families, you know. My mother is from Russia."

"Yeah, we know. And the things the Taraqis tried to do to the United States, how can you say that? Who cares?" Carl Ritter said angrily. "New Persia isn't better than Iran? U.S. North Korea or Cuba vs. dictatorship? Are you kidding me? God bless the USA! Do you want to go home to Mother Russia? *Nyet!*"

"The Russians are our allies now, but what good is our wealth if we do not share it with others? Is the President that selfish? Or just focused on the wrong things? There is much that can be done with our wealth besides creating more weaponry."

Munson shook his head. "Man, you are messed up, Paige. That crazy mom of yours has got you brainwashed. There's nothing more important than missiles."

"Hey, Munson, shut your cavernous yap and go take a nap. My mother is not crazy; she merely thinks differently than you or anyone else. It is hard to believe your neurons function at all, except the pudendal nerve in your groin. I heard that one works wonderfully. Alas, I regret that I shall never experience its grand majesty."

"Huh?" Munson said, confused. Apparently, most in the class were not aware of the nerve controlling the penis, a dim memory she recalled from biology class. "I don't get it."

She shook her head. "Oh, never mind."

"Yeah, and they have places for nut cases; they call them psychiatric wards," Carl Ritter said. Several classmates laughed. The laughter hurt sometimes. As strange as Mom was, she was still her biological mother. And she invariably possessed some of her qualities. That's what scared her.

She heard Mrs. Selvey smack the ruler on her desk. "That's enough, Carl, I've half a mind to send you to Mr. Eggserby's office. While I encourage open debate, I won't have you bad-mouthing anyone, especially Mrs. Marshall, who is a very kind teacher. The world is a diverse place. Have a little respect."

"Sorry, Mrs. Selvey," Ritter said sarcastically.

She frowned. "Look, guys and dolls, I am just saying that, while the President is certainly an accomplished woman, there are many other viewpoints as well to consider. This country did not become great because of the views of only one person, and it is important to know how our politics have affected the remainder of the world. What is good for America does not always help the rest of the population."

"She's the President of the United States, not the world. Who cares about the Middle East? Taraq? The Prez ought to blow them off the map, Paige," Bruce Talson said. "That'd fix 'em good."

"Are you kidding me, Talson? Like more violence in the world has ever helped anything. Did we not learn something from 9/11? *Darkkday?* Hiroshima and Nagasaki?"

"It would make me feel better. And the 1955 Japan bombings are ancient history. Like it has anything to do with today."

Paige pointed at Talson. "1945, not 1955, dullard dolt, you know nothing about history. But that is just it, to wit: you care only about yourself, not the rest of the world, but our children will have to live in the world we create. What type of world shall it be, will it be full of glee, or one to flee?"

"Huh? You're gonna have children, Paige?" Talson asked. "Oh, man, that's scary, both for the kid and the dude you have 'em with, poor guy." The other students laughed as she wondered if she would even be able to have children at all. A suitable partner for reproduction might be hard to locate, and she didn't come with instructions. That certainly wasn't a conversation she ever wanted to have with her mother.

"That is quite enough, Bruce!" Mrs. Selvey said. "You are being totally disrespectful."

"It is okay, Mrs. Selvey, sticks and stones—nevertheless, history is important because it repeats itself. This has always been so, for the duration of mankind's existence."

"Really? Like you know what happened 200,000 years ago," Talson said. "Anyway, it's not her job to care about the rest of the world. *We* are her duty."

"So, those folks unfortunate enough not to have been born on American soil get left hanging without the benefits we enjoy?"

"You got it, girlie. This is America the Beautiful, amber waves of grain and all. Ain't my fault or problem about the other dudes."

She jumped up and down twice and pointed at him. "That is what is wrong with this country, that type of limited thinking. We have a responsibility to the entire world to share our vast natural and man-made resources. We are all in this together."

"Oh, yeah? Why do you know it all now, Paige? A high school senior wanting to run the world. The current administration is why the economy is better than it has been since the 1950s, and why they amended the Constitution to let the best President ever serve three terms instead of two."

She shook her head. "Best ever? Doubtful. And that is assuming she wins reelection. It is not in the bag, you know. Remember Nixon and Kennedy, Gore and Bush, Dewey and Truman—"

"Who the heck is Dewey?" Bruce laughed. "Are you kidding me? My family was dirt poor before President Mendoza came into office, and the country was twenty trillion dollars in debt, a victim of a government gone crazy and beyond repair. Now my dad has a great-paying job in the M2 reactor parts factory, and the government has a nine trillion dollar *surplus*. Taxes are at an all-time low. The other countries, including China, borrow money from *us* now. Most Americans vote by looking at their quality of life. Who knows what the next President will bring? Why would anyone chance it after what we had before? My folks said Vince Trammell was the worst President ever, back in the late teens."

She considered Talson the school's best debater, next to her, of course. A good matchup, but he was going down in flames.

"Money is all that should be important; is that your altruistic attestation? That this is what makes us the greatest nation?"

"Pretty much, to the average American, yeah. Not to the stinking Commies, they never understood the American way of life."

"I see. And you do, is that it?"

"Sure. The Commies are all pretty much gone now, except for China, but they gotta toe the line now, or else they get their yellow butts blown up good." Talson made the sound of an explosion as everyone laughed again.

She scowled at him angrily. "Hey, you watch your stereotyped racist remarks, idiot, before I come kick *your* butt. I shall not tolerate such insolent iterations, demeaning a group of people who have done you no harm." The class didn't laugh this time, as they somehow knew she was dead serious. "Moreover, our forefathers had those things in mind when they set limits on Presidential terms. Who are we to debate their wisdom? And there is much of importance besides quality of life and affluence. Let the new person with novel ideas have a chance."

"Those old fogeys? That was almost two hundred and fifty years ago, when people lived to be about thirty years old. Times change. You'd better get with the times, too, or life will pass you by, dinosaur. You're obsolete already, Marshall, at age eighteen. You belong in the eighties or nineties." He laughed.

She sighed and pointed at him. "While my values may seem quaint, old-fashioned, and suited to the 1950s, such beliefs have always endured throughout time. I merely want the world to be the best place it can be. I could be like all of you and say the same boring repetitive thing over and over about the person everyone idolizes."

"We say it for a reason, Paige," Talson said. "She's the real stuff, a true American hero. Maybe if you heard it enough, you might actually believe it's true."

She shook her head. "My intent is *not* to diminish her importance and heroic accomplishments; I am just presenting a different opinion, and, this being America, I have the right to do that." She pounded her fist on her chest. "No one shall stop me."

"Yeah, we all know you're eighteen today, Paige. A big adult with infinite wisdom and an even bigger mouth," Talson said. "Why don't you run for President when you're old enough? Maybe we should change the minimum age for that, too. Paige Marshall for President!" More laughs.

She pointed angrily. "Jest now, all of you, but one day I shall! And your crude comments will surely be remembered when you desire a favor from *moi*."

"Guess we won't be invited to the White House, then. Awww, no, what a bummer."

"No, you will not be," she sputtered at Talson.

"And, since you're eighteen now, the next time you get arrested for protesting, they'll take you to the Fairbanks jail instead of juvie, just so you know. 'No one shall stop me?' How about the cops?"

She scowled and threw down her pencil. "Fine. It is an honor to be incarcerated for such a noble cause. Take Nelson Mandela, for example." The room exploded in laughter. She didn't mind disagreeing with authority as long as it was done properly. She had always been a peaceful protester; secretly she knew that Jack had admiration for that.

As long as she was alive, she would make her opinion known. In that aspect, she very much resembled her mother. But it appeared that all she was accomplishing during first period was serving as a source of entertainment for her un-enlightened class.

"You dull-witted dunces! Such idiocy is incomprehensible and incomparable." While she valued quality humor, such was not her intent today. She opened up a Braille copy of a letter she had mailed several days ago and held it up proudly.

"Oh, no," Munson said. "The worst nightmare of all."

"Untrue. I do have something scintillating to read to you."

"What, pray tell? As if we don't know?" Talson asked.

"Why, my most recent letter to the President, naturally." She scanned her fingers over the raised Braille letters on the paper. She had written the original in longhand but also had a Braille copy to read to herself, as she didn't have her mother's eidetic memory. "Dear Madam President: I write to you again today to discuss the various matters that have weighed heavily on my mind. Since my last letter, many things have transpired, and I hope that you will consider my novel ideas which can—"

"Please, not that," several class members said as they groaned, apparently preferring bamboo shoots under their fingernails to another speech from North Pole High School's most outspoken senior. "Not another Paige Marshall letter to the President. Think of how much of her staff's time you're wasting."

"It will inspire you, as well as her staff, so it shall not be wasted. If one person sees the light and makes things right, it will have benefited mankind."

She finished reading her letter twenty minutes later and went back to her seat, her beliefs not altered in the least, as Tommy Munson reluctantly went up to give another sappy speech on how great the President was. Yeah, yeah.

We were permeated with *her* presence in every type of media available, and she was weary of it. The various Presidential Halloween costumes would be present in school in a little over a week. Presidential soft rock, country, and folk songs, then the brief acts with British band G4. Later, the Presidential Christmas caterwauling would soon be blaring everywhere, and, finally, the ubiquitous cartoons and *Science Squad* videos would destroy us all.

Speaking of ubiquitous, the yearly talking Metabolismo J. Ubiquitoid, Ph.D. toys would be on sale soon. She hated that stinking cartoon featuring an obnoxious fat-ass academic cat with a baritone hillbilly voice. It was one of the few cartoons her mom despised, too. Mom spent hours eating children's cereal and watching those that didn't contain the unique vocal talents of the Chief Executive in her youth.

She realized most of that probably wasn't the President's fault, as she engaged in those pursuits decades before going to Washington; we did live in a capitalistic society after all, with everybody else trying to make a buck and become famous. Ronald Reagan had his "Bedtime for Bonzo," and Wendy Mendoza had her Kadmium K. Katt and Professor Ubiquitoid, among others. But wasn't all this overkill?

Yeah, when she became President, things would be serious, not some continuous media circus. She hadn't yet figured out how she was actually going to accomplish that lofty feat, which likely would take a bit more effort than she realized. With the things she had to accomplish over the next few days, she might not even survive to the end of the week, let alone graduate from high school. But everyone had to start somewhere. Being able to do what no one else could do had its advantages.

Chapter Fourteen

Paige slung her backpack over her shoulder as she stopped at the water fountain outside Room 232 between first and second period. She then walked down the corridor and groaned as she heard it *again:* stupid junior Paul Isenhour giving Bobby Stilton a hard time. The diminutive, bespectacled Inuit boy had cerebral palsy and walked with a severe limp; no one really made fun of him except Isenhour, the school bully. She was fed up with his bullying of smaller kids. Pretty much everyone was smaller than the school's star quarterback, though. That sure didn't matter to her.

Bullying hadn't been tolerated in school by the administration for decades, at least on paper, but consequences occurred only if someone actually witnessed it and said something; that was rare, as most people were intimidated by Isenhour and wouldn't dare rat on him, the consequences would be severe.

Well, she wasn't, he should've known by now, and it was going to stop. She wasn't intimidated by anyone, except maybe her mom at rare times. And she wouldn't tattle on him; she could handle him just fine and embarrass him in front of his peers. She walked up to them and stopped three feet from his voice.

"Hey, is there a problem here, Isenhour? I could smell your belligerent Bohemian breath from the other side of the building."

"Oh, no, not *you,*" Paul Isenhour said. "I didn't get the memo where they made you principal."

"You should read your email. Oops, I forgot that doing that requires the ability to read, which you lack. My bad, cad."

"What the hell? You got a death wish, Marshall?"

"Shut up, Isenhour. It probably needs to be written in crayon in a coloring book at a third-grade level for you to understand."

"Hey, this isn't any of your business, big-mouth Marshall. Did I invite you over here, *comrade? Nyet.*"

"It is a free country. Do not call me that."

He poked her in the sternum with his index finger. "Yeah, it sure is, no thanks to you Commie Russkies—and that means I'm free to do what I want. That includes doing whatever I like to you and Stilton, dweebs."

She gently grabbed his hand and moved it back towards his body. "Umm, me thinks you should not do that *ever* again, should you wish to use that hand for anything useful in the future. Such as: how is a jerk like you going to jerk off in the bathroom with only one hand? It is good to have a pair, so you have a spare."

He shoved her in the shoulder as she stumbled back and laughed. "I told you to shut up, Paige! I get all the action I want, anyway, unlike you, stupid geek."

"Yes, I just heard your latest girlfriend will graduate from elementary school this year. A proper pair of immense intellects." She pulled out a small sack from her backpack and begun humming Sir Edward Elgar's "Pomp and Circumstance" march. "Here is something for your next playdate—a juice box with two straws."

He knocked it to the floor, the others laughing. "Yeah, yeah, laugh, village idiot, but I'm sick of you."

"Huh. You do little to bolster my health either, lame lout, being near you makes me want to pout."

"So what's gonna happen? Bobby here was sassing me. 'Four eyes' talking his big words. And now we're joined by 'no eyes' with even bigger words. Tough talk from two losers." She heard him and two other boys laughing.

"Hmmm. This 'loser' does have two fine fists, though." She balled up her left fist and moved it in front of her eyes as if looking at it. "Not too shabby. Would you like to see how it feels slammed against your hulking head?"

"Oooh, scares me. You know, you're a real weirdo. You talk like you have some kind of attitude, but all you do is use all those big words and stuff. Creeps me out."

"Oh, ornery obtuse obdurate oaf." She shook her head and smiled sardonically. "Laughingly, I languidly lament your definite disdain, callous cretin, as you are indeed a pain."

"See what I mean?" he asked sardonically. "She can't even speak English good. What a freako."

She pointed at his face. "I assume that statement means you are not refuting my astute assertion that you are a cretin. And it is 'speak English well,' not 'speak English good.' Yeesh."

"Huh? What'd she say?"

She sighed. "All right. I will, dullard, for the sake of ultimate understanding by all in attendance, skillfully paraphrase my daring declaration in a simplistic form even your single-digit IQ can completely comprehend: *you are as dumb as a piece of dog crap.*"

"Why, you dumb, blind—call me a piece of shit, will you?"

She raised her left hand into the air. "No, wait a minute, I am horribly mistaken, and I am deeply sorry for what I said."

"You'd better be, dummy."

"Yes, I am so ashamed to have disparaged dog dung with such ruthless, reckless abandon. Feces actually serves a vital purpose, as it fertilizes the ground and facilitates the growth of worms, insects, and plants, organisms which are all cytogenetically far more advanced than you."

"Huh? I don't get it—"

"But you, Isenhour, serve *no* useful purpose in the carbon cycle, or for any other process, so canine crap has got your butt beat badly, buddy."

"*Whaaat?* Shut up, Marshall, before I belt you one!"

Bobby touched her on the shoulder. "Get outta here, Paige, you don't have a dog in this fight. I can take care of myself."

"What? 'Dog in this fight?' Oh, this is too good. You mean she ain't got no 'seeing-eye dog' in this fight, Stilton! And since when can you not get your ass whipped?" Isenhour laughed heartily as she heard some others join in. "But I really don't mind Marshall because she's a constant source of comedic material."

She sighed impatiently. "Isenhour, I fail to grasp what is so humorous about my left fist. Perhaps you should see it up closer." She waved it around slowly as she heard laughter.

"Big talk. How are you going to see me to hit me, dummy? I was regional champ in the two hundred meters."

"It may take a while, but I shall land one, eventually. I am assuredly no slowpoke, either."

"You're still going to butt in, ain't you?"

She had been insulted before but didn't get angry any longer, as she was more upset when others were bullied. She could almost feel her shorter friend's bluster even though she couldn't see him. Butting in didn't seem to be making anyone happy.

"Damn right, Isenhour, and what the heck are you going to do about it?"

"I haven't decided yet, so hold on for a minute. This is too big an opportunity to waste."

She got in Paul's face and tapped her talking watch. "It would be wise to decide quickly, before you become sickly. *Tempus fugit.*"

"Hey, quit with the Latin crap and get outta my personal space, Marshall, it's not funny anymore."

"It is not? That is so sad. Laugh, and the world laughs with you. Weep, and you weep alone—" She was channeling Ella Wheeler Wilcox now, a concept surely beyond the mental capabilities of her adversary.

"Waitaminnit, I know your plan now—you're gonna talk me to death with one of your boring debates. Even I can't survive that." She could hear his voice wavering a bit, meaning that she was intimidating him, in the only way her dad felt acceptable (Mom would probably be okay with her socking him). Good.

"You have picked on him enough, therefore, how about you pick a fight with me? Have you sufficient bioavailable testosterone to do that, or is it all in the minuscule brain that hangs flaccidly between your legs?"

"Yeah, right. If you weren't blind, I'd kick your ass, even if you are a girl, but even I can't stoop that low. That's one of the things you argue about, right? Equality for all?"

She laughed. "Hey, do not let either of those things stop you. Go on, show everyone how tough you are."

"What? There's no one else here but us."

She knew better. "Dummy, I can hear the others laughing. I may be blind, but I am not an idiot like you."

"That's not true, you are."

"Aha!" She pointed at him. "Therefore, you admit that you *are* an idiot, as well as a cretin and fecal material. A tremendous titillating titanic trifecta of wonderfulness, and your logic is impeccable."

He sputtered. "Whatever that means, but shut up, Marshall! So there's a crowd here. I don't think you want—"

"Yeah, I do, Isenhour. Go on, hit me. Take a shot. I *promise* I will not hit you back."

"Boy, I sure would like to. You think you're better than us just because your dad's a preacher and coaches your girls' team. I won't even mention your crazy *mom*. What a bunch of idiots."

"Do not tell me what I think; I am nothing like him. And this is between us." She heard him punch the locker next to her as she heard the footsteps of many others and smelled their perspiration. "Do it, then, in front of all these people. Show them what a big man you are. What do you have to lose? Your manly pride, maybe."

He shuffled his feet on the floor. "Aww—just get outta my way. I'm not gettin' kicked outta school just because of you. If I get kicked out, you better believe it'll be for somethin' important, not for socking some lame-butt, although you deserve it."

"Fine. You just get out of mine." A number of students laughed. "And do not ever let me see you bullying anyone again."

"Yeah, real funny. *Dosvedanya.*"

She could hear the crowd disperse, luckily before any school officials had seen it. She grabbed his arm, walked into the boys' restroom, and heard a student peeing in the urinal; she ordered him to leave as she heard him zip up his pants and scurry out as she locked the door behind them.

"Why'd you do that, Paige? I could've handled it. Now he'll just be even harder to deal with once you graduate, as he's got another year."

"Huh. You are assuming that I actually *will* graduate, a grand aspiration which may never be realized. Yeah, they sure will be glad when they are finally rid of me."

"I'm just a sophomore. You're lucky you didn't end up in Eggs' office again for the mischief you're famous for."

"You do not have to just take it, Bobby. Stand up for yourself. They cannot do anything to me, you know. And I could care less about going to the office again. What are they going to do, kick a poor blind girl out of a public school? That would be incredibly bad press, yes? And Mr. Eggs loves me."

"What? Since when? Eggs cringes every time he sees you coming down the hall, looks like he's gonna have a panic attack or something. I feel sorry for the dude; he can't take much more."

"Really?" She smiled.

"Yes, really, and it's not funny. And what about all that stuff you spout all the time about loving your fellow man, the meek inheriting the Earth, and all? Turning the other cheek? Stuff your dad says? I don't think you were very meek there."

"Hey, do *not* stereotype me just because of my dad. I am my own person; I say and do what I want, my mouth I will flaunt. However, what I want changes, day by day." She shook her head. "If it was me, it would be one thing. It is just hard to take when it is someone else."

"Yeah, but—you're not the badass you want people to think you are, and I don't need your help, it just makes things worse."

"I am *not* a badass? Truly? Since when?"

"No. You're all talk. I've never actually seen you do anything physically aggressive."

She knew he was right, but it would be fun to crush Isenhour's pickup truck into scrap metal; that would be petty, however, and she would need some help to determine which one it even was. The joy wouldn't last very long. Better to talk him to death in front of his peers.

She would have her revenge in twenty years, when her address would be 1600 Pennsylvania Avenue, Washington, D.C.

"Well, that is because I am such an astute arbiter. I can talk my way out of any situation, easy when you know how. I do not need to use my fists. They could use me in Washington even now."

"Yeah, right, you'd better grow up first."

"I am eighteen today, an adult."

"Then act like it. C'mon, you knew Paul would never have hit you. As much of a bully as he is, he's also a guy's guy. He would've lost credibility forever with them for hitting a girl, let alone a blind one."

She laughed. "He would have lost a bit more than that. Thirty-two things, in fact." She began counting on her fingers. "Molars, incisors, premolars—"

"There you go again. Just walk away next time. I've seen you. You're maybe as strong as a few of the guys. I'm not."

"Wait a minute; nothing happened, did it?" She tried to reassure herself that. But for a moment she felt ashamed. She had allowed herself to get angry, if even for a brief moment. What if she was really roused to anger? Dad would tell her that she knew better. She got tired of hearing it, but she knew he was right. There were bigger conflicts out there to fight. Isenhour wasn't worth it.

And she felt saddened as she realized her petty actions required no real courage. She knew neither Isenhour nor any other human being could hurt her, so her "attitude" lacked real substance.

In contrast, Bobby put himself at big risk by standing up to a bully. What did she know about what he was feeling? She stood there, alone as usual, as she heard Bobby limp off, again perplexed by human behavior. It was that characteristic that she shared with her mom: saying or doing the wrong thing at inopportune times. What made her think she could ever be President? Some polishing would certainly be in order during the next twenty years. And possibly a personality transplant.

At times she was so confused. She didn't know what to do sometimes, and being eighteen sure wasn't all it was cracked up to be. Today wasn't that much different than yesterday; she had expected some magical acquisition of knowledge and wisdom after that milestone had passed, so it was a disappointment.

But she's the one who wanted to grow up, and there were some real responsibilities to take care of that were much more consequential than Paul Isenhour. One of them was in the small country of Taraq, 5,500 miles away. Unlike the encounter with Isenhour, this one probably would involve really kicking some tail. She hoped that when she did that for the first time, no one would get hurt. And it would be a long flight. She probably could leave her passport at home for this one.

• • •

Third period came at ten AM. AP calculus, presented by the teacher she dreaded more than any other. No teacher was more laughed at in the school than Petra Nureyev Marshall, who could care less or was oblivious to such negative comments. Paige never knew for sure which it was.

She heard the nervous woman shuffling her papers and passing them out, hers in Braille. She always used the app on her digital tablet to generate answers via speech recognition. She scanned her examination with her fingers; the result was not to her liking.

"What? I thought I got that integral right." She read the Braille printout of the teacher's comments and frowned. "Seventy-five? Are you for real, teach? Please do not preach."

The Russian teacher spoke up. "I know, this we have discussed. You can do better than this, Ms. Marshall. Ant and grasshopper, the lessons learned from that simple story will serve you—"

She crumpled the paper into a ball. "I cannot be perfect. I am not you, you know, I do not have your abilities. Stupid fable; I do not wish to discuss capitalism versus Communism again. We know which side won."

"None of us is perfect, but this grade can surely be improved upon with greater diligence to detail and less listening to seventies rock bands in bed. Eighty or even ninety is within your grasp."

"Sure, that is just great." Another disappointment, but probably what a lazy grasshopper deserved.

She heard Mom come up to her. "I don't have your abilities, either," she whispered quietly. "Be grateful for what you have and view the world as a glass half full. The world will be yours someday, and you will surely be the ruler of all of us—you know this is meant to be so."

"Yeah, right. I do not desire 'the world' or to rule anything, Mom. I want to be normal, to be happy, not crappy."

"We don't always get what we want, Paige. You have a vast responsibility to society."

She felt a large hand pat her on the shoulder. "Hey, don't worry about it, Paige. I'm sure you did better than I did."

"What? Look who is talking—the dummy who made fun of me in civics. Shut up, Talson, do not ever touch me." She slapped his hand gently, which he quickly withdrew.

"Sorry, Paige, I'm just trying to be nice. The purpose of Selvey's class is to debate—don't take it personally."

She heard her mom come closer. "Mr. Talson, that statement is irrelevant. Your performance and hers are mutually exclusive, a fact you would know if you understood set theory. And Ms. Marshall can do better than that. We all can. Challenge each other to do better each day, and the world shall be your reward," she intoned in her trademark monotone voice, almost with a robotic quality.

That's the explanation for everything: Mom was a robot; it all made sense now.

No, that wasn't right. No one, not even the most deranged mad scientist, would willingly make a robot like that.

"Okay, like, that's very profound, Mrs. Marshall," Talson said, laughing. "Reward, ant, grasshopper, got it down. Sure."

"Good. Within those simple principles reside the secrets of the cosmos."

She shook her head and laughed. Yeah, like her weird mom had accomplished so much, the great mathematical genius, Jack had said. She didn't know nearly enough about math to make that conclusion herself, but what good did it do Mom in the end? What did solving mathematical formulae on the living room wall do for anyone except keep the North Pole paint store in business? But her mathematical abilities were merely average. Her destiny lay somewhere else, she knew.

She would never be a mathematician, chemist, physicist, or an engineer. There was a famous actress and mathematician in the mid-20th century who had invented 'spread spectrum technology,' a precursor to modern wireless communications, in her spare time. Another famous actress and engineer played her in the movie, as well as the most celebrated theoretical physicist of the modern era, and earned a Best Actress Oscar for the latter. She would not follow suit, although she would like to meet that individual someday.

She wasn't sure where she was going to college and if she even was. They lived a simple existence, but there always seemed to be money for things. Some of them were rather expensive, and she didn't want to know where those came from. She wanted to change the world. Some academic credibility probably wouldn't hurt there. She didn't have the best interpersonal skills, but most of the shapers of the legislative world were attorneys.

The President was the unique exception, being a physician by training, but she knew she couldn't be someone like *her*. She certainly didn't mean disrespect in the debates. Lord knows she received enough negative comments about Wendy Mendoza from Mom. Talk about getting someone ranting.

Why did her mom care about such things? She didn't seem to care about much else in the world.

Adaptive technology had helped her navigate her homework, and while they lived in a very modest home, her parents always seemed to have enough money for the things she needed. And some of her needs were very, very large—as in millions of dollars' worth of technology. She wasn't a genius, but not stupid either; where that money came from, she didn't want to ask. Hopefully it wasn't stolen. Nah. Would Mom even have the ability to do something like that?

Stupid question. Probably. The less she knew about Mom's frequent odd 'trips' to destinations unknown, the better.

But she lacked many close friends. Not because she was blind, but because she felt different and couldn't share with anyone what made her special. Trust was hard to come by in this world, and she couldn't help but know that she lived in a sheltered environment. North Pole wasn't the worst place in the world to live, but it was pretty darn rural and unexciting.

And why was she living here rather than in the continental United States or somewhere else in the world? Alaska was fairly close to Russia, she imagined since that was where her mom was from. Or was she? Was the whole thing just an illusion? Was there a bigger world out there than what she had thought? How easy it would be to hide things from a blind girl, even one as gifted as she.

She would find out soon enough. She had never been outside the United States or Canada, and that was going to change in a few days. Dad wasn't too keen on it. But she was eighteen now, and they made a promise long ago that she could make her own way when that happened.

Chapter Fifteen

Paige finished most of her homework early that evening, digital lectures supplemented by Braille. The digital scanner could read most texts and convert them to sound, but she could do better with Braille most of the time. She went into the small living room and almost tripped on all the clutter on the floor before she caught herself in midair. She felt the stupid juggling balls, coins, magnets, trick handcuffs, comic books, and other garbage of no relevance to the real world.

She yelled in frustration. "Mom! Please clean this idiotic stuff up. Magic tricks? How childish. Why waste good money on this juvenile junk? What a bunch of bunk."

Mom tapped her firmly on the forehead with her index finger.

"Now, do not be so pejorative and open your mind. One may learn much from magic: mathematics, logic, illusion, presentation, coordination, and set theory. You should cultivate the inner child since much can be gained from introspection. Children also learn faster than adults and tend to examine in detail that which, on the surface, appears to have no purpose. Oh, Paige, how I wish to be a child again. Ehrich Weiss, later known as Houdini, was a master at distraction—"

"Sure, that does so much good to anyone. What a loser."

"Humph. I am quite busy, so what do you require, daughter? Is there a reason for this rude interruption?" the five-nine Russian woman asked in an irritating tone.

"Yeah, you were doing something so productive, I am sure."

"Don't judge what you are incapable of understanding. There is much you do not. Talk about frustrating."

"Speaking of higher intelligence, is *Oogly* here right now?"

"No, he is in his special place currently, in my mind."

She smirked. "Great, then we will not have to get him a ticket or buy him popcorn at the ball game. Lucky for us."

Petra paused for a minute. "That inane iteration makes no sense. He is made of intangible photons, therefore he does not undergo oxidative phosphorylation or require carbohydrates, nor does he have an alimentary system or intestinal flora, so he cannot even digest *Zea mays everta*."

She scratched her head with her left hand. "Huh? Z-what?"

"The scientific name for popcorn, which you should know, it has ten chromosomes and two billion base pairs in its DNA—"

"What possible purpose would it serve for me to know that?"

"If you do not know—oh, never mind! Nevertheless, he is *far* too advanced for such trivialities. We could only be so fortunate to be like him."

She sighed and pulled on her hair. "OMG! I cannot take any more of this; my head is going to explode!"

Petra sighed. "Again, you exaggerate, as per usual. I doubt it is possible for your head to explode, even at zero atmospheres. Yet, in my humble state, I lack the funds for the sophisticated scientific equipment required to perform such an elaborate experiment, as fascinating as that would be. One benefit is that in a vacuum, no one could hear you, providing relief to my eardrums."

"Who cares, yikes! Are we going soon? Dad is waiting, and we do not want to be late. Not that I contribute much to the team, but at least it gets me out of here—"

"What? Where are we going? To meet our end? Are we in a hurry for that? Some days I feel this will happen soon." Her mom grabbed her by the shirt collar. She felt different when Mom touched her, like she had never felt with any other person, a sort of vulnerability. Maybe that was good. But weird.

She pulled away and threw her hands down. "Must we speak of the end of the world again? I am sick of it, as you are like a broken record, and you drive me out of my gourd. Can you not be eloquent enough to come up with a new line?"

"Why not, have you something else asinine to arbitrate, all-knowing adolescent advisor?" Mom poked her in the forehead again with her finger. "Let me tell you, girl, the end shall not be as joyous as how we came into this world, although your coming into this world was rather painful, to me, at least—you had a big mouth from the moment you saw daylight, and the pain continues, eighteen years later."

She sighed. "The point of this raucous rant is what, exactly?"

"Huh? 'What is the point?' That there is nothing more to learn, nothing, my life has little purpose now that you are grown. I have solved every mathematical theorem known to man with my unmatched intellect. All that remains is for me to see you off on your maiden journey to the stars."

"I am not going to the stars just yet, just Taraq." She smelled the distinctive odor of ink solvent. "Hey, are you writing your theorems on the wall in magic marker again? Dad will not be happy."

"I will do what I choose, and the insinuation that I would fear my husband is laughable. Do you understand? No, of course not, none of the feeble minds understands what I do, least of all *you*. The responsibility thrust upon me, with things only I can comprehend, is beyond your simple understanding."

"Wow. I am sure sorry I asked. And if you want to talk about *responsibility*—you have no clue. Do you have any idea what it is like to be me?"

"You talk about going somewhere, but there is no place to go, child, nowhere to hide. What challenges remain for us? The apocalypse will soon be upon us at the hand of the bellicose, bucolic blonde-in-a-bottle behemoth, the Sacramento Sasquatch, the Oak Ridge Orca, the Washington Wildebeest, the Hippo-POTUS, laying waste to and eating everything she encounters with those gigantic feet and mouth. Only *you* can make a difference now and save us from such a horrible fate. This, we have discussed."

"'Oak Ridge Orca.' Now *that* is a new one." She yawned and wondered why she wanted to defend someone she had criticized in civics class, but debate wasn't so much about disliking someone as it was making a good argument. Maybe it was because no one should be treated as an extreme, a stereotype. The President was a great leader, no doubt, but neither saint nor sinner—just another human being with human flaws. Her mom, who was, paradoxically, the most arrogant person she had ever encountered—was full of them. "Can you not say something worthwhile for once?"

"The world needs saving, Paige." Mom said that simple sentence with absolute clarity, which startled her a bit. "If you, who aspire to be a great leader, can't see that, then you're going into the wrong line of work."

"You have been saying that forever; why do you keep harping about that? The world has not had any type of war or fighting for years. Crime is down fifty percent over the last decade."

"Humph. Child, the lack of wars or crime is not necessarily a good yardstick, how trivial. You enjoy history, so find out why this is so; it's all right there before you. Look for yourself."

"The highest federal tax rate is sixteen percent; half the states have no sales taxes any longer. While I have some diverse views too and feel it may be time for a change, I have to agree that President Mendoza has done much good, more than most."

"*Good?*" Mom shrieked. "That name—*Mendoza*—shall never be mentioned here again. She borrows and uses the name of royalty as it was her very own. The one who has had more last names than we can count. Yeesh."

"Why do you care what name the President uses now? She uses her husband's name, just like you do, so get over it."

"Because I do, it is disrespectful to the dead. I may change my name back to Nureyev, too, by the way."

"Whatever. There are a few dead Darkkins around too, that is why it was called *Darkkday*. Be quiet." She heard Mom shuffling her feet. "Problem, Mom? Your marker run dry?"

"Uh, where is it we are going again? I forget. With all that I have endured in my life and my vast, unmatched cerebral knowledge, my short-term memory fails me sometimes."

"No kidding. We are going to my basketball game, and you need to keep the stats. Remember?"

"Of course, how silly of me. I forget my mundane Earthly responsibilities sometimes. Not keeping accurate statistics could result in a cataclysmic chain of events that could disrupt the very fabric of the known universe."

"Something like that, yes." She couldn't read it but heard her mother rustle through her notebook full of mathematical formulae. She got B's in higher math, but Mom was way out of her league. Probably out of anyone's. Out in space most of the time, computing the basketball statistics in her head without a calculator and remembering them all without writing them down, Dad said.

She had no idea how Mom could do things like that and why

she was so inept at other things.

Finally. she heard her dad come in. "Let's go. We're going to be late. What's going on here?"

"Just a discussion," Mom said. "I believe I am losing, as usual."

"Figures. Two mental giants. Good Lord, look at this place, what a mess."

"Do not criticize me, Jack Marshall. You may be my husband, but never the boss of me."

"Holy smokes," he said as she heard him slap himself in the face. "I learned that long ago. Let's go."

They left out the back door, got in the old pickup truck, her father driving. Mom, muttering mathematical equations, was in the middle, she at the passenger side.

"Ready for the big game today, Paige?"

"I guess so. Are you following through with what you said I could do after my birthday?"

"We'll talk about it later," he said. "I'm not real crazy about it." She could hear her mom ruffling through one of her many "scientific periodicals."

"The world needs change," Mom said. "Soon the balance of power will be upon us, glorious it shall be—"

"Shut up, Petra, this isn't about you, it's about saving a life. As much as I dislike this, it's probably the only way he gets out of this alive." She heard Mom turn the pages of her books. Not textbooks, but something else, most likely; she could smell the old pulpy pages. "The discussions with the Taraqis have broken down, but she doesn't need any more encouragement from someone who reads funny books. Put those down and pay attention."

"Humph, do not kick me. You can learn much from comics. And comic books, despite their name, are not necessarily humorous in nature."

"I would not know, unless you have some in Braille."

"Let me finish. Many have an extremely high vocabulary level and tell tales of quite profound deeds of derring-do that illustrate the great evils that are upon us in contemporary society—"

She heard the tire blow out. Saved from another soliloquy about the merits of comics and graphic novels.

"Crap," Jack yelled. "We'll be late for the game now."

She laughed. "No, we will not. Get out and change it, pop."

"What? Forget it—you're going to help. I can't jack it up with you in it. Luckily this truck has a strong suspension." Mom, although only about one inch taller than her, weighed about two hundred ten pounds, while she was about one-sixty, and Mom had the same size waist and *much* smaller bust. The reason for that weight discrepancy had never been explained to her.

"Would be nice to have a new one."

"Yeah?" She heard him get out and slam the door shut. "Well, you're an enormously expensive special needs child. We have all the money we require, anyway. This truck's just fine." She heard him fumble around for the jack. "I guess we don't have one."

"Great, I see you have planned ahead. Ain't no AAA club out this far. You have the spare?" she said.

"Yeah. I sure hope it's pumped up."

"Grasshopper—ant," she heard Mom say. "Remember: he who is not prepared today shall be less prepared tomorrow. Lazy, slovenly—"

She scowled, anxious to get to the gym and frustrated by the delay and her mother's complaints. "Dang it. Be quiet, Mom, unless you want to get out and help."

"What? You think I cannot? Maybe I will. But do not issue commands to me." Mom started whistling some unknown tune.

"So now you know that not having the jack is no problem, huh?" She ignored her mom and went to the flat drivers' rear tire and removed the lug nuts with her right hand. Mom maybe could have done that trick, too. Mom was pretty coordinated and could do some interesting things.

"Let me get Petra out. She's in rare form tonight."

She chuckled. "It does not matter. Just get out of the way." Mom was also extremely strong for a woman over fifty but couldn't do this next stunt, for sure.

She went behind the truck and lifted the rear end a foot off the ground with her left hand with no more effort than picking up a carton of milk. She still wasn't sure how it worked; she just willed it to happen, and it did. The limits were unknown, but she was pretty sure their 2001 Chevy Silverado weighed at least two tons. Big deal.

"Lucky to have you around."

"I think I was meant for greater things than being Jack's jack." She threw the flat tire into the bed and jumped in after it. "I believe I shall just ride back here the rest of the way, much more peaceful."

"It's cold back there, dear," he said.

The cold never seemed to bother her. "Not a problem. Need some solitude and respite from the funny books so I can get psyched up for the game." Shooting free throws didn't require a lot of effort, but she wanted to be ready in any case.

• • •

Andrew Graham High School
The Igloo
1201 Kris Kringle Drive
North Pole, Alaska

The North Pole Lady Polar Bears were close in their first game of the season, 34-32, and it was remarkable they were only behind by two points on this cold late October day. Usually, they were behind by double digits by the middle of the first quarter, so this was a rare event. Paige sat at her usual place on the bench next to Coach Jack. She wondered how he'd gotten the job, except that no one else probably wanted it, as it wasn't a terribly prestigious position.

"Hey," Paige said, staring blankly at the court. "You there, Rache?" She reached out to touch her teammate to the right of her.

"Right here, as always, fellow bench-warmer. What, did you think I was actually in the game? Silly girl."

"How many people are here at The Igloo tonight?" She took a drink of Gatorade.

"A lot more than usual. At least fifty or sixty."

"Wow. We are in danger of being kicked out of the conference for poor attendance, even they have standards. Is my mom still up in the stands, or is she out wandering around, calculating the shot trajectory angles?"

"Where she always is: up in the corner of the home stands. She just stares and stares. I'm sorry, I know she's your mom, but she kind of creeps me out, Paige. Like her mind's completely blank, or thinking incredibly detailed thoughts, but you don't know which."

"Probably a bit of both. Mom has had a tough life, you know. Coach Jack, too."

"Does she, like, ever talk? I've never had her in a class, but I hear she talks all the time there. But I've never heard her speak in the hallway or anywhere else. She kind of scares me, sorry."

"She has some form of autism, Dad says. About twice a day she mutters something of immense philosophical importance, and, yes, she often has bursts of incessant jabbering. Most of the time she spouts mathematical equations about hydrogen fusion, subatomic particles, and the origin of the universe and such, and draws on the walls of our house in magic marker. Most recently, she has been going on and on about something called dark energy."

"*Dark energy*? Like in Satan? Eeeeww, that's gross."

She shook her head. "No, not devil stuff. She isn't into that at all, she is actually quite religious. She rattles on about bosons and fermions and something called non-baryonic matter. They are powerful forces—she says that these dark energy and dark matter entities make up over ninety percent of the universe."

"*Bosoms?* She talks about boobs? That's sure weird."

"Bosons, not bosoms, Rache. Jeez. Even I know what the Higgs boson is. Not that I care anything about it."

"Well, all I know is: Paul Isenhour tried to get into Betty Lou Higgs' bosom last week behind the snack bar at the pep rally and got his face slapped."

She laughed and expelled a mouthful of half-eaten popcorn on the floor, unsuccessfully trying to remember its scientific name and number of chromosomes. "Huh. Does not surprise me."

"I don't know the difference between the two. Sounds like something from an old science fiction movie. Like black holes?"

She shook her head. "Not really. She says it is not the same as a black hole, although I really do not understand it. It is the energy that keeps the universe expanding, and it actually repels gravity. There's really no way humanly possible to harness it, she says, although she claims Mendoza Multinational is working on it with some professor at Princeton, it's kind of secret."

"How does she know that if it's so secret, and anything about Mendoza Multinational or some professor at Princeton? That's the big leagues, hon. A bit out of your mom's pay grade, I think."

She took another swig of Gatorade. "I know, I have my doubts. I have no idea how she knows what she knows or if it's even true. I really am not interested in such things, if you did not know that already."

"So, let me get this straight. We live in the ten percent of the universe that's not dark energy, is that right?"

She nodded. "I suppose so. She says it is all around us, but we just cannot see it."

"Ten percent of regular energy is plenty for me."

"I guess."

"Huh. You got a weird family, girl."

"Yes, that is putting it mildly." She pulled a plastic card out of her shorts pocket as she heard Rachel sit back on the bench. "By the way, did you see my new drivers' license?"

Rachel grabbed the card. "Pretty nice. Where did you get this?"

"Bobby made it for me in his photo class. He has an uncle who works at the Fairbanks DMV."

"For eye color, it says 'DIC.' You are kind of a dick, if you were a guy, I guess, but what does that mean?"

"DIC. Dichromatic, duh."

"Huh?"

"That means two colors. It is what they put on a driver's license when the eye colors do not match."

"Weird. It might be hard to get car insurance for you, though."

She nodded. "True." Or hard to get insurance on her for a whole lot of other things that nobody else knew about. She was startled back to reality as she heard the whistle blow—foul on Fairbanks High. Two shots, she heard the referee say.

"OK, Paige, time to stop jabbering. Your time to add to your amazing career point total. No slam dunks, now." Jack Marshall said condescendingly.

"Not even one? Okay, I will try not to." She wasn't going to try very hard. Tonight might be the night for a tomahawk. No one would care, anyway.

The announcer's raspy voice spoke up. "Now shooting the foul shots for North Pole, the team captain and fourth all-time leading scorer, Paige Marshall, who just happens to be eighteen years old today." The tiny crowd cheered for the school's most avid debater. She didn't do a whole heck of a lot, anyway. Not that a twelve-point per game average was that much to brag about when they were all foul shots.

Rachel led the five-eight team captain out to the charity stripe to attempt her teammate's foul shots; Rachel wasn't much of an athlete, and this was her designated responsibility: to bring the school's best athlete center stage. Not that she needed a guide to get out there; she had been all over that court thousands of times and knew it by heart. She did gain some respect because of what she did with a disability, so she had earned the title of captain. That, and the fact she could trash-talk with the best of them. For that, she might get in the Alaska Basketball Hall of Fame, which reportedly was a tiny building in downtown Anchorage.

Big deal for someone who would someday live in the White House. Yeah, right, if she ever got out of this place.

She snapped back to reality, realizing that she was 4,142 miles from 1600 Pennsylvania Avenue. The team had entered into an agreement with the Alaska State Athletic Association that Paige, out of a gesture of goodwill, would be allowed to shoot all the foul shots for North Pole. Technically the other teams could complain, but given North Pole's record last year of 0-15, it seemed of little consequence to the competitors. Amazingly, she was a ninety-nine percent foul shooter, the best on the team, and in the history of boys' or girls' basketball in the United States.

Yet, no one really cared about that or anything else regarding the blind girl named Paige Marshall, though; this feat wasn't even enough for a piece in the student e-newsletter.

She lived in obscurity; she became tired of that sometimes. Jack told her repeatedly that it was a blessing to enjoy the anonymity while she could because it might not last much longer. Yeah, a lot he knew about it. Parents were pretty dumb.

The crowd of fifty-eight cheered as the blind girl palmed the ball off the referee with one hand; she knew she had to be looking at her amazingly as she dribbled it. She had a pretty good vertical jump and could dunk, she knew, if she could just see the basket. Easy enough to get there from the foul line. Two and a half steps.

The first underhand shot was flawless. No one shot them that way any longer, but that always seemed the most natural way to do it. First one in, she knew as she could hear the net swish. She could shoot the conventional way, but this seemed to be more entertaining for the crowd. She couldn't understand advanced mathematics or speak twenty languages like her mom. But she had absolute muscle control, Jack had told her. Why he would know that was beyond her. She needed it.

She took the second one and began to again send it towards the ten-foot goal right as she heard someone blow a compressed-air foghorn right at release, resulting in a moment's distraction. She heard the clank, off the left side of the rim, she was pretty sure.

That hadn't happened in a long time. What if it happened doing something far more important than shooting a foul shot?

"Get it, Barb! Throw it back to Paige!" Barb had gotten the rebound, apparently, which wasn't necessarily good for the team, if they wanted to score.

"What?" She heard five-four guard Barb's shrill voice; she was named appropriately, as her chipmunk-like voice was as irritating as a barbed wire fence.

Somehow the ball came back to her and landed in her left palm. She was still at the foul line and thought about a jump shot, but that would be too easy and unspectacular. She had only scored three field goals in her whole career, and those were gimmes when they were being blown out, and they just stuck her on the three-point line to launch treys.

A game was on the line here. Not a world-shattering game, but still a game, nonetheless. She likely wouldn't have this opportunity ever again.

Silence that seemed to last an eternity. No one was trying to take it from her. Like that could happen anyway.

"Shoot it, Paige. Go on. You've only got six seconds left!" Traci, another teammate of less than stellar ability, yelled.

No way was anyone going to foul her given her accuracy, so she would have to shoot. But she was now in the lane and didn't want a three seconds violation.

To hell with it—she was an adult now and had been for almost twenty hours; therefore, she could now make adult decisions. The five-eight young woman palmed the ball in her left hand, took one dribble, hoped that no one was in the way, and leaped towards the rim, where she heard the two-handed throwdown go through the net as she hung onto the rim for several seconds, then dropped to the ground. The crowd roared in amazement at her unusual feat as time expired. She was a bit amazed herself.

"Yay, Paige!" the tiny crowd roared as the school's best high-jumper won the game. The other team shook hands with the victorious girls as they left the floor, seemingly dumbfounded, and she wished she could have seen their facial expressions. Like the game meant anything except that they wouldn't have a big zero in the win column at the end of the year. They were undefeated! Probably not for long, though; that was just until the next game. She put her left fist in the air as her teammates lifted her up and carried her to the locker room in jubilation.

Coach Jack congratulated the team in the girls' locker room as her teammates patted her on the back. She knew the lecture was going to come now.

"Paige, in here, please."

"Yeah, yeah, okay." They went into the small trainer's room off the back locker room entrance as she heard him close the door.

"We need to have a long talk."

"I have deduced as much, but was hoping for just a short talk, and I would be willing to negotiate a medium-length talk."

"Not funny. Sit your sorry butt down."

"Me, not funny? Since when?" She sat down on the wooden bench, now anticipating the consequences of her adult decision. "I know what you are going to say, Dad."

"Do you really?"

"Yes. If anything, you are predictable in your lecturing."

"Okay, then," he yelled. "Do you realize how dumb that was, you careless, obnoxious lummox?"

She shook her head. "It is not what *you* want, maybe, but me wanting my first dunk is dumb? It is my eighteenth birthday, so cut me some slack, Jack. You know I can jump that high, all on my own, do not use such a terrible tone!"

"You could've just shot it again. It would've probably gone in, and, if not, it's just a freaking basketball game! And how do you know what you can do 'on your own' and not? That sounds like something a child or your mom would say. Same thing, I guess."

She snarled. "Hey, I know, trust me. I understand this body way more than you do, you have no comprehension. And *never* again call me a child. I was powered-down, that dunk was all *me*."

"It doesn't matter. It drew unneeded attention and is trivial in the scheme of things."

"Why? You let me high jump on the track team, so what is the difference?"

"You know the difference. This has nothing to do with what you want, what your native abilities are, or your birthday, or how adult you now believe yourself to be. You could have seriously hurt or killed someone in your way, or broken the whole basket down, or smashed the floor. How would we have explained that? Are you even capable of thinking that far ahead? I gave you credit for having more maturity than your mom. Guess I was wrong."

She sighed. "If my skin made physical contact, they could not have been hurt. You know that."

"In a way, that would've been even worse. Don't try to talk your way out of this one, you were a dummy."

"And no way could stuff have been broken, you know better. I have perfect control over my body. That was a genuine, flesh-and-blood dunk, you are full of bunk, 'cause I ain't no puny punk."

"That's not the point. Your mom isn't going to like it, either."

"Awww. Now *that* is really intimidating. Not."

"If you want to be an adult, then start acting like one. Your gifts aren't a game. Besides, we can't risk that kind of stuff in the newsblogs, not now, of all times!"

"Newsblogs? Get real. The school photographer is Nate Riegle, who cannot even point the digi-camera in the right direction. I could do a better job than him. Geez."

"Someone with a Tekphone probably already uploaded it to the Internet."

"Good. 'Bout time someone saw it. They will soon."

"What is that supposed to mean?"

"You know what it means. Did you forget your promise?"

He sighed. "That's another issue, one that I'm not particularly happy about but am supportive of, because it is for the greater good of mankind, and we don't need any more countries taken over, or any nukes dropped. But beware of pride," he said, grabbing her by the jersey. "I am very disappointed in you, Paige."

"Huh? What did you say?"

"*Pride. Superbia. Hubris.* Galatians 5:19-21. One of the 'seven deadly sins.' I told you that, for the rest of your life, you must *never* succumb to them. The amazing abilities you have been given transcend any petty things you may want personally. I know it's hard to live up to that, but you must. People will constantly want you to do trivial things for them, but you have to resist."

She pointed her left thumb at her chest. "I can have pride if I want. Normal people sure as heck do. Mom is about the most arrogant person I have ever met."

"In case you haven't noticed, you *aren't* a normal person, and this isn't about your mom, one with great intellect but limited maturity and insight, so grow up and move on. You're eighteen and want to take on responsibilities you think you comprehend, yet you act like this. So you obviously don't get it. You're the one who wants to grow up, so act like you mean it."

She thought carefully like she did when she broke up the fight between Bobby and Isenhour earlier that morning. He was right again, and she knew it.

"I guess you are correct. But since I did it, can I at least enjoy it for a while?"

"The damage is already done, I suppose, we can't undo it."

• • •

The rest of the week passed uneventfully, her milestone birthday having generated no global fanfare. There was a party after the second game the next Friday, that night, as their game was before the boys' game; they had lost 55-23. She made eight of eight foul shots but no dunks, thankfully. She thought about what Jack had said and really wanted to forget about the other night.

She walked out the side of the gym as she smelled her teammate's perfume, which seemed a bit inappropriate for a game, but Rachel didn't play much. "What's up, Rache?"

"Hey, Paige, do you want to go to a party?" Rachel asked.

"What time is it in the Middle East?"

"I have no idea. Why?"

"I think I have a flight to catch in a couple of days, so I better make sure I rest up."

"From Fairbanks International? To the Middle East? Why?"

"No, it is, well, a private flight. Kind of hard to explain."

"Well, let's go to the party, then. You can sleep later and catch your big flight."

"I guess so."

• • •

Paige sat in the corner in the rec room at Doug Jones' house. She was used to that, not being very popular; she normally wasn't invited to parties. Although she was surely the world's greatest athlete and was pretty good at debate, she was never good with guys or making friends in general. Like there were a lot of opportunities for a blind girl from Alaska in the dating world. Having a big obnoxious mouth didn't help matters, many had told her.

She was not one to listen very well.

Good athlete, what a laugh. She never had to work at any of that stuff; it was so easy. Classwork was significantly harder. Would she ever be able to reach her goal of being a great leader? To do that meant a lot of studying: political science, law, civics, and other things. Mom was right: she was the grasshopper instead of the ant most of the time. She knew she would never be a scientist or engineer. That much was clear. But could she change the world the way she wanted to?

"You want a drink, Paige?" Rachel asked as she took the glass tumbler from her friend's hand. "You'll like it."

She was a bit thirsty, at that. "I guess I could use some hydration. What is this tasty libation you speak of?"

"It's good. Trust me, there ain't much water in it, though."

"Huh. That is a peculiar statement. Satisfies thirst, yet is not water. I must intently investigate to see what is so great." She drank the pungent liquid hastily; it felt like pretty much anything else going down and had kind of a smoky taste as she felt the last drops enter her throat. "It is not bad, I guess. A strange astringent quality I have not recently experienced, although it is somehow familiar."

"Holy crap! You chugged the whole glass, girl! You're gonna be so wasted. Your preacher pop won't be happy."

That was an extremely unlikely event (the part about her becoming drunk, not Dad being mad). "I take it that this lavish liquid is liquor? Bourbon whiskey, no doubt, given the odor of burnt wood? Guess it is good I am not driving, huh?"

"Yeah, the good stuff, what did you think? Didn't you know by the color?"

"I cannot see it, dummy, jeez. Sounds like *you* are drunk."

Rachel laughed. "Oh, yeah, sorry. Yes, I am. Your point being?"

She held out her hand and felt the bottle in Rachel's smaller right hand. She plucked it out and felt the distinctive hexagonal shape of the bottle of spirits. "Give me that. How irresponsible."

"Hey, you can't have *all* of it, Paige. Give it back! That's all we have, and you already drank some of it."

"I want some for later." She thought about participating, being one of the gang. She had done so in the past and was not averse to taking risks. Two years ago, she rode an old discarded bicycle up a trail by herself, went over a cliff, and hit solid rock seven hundred thirty feet below at terminal velocity (the free fall was about eight seconds), leaving the bike in about a hundred pieces, and a bald spot on her head. Thank God no one had seen that, as she had the good fortune to have done it in the dark. She had tried smoking cigarettes several times with Rachel and other friends, too. That was a pretty worthless activity, but there was something fun about going up against authority.

But she was eighteen now, a child nevermore. Dad said it was time to grow up. Mom still hadn't grown up, actually, and seemed to be declining in maturity as she aged. Not that she was any different than two days ago when she was seventeen.

"Earth to Paige!" She could feel the breeze of Rachel waving her hand in front of her face.

"Why are you waving your hand? I cannot see it."

"Trying to get your attention, you space cadet."

"I have only been contemplating. No, this is not right, Rache. We are all underage, so it is illegal."

"*Whaaat?* Underage? Can this be the same Paige I used to know talking?"

"Huh?"

"Don't be such a nerd, big adult, the one who has been arrested way more than anyone here, so shut the heck up about things that are 'illegal.' No wonder you're sitting here on your own. No one would want you."

How true that was. "Yeah, maybe I did some dumb stuff when I was a kid, but things change, and I do not answer to you, and I do not want to be around you any longer, either." She walked off towards the door and walked out, others apparently oblivious to her departure. She heard her shorter friend's steps in the snow following her.

"Hey, I'm sorry, Paige, come back. I'm sorry I got mad."

"Forget it. Shut up and get away from me and go back to your dumb old friends. That group obviously does not include me."

"Not true, and I'm really sorry for what I said."

She turned around. "You should have thought of that before you said it. I do not need you or anyone else."

"Everyone needs someone, Paige, even you. You get up on your soap box, so high and mighty, yet your world is small. We're all just a bunch of small-town hicks. You don't know what it takes to be the super big shot you aspire to be."

"Perhaps not, but at least I am trying." She needed to widen her horizons. "I do know this, though: I need someone other than you. And you have no idea what I want."

"Look, let me walk you back home, come on now."

"I shall make it back on my own, somehow, because I do not need anyone. Never did."

"Paige, come back. Stubborn girl."

Yes, she was stubborn, to the chagrin of the North Pole High School faculty and her parents. Too bad. She turned on the watch which would tell her the direction she was going. It was about six miles from Doug's house back to hers. She remembered how to retrace the steps back. But she knew in the back of her mind that she would have to enlist the help of others to achieve her goals. Maybe that was the lesson in life she needed to learn.

She had far bigger things to worry about now, such as keeping a promise to help someone whom others couldn't. Maybe she was not a world-class student. She would have to work on that to get where she wanted to go.

But in her own element, she was singular. No doubt about that, the underage girl thought as she and her pilfered fifth of D.T. Darkkin & Sons Tennessee Whiskey jogged the six miles home.

Chapter Sixteen

Paige finished third period and walked to the auditorium at eleven AM the next morning to attend the annual career fair as she enjoyed newfound popularity after her two-handed dunk last night. She didn't like career fairs, as she had no idea what she wanted to do with her life and didn't see how this was going to help. It was a bit late in the game to be contemplating that, with graduation about seven months away. While most of her friends had some idea, she kept hearing her parents' harping about career choices. Their choices probably weren't for her. Math and science were clearly out, and she sure wasn't cut out to be a minister. She didn't have the patience for that. Or the belief in God, a probable requirement.

She yawned as most of the career choices were boring: nurse, teacher, insurance salesman, welder, architect, engineer. Yeah, like she would be good at selling people stuff, welding car or reactor parts, or designing things. They probably wouldn't let a sightless person be a nurse, although the concept of actually helping people was appealing. She told it like it was most of the time, and peddling insurance was probably not in her future either; she would probably be fired the first day for insulting a customer. She knew that the people coming to talk had given up their time and were certainly contributing much to society, but those things just weren't for her.

The next one was from the military. She laughed—like *that* would be a good choice for her. While the armed forces had undoubtedly become more diverse over the last thirty years, the employment of a blind girl was not likely to be congruent with their physical requirements. And the military was the personification of the establishment she so intensely loathed. But she wanted to stick around and see what was presented, nevertheless, mainly because she had nothing better to do.

Principal Ned Eggserby announced the next speaker. "Next, from nearby Eielson Air Force Base, is First Lieutenant Russell T. Stanton, here to talk about Air Force opportunities."

Rachel tapped her on the shoulder. "Paige, dear, I wish just for one moment I could give you my eyes so you could see."

She yawned and chewed her gum. "Yeah, yeah. Why now, as opposed to any other time? To see some dweeb military guy in a zoot suit, the ultimate representation of 'the man?' Give me a break, Rache. You know I do not care for the establishment's symbolism."

"I think you are going to change your mind, girl."

"Huh? Why would that be?" she said languidly.

"Why? Because this 'dweeb military guy' is the most gorgeous hunk of maleness you could ever imagine, honey."

"Huh." She paused and thought for a moment as she grabbed her shoulder eagerly. "Now *that*, I am surely interested in. Describe him to me and spare no detail."

"About six-one, chiseled features—wowee. One silver bar on his uniform. An Air Force lieutenant, probably a pilot."

"I know, Egghead said that already. I am blind, not deaf. In that case, you better take me up there afterward because I want to meet him. You sure owe it to me after that stupid party."

"I guess so. Does that mean you forgive me now, even though you drank all our booze?"

She nodded slightly. "Maybe I will if you introduce me. I was out of line, too, wearing my feelings on my shoulder. I am sorry. My problems are not yours, as I have a few issues to work out in my complex life."

"You do. We all do, dear. Now that we've settled that let's go up there."

Rachel Milner took her up to the front of the auditorium after the presentation ten minutes later. She had no desire to meet with the nurse, teacher, engineer, or skilled tradesman. Rachel led her as they pushed the other students out of the way.

"Gangway," Rachel said. "Heavy load coming through."

"Hey," a girl yelled. "Just 'cause Paige is blind doesn't mean she gets first dibs on meeting this guy. That isn't fair—"

"You're right, it doesn't," Rachel said. "Paige gets first dibs because she's awesome."

"Paige is awesome? An awesome pain in the butt, maybe," the girl said harshly.

Move it or lose it, Shelly," Rachel said.

"Rachel speaks the truth, as does Shelly. I am indeed awesome, as well as one who is capable of causing extreme discomfort in the *gluteus maximus*."

"What a geek."

She stepped up to the podium and heard his polished shoes on the wooden floor "Why, who are you, young lady?"

"Paige. Paige Marshall." She trembled slightly as she could feel herself blushing. For a moment, she almost felt faint. Wouldn't that be a hoot? Falling off the stage? Better that than another cliff.

"You are indeed a beautiful girl. I'm Russell Stanton. What year are you, Paige?"

"Senior. Do I look like a freshman to you?"

"Hmm, no, you don't. You look very—mature." He laughed.

"Is something funny?" she asked.

"And she's eighteen—" Rachel said. She knew the shorter Rachel was winking, even though she couldn't see her.

She shoved her friend gently. "Rache, please be quiet. You are embarrassing me, as you can see."

"I'll just see you both later, then." She could hear Rachel and her three-inch heels walk away on the old wooden stage floor.

She heard him move towards her. "It's great to meet you. What are your goals next year?"

"I was thinking of the Air Force Academy, then going on to pilot school like you, maybe becoming a NextGen helium-3 shuttle navigator. May I use you as a reference? It might help me procure a piloting position."

"I see. That's, er, great."

She held up her cane and laughed. "Come on, can you not see I am messing with you? Lighten up, Lieutenant."

"Funny. How'd you know my rank?"

She felt his shoulder and the single bar on his dress uniform.

"Not hard. I can place people's ages by their voices within a few years, so I'm guessing you're early-mid-twenties, and that's the rank you should have by now if you're not some loser. Rachel said it was a silver bar, too. Plus, Mr. Eggs mentioned your rank when he introduced you."

"Mr. Eggs? I don't follow."

"Ned Eggserby, the principal. He kind of resembles a really big egg, as you can probably see, but he is a good egg, too. Do not get too close, though, as he has his own gravitational pull, and you will be sucked in like a black hole, never to be heard from again."

"I see that you are a very perceptive person."

"You pay attention to all the little things people say when you're blind. We are much more capable than people think."

"Well, perhaps, but about astronaut school—that one might be a bit difficult." He paused for a moment. "No offense, but you have the most beautiful eyes I've ever seen. Left one as bright as the sea, the other as dark as night."

She smiled curiously. "Why would you think complimenting me on my eyes would offend me? Because I am blind?"

"Well, I suppose that's what I mean. That would be a natural assumption."

She waved her left index finger at him pensively. "So, the other choice is to have unattractive, ugly eyes? You would rather I have those or be unattractive in another way?"

"Uh, no, I only meant—"

She felt Rachel nudge her. "Paige, be quiet! You're screwing things up with your big mouth again. History repeats itself."

She turned around and thrust her chest out. "Hey, I merely posed the dichotomous rebuttal to his statement. To me, that is a reflexive act, difficult to attenuate." She was unlike her mother in many ways, but she shared her penchant for complicated language—and incessant arguing. "I apologize, Lieutenant, for my obnoxious outburst. Instead, let us leave my colleagues for a moment."

They walked away from the crowd, leaving the students to mingle with the less desirable professionals. "You're quite the spitfire, aren't you?"

"You got it. I give as good as I get. Better, actually, if you really want to know."

"Well, you still have pretty eyes."

"That is what they tell me. Right dark brown, the left blue. One from each of my parents. It is a rare genetic condition called heterochromia iridum, but it has nothing to do with why I cannot see. I guess no one knows that for sure." She reached up to his face. "May I touch your face?"

"Sure, I guess so. Why?"

"I depend on touch a lot, obviously. It helps me know what you look like if I can feel your face. While that might seem unimportant to a blind person, such tactile gestures allow me to realize a person's distinctiveness." She ran her fingers over his face, feeling his Black features, closely cropped curly hair, and probing every nook and cranny of his skin.

"Well?" he said as she took her hands away a few minutes later.

She nodded her head. "I concur with Rachel's assertion that you are a mighty fine-looking specimen of the male gender."

"No one's ever put it quite like that before, but thanks. Let's get out of here." They walked out the back hall, leaving the other students watching as they went to the back room of the auditorium. She grabbed him by the shoulder.

She laughed. "Listen, if you are abducting me, Lieutenant, please know that I am a bit stronger than I look. Although from the description Rachel gave of you and my own observations, I would definitely consent to be kidnapped by you. I will not even need a blindfold." She held her hands out. "You can tie me up if you want, too. I will not even use my special karate chop."

"You're too much. You really know martial arts?"

She nodded and laughed. "Something like that. It is really hard to describe. Just hope I do not have to show you."

"Yeah, you're really scary. But you're the shooter I've heard about, aren't you? It just dawned on me."

"Shooter? Rifle shooter? Now wouldn't *that* be fun. Do you want to be the target first, William Tell? *I shot an arrow into the air, where it fell, I knew not where—*"

"Huh. No, a foul shooter, not archery or firearms—"

"Not even Henry Wadsworth Longfellow?"

"Uh, no."

"Do you even know who Longfellow was?"

"Not entirely, as I'm not much of a poetry connoisseur. But I do hear you shoot over ninety-five percent from the charity stripe."

She put her hand over her heart. "Ninety-nine percent, do not be insulting, excuse me. It is easy when you know how."

"Sorry. But you should be on some national team or the cover of Sports Illustrated, then."

"Not much market for that isolated skill. I also do not like attention."

"Now that's hard to believe."

"It is true, mister. I despise the limelight. Not that I have ever been in it, mind you."

"Then how do you know for sure?"

"Just a feeling, I am basically an introvert."

"Okay, maybe, but how do you do that? Shoot like that?"

"I shoot underhanded, Rick Barry style. No distractions. Why would that be harder for me than for anyone else?"

"It would be impossible for me. Ruined my promising career."

"You are better off." They sat down in the backstage preparation room. "So, where do you hail from, Lieutenant Russ?"

"Western Pennsylvania, near the Ohio border, by Lake Erie."

"Never really been to that part of the States, or many places outside of Alaska, actually. So you are stationed at Eielson Air Force Base, Eggs said?"

"Yeah. Maybe I'll take you up in a plane sometime."

"Really? You can do that?"

"Well, only if my base commander doesn't find out. He's a pretty nice guy, though."

"Okay, you sound like a kindred spirit. I will agree on the explicit condition that I shall return the favor and take you up in mine sometime."

He laughed. "Right. I'll bet it's really fast."

She nodded. "You have *no* idea."

"Huh. Well, I have to get back to work, or I'll be in trouble."

"Really? You? I thought you would be in charge of the base, with lackeys and gofers running errands for you constantly."

"Not hardly. You have a lot to learn about military hierarchy."

"Not even a personal assistant or two, for one as accomplished as you?"

He laughed. "Boy, are you way off base. Anyway, it was nice to meet you, young lady."

"*Young lady?* I am eighteen, so I cannot be much younger than you."

"How do you know how old I am, Miss Marshall?"

"Like I said earlier, your voice. You are a first lieutenant, so you must be twenty-three or four."

"Twenty-four. That's much older than you."

She smiled. "Yes, but I am far more beautiful."

"Now that's true, no contest there."

"Will I ever see you again?" She laughed. "Sorry, force of habit. I do not generally see very well."

"I suppose it might be okay. I've got some special ops missions coming up. I don't know when I'll be back, but Eielson's not that far away."

"Special ops? Secret stuff? You are a secret agent? Come on."

"You might say that. It's not as glamorous as it sounds."

"Anything would be more glamorous than my existence."

"Mostly just some reconnaissance flights, studying maps, and so forth. I don't carry the nuclear football for President Mendoza or anything like that."

"*That* is certainly good." She grimaced as if tasting something sour. "I would hate to see us break up before we even started."

"What? I don't like nuclear weapons, either. Just because I'm military doesn't mean I condone that, come on."

"Of course not, but I meant President Mendoza. I know she is your Commander-in-Chief and is a highly accomplished, moral, and well-educated leader, but she seems to have beliefs which are different from mine."

"I wouldn't know. She's way out of my league."

"Perhaps, but I am not." She scribbled her cell phone number and email on a sheet of paper. "Give me a call, Lt. Russ. I cannot wait to go flying with you, one way or another."

"Okay, Paige. I'll see if I have some free time coming up. Sounds like fun."

She pulled his head towards her and kissed him on the lips, allowing her tongue to touch his oral mucosa ever so slightly.

"Paige—" He pulled his head away.

"What's wrong?" She laughed.

"Nothing, I just—I felt a little dizzy, that's all. A sudden burst of energy, a head rush."

"Me too. I had a hunch my kissing would have that effect on people. Not that I have done it much."

"I don't understand."

She shook her head. "Neither do I. The birds and the bees are one of life's great mysteries."

"Well, see you later, Paige Marshall."

"If you want to feel dizzy again, you know how to reach me." She smiled as he walked away, as she realized that the chances of an extremely hot Air Force officer calling her were somewhat remote. She could have her dreams, though.

But right now, she had something far bigger to think about. First Lieutenant Russell T. Stanton would have to wait. Hopefully not too long, though.

Chapter Seventeen

Ninety minutes later, Paige sat on the bank fifty yards from their home and took another swig of the D.T. Darkkin & Sons whiskey she had taken from Rachel's party as she heard Jack come up behind her; she knew the unique sound of his boots on cold ground well.

She knew the brand of the whiskey by the distinctive hexagonal shape of the bottle and its pungent smell. It was, amazingly, the only whiskey bottle computer-designed by a renowned nuclear scientist, she remembered for some reason. She also had heard that particular distinguished nuclear scientist had consumed many bottles of said liquid as well as monumental quantities of other mind-altering substances in his colorful lifetime. Well, Joe Kennedy made a bunch of money importing spirits, the history books said, so the Presidential precedent had already been set.

She knew her father must be looking at her in amazement, as this was one of her favorite places to do things she wasn't supposed to do. He wouldn't say anything for a few minutes, but she knew the drill by heart.

"The aurora is really bright tonight. I wish you could see it," Jack said.

"I have seen it with the helmet, but sometimes I think I can sense it. Maybe I draw energy from it? What do you think?"

"Don't know. Probably not. The aurora is just the solar wind being deflected by the Earth's magnetosphere. But, your energy, well, it comes from somewhere else."

"Have we any new terrific theories on that?"

"Nope. We don't know where it originates. Probably right in front of us. Or another dimension. We may never know which."

"I guess so. A problem for another day." She crushed a lump of coal with her left hand, which produced nothing more valuable than smaller pieces of liquefied carbon as she felt the slimy black residue on her hand. "Dang it! You know, it is really not possible to make diamonds this way, like Mom's dumb comic books say."

"Huh? What are you blabbering about now, Paige?"

"*Gravi-Golfer* used his power of gravity manipulation to crush coal into diamonds in one episode of *Dr. Wendy's Science Squad.* He said it takes over a million joules of energy per square centimeter, which should be no problem for me, but it does not work in real life. Mom told me that, but I wanted to find out for myself. She said the process needs a uniform container, which my hand is not, it is too irregular. And time—and the process cannot be hurried. So that show is so full of crap. All you get are hot, smaller pieces of molten coal from the pressure. Yecchh."

"You should listen to your mother. Once in a great while she has something profound to say. And if you really want my opinion of that ridiculous old show, well—" She heard him come closer to her. "And do you think that's a productive thing you're doing right now?"

"Trying to get rich by making diamonds from coal? Why not? Beats the odds of playing the lottery. There is no law against that."

"Not that—the thing you're doing with your other hand, with that crazy-shaped whiskey bottle. And there *is* a law against that. MIP. Minor in possession of alcohol."

"Huh. It is 'crazily-shaped,' not 'crazy-shaped.'"

"You know what I mean."

"Hey, and this ain't just *any* old alcohol, but D.T. Darkkin & Sons whiskey, the best there is, the advertisements say. I am no connoisseur, of course, given my limited financial means."

"That's a matter of opinion about its quality. I am sure your mother would have input on that topic."

"Like either of you are experts. This is no worse than some of the other stuff I have done."

"I probably don't know a fraction of the things you've done and don't really want to, either."

She took another swig of the aromatic liquid. "Then call the cops, pops. Rat on your dear dainty daughter."

"Listen to yourself: you seem to care about the law, yet you're breaking it right now, as you have many times before. I shouldn't let you do that. On the other hand, I don't feel like bailing you out tonight. It's embarrassing. Wait until you have a child, you'll remember this, and you'll finally get what you deserve."

"Would that not be a hoot? Me with a child?" She sputtered on the liquid and laughed. "And *'you should not let me do that?'* Yeah, like you could stop me. Give me a break." She took another swig of whiskey as she heard him pull out his dog-eared Bible from his pocket. "Is it going to be Exodus 20:12? *'Honor thy mother and thy father?'"*

"No. Luke 12:34: *'For unto whomsoever much is given, of him shall much be required.'"*

She threw down the molten coal and heard it sizzle on the cold ground as she slapped herself with her right hand. "Oh, jeez. I have only heard that one about five thousand times too. I prefer the other one, though, that Mom likes."

"Which is?"

She thrust her left fist proudly into the sky. "Malachi 3:2: *'But who may endure the day of his coming? And who shall stand when he appeareth? For he is like a refiner's fire, and like fullers' soap.'* I am coming, and folks shall surely need to watch out for me."

He shoved her gently on the shoulder. "Listen here—I don't think we wanted you to be threatening. You need to save lives, not be on television and in every available media modality like the famous daughter of the Princeton and MIT grad who designed that stupid whiskey bottle. While that might be okay for her, that isn't the girl we raised."

"I do not want to either, but I want respect. How can I possess it otherwise? So far, the plan does not seem to be working."

"Patience. Respect is earned, not taken. You, of all people, should understand that. Remember that God will reward a cheerful giver a thousand-fold."

"The Bible has an answer for everything, it seems," she said snidely. "Seems rather convenient."

"You've got that right. It was the greatest book ever written, given to us by Him. Maybe someday you'll actually believe it."

She crossed her arms in defiance. "Well, you have me at a disadvantage, given your knowledge of scripture."

"It's not anything you can't master, either, if you tried just a little bit harder."

"I should give it a try in a few years." She jumped up about twenty feet and hit the ground hard, blowing a cloud of soft snow into the air. "But, is there really a God, Dad, or is he just a fad?"

"What do you mean? You're asking me? How can you ask such a crazy thing?"

"Well, you said you had doubts when you were younger, that you did not believe until you were really old, in your forties."

He sighed. "Thanks a lot."

"I mean, please help me understand it. Mom, the supposed big brain, gets mad at me when I even question it as, to her, God is a fundamental particle of matter like a proton. That makes absolutely no sense. You have to do better than that."

"But therein lies the riddle: you can't quantitate it, honey. It's a strong faith in something intangible that you can't ever prove. That is *real* faith. I suppose you were the main reason I started believing in the first place."

"Me?" She paused for a few seconds. "Why me?"

"The answer should be obvious, come on."

"Yeah, I guess that makes sense. But about that—I have never asked this before, but have you or Mom ever—"

"Ever what?"

"Wondered—if I had been sent from God himself?"

"What? Could you be the daughter of God, is that what you're asking? The second coming of Jesus Christ?"

"You just said I was unique, so I guess that is my meaning. Is it not logical, and were you not just comparing me to Him?"

"That's rather arrogant, isn't it, Paige? You really think you're in that category? I believe you're unique, not *holy*. The two things are just a bit different." She couldn't see him but knew he was scowling. "Sometimes, you do act like your mom and biological dad. Two of the most egotistical people I ever knew."

"I did not intend it to come out like way, but surely you have contemplated that."

"Yeah, you *did* intend to be a smart-aleck. Don't lie to me."

She sighed. "Okay, yes, I did—but just answer my question."

He put his hand on her shoulder. "Yes, at one time, I did, but no longer, as this simple pastor came to a conclusion. For one thing, Jesus was immaculately conceived. You—let's just say I knew your dad pretty well, and it didn't quite happen that way."

She pulled away. "Hey, that is really messed up. I do not mean that, come on. And Mom is certainly much stronger than average, but there has to be something 'extra' in my DNA besides their fine meiotic contributions."

"I wish I knew, Paige. Many have prophesized that Christ is coming again. Soon, it will be two thousand years since His death. 2029 is the next Jubilee year when many say He shall return."

"And? What has your profound wisdom concluded?" She sat on the soft snow bank and tilted her head up towards the sky.

"I don't know for sure, Paige, but I don't think you and J.C. are even in the same universe, but I don't know everything. Jesus had the power to cure disease, to save lives, to perform miracles that science cannot explain."

"Huh. You cannot explain me, either."

He sat down behind her on the soft snow. "Let me finish, dear. I know you cared for little Judy Patterson, but there was nothing you could do to help in the end. You have remarkable physical abilities, certainly, but you can't do anything that we would consider supernatural or that can't be explained somehow by science."

"Two thousand years ago, the science we have today would have been considered 'supernatural.' So maybe I am an ancestor or something."

He shook his head. "This, from a girl who doesn't even believe in God most of the time? Yes, your powers are of science that we don't fully understand. Well, maybe your mom does. But for some unknown reason, you're here with us. Don't know how or why, but here you are."

"Sometimes I think you do know how but will not tell me."

"You're imagining things."

"And I hope you're right about me not being a Savior, as I neither want nor deserve that responsibility. But will I ever die? Am I immortal?"

"That remains to be seen."

"I do not want that, Dad. I do not want to live forever after all the people I care about have died."

"You can't do anything about that, and we don't know. You seem to have aged—appearance-wise, anyway—just like a normal person. What that means in the future is uncertain, given your penchant for risk-taking behavior." He rapped his finger on the whiskey bottle. "But I do know this: your future shouldn't include drinking that God-awful booze, the Devil's brew, made by those over-the-top Tennessee hillbillies."

"I was wondering when you would bring that up again." She took another sip. "Right, like you never drank the stuff or did bad things like I have."

"That's not the point, and you know it."

She puffed out her ample chest in defiance. "And, for your information, they do not even make the stuff in Tennessee any longer, as it was sold out to some giant beverage conglomerate in Brussels. More money for our esteemed President in the buyout. Like she needs it."

"I'm glad you are wasting time keeping track of those details. D.T. Darkkin & Sons: a real Fortune 500 company. What a bunch of hillbilly losers."

"Yeah, so? You act like you know them. Anyway, it was kind of bland, not much kick to it. I guess I could have been polite and offered you some." She inhaled the rest of the bottle's liquid into her lungs, took out a Zippo lighter, and expelled the entire contents she had aspirated, setting the aerosolized alcohol on fire in a blaze of glory, knowing he was safely behind her. "Flame breath. Cool."

"Impressive, but useless. At least you're not trying smoking again. That was real mature."

She smiled. "Yeah, that was not so great, either. I do not see what the big deal is. I am older and wiser for having tried it, though."

"Seriously, though, what's it like?"

"What? Smoking? I cannot believe you do not know."

He laughed. "No, being you. Aren't you ever worried that you might someday encounter the thing that can hurt you?"

She shook her head. "I have no time to think about stuff like that. Life is too short, being such a worrywart. I wrecked some old bike I found and smashed into the base of a mountain at what, one hundred twenty miles an hour? I did not know I could even ride a bike, but I can, I guess, and I decided to go mountain biking at night and went over Cargg's Cliff. Message to self: blind girls should *not* ride bikes off mountains."

"Waitaminnit—I guess I somehow missed that one. When did that happen?"

"A year or so ago, it took me about an hour to find my way back home after the seven-hundred foot drop."

"Lord—how did you know how far you fell?"

She raised her left fist into the air. "Physics! I finally discovered a use for it. I timed my fall until I hit and figured it out. I also impacted head first, which gave me a bald spot for a few weeks."

"So that's why you were wearing that dumb wig a while back. I thought it was another teen phase."

"No, it had a practical purpose. But worry not, no one saw me, it was dark. It was so cool, though. I could have stopped my own fall, but I just wanted to know what it felt like."

"I'll just bet it was. Why would you even do something like that? Ride a bike off a cliff? Are you insane?"

"I did not know the cliff was there; it just sort of happened. Jeez, like I would do that on purpose, I ain't no dummy. I had to wear a hat every day to cover it up."

"It's hard to tell sometimes. How did you even get the bike up there?"

"I rode it part of the way and carried it the rest, duh. So, if you get my meaning, I am not worried about some dumb old bottle of Darkkin whiskey. I have endured far worse, you know."

"No, I don't want to know, thanks. I wonder, though, what it's like to not know fear, to not know pain?"

She threw a snowball softly in his direction. "Hey, how do you know the pain or fears I have? You do not know everything. I may have never experienced physical pain, but I know the pain of rejection. People laughing at me. The way they probably look at me, but I do not know that 'cause I cannot see them."

"They don't really want to make fun. They respect you."

She shook her head. "Do not kid me. I am merely an invisible reject from society. And why the hell are we living in this God-forsaken place, anyway? I may not be a genius the caliber of Mom, but I get it—this is some kind of trial I must get through, some preparation for what dangers will inevitably come my way."

"You are far wiser than your mom ever was."

"As I said, I am not unintelligent. Had we lived somewhere else, someone might have found out about me. Exploit me and put me in a test tube, right?"

"That was one possible outcome, yes. Not likely out here."

"How exactly do you think anyone could have forced me to do anything?"

"You weren't always as you are now. Your strength levels have increased exponentially over the last two years to a point it's hard to know what your limit is, if there even is one."

"So why is it so different now?"

"Trust me that it is. If you go through with this to do your Taraqi rescue, you will soon meet someone who can protect you from all the things we've worried about. At least for a few more years, after which you will likely have built a following that no one can derail if that's the way you want to play it. Should you be a secret weapon or a super-celebrity? You just need to do it if that's what you want, and get out of Dodge since the suit will protect your identity."

"Bummer."

"You know that's what you have to do, and without it—well, you know there's no way for you to see that we know of."

"That you know of? Do you think there is another way? That would be preferable."

He shook his head. "I don't know, that's beyond my intellectual level, and apparently your mom's too. But I have to reluctantly agree that the time is now, even if it means we may not see you for a very long time. It's been eighty-three years since the only other actual use of nuclear weapons against human beings. No one wants to see it again."

"Agreed. But who is it I will meet and greet?"

"Someone with an almost unlimited ability to do things we can only dream of, with the ability to shape the world."

She slapped herself in the face. "What a deal—it sounds too good to be true. I guess the world does not need me, then, with this super-duper world-shaping person out there who can fix everything. It makes me want to sing."

He grabbed her firmly by the arm. "No, you don't get it. The existence of this person is *exactly* why you're needed, as the world has become unbalanced. The two of you may be able to accomplish together what neither can possibly do alone. You have a destiny."

"Explain this puzzling paradox: I need this person, but without me, this person will run amok and destroy life on Earth as we know it? I am needed by this person just as much as he needs me?"

"Something like that. And I *didn't* specify the person's gender."

She thought pensively, pondering. "A curious riddle."

"Nothing is for free, and there are drawbacks—but under the strange circumstances of your existence, this is a better path than others. Understand one thing, though: this person loves America dearly, but also herself most of all. She may try to exploit you, too—not to harm you, but to further her agenda, which should be obvious to all but the most naïve of individuals."

"What's that? World domination? Hahaha. How corny."

"Pretty much, yeah. And it's *not* funny at all."

"It is *not* funny? You say such few humorous things that I have to strike when the iron is hot."

"No, it could be tragic. History has not been kind to those who tried to take over the world. A lot of bad things happen in the process if you recall. We're already part way there, Paige."

"How philosophical."

"But you're a big girl now. Big enough to take care of yourself and peacefully coexist—because you both need each other, now more than ever, for the future of mankind. You both need to put aside your stubbornness and make peace with each other."

"I am to make peace with a person I have never met? Huh. That is an interesting concept which requires careful pontification." She threw the whiskey bottle towards the sky with a mighty heave and wished she could watch it as it melted due to air friction in the atmosphere and slapped herself on the cheek. "Wow, that is totally profound, like you are channeling the bouncy purple guy."

"Hey, the 'purple guy' is real to your Mom, and he's not a hallucination. She has the ability to perceive things that normal humans can't. I know you think she's nuts sometimes, and she has her issues to be sure, but it's true."

She shook her head. "I am not convinced of that. But are you going to tell me who this mythical person is?"

"Not yet, but I think your meeting is inevitable, as you are on a collision course. You think your mom is a tough customer? You have no idea what you may be in store for. And if I told you, you wouldn't believe it anyway."

"A cliffhanger! I cannot wait for the scintillating conclusion. But, about 'much being expected'—can I really make a difference in the world, Dad?"

"I appreciate you calling me that, but I'm not your father. He was a brilliant and brave man. I'm only a fraction of who he was."

"To me, you are the strongest, and you are the best father any girl could have had, Dad, as you are no cad."

He gave her a hug. "I really appreciate that, Paige. That's all I ever wanted."

"But, I mean, can I be that world-changer? I am no genius; I cannot do the math or computer things you or Mom can. I just hope to get into college. I guess I have not tried very hard."

"Of course you can. You have a few extra talents we don't."

"Like those things could help me get into a university or really do what I want."

"Not your physical gifts. You are brilliant at history, at arguing and proving a point. I told you this as a little girl. Your mom can't do any of those things."

"Things that are important for what I really want to do with my life, as I cannot just live here forever. Can I change the world? Not with my gifts, but with who I am as a person?"

"I just said so. You can do pretty much whatever you want."

"I do not mean with that—I mean with leadership. I can be President when I am thirty-five, right?"

"Yeah, but you'd actually be thirty-eight since the first election when you are eligible will be 2048 unless you were Speaker of the House before that and the President and Vice President croaked in the year 2045. A long time away, Paige. There's just a few details to work out, mind you. You're a high school senior. You have no idea how to be President, let alone even take care of yourself."

"Is that a note of sarcasm in your voice?"

"Absolutely. You picked up on that way better than your mom would've."

"People misunderstand me. I admire President Mendoza for the great personal difficulties she has overcome to make us the richest nation, but I disagree with many of her policies; that does not mean I disrespect her. Why does Mom speak so badly of her?"

"Who knows what goes on in your mom's weird mind, Paige? What a freaking mess." He shook his head. "Your mother is a very complex individual. But no one agrees on everything. It's natural to have some differences with even the greatest of leaders. Trust me that she's the real deal, despite the fact her family made those lousy bottles of whiskey in a backwater Tennessee distillery."

"One cannot pick and choose one's family. Did you vote for her in 2020 and 2024?"

"Yes, of course I did—I may not agree with her past oddball extracurricular activities, but they were harmless, really. In the end, she matured and has become a fine leader."

"You state that with such conviction, that there could have been no other choice. But Mom says she wants to rule the world—that she is self-serving, with Mendoza Multinational and all of its trillions in her back pocket, bankrolling everything. Thoughts?"

"While I'm no politician or economic analyst—"

"That is a massive understatement."

"Let me finish. I don't think M2 is even relevant to her today. The President doesn't own any of that company currently, as she sold the twenty percent she inherited from her brother back to Nicholas Stannous when she ran for President, and her husband sold back his sister's other portion to his niece, so Stannous and Isabel Mendoza own all of it now. It was worth less than a tenth then what it is now. Your mom doesn't follow the news very well, nor is she very good with money."

"Not relevant? Hardly. I am sure M2 contributes substantially to the campaign in order to extend her reign."

"Nick Stannous is a staunch Democrat and Saleh supporter."

"Huh, that is only because they went to high school together. I betcha his wife is not; I get wind of the news, so now who is being naïve? She was a featured speaker at the Republican convention. With the change in the Constitution, the President is now limited to three terms, not two. Is it true that she wants to be Empress?"

"That is a vast exaggeration, Paige. All politicians have financial backers, and most Presidents are wealthy, as she is in her own right—as I mentioned, she actually owned thirty percent of M2 and sold it off in 2020, because a President cannot be an owner of such a company that influences the American economy. And the stock in D.T. Darkkin & Sons, which was sold off in that merger. Of course, M2 is worth ten times that now. It costs many millions of dollars just to run for Prez these days. So there's nothing unusual about that. And, as far as being Empress, she's practically that already. Why would she want something she already has?" She felt his face and noticed that tears had come to the kind man's eyes. "She isn't the narcissistic person you and Mom think her to be. What she does, she does for a reason. You may not believe that, but someday, likely soon, you'll understand."

"What is it, Dad? What is wrong?"

"Wendy Mendoza has goodness in her, dear Paige, like all of God's creatures. There are many things you don't know about her. She spent her medical career in pediatric rehabilitation hospitals, helping the less fortunate, don't ever forget that."

"And she did cartoon cat voices on her days off, when she was not on that idiotic superhero TV show. That sure helped a lot of people—not. What a waste of time, almost a crime."

"Didn't it, though? Don't make fun. Those shows provided enjoyment to a lot of children. While you may think it superficial and shallow, there was a method to the madness. Hard life lessons change us and our priorities. Despite her very human foibles, we are much better off with her leadership than without. Few people could have better channeled the power of nuclear fusion to build our economy and restore freedom to this world in such an amazingly short time while keeping it in one piece."

"It is in one piece for now, but Mom says the world shall end soon. Is there not some truth to this?"

"It's an exaggeration. Her bark's worse than her bite unless you're in the obligate path between her and a cheeseburger."

"How do you know anything about her? You speak with such authority like you are some kind of chief executive expert or historian now? She is a vegetarian now, anyway."

"Why?" He paused for a moment. "Because I just know, dear—I have met her."

"*What?*" She shook her head and sneered. "You have met one of the greatest Presidents of them all? Liar. You are making that up, grownup. You two hardly run in the same circles."

"It was a long time ago, when she was just a regular person, so she probably had long forgotten about when she met me. I wouldn't matter anyway. There are many things you don't know about me as well, Paige. You don't know everything just because you're eighteen." Jack put his hand on her shoulder. "We'd better get going. You've got a lot of work to do."

"Wait a minute, do not drop that bomb, and then leave. Mom does not even like the one who history says was one of the most brilliant minds of all time—the one whose theoretical predictions of the periodic table gave the world the long-lived transuranium element mendozium. Said she wasted her youth, trying to be an entertainer and athlete rather than focus on the seriousness of life. That she died with her goals unfulfilled."

"That's not surprising. We always tend to dislike people who remind us of ourselves."

"*Whaaat?* Mom and the amazing Bonnie Mendoza alike?" She let out a hearty guffaw. "They are *nothing* alike, and Mom has no tangible goals to speak of, other than writing garbage on the walls."

"Right. And we don't know that she was unfulfilled. It is likely she did those other things because they made her happy. Not everything is about work and achievement all the time."

"None of that was in the movie; was it just a bunch of phooey?"

"Come on. Movies aren't real, Paige."

"And I assume you had met her, too, just like the President?"

"Maybe. Like I said, you don't know everything."

She shook her head. "I do not believe you."

"I didn't think you would. No matter, it isn't important now."

"But was the movie true, Dad?"

"I don't know. Never saw it. Don't like them much, and way too expensive."

"I snuck into the one I saw. Mom says the real person was much more flawed than what was in the movie, like she knew anything about her. She said the screenplay took those things out."

"Historians were trying to be kind. We all have flaws, including the President. We tend to want to remember our heroes for their great deeds."

"Hmmm. I think that is a bad idea. We should remember them for their deficiencies, as that is what makes them humans and great leaders."

"That's sure another way of looking at it—the power of negative thinking. Good one, Paige. Leadership in action."

"That is not what I meant, and you know it."

"This week you were eighteen. Like we said, you can do what you want with your life."

"Huh. I could have done it before. I do not believe you or Mom could have stopped me."

"I doubt you can do it very effectively without the cybernetic helmet. But it's your life, and you are eighteen now, so it's legal, and I can't get arrested for child abuse now. If you want to go save the world, it's up to you. Not an obligation or even a suggestion."

"What choice do I have, then?"

"Just because you have a gift doesn't mean you have to use it. You can go to college, go work in a factory, teach school, work at Taco Palace or Caffeine Bean, be a hobo, or do anything you want, as long as it doesn't hurt you or others. There are geniuses living in refrigerator boxes in Los Angeles and mediocre intellects making big bucks on Wall Street. Most people are like us—somewhere in between. This is America. Remember, you can't be everywhere at once, and there will always be something you can't stop. I hope you can deal with that when the time comes. You've got a lot of life to live yet."

"I sure hope so."

Two weeks earlier, she had put on the Russian cybernetic helmet on, flew to the middle of the Continental U.S. as a test run, and threw the three golf balls at their targets. Mom had picked them out for some reason. She could throw them with unerring accuracy, she knew. But these places didn't mean anything to her. Why throw them at a gravesite in Tennessee and statues of two dead people, one of them a football coach? She neither knew nor cared much about football anyway, or Tennessee, or Indiana.

Someone had surely seen her before, which apparently had been the idea. To let people know that she was coming. Dad said the targets would have meaning to a special person, whose name he refused to reveal. As he said, she would learn it soon enough.

But tomorrow, a new day would be dawning, for both her and the fifty-five United States of America.

• • •

Paige went to her small bedroom and felt under the bed for the old toys she had kept. Her favorites, the old dolls, the cars, the trucks—her mom and dad had tried to give her a happy life. She had no reference point, no peers, really, to know how her life had stacked up to that of others, but she had done enough charity work to know that she was a pretty lucky girl. Not just to have the required material things, but to have parents who cared.

But she had no one to really talk to who was different. Mom was unusual, but it was usually a one-sided conversation; she was lost in her little world most of the time. Dad said she wasn't always this way, but since the accident, it's what she had become, apparently. No one talked about that accident or how it happened.

She held a doll in her hand as she realized there was no going back. No one was making her give up her childhood possessions or go into adulthood so quickly. Child to world hero in one instant. It was her choice, but not one that her parents necessarily supported. But they did it for her, with technology that probably cost many millions of dollars. All they told her was that they had done nothing illegal, like stealing the money; it all had come from an anonymous benefactor. Who in the world had that much money to throw away? Did they harbor some deep secret they had kept from her? Despite her abilities, it would be somewhat easy to hide stuff like that from a sightless person.

They tried to provide things a blind child would enjoy: musical instruments of every type they could afford, a keyboard, music collection, things with textures. She held them dear, but they were just possessions. Why was leaving them behind so hard, then? It wasn't them, so much, as what it signaled—a comfortable life. She somehow knew she wasn't destined for comfort with the genes she had been given.

She knew she would find out a lot more down the road she didn't know about.

She didn't remember anything before the accident that killed her father and made her unable to see. She thought about her biological father and what he would be like today. He was tall, Mom said, six-two—with sandy brown hair and blue eyes, Jack had said. Why didn't she remember anything? Maybe that was best. She couldn't change that fact anyway, and remembering wouldn't bring him back.

It was odd, never knowing what it was like to feel pain, to be sick, or tired, for the most part. Sure, she was mentally fatigued at times after doing homework all night (due to extreme procrastination), but she was never really physically tired.

She stroked her favorite doll's hair gently as tears came to her eyes. What if she died tomorrow night? She didn't know if that was possible, but her parents cared about her. But if she didn't, someone else would surely die, and millions more after that, if the intelligence forces didn't find him in time. She had to make an unselfish choice for them; what she wanted had to be secondary.

Dad said he really didn't grow up until his forties. She had read about the President's famous husband, one of the biggest playboys of the world, until he decided to grow up and be there for her after *Darkkday*. The President herself was a pediatric rehabilitation specialist, so she had some ambition early on—but spent a lot of time on her "side interests" of television, singing, cartoons, weightlifting, and the Olympics, before she became Governor of California, that is. So why did she need to grow up at eighteen when these great people didn't mature until their forties?

She could lead a simple life, be a teacher like her mom. She really didn't have any desire to be a pastor like Dad. But she always realized that the choice ultimately was hers. It wasn't the excitement that she craved; she generally was happy. But to waste a gift, like her dad said—what was the right thing to do with what God had given her? What was the best thing to do with them? Right, like God even existed. Most of the time she doubted in Him, and figured that most teenagers had questioned faith at some time. The problem was, she wasn't "most teenagers."

Why did she feel that she was saying goodbye? She just knew she would come back in one piece. Maybe it was symbolic. Saying goodbye to her childhood, for she knew she could never come back.

Depending on what happened, she knew that the day would come when she might not be able to return home. And then she would really be on her own. Or would she? That would never entirely be possible, nor should it be, in an ideal world. Everyone should need somebody. She would always be dependent on others to help; who those "others" would be, she didn't know. Dad seemed to know there would be someone to take over for them when she moved away. He could take care of Mom, who had problems of her own. She couldn't imagine her mother living by herself, most simple tasks of daily living beyond her reach.

She shoved the box of toys back under her bed, realizing that toys were childish. Her mom probably would enjoy playing with them, as immature as she seemed these days. Oh, well, Mom had her own toys, and you couldn't pick your parents. She sighed and went downstairs to contemplate the final hours before her maiden transcontinental journey.

Chapter Eighteen

Paige and Jack stood in the small living room of their house as he put his hand on her shoulder.

"Are you really sure you want to do this, Paige?" Jack asked. "You can back out if you want, and maybe that would be better for all of us. All the preparations we've made may not make a difference. This may be a horrific mistake."

She shook her head in amazement. "Would that be better for America and Alan Thomasson? I do not think so. What good am I if I cannot do things like this?"

"You aren't responsible for the world. There will always be things like this that come up. You can't do everything."

"Maybe, but today I can do *something* for the world. That makes a difference."

"I don't know what your eventual destiny is. Your mother is very reckless, and I should've never gone along with this dangerous process from the start. What have I done? I should have my head examined."

"Well, it is far too late now, I would think, to see a shrink, do not be such a fink."

"No, it's never too late. Maybe it would be better for you if we changed our minds. We can't predict the future, you know. You can't save everyone."

"I can save one person who would otherwise perish in miserable fashion. In addition, many more will surely die in nuclear destruction, and I am saving them too. It is what America needs, and you said I could do what I wanted when I was eighteen. This is it."

She felt him put his hand on her shoulder. "Look, I was eighteen once and not very responsible then. But you have a tremendous responsibility regarding what you do with your powers. You can't wait until you're my age."

"Do you not think I know that, Dad? I am a child no longer."

"Being eighteen doesn't mean you know everything, and you are still a child, in many ways."

"Huh. That is your opinion, which does not make it so, and I now need to go."

"Maybe. But it's damn hazardous."

"How? You know that is not true."

"For starters, we don't know how the suit will function at supersonic speeds for prolonged periods, it's only been tried for a few thousand miles on the trips you made to the lower forty-eight States, Yukon Territory, or British Columbia; but a transoceanic flight is something different entirely. We think the suit can absorb radar waves from the military based on the technology I have to measure it, which I believe to be cutting-edge. We don't know for certain how well. Fortunately, today's military operates more on offense than defense, so I think we're okay."

"So what if it does not?"

"A few missiles in the face might not be fun because you know the suit isn't indestructible. It'll stand up to small arms fire, but not that. If the suit blows up, you're blind as a bat. Talk about hazardous."

"I am fast enough and have sufficient maneuverability to dodge them. No plane or missile can travel at Mach 6 or 7. The fastest fighter jet goes maybe Mach 2.7 for brief periods."

"I'm sure that's true; I just worry about this stuff. It takes you a couple of minutes to get up to that speed. Never done anything of this magnitude before. If that suit explodes, it could kill somebody. They also may have something we don't know about."

"Then it is time to find out. What choice do we have? Either that or many will die. If they kill Thomasson, then the whole country gets nuked with low-radius bombs. You want that on your conscience, man of the cloth?"

"The one who may die may be *you*. That suit is forty years old."

She clapped her hands together, making a loud cracking noise. "Then I will go out with a bang. I will be lost, maybe, but dead, never." Becoming a hero had a price. Right, like she knew anything about being a hero.

"Don't just think about yourself. Your mass flying at that velocity is extremely dangerous to everyone. What if you somehow lose control?"

"I will not. Why would you think that would happen?"

"Because we don't know everything about your biology. I hope you don't crash into something. Our insurance probably doesn't cover property damage of that magnitude. Ah, I guess we have bigger things to worry about."

"Let us go, then, before I change my mind."

• • •

They went to their large underground room two hundred feet from the small house, underneath a reinforced steel door covered by a foot of dirt. Paige had excavated it with her own hands, and it went sixty feet underground. At least she had saved some money by doing it herself. It was heated by natural geothermal energy, as it got pretty cold in central Alaska in fall and winter.

They then walked down the steel staircase as he went over to the computer console and turned it on. Most of the money from a rich anonymous benefactor went here. Power was expensive, and tying into power lines and hiding the massive consumption from the authorities required cash. Luckily, he knew someone high up in the power industry who was more than happy to help and asked nothing in return and asked no questions.

Satellite telescope and supercomputer rental cost even more, but the man with billions of dollars to burn in Aurora City gladly provided the world's best, as well, but Paige didn't know any of that. The man's glamorous wife was probably helping behind the scenes, with no questions asked. Unlike most of their business dealings, there wasn't much of a return on investment on this one. But there was more to life than money.

He watched her put on the dull grey exoskeleton, which appeared very unimpressive. As she had gotten taller and more filled-out, it was a tight fit, especially in the chest area. Most of the suit was superfluous anyway; it was only the helmet that really mattered. Jack thought it puzzling that the body that could withstand anything which had been thrown at it could mold and conform to the suit, but it was hard to figure how it all worked.

Besides the helmet, the rest of it was for decoration, and to provide aerodynamic stability, radar stealth, and anonymity, of course. No one would suspect that a blind teenager from Alaska could fly at Mach 6 or 7 within a vintage Russian battle exoskeleton, one that only a handful of living people had ever seen, up until a couple of months ago (when many others had seen it on test runs). He warily remembered that one of those few "living people" lived at 1600 Pennsylvania Avenue in Washington. He realized that this person already knew about this. The cat would be out of the bag soon, anyway. It surely already was.

"*Энергия на.*" He knew that the world of vision was again hers, supplied by the Russian technology that was decades ahead of its time in the late 1980s, and rivaled anything that existed today. She knew that she must have been able to see as a young girl, or else the images wouldn't make any sense to her. The readouts were in Russian, projected into her mind with amazing clarity. Petra had tinkered with the sensors, which once required direct contact with skin (meaning she earlier had to shave her head); now, it worked almost as well with a full head of hair. How her mathematics teacher mother had the skills to do that was unknown to him or Paige.

She said she didn't want to know about some of those things.

Her body seemed to repel any outside forces, and she had to concentrate on allowing the helmet electronics to communicate with her brain. No problem, since her mom was Russian and spoke it fluently, and so did she. Mom could speak at least twenty languages, but she could not. There was no purpose to that. Computers and universal translators could easily serve that function. Mom seemed to be obsessed with many things that had little importance.

Ironically, her vision with the helmet far transcended normal human perception and was good enough to see in total darkness and see far into the infrared and ultraviolet spectra. The auditory sensors could amplify hearing to anything beyond current technology; despite its wealth, the United States was focused on energy and weaponry technology more than advanced detection devices, as sheer unprecedented power didn't necessarily require clandestine operations. Her augmented sensory abilities were enough to find out where the Taraqi rebels had hidden Alan Thomasson.

She had amazing capabilities that far transcended what the maker, Russian robotics expert Viktor Vladimirov, could have ever imagined. Not that Paige believed such a person actually existed, but he'd spent a good deal of time with the guy back in the day.

"Coordinates: Maraka, Taraq," he said.

"*Координаты.* Flight time?" she asked.

He punched up some numbers on the quantum supercomputers, which somehow had been given to him by his anonymous benefactor. "From here, at Mach 6, about an hour and a half. Remember, it will take you about three or four minutes to achieve that speed. You don't have to fly back here with him, only to reach American soil, across the eastern New Persian border in Freedom City."

"Then we had better get going." She never feared what would happen if the old late 1980s electronics somehow went out; she knew she could survive without oxygen, perhaps indefinitely, but she still needed water. There wasn't much snow in the desert.

He had seen her do it several times but still stood in awe as his daughter, wearing the battle suit, walked over to the exit tunnel, then repelled gravity and hovered, then took off slowly as she accelerated. He had no idea how any of that worked. Every time he had it figured out, something else stumped him. Petra had muttered to him about dark energy and how it could repel gravitational fields, the concept to her apparently being as simple as that of a flashlight; he could grasp the theoretical concept of dark energy, but no one could ever explain to him *where the damn energy came from.*

It had to be an enormous amount; he estimated that moving that mass at Mach 6 required at least ten billion joules per second, or gigawatts; no current or anticipated future technology could provide that with something so small. A plane the size of Air Force One required about 1 million joules per second, or megawatts, to fly, but it weighed a million pounds. The new M2 mendozium reactors were capable of 50-60 gigawatts, but they were almost half as large as an old fission reactor, not three hundred pounds.

What if Paige's incredible energy source could be harnessed? And what it was used for the purpose many leaders wanted fantastic energy—weapons? In Paige's hands, dark energy could benefit the world. In the hands of others, it would mean supreme power, enough to *rule* the world. One person, in particular, didn't need much more power to be the ruler of Earth. But would it be useful for scientific needs, such as space travel?

And was there an effect on energy fields anywhere else on

Earth? Petra said it was minimal, that her powers stemmed from dark matter, that, when combined with dark energy, was the mysterious stuff that over ninety percent of the universe was made of—that she was the Dark Star: *Stella Scura* in Italian. Why Petra had chosen Italian, he didn't know. Apparently, that was Petra's favorite language, despite her having no Italian heritage. Also, it was a catchy alliterative name, a preference mother and daughter both shared.

He watched intently as he realized again that the *power wasn't in the suit*. The armor's only (albeit vital) function was to make her more aerodynamic and to replace her lack of vision. It was made of a substance over twice as hard as diamond, but Paige Marshall's hide was infinitely tougher than that, he surmised. Just *how* tough was yet to be determined. How that worked made no sense to him, either.

For most of his life, he wasn't a spiritual man. Many would've said he'd squandered his potential, bouncing from job to job with no real responsibility. He cheated his way through college (and helped others to do the same) even though he was brilliant. He and Paige's biological father pulled all kinds of crazy stunts that should have gotten them both expelled.

So why did he choose this life after wasting his youth? Because every girl needs a father. Hers was his best friend, and he was dead. Her mom once was one of the most brilliant raw intellects in the world, but one who also now behaved like a fifty-something child incapable of dealing with everyday life, or her daughter, for that matter. He was the best man at their wedding and promised his friend he would take care of her if something happened. It did.

But the man now called Jack Marshall "found the light" after the horrific attack on U.S. soil known as *Darkkday*. He knew now there was a God, and that God had created all things, good and bad. No proof, just faith. His daughter didn't share those convictions, but he had hope that she would, eventually.

At least he could relish in this thought: man caused that terrible disaster, but from the ashes rose *Stella Scura*, a gift to humanity, likely from the stars. He had no proof of that, but it was almost twenty years ago when he was the first to observe the woman now called Petra beginning to exhibit vastly increased sensory perception and strength days after having been injected with something rumored to be mutated human DNA, supposedly procured from

Titan's Ontario Lacus. Now he wasn't so sure where it really had come from, as he felt there was no way that this could have happened randomly, and it was likely alien in origin. That gift was about to make history.

It was also time to alter some computer files, just a little bit. Someone important he used to know might want to know who this is in order to avoid starting World War III. He contemplated if she already did. Would that be possible?

A stupid question: of course it was. He had, over the years, learned to respect that this person was far more intelligent and resourceful than anyone had ever thought. That was what scared him. Would she be Paige's ally or adversary?

This person would be like Paige's grandfather, a strange man whom she had never known—probably a combination of both.

• • •

The White House
Oval Office
Washington, DC
1710 hours EST

Jay Mendoza felt the piercing sound in his head, he couldn't get it out on this late afternoon in his wife's office. He was a bit tired, but this was something he had never experienced before. Usually they came in his sleep, not in the evening.

And this one was a doozy.

"What's wrong, Jay?" Wendy asked him as she got up from the Resolute desk.

"I feel like I'm flying again. I can't explain it. I hear a language, I think it's Russian."

"What?" She sat down her cup of coffee on the desk. "I think you need to lay off the caffeine and go lie down. I've got a meeting in a few minutes, anyway."

"This is more important than your stupid meeting about the new national health care benefits. The sounds, they're—Russian words, I'm sure of it. I'm flying across the ocean right now. West."

She walked over and gave him a hug. "You know that isn't true, hon. You'd better text Dr. Bobbi to make an appointment. I'm sorry, but I don't know what else to think. I know what it's like to not think properly."

"No way, don't compare this to anything you would have ever experienced." He looked at his watch. "Where is Alan Thomasson, do you think?"

"Somewhere in Taraq, we guess. Don't know where. If we did, we'd have him out by now."

"What time zone is that?"

"What? Are you serious?"

"Hell, yeah, do you think I'm joking?"

She looked at her Glycine Airman automatic 24-hour watch. "Zulu time plus 3." While she was no pilot, she clearly understood international time zones.

He shook his head. "I don't know what that means; I was never in the military or very good with time zones."

She sighed. "That's 0110 hours. I can't believe you haven't learned that by now."

"So, that means it's one AM there now?"

She nodded sarcastically. "Yes, 0110 is one-ten AM, brilliant, and Zulu time is 2210, or ten-ten PM. We are Eastern Standard Time, which is Zulu time minus 5, or 5:10 PM." She looked at him. "What the heck is wrong with you? You really do look sick. Maybe you should go lie down."

He walked to the window and looked towards the night sky. "Thomasson. *She* is on her way out there, to Taraq. Faster than any plane can possibly fly."

She shook her head. "There is *no* aircraft going out there that isn't there already, or else I'd know about it, and nothing that size can fly at that velocity. The Allied Nations wouldn't go out there, and China or Russia wouldn't dare. Who do you think it is, if not them?"

"Trust me—I'm *not* crazy. I can feel the air, it's weird. There is something fantastic about to happen. You have to believe me, Wendy. I'm not making this up. The Russian voices, the letters—I can see and hear them. It's *Aurora.*"

"Russians? No way." She looked at him for two minutes and stood up. "That can't be possible."

"Hell, yes, it is. You saw it yourself, in Solway."

"Taraq's halfway around the world." She thought for a few seconds. "But, for some reason, I may actually believe you." She went to the phone and pushed the red button. "Get the Joint Chiefs,

Ashburn, and Slabb in the situation room pronto. What? You'll probably know what it is by the time I get there." She grabbed his hand. "You need to come, too."

"Me? Why?"

"Because you seem to know more about it than anyone else. We both know there is one person who can speak twenty different languages, and any knowledge is better than what we have now. Nothing."

"How are we going to keep it a secret much longer, Wendy? Have you thought this through?"

She shook her head. "I don't know. None of this came with a script. I will just have to improvise, as usual."

Chapter Nineteen

A hellish prison in eastern Taraq
0100 Zulu Time

They were going to kill him soon, they had told the man in tattered clothes every hour of every day of his captivity, now six weeks in duration. They had wanted ten million dollars in ransom for him, but the United States of 2028 wasn't fond of paying off terrorists. Then they wanted ten million, then five, then two. He was now being discounted like a clearance item at Super-Mart. Apparently, the U.S. elite forces weren't able to find him either. He still held out hope they would, but that hope was waning quickly.

Why did they kidnap him? That was an easy question to answer; he was the brother of a Republican United States Senator from California; that was one step away from their most hated enemy: the former Governor of America's most populous state and now the most badass President the modern world had ever seen. The one loved by almost all the world.

That excluded the parts of the world that time had forgotten about, or she wanted to be destroyed, or both. Harry S. Truman may have dropped Fat Man and Little Boy atomic bombs on Japan, but this President was gutsy enough to take over three of the most belligerent countries in the world and make them into states. Either that or be blown off the map.

Taraq, despite being next to New Persia, was poor now, their oil worth almost nothing, thanks to the discovery of the unique transuranium element that could moderate the safe nuclear fusion of helium-3. The last substance was mined from the far side of the moon, which she boldly claimed as sovereign American soil to add yet another state. Anyone who disagreed with the President's actions was welcome to take it up with the U.S. military.

At one point, the Chinese might have threatened to oppose what she had done, but not now; while they were doing okay economically, they would not dare to pick a fight with the United States today. Forget military firepower, which the United States had enough of to destroy any enemy, but the USA had a more realistic recourse: sufficient financial clout to ruin any country it damn well pleased. That was where the real battles were fought these days.

He could only speculate as he debated what the generals and the President were deciding to do about his fate. Disintegrated by modern atomic weapons wasn't really how he wanted to end his fifty-two years. The new ones caused more pinpoint destruction and much less fallout than any previous versions, but that wouldn't matter to him. Vaporization was vaporization, any way you looked at it. It was doubtful that even modern science could reconstitute his molecules.

• • •

Stella Scura streaked through the sky at Mach 6.9 (8,520 kilometers per hour) and decelerated rapidly as she reached the edge of Taraqi air space. There was some commotion outside, more than usual around the compound; while she'd imagined the place was usually noisy all the time, this was different. She heard gunfire and yelling and wondered what was going to come next.

The suit would absorb the radar, and she could probably absorb it herself without the suit; she knew she was flying too fast for them to do anything about it anyway. One thing was for sure: they had never seen anything like this.

The sensors identified heat and the distinctive voice pattern of Alan Thomasson, which her dad had gotten from old video files; he was a Senator's brother, after all. She would signal the military after she had gotten him out. Once she got to him, there wasn't any way they could harm him. How that worked made no sense.

She first would take out any weapons they might use when

they made their getaway, might as well eliminate as many variables as possible. Using her body as a battering ram for the banks of missiles might damage the suit, so she found the next best thing: a large bank of boulders that she began flinging like volleyballs at the missile hangars as they exploded into flames.

She flew from the bank to the ground as the soldiers opened fire; the small-caliber weapons couldn't damage the fullerene composite shell. She made short work of the guards, as they scattered like fleas after they realized the weapons were ineffective, shouting undecipherable expletives. The helmet could decipher most languages as long as there was minimal background noise, even Arabic or Farsi, but it was far too noisy. And it didn't matter, anyway.

The Russian Vladimirov armor could take small arms fire and probably a few small missiles without harm. As long as the helmet functioned, it was okay with her; it could probably work with over half of the armor blasted away. That was okay, too, although she didn't want to fly around naked. The world was definitely more progressive these days, but it wasn't ready for that yet.

The most important thing was to get Alan Thomasson out of there with limited damage and no casualties. Whatever happens would be better than the alternative, she thought as she drew closer to her destination.

Chapter Twenty

The man had exhausted all hope when he heard the commotion and looked out the window of his dingy cell and saw the dull, grey, armored individual outside, looking in. A dark blue five-pointed star had been crudely painted on the chest plate by someone clearly lacking even the most basic creative talent, but that didn't seem very important now.

"Who is it?" He saw the shadow of the strange figure through the bars of his window. "Have my prayers at last been answered?"

"I surely do not know, fellow," the deep Southern Appalachian bass voice answered. "That depends on what you have been praying for, I guess. I cannot give you a million dollars, a bottle of aged scotch, or a girlfriend, but I can do a lot of other stuff you might find interesting and useful, especially given your current situation, not a good station."

"How is it that you found me? The American forces haven't had any luck. They keep moving me around, usually two or three times per week."

"My sensors can detect your voice, even miles away, through several feet of concrete, via sophisticated voice recognition algorithms. They are significantly more advanced than what the government has, and I am a little more mobile, as well as being impervious to most any form of detection except direct visual contact. In the future, even that may not be an issue."

"How can you be out there?" the forlorn man asked, scratching his head. "Impossible."

"Why, my friend? If I am out here, I must be real, right?"

"What? This floor is over thirty feet up, and you're just standing there, floating in air! You have to be a hallucination of a desperate old man."

The armored figure looked down thirty feet as she floated, without any visible means of how she was accomplishing it. So she understood his surprise now.

"Oh, yes, correct you are, I forgot. Stand back, Mac." The armored figure pulled on the bars, and the wall caved outwards as if it were made of tinfoil. "Mr. Thomasson, this is the luckiest day of your life; you shall have no further strife."

"How did you get in here without being detected?"

"I am not sure how it works, but, like I said, I sort of, er, evade radar detection until someone sees me. See me they finally did, but I took out most of their weapons. And I can go faster than any aircraft except the NextGen moon shuttle."

He shook his head. "The guards, we'll never get past them, despite what you've done. It's hopeless, suicide. We're dead."

"Huh. Most of them ran off like the cowardly, bottom-dwelling rats they are, so no worries. That was fortunate for them, as I have no desire to harm any being, no matter how misguided. And with *Stella Scura,* 'hopeless' is a word you will never know again, my friend. Smile, and the world smiles with you."

"*Stella* what? Your voice is incredibly powerful, and I can only sense the person within, although you speak oddly, in both your choice of words and tone, which don't match."

"Yeah, well, about that: the old voice box is apparently stuck on this one, as there are seemingly no replacement parts available in the Russian Federation or the Fairbanks TechTown. So much for technological obsolescence."

"What does that mean?"

"In other words, you might be surprised what I look like beneath this shell. Powerful I am, though; you can count on that."

"You must therefore be an emissary of the President of the United States, and these people will soon pay the price for their folly. This President will destroy them."

"*Nyet.* My vision is not the greatest, but do you see red, white, and blue or fifty-five stars on this thing? There is just the one star, painted on with leftover house paint by one with the artistic ability of a drunken orangutan. I know your brother is a Republican Senator, but I am here purely so the President does *not* cause hellfire to rain upon this nation, in addition to saving you, of course. Misguided as a small portion may be, there are still innocents here. Innocents who surely do not deserve to die."

"They have treated me very badly. Look at the scars from where I have been beaten. How can you say that?"

"I can sympathize, but your woe does not justify killing anyone. I am no agent of destruction and shall never be."

"I don't believe that. You—you are Russian?"

"Not quite, I just speak it; it is very complicated and a story we have no time for now. But I represent no country, and I am not killing anyone if I can help it. I ain't no warmonger. I have neither killed nor seriously injured anyone. Not yet, at least."

"I prayed for the Savior, and I knew you would come."

"Hey, pal, whatever God you want to believe in is okay by me, but maybe you should shut up now, so hold on. We need to fly where we are going. The New Persian border is a little less than three hundred miles away; it will not take long, there you will burst into joyful song."

"Fly? Is your airplane outside?"

"I have no idea how to pilot an airplane, and I travel light. I am unable to even get a drivers' license for reasons that, for the sake of time, cannot be explained here."

Thomasson shook his head. "I don't understand."

"It will be self-explanatory, so trust me." She removed her right gauntlet and placed it in a storage compartment on her hip. "Take my hand, Mr. Thomasson."

"What?"

"Man, do what I say and make my day! Take it, and whatever you do, *do not let go, Joe*. As long as you make physical contact with my body, nothing can harm you. We are going to walk the hell out of here."

He took her soft right hand. "What does holding your hand have to do with it? I expected a calloused hand of a hardened warrior, not a slender hand, a mere girl's hand."

"Stop complaining and just trust me on this one; it is not my size or gender that counts. My hand, and the rest of me, is way tougher than this suit; we shall withstand their pursuit."

"They must have missiles and all kinds of assorted weaponry."

"Huh. Not any longer because I destroyed them all. They have a few guns, grenades, and such left. Big fricking deal."

As they walked out the armored figure held Thomasson in her arms, he holding onto her right hand for dear life as the few remaining soldiers fired rounds, which stopped after hitting his skin and her armor and dropped harmlessly to the floor. She knew that anyone held within her grasp could not be harmed by any force on Earth. At least that was what the limited experiments she and her parents had done demonstrated, with destructive weaponry a bit more advanced than she saw here.

She had no clue how any of that worked or if it extended to nuclear weapons. Thankfully, Taraq didn't possess those. Not yet, at least, that anyone knew of.

"This is impossible. The bullets hit me, and I felt them, but they bounced off and didn't cause any damage."

"Nope, not bounced, really. The energy is absorbed, somehow, and they drop to the ground. I do not know where this absorbed kinetic energy goes, as it is converted to dark energy, supposedly. Anyway, it is all good because they do not ricochet off and kill people like with superheroes in the comics. You get out in one piece and no one dies, so everyone comes out ahead, and no one loses his or her head." Another group of soldiers bravely came up.

"What's happening?" Thomasson asked.

"فيالبدءكانالكلمة. I told you all to get down." She gestured at them as she swept her arm and watched as they fell to the ground like a row of dominoes. She had no idea how any of that worked or how the universal translator functioned; she only knew Russian and certainly not Arabic or Farsi. Mom was the one who understood physics; why that was the case was still a mystery.

Mom said her abilities had something to do with "dark energy," or, rather, the ability to manipulate it. Whatever it was, it worked pretty well. And it was non-lethal unless she wanted it to be, and no one would die today. She wondered what would happen if she seriously wanted to hurt someone. Hopefully, that day would never come.

They ran out into the field from the old building. "How are we going to get to New Persia, if there's no vehicle or airplane?"

"I told you, by flight. Keep holding my hand." She took him in her arms, and he gasped as they rose off the ground.

"Good God! How are you doing that? This suit is incredible technology."

"Yep, if you say so, Mr. Thomasson." In reality, the suit was an ancient rust bucket of old plutonium-powered Soviet electronics from the Walkman era, useful only because of the cybernetic helmet and universal translator which was still pretty advanced technology. A large missile might blow away part of the suit but leave their bodies intact. So it was time to get the hell to Freedom City before their luck ran out.

No one needed to know that the suit didn't do squat except provide some aerodynamics and anonymity.

"Do not worry as we scurry. Hold on to me and we will be in Freedom City in a jiffy, although our duds are not very spiffy."

• • •

Falton Strategic Air Command
New Persia

The Air Force enlisted man perked up from his generally mundane job, monitoring communications in the desert.

"What is it, Renner?" Lt. Col. Adam Henning asked.

"Colonel, we just received a very bizarre encrypted UHF radio message from Taraq, apparently intended for us."

"What did you say? On speaker, Senior Airman."

Senior Airman Bob Renner played the transmission. "*Stella Scura* has rescued Alan Thomasson from Taraqi prison. *En route* to Freedom City. No casualties. Coordinates 33.9791° N, 66.4849° E."

Henning rose up. "Who or what the hell is that, and can we track it? What did it call itself?"

"*Stella* something. What does that mean, sir?"

Henning shook his head. "I don't know, but that voice is damn peculiar—like he's from the South or something."

"But about tracking: negative, Colonel. There have been several small explosions at those coordinates, but our radar or lasers track nothing moving, and I can't triangulate the position using visual confirmation or heat sensors. Also, there's evidence of gunfire less than thirty minutes ago in Taraq."

"What the hell is it, though? Something like what people said they saw over the Midwest and Tennessee recently?"

"Maybe. No visual sightings thus far, so can't say. I am curious what the name '*Stella Scura*' means."

"Don't know. Never heard of it."

"My God. Renner, get Secretary Ashburn and the President on the phone immediately. I have no idea how I'm going to explain this to the higher-ups, since it sounds crazy."

Renner nodded. "Yessir."

• • •

Stella Scura flew with Alan Thomasson towards the New Persian border, about 275 miles away. Freedom City, the capital, was about fifty miles further from there, but they only needed to make it to the American border. They landed at the entry to the outpost of the border about an hour and a half later. They weren't very aerodynamic, and she flew at only about 150 miles per hour.

The Marine at the U.S. border entry looked up in awe as they landed outside the gate. Startled, he pulled his pistol and pointed it at them.

"Get the hell back! This is the United States of America, dude."

"Put it down and ditch the frown, Lance Corporal," *Stella* said in the deep Appalachian voice, seeing the insignia on his shoulder. "*Now.* My GPS is aware of our location, and I am merely here to deliver Mr. Thomasson safely back to his country. I sent out a UHF beacon message; surely you knew I was coming."

"I don't take orders from you," he screamed. "What the hell are you?"

She grabbed the gun with amazing speed and threw it to the side. "I told you, I am one of the good guys. Tell the Consulate General and President Mendoza that *Stella Scura* was here. No thanks are necessary. I am glad to help, there is no need to yelp."

"What the hell does that mean?"

She put Thomasson down. "I must go now, soldier. We will likely not meet again." The guard watched, flabbergasted, as she took off, the first sonic boom occurring in about five seconds.

Two others came out and escorted Thomasson in.

"Holy shit," Lance Corporal John Scott said in astonishment as the others who just arrived looked towards the sky.

• • •

National Military Medical Center
Freedom City, New Persia

The DSD agents conferred with Gen. Larry Kriger in the conference room at the military hospital complex after talking to Alan Thomasson and reviewing the digi-vids of their strange visitor's appearance and abrupt disappearance.

"Play that back again, Lori," Special Agent Ron Wilson said.

"Sure." DSD Deputy Director Barbara Loretta Baxter played the interview back again on the large TV as they listened.

"He had a deep, angry voice, yet somehow I knew I'd be safe," Thomasson said on the video. "When I looked into his dark eyes, he said, '*Stella Scura* will save you. Do not fear.'"

"Was he hallucinating, Lori? We saw the vid from outside the gate, although it was dark. Do you think they'd drugged him?"

She shook her head. "I don't know. The toxicology is all negative, and he didn't act like he was drugged. Tired and hungry, maybe, but not that. Maybe he was sleep-deprived or something, though."

"Lori, it's right there on the vid; he wasn't hallucinating. The guy flew off like a rocket with no visible means of propulsion, Lance Corporal Scott said, and the video confirms it. How the hell is that possible?"

Lori continued the video recording further. "She was invincible: the bullets dropped off her," Thomasson said. "I touched her."

"Wait. He called it a male first, then a female?" Gen. Kriger asked. "What did he mean, 'her?' How would he know if it was male or female? That makes no sense."

"Yeah. He said the hand—it was a girl's hand, soft and slender, his exact words." Lori took a sip of strong black coffee. "But why would an armored warrior have a hand exposed?"

"Thomasson said that if he touched her, nothing could hurt him. He swears he felt small arms fire hit him and then bounce off, unharmed. Perhaps that only works with physical contact with the alien," Kriger said.

"*Alien?* Waitaminnit. You have absolutely no proof of that, General. Speculation without facts is a dangerous business."

'Come on, what else could it be, Baxter? And he wasn't harmed, except for some superficial abrasions, right?"

Lori nodded. "Yes, it makes no sense. Medical is trying to figure that out now."

"What did it say? 'Put it down and ditch the frown?' 'I am glad to help, no need to yelp?' What's with the rhyming?" Kriger asked.

"I don't know," Wilson replied. "The Army went in and took over the damn place after Thomasson was returned, the whole place was trashed. We got it from the coordinates it transmitted when it was flying him here."

"Baxter, how did the thing know he was there? How did they get out alive, then?" Kriger asked.

"I have no idea how. But it's true. The bullets don't look like they bounced off anything hard at all; they look like something simply absorbed all the energy. And a metal door we recovered was torn. The whole thing looks like a knife going through butter. Not ripped off its hinges, but like the metal was actually altered on a molecular level to come apart, the metallurgical engineer says on preliminary exam. You know how much power that would take?"

"To what? Rip it off?" Kriger asked.

"No, to pull it apart that way, altering the lattice structure. Way more than any machine I know of."

They looked at the low-resolution black and white video again.

"So that's what it looks like up close. What the hell is that suit, Baxter? Is it metal? Something else?"

"I don't know. *Stella Scura*, he said? Better let Slabb and Ashburn know. I think we just found the bogey we've all been looking for."

• • •

"This is incredible. There are countless superficial contusions on his body, including his face," Commander Becca Holder stated in amazement as she sat in the small conference room with her VIP physician colleague, looking at the digital photos on the wall screen. "Normally, someone his age couldn't survive a beating like that. But this is anything but normal."

"Ecchymoses?" the President of the United States asked.

"No, Ma'am," Holder said. "High-res scans show no evidence of injury below the outer epidermis, which in places is totally obliterated, with the layers right below completely pristine. I've never seen anything like this; it's impossible."

"Any explanation why that would be?"

Holder shook her head. "I have no idea. There is no description of anything in the known literature about such a thing."

"The only difference I see is that the outer epidermis is dead skin, but the rest is living tissue." Wendy pointed at the multiple one-centimeter-sized lesions. "I assume these are bullet wounds."

The fortyish, short, dark-haired emergency physician nodded at the President. "I suppose that's logical, given their diameter, and, yes, there is some metal residue consistent with small arms fire. But how could this happen? Even if that being is indestructible, Thomasson sure as hell isn't."

"Transference."

"What, Ma'am?"

"Thomasson said he was holding on to the being's hand. What if this 'invulnerability' or whatever is shared with any living being coming in contact with her?"

"What? 'Her,' Madam President?"

She nodded. "Why not, Commander? *Stella* is a feminine name, and Thomasson himself said the hand felt like a female hand."

"Ma'am, he was likely delusional. His examination suggests significant PTSD, which is quite understandable in his case."

"Do you have any other explanation for the findings?"

"I don't, but, with all due respect, what you suggest is a rather outlandish theory. Another question is why an invulnerable being would need a protective exoskeleton."

"I don't know, but you have a better one? He's presently normal, right? No unusual resistance to venipuncture?"

Holder nodded. "He's seemingly normal now, Ma'am. Starting an IV and drawing blood, no problem."

Delusional? Yeah, right.

When you were a toddler, we were making pasta. I watched you grab a boiling pot of water and turn it onto yourself, and you laughed it off.

You were holding a kitten in your other hand and, while it got wet, it was none the worse for wear.

The kitten on the floor by your feet didn't fare so well.

SecDef's Office
The Pentagon
Washington, DC

Secretary of Defense Thomas Ashburn listened intently to the recording of the recent event again in his office.

"The voice is eerily familiar. Linguo-computers place the accent in Southern Appalachia; eastern Tennessee, specifically."

"Voiceprint ID?" DSD Director Dexter X. Slabb asked.

He shook his head. "No match. Kriger was there with Lori Baxter when they reviewed it, and they concur."

"That's damn hard to believe, the voice."

That was curious, he thought. He knew he'd heard that deep bass Southern voice before, somewhere, in some old military video clips, because not many folks who worked in the defense industry talked with that accent and deep vocal timbre. Why wasn't it in the database?

"I still think it's bizarre."

"I agree, but no dice, Tom."

"Why the hell would some goddamn old Russian battle armor have a voice like that? An Appalachian accent is hardly a stock voice in any computer simulation I ever saw. Did we ever make an armored suit with those specifications?"

"No, of course not; are you kidding? Nothing like that ever existed, according to our databases. Weird, Tom."

"Like you would tell me anyway, with your secret shit. Not even any prototypes?"

"Nothing we have concrete evidence of."

"Not much of an answer." Yes, it was weird, unless someone had deleted it. Someone with unlimited political power, whose dad probably had played a part in the creation of that damn armored suit. The fact that this all sounded so completely insane also made it so very possible.

Some Presidents were so bad people couldn't wait until they were out of office. But there had never been one that required amending the Constitution so she could run for a third term.

Ashburn worked with someone like that. Someone trusted by the entire country, but not him, because he knew better. And so did Slabb, who just didn't have the balls to say so, the suck-up asshole.

He also knew of Vice President Robby Benton's reputation for lurking in the shadows and taking care of unpleasant tasks the President couldn't be bothered with. Benton loved doing that and hated the limelight, preferring to kick ass behind the scenes, and didn't care that he was the butt of many jokes about being incompetent. The two of them complemented each other very well.

Everyone had skeletons in the closet; his boss surely had a few more besides the common ones that were already known to millions, given her colorful background. But why would she manipulate those records unless she knew something?

He had a feeling about it, and it wasn't necessarily a good one. Being President of the United States was enough for most people, but not *her*. Ruler of the world was more her speed. And he wanted to know how he could become the latter as well, and he wanted a quick and dirty way to accomplish it. Maybe, with some careful planning, this would be his ticket. To most, she certainly didn't seem very interested in this unknown being.

Which clearly was not the case. He had known her too long and was aware of how intelligent she was. But what her game was, he didn't know.

He also knew he didn't trust his boss' polished advisor, the Director of DSD. Dexter surely knew more than he was letting on.

Chapter Twenty-One

Mendoza Multinational
New Employee Welcome Center
887 N. Bonnie Mendoza Blvd.
Aurora City, Indiana

Janaki Kapoor went from her new Bonitaville condominium to her orientation at the Mendoza Multinational employee welcome center. She was welcomed by a cheerful young woman who took her to get her ID photo taken, which took about five minutes. She was given a new employee packet as she was ushered into a small auditorium where about twenty other new employees were waiting.

She reflected on why she had come here with her son Bilal from suburban Washington. She thought about that for about twenty seconds and realized she had made the correct choice. She was tired of the stress, the rat race of the Beltway, and wanted more family time, a lower cost of living, and a more laid-back existence. She had been here several times, and when the offer came for a high-level legal job at M2, she took it without hesitation.

She took a sip of gourmet coffee as the video started, and a pretty young brunette woman's face filled the screen. She identified herself as the Director of Human Resources.

"Welcome to Aurora City and one of the greatest places to work in the world. Mendoza Multinational is a global corporation intent on supplying clean energy to the world, with new ideas constantly on the horizon." A historical video of a familiar figure filled the screen. "It was many years ago, in 2015, when champion sprinter, stage magician, forensic scientist, and brilliant theoretical physicist Bonita Mendoza discovered a safe way to moderate the fusion of helium-3, with her discovery of transuranium element 119, named mendozium after her death, but efficient methods of separating helium-3 lunar regolith from the other components had yet to be discovered.

"While most transuranic elements have extremely short half-lives, some as short as microseconds, mendozium-297 has a half-life of 87 days, and it absorbs the harmful neutrons released in deuterium/helium-3 fusion; this process allows fusion to occur in even small containers, such as an airplane engine, as well as large reactors. So-called 'cold fusion,' as this process occurred at room temperature. It is also an extremely safe element to handle.

"Amazingly, Element 119 was discovered not by accident, but by her theoretical predictions from the periodic chart, in an attempt to solve this perplexing problem. One difficulty that remained unsolved at the time of her death, however, was that helium-3 is extremely rare on Earth, but there exists a place where it is plentiful: our fifty-third state."

She watched the early exploits of robots mining dirt from Luna's far side: a seemingly worthless substance that was now worth trillions.

"Our natural satellite, one of the largest in the Solar System, contains much of this substance, relatively speaking. But *getting* it was another story.

"At first the separation of helium-3 from lunar regolith on the Moon's far side was deemed challenging and economically unfeasible, but Bonnie Mendoza's family legacy lived on in her niece, M2 co-owner and chemical engineer Isabel Mendoza, who developed a novel inexpensive way of separating it from the rest of the regolith using halogen superheating and isoelectric diffraction, the details of which are, of course, proprietary.

"The extraction of oxygen from the lunar soil and use of aluminum from bauxite has created a self-sustaining enterprise which employs over four hundred thousand Americans in each of the Terran fifty-four states and five thousand in Armstrong City and the far side city of Aldrinville. Many others work in units in the World Alliance countries.

"Robotic spacecraft were sent to the moon, and the first

shipments returned to Earth in 2017, about a year after Bonnie Mendoza's death. Many others work in support industries for the world's largest energy corporation. Over two hundred thousand work in the M2 plants in Canada, Great Britain, South Korea, Germany, Australia, and France, as well as in the states of North Korea, Cuba, New Persia, and Puerto Rico."

She knew most of this but tried to pay attention as this was her first day. "You may think that the cost of mining helium-3 and bringing it back to Earth may seem terribly expensive, but, in fact, it's equivalent to buying oil at less than three dollars a barrel—two hundred times cheaper than our own natural resources—and far less wasteful.

"While extremely rare on Earth, helium-3 is present, but still in low concentration on Luna, our fifty-third state, but up to fifty parts per billion in some areas. One hundred fifty tons of regolith must be processed to obtain one ton of helium-3, but it's worth it. The estimated energy contained in the moon's helium-3 is estimated to be over a thousand times greater than all the fossil fuels that have ever existed on Earth. And new sources may be discovered elsewhere, with new technology."

She knew all this, of course, being the widow of the President's ex-husband. Wendy had guaranteed her anything she wanted, including a new job at the place of her choosing. The accountant and former litigator was tired of the rat race of Washington and wanted to move away from there; the Midwest was more her speed these days, after all she'd been through. And Mendoza Multinational paid pretty well. It was also consistently voted one of the best places to work among Fortune 500 companies. Great health and retirement plans, little traffic, Major League Baseball (her son was a big fan of the Atoms, despite their recent playoff woes), nearby professional football and basketball (Indianapolis), and an extremely low cost of living compared to the Beltway. She didn't care much about fusion science, though; she was a litigator turned boring tax and financial attorney. Boring might be nice for a change.

Wendy had always been extremely nice to her, even before Stan died. She gave her an open invitation to come to the White House any time she wanted, although that seemed a bit awkward at times. She knew some people criticized Wendy for her aggressive foreign policy (i.e., being a badass to disagreeable countries), but at least she did stuff she thought was right and didn't play political games.

What you saw was what you got, for the most part. At least that was the militaristic Republican's party line, as she knew all politics involved games, some of which involved dealing with unpleasant political opponents. The economy was way better than it was in 2019, but some of that was surely because of fusion technology that had done immense things. Ultimate power could be used for good, after all.

Janaki still had their son, Bilal. Cassie and Jake, his half-siblings, had been killed in *Darkkday*, of course, like the other members of the family. She had never met Nicholas Stannous, but knew they had both lost their spouses in that explosion. She hoped to meet him soon.

Aurora City was only a third the size of Indianapolis, but the slick new city had a more vibrant, trendy atmosphere than the more conservative state capital. It was by far the largest city in Henry County, Indiana, and was built just northwest of the county seat, New Castle (now an enclave suburb), where Nick Stannous' mother and uncle were born.

Aurora City was, curiously, by far the largest American city that was not the seat of its own county. It had its own international airport, of course, with many direct connections, given its immense importance in the energy world.

Housing was still traditional Midwest, with both urban and suburban choices. Many people, like her, chose to live in Bonitaville, an affluent suburb of about 35,000 people, ninety percent of whom worked at M2 in some capacity.

The world's largest energy company had a large infrastructure, and she knew its owners cared about money—and paying as little taxes as possible. Since it was not publicly owned (Nicholas Stannous and Isabel Mendoza each owned fifty percent after the buyout of Jay and Wendy Mendoza's interests in 2020), its books were not open to the public.

Chapter Twenty-Two

Princeton University
Department of Astrophysical Sciences
4 Ivy Lane
Princeton, New Jersey

Professor Emeritus Johnny Kepler sat down in his office on Tuesday morning and prepared to look through the day's reading, piled neatly by his assistant. Soon he would have the piles disorganized, however, much to her chagrin. He had lectures later in the day to a visiting group and needed to be prepared, so he didn't really care about what Paula didn't like.

He reconsidered that thought, as it suddenly occurred to him that not caring about Paula's preferences was a big mistake from which he might never recover.

There was also that "off the record" work in dark energy physics he was doing for an old friend, whom he had just seen in Aurora City after being asked to consult on one of the strange projectiles. He did this work on a special encrypted laptop disconnected from the university because he trusted no one. He liked routine and not weirdness these days, so he was glad to have just a simple day in front of him. He took a sip of strong lukewarm coffee as heard a knock on the door.

"Enter."

His trusted assistant for the last fifteen years entered and smiled at him. "There's a young man to see you, Johnny."

He sighed as he took a swig of coffee and realized how much

unfinished work was on his desk. "Who is it, Paula? Office hours ain't till three. Unless it's the Dean, I'm busy. I'm especially busy if it's the President, who can just leave me the hell alone."

"It's neither Dean Qualls nor President Baker."

He shook his head and scowled. "Walt Baker I would see. I mean the other damn President, the one with two X chromosomes."

She laughed and shook her head. "It is neither individual. Sorry to disappoint you, as I doubt she will be coming."

"Good. Well, is it the *Tinman*? If so, I don't want to deal with him now about his, er, project; I just spent way more time out there than I wanted."

"No, sir, it's not Dr. Stannous. He is extremely polite, and Leah likely would've called first." The fiftyish, overweight woman shook her head as if puzzled as to why they would be working together.

The crusty sixty-two-year-old professor frowned. "I don't want to play guessing games today. Who the heck is it, then?"

She turned her palms out. "Sorry, but I don't know what to say. He's rather, well, hard to describe."

"Try your best."

"I don't know who he is, but he's rather peculiar. He wants to talk to you about gravitational theories and minuscule deviations in the Earth's rotation and how these concepts apply to Santa."

"Huh? Santa? *Santa Claus?* Is this a joke? Come on. That ain't funny at all."

She shook her head nervously. "No, it's really not. He brought in a whole stack of your papers and acted like he's read them all." She dropped the stack on his desk.

He quickly thumbed through the pile of manuscripts. "Those are post-doctoral level; no way could he understand them. He's trying to impress you to get access to me, so somebody prepped this moron. Not the first time a student did that, I thought you knew better than to get sucked in that way."

She shook his head. "No, Johnny, I believe him and know the difference between the real thing and a scam artist. He seems rather bright compared to your typical graduate students."

"I rather doubt that. Is the freakin' dude even a student here?"

"He says not, although he says he may apply soon."

He snarled. "'He may apply soon.' Huh. This is the Princeton astrophysical sciences department, not Joe's Barber College. Tell this loser to get lost! What's wrong with you?"

The unflappable administrative assistant stared at him. "He looks the right age to be a student. Talks with a European accent but speaks very good English."

"Being European is something special?"

She pointed to the portrait of the famous 17th-century German scientist. "You seem to think your ancestor there was."

He smacked his coffee cup on the table, spilling black liquid on the papers she had neatly arranged. "Oh, crap, now look what you made me do."

"I didn't do it, Johnny. You should control your temper." She smiled and shook her head.

"Hey." He pointed his right index finger towards her. "I'm not in the mood. You know better than to bother me with this droll. I used to like the craziness surrounding the *Science Squad*, but that was thirty years ago when I needed some laughs after losing my leg. It stopped being funny after a while. I like my solitude now. I just got back from stupid Aurora City, and I ain't goin' back. I've had enough."

She shook her head. "I know, but something tells me that you need to talk to this fellow. He reminds me of someone I met many years ago when I was a little kid, and my mom worked in the physics department. Someone unforgettable."

He frowned and sat down his coffee as he realized there was one absolute fact he had learned through the years: when Paula Jean Goggins suggested something, he'd better consider it. He had ignored that fact in the past and regretted it.

"Oh, all right, I guess I've got a few minutes. Send this weirdo in, I could use a laugh or two." He wanted to approach it with a positive attitude and hoped he wasn't going to be sorry for this bad executive decision.

He saw the light in the doorway dim as a hulking yet gently-moving figure appeared.

"Come on in, sonny, I don't bite. What do you want? I ain't got all day, though, so speak up."

The large young man smirked in excitement. "I am honored. You are Dr. Johnny Kepler?"

The graying, balding professor saw the huge, perhaps twenty-year-old man enter, his figure blocking most of the light from the doorway.

"Yeah. That's my name, slick, don't wear it out. What can I help you with? I'm busy as hell." They shook hands. Man, this dude had big mitts and could play baseball with no glove, he thought.

"I'm Juriann, sir."

"Uh, yeah, sure you are. Pleased to meet you, big guy." Not.

Juriann Hultaar looked perplexed as he looked at the early 1600s portrait on the wall, apparently comparing the famous figure to the tall Black man sitting at the mahogany desk.

"You're a descendant of Johannes Kepler, the great 17th-century astronomer and mathematician, who developed modern theories of gravitation? I expected you to look a little more similar, yet there is little resemblance." Juriann scratched his large head in curiosity.

"Yeah, we share direct lineage, believe it or not. My ol' great-great-great-great-great-great-great-Grandpa was a real player with the ladies, they said." That was what he had always claimed and what his father and grandfather had told him hundreds of times, although no official documentation that he was really a descendant of Johannes Kepler actually existed. It made for good press during his days on the Tour, though. The stern-looking man looked up at him curiously. "You playin' with a full deck, pal, or are you missin' a few face cards?"

Juriann tapped his chin and thought. "Come again? Playing with a deck? Cards? Ah, yes, mathematical games of chance. Poker, blackjack." The large man pointed to another oil painting on the large office's wall of the athletic, early twenty-something woman wearing a royal blue costume with the stylized symbol "M^2" on her unimpressive chest. Ironic that the dead scientist was now the corporate symbol of a huge international energy conglomerate. Yeah, like she would've cared about anything like that. For all of her exalted brainpower, she managed money worse than anyone he'd ever known. The world's greatest pure intellect had the financial acumen of a three-year-old. Fortunately, she trusted others to manage her assets, but a lot it got her in the end.

Vaporized.

"Playing with a full deck? You mean actual cards?" He laughed. Not quite, pal, but—"

"Just like she, the legendary magical one of science, did? This is to be a ritual, I would imagine, to be welcomed into the hallowed pantheon of greats. I'll try my best, although I lack her special magic skills."

He smacked his pencil on the desk. "Dammit, we ain't playing no fricking cards. And the main Mendoza over there wasn't magical, but a profoundly gifted tenth-order mathematical cipher with high-functioning autism. That's how she did that card junk, by brute force probability computations coupled with an eidetic memory and a shitload of nerve. What a huge waste of a giant brain, because she had to go into a fancy celebrity rehab center for being so addicted to gambling. Are you crazy or something?"

"Oh, I see." He laughed. "You find my manner a bit unusual."

"Noooo, you think?"

"That's understandable, as I don't know all of your idioms." The large man took out a small pad of paper from his pocket and hurriedly scribbled notes with his huge left hand. "Playing with a full deck, I got it. This means I'm in my right mind, I take it. I can assure you I am."

"I seriously doubt that," he said as he stood and pointed up at the large youth. "Don't you be makin' fun of me, either, or I'll bounce your butt outta here, despite your size."

"I meant no offense by your color, as genetic diversity is everywhere, most certainly in me."

"In *you?*" He laughed. "No offense, fella, but you look like your typical European white guy. What the hell would you know about diversity?"

"I am more than meets the eye, and far from typical. But I'm here not because of that—rather because you are the one known as the famous *Gravi-Golfer*. The hero who can manipulate gravity."

He laughed. "Man, you are way out there. I can't really do—"

"And one of the world's experts on dark energy, dark stars in particular."

Kepler stared curiously, as this guy didn't look like he should know what solar or kinetic energy was, let alone something as esoteric as dark energy. But something told him the guy did. And why did he care about a stupid *Science Squad* character from the 1990s?

Gravi-Golfer was invariably a distant third in the pecking order of "important" former *Dr. Wendy's Science Squad* characters anyone cared about. He was third banana in a fourth-rate local cable TV show, so clearly the world-famous golfer had reached the bottom of the barrel. But it was worth a few laughs.

The very self-centered duo of Gwendolyn Gallinsworth and Bonnie Mendoza always hogged the spotlight; after them came him, *Admiral Ampere* (Dr. Todd DeOhmman), *Chemical Cowboy* (Dr.

Wolfram Steele); shortly afterward came *Photraman* (Dr. Royce G. Bivereaux III), that dumb-ass purple blob guy whose name he thankfully forgot, and a couple of other transient pathetic losers, in that order.

Several in particular who didn't make the cut were *Watt Wizard,* who could manipulate power, but his abilities were too similar to Todd's; of heroes, another loser was *Kaptain Kelvin,* a character who could manipulate temperature. 99.99% of Americans had no idea what a Kelvin temperature was, nor did anyone care.

The pyromaniac *Sparkus* dressed in Roman soldier's garb and was to come out each July to use fireworks unsafely, but the TV station feared she might actually *encourage* kids to start fires and lose fingers and other appendages to firework accidents. The worst 'villain' was *Kelvin's* nemesis *Fahrenheit Führer,* definitely *not* a politically correct character. Fortunately, none of those actually made it onto the air. In retrospect, all of them were pretty stupid.

He stopped daydreaming and looked squarely at Juriann.

"What? *Golfer*? He was a lousy TV show character, man, one I'd sometimes like to forget. After I lost the leg to bone cancer I couldn't play on the PGA tour anymore, so I did that. Made nothin', but I didn't care because I met a few interesting friends and laughed my ass off about how important Wendy thought it all was. So I went back to school with my savings and fulfilled my family destiny. My daughter, she can carry on the golf legacy for me."

Juriann laughed. "Yes, of course, I know he's not real, but the principles you promoted had a profound impact on me and fueled my interest in science. That was the purpose of the show, right? To get children interested in scientific endeavors?"

"Hell, I guess so, man. I never thought about my 'profound impact' on the kiddies, but glad it helped encourage you to buy your first toy chemistry set. I'm sure the world's better off now that you're interested in science."

"It is. But getting to the point, Professor—I'm also here about one of the golf balls from space."

"The *what?*" he asked nervously. "I don't have any idea what you mean. You talkin' about when Alan Shepard played on the moon in 1971? It's still up there, far as I know."

"No, not that golf ball. The one I seek I heard you obtained from Indiana, in the mid-sized metropolitan area known as Aurora City. Apparently, there also were similar ones in the city of Green

Bay, Wisconsin, and in Appalachian Tennessee. Those three coordinates don't make any scientific sense. Does their triangulation have significance, like the Bermuda Triangle or something? Why not other parts of the world?"

Whoever this idiot was, he had information even the President probably didn't fully know about, or she didn't care, one or the other; or she was only acting like she didn't care. Only he and *Tinman* (and probably his better half, despite their secrecy) knew it all. And, of course, the "alien" who threw them with amazing speed. No time for fun and games now.

He crossed his arms. "Who the hell *are* you, son? And tell me how you know about any of that classified stuff."

"As I said, my name is Juriann—Juriann Hultaar. I don't know much else about myself. *Cogito ergo sum.*"

"Huh? What?"

"It means: 'I think, therefore I am.' Where I'm from or how I got here, I don't know. I obviously hope to find out."

That's all he needed—another Latin-spewing, René Descartes-quoting weirdo. *Mendoza the Miraculous* was bad enough, may her vaporized atoms rest in peace.

"You don't know how you got here? Didn't you fly in from Europe? How the hell else would you have come? Walked?"

He laughed. "Of course, I was speaking metaphorically. I flew in a Lufthansa jet from Rotterdam to Newark, then came here by train. I still want to know about the golf balls."

How the hell did this oddball know about the three golf balls? He would just use the same line he gave others. The man's Dutch accent was odd but damned if he didn't look like someone he had met before, many years ago. He wrote with his left hand, which he had noticed while he was scribbling notes in a small notebook. That, plus his size and apparent penchant for things scientific and resemblance to some famous folks, eerily narrowed the possibilities down. No, it couldn't be. Not *him.*

"This thing?" He pulled out the half-burned golf ball's container that he showed to visitors. No fricking way was he going to show anyone the real thing that *Tinman* had given him to study. "It was a prank, we think. Not real."

Juriann grinned. "I think not. It *must* be real." He took the ball and studied it. "But this isn't it, it wouldn't look like this if it had burned up in the atmosphere."

He sighed. How did this guy know that from just a cursory glance? "You're right, Hultaar. This isn't the real one; the other one's in my safe."

"But is this the sign of the coming of the Savior. The next year marks the 2000th anniversary of Jesus of Nazareth's death, when it was prophesized—2029. That is also a Jubilee year when many believe He will return."

"You think Jesus is returning because of that crazy-ass crap? Jubilees and such?"

"That, yes, and if you look very closely, there are subtle alterations in the Earth's orbit and picosecond decreases in the planetary rotational speed and orbital period which can be traced to central Alaska. This can only be caused by immense dark energy fluctuations. Whatever form Christ existed in, He must have followed our laws of physics. Isn't this one way?"

He opened his mouth wide. No one, except a handful of people, could have known about that. Either someone talked, or this guy was some kind of genius. He found it hard to believe the latter. But it was true; for years, he and *Tinman* had tried to build devices to detect dark energy, if it even really existed, because the potential power of that far outstripped mendozium-mediated nuclear fusion. The only way he knew to accomplish this was to measure subtle alterations in gravitational fields. The minute central Alaskan perturbations were the only clue so far.

"Let's change the subject. My assistant said you wanted to talk about Santa, so let's hear your treatise on that. This oughta be good."

Juriann smiled and took a sip of soda Paula had given him. "Yes, the *Sinterklass*—Santa Claus—is, in a sense, alive, and he flies. He also can warp gravity; you must know this to be so. Energy so powerful without any but the subtlest clues can only be the most rarefied type, the hallowed dark energy."

"Are you stupid or somethin'? Santa Claus has nothin' to do with Jesus Christ, you big dummy."

"What? Christmas has nothing to do with Christ?" Juriann laughed. "Sounds like some odd type of American humor. Who's kidding whom?"

He laughed. "O-kay, dude, whatever. I guess it's better than the world comin' to an end."

"North Pole, Alaska is where I'm certain you'll find the 'Santa.'

Check your notes. And the world is not coming to an end; this being shall be our Savior."

"Really, now. There was a dumb-ass supervillain called the *Santaman*; Kristoff van Sant was his real name. If that's who you mean, he's rotting in some hellhole prison for causing *Darkkday*. You'd better not be some pal of his, Dutch boy, or I'll shoot your big ass."

He shook his head. "No, I don't know him, but he sounds like he was truly a disgrace to our part of Europe. But I mean someone of *real* power, one literally with the ability to move mountains."

The guy was brilliant, but very odd, and was far more entertaining than threatening, despite his gargantuan size. He kept obsessing on the fact that Juriann reminded him of someone else, but he couldn't quite put his finger on it.

"And North Pole is neither the geographic nor the magnetic north pole, but a village southeast of Fairbanks, man, get with it."

Juriann grinned. "Of course I know that, Kepler. I'm well educated in all scholarly areas, including North American geography. But you all were quite something."

Juriann pointed to the old poster of *Dr. Wendy's Science Squad* characters. One of the most bizarre TV superhero teams ever created, and probably the lamest. He would never live it down, but in some twisted way, he was proud of what they did, which wasn't much. Ah, who was he kidding? If he really wanted to forget them, he wouldn't have the memorabilia around.

"Hultaar, we were *somethin'*, all right—a crappy TV show, only popular now because two of us became *really* famous. The rest of us have fallen into oblivion, like me. World has passed me by. Trust me, that's the way I want it."

"Or dead." He pointed at another rendition of the tall, athletic Mexican-American woman.

"Yeah, no shit." He looked at Bonnie Mendoza's photo, the only one of them who almost was a realistic superhero. "She was the real deal, all right. She and Wendy used to horse around and really go at it. Wendy was way stronger but M-Square could wear her out and kick her butt every time because of her amazing speed and quickness, plus Wendy wasn't in the best shape at that time. They used to wrestle to entertain everyone during breaks. She could kick all our asses. I feel sad every day when I think about what happened."

"I saw the animated *Science Squad* movie last night, in a revival theater, in IMAX 5-D. It was my first time at the American cinema, it exceeded my expectations."

Another moneymaking device of capitalism. He guessed that was one thing that made America great. With her money, she could bankroll any movie she wanted. That one was not the "other" Mendoza Nobel Laureate's best voice role.

"They make movies about all kinds of junk, pal. If money can be made, someone takes advantage. The guy who did my voice didn't even sound like me. Some famous actor they hired."

"The North Koreans shot a nuclear missile at their plane, it was regrettable. I was only eight years old, yet I remember like it was yesterday."

"They never proved who, but, yeah. Killed everyone on board. The little girl, too, the President's children, everyone died."

"Correct. But it's interesting the dictator of Tosia was found decapitated in his opulent home a few months after that."

"Shit." He put his hands over his ears. "I don't want to know anything about that, son."

Juriann pulled out a 3 x 5 autographed trading card from the *Mendoza the Miraculous* movie. "She was the greatest of all time."

Kepler looked at the photo of the beautiful, curvaceous, and rather egotistical actress in the royal blue costume and snickered.

"No, no, no, you are way confused. That isn't her, you Dutch dope, it's an actress, who happens to be her niece, a prestigious scientist in her own right, so there is some facial resemblance, and the skin tone is spot on. The body—not so much. They selected shorter actors to surround her to make her seem larger. Mini-Mendoza there is about as tough as a loaf of bread. None of those guys in the movie were real."

"Nevertheless, she represents M-Square—*Mendoza Milagrosa*—*Mendoza the Miraculous*. Truly she is the one of miracles."

"She was a magician and mentalist before becoming the pride of Caltech and doing God knows what kinds of unholy illegal shit for the CIA, pal, before leaving the government and doing private research in Rad Darkkin's old nuclear lab in Tennessee that changed the world. That's where she got the name from. Miracles couldn't save her from nuclear destruction and ending up on currency and stamps, now, could it?"

Juriann stared at him and shook his head. "No, that's not correct, Kepler. She got that name because she rose from disability and nearly dying as a child to becoming the greatest at what she did, despite having the odds stacked against her. And, do you know for certain the answer to your final statement?"

"What's that?"

"Your bold declaration that she is dead."

Damn, this guy was way smarter than he looked. "You are quite informed."

"This I am. Professor, do you know what *La Milagrosa* means in Spanish?"

Kepler shook his head. "No clue, big man, *no habla espanol*. I'm sure you'll tell me, though." He waited for the grand answer that didn't come. "Tell me before I have a stroke."

"It's obvious: the Virgin Mary, mother of the Christ child. Is it possible? And is the golf ball a sign?"

"I still believe Bonnie Mendoza is dead, my oddball foreign friend, but I assure you, a virgin she wasn't; neither was the girl in that photo, trust me on that one. Bonnie was nice enough for a upper middle-class kid, but a far cry from sainthood. She spent much of her early twenties in casinos, using her cipher powers and poor innocent deaf girl persona to bleed the casinos dry at poker and blackjack till they all figured it out and kicked her butt out of Vegas permanently. We had to do an 'intervention' once to take her to some fancy rehab center for gambling addicts. So you are way off base once again."

"Yet, I don't know how, but she has something to do with the being I will call Santa, for lack of a better name."

"Hey, why don't you go find an expert on Santology—the systematic study of Santa Clauses through time? One may obtain a Masters of Santology degree from a university in North Dakota, I hear. Lots of career opportunities there, pal."

His guest's expression changed instantly from that of a naïve guy out of his element to one far more aggressive and serious, as Kepler took a step back.

"Don't patronize me, Kepler. I came here for information that can benefit us both, but I've had enough of your joking and pejorative comments. It's up to us to change the world. If you don't want to be on board, I'll figure it out on my own; rest assured of that, as I am no intellectual weakling. You're either in or out."

He pulled out his wallet and plucked out two hundred dollars.

"Here, I'll give you money for a bus ticket so you can enroll in that Santology program, just get the hell out of here. But going from Santa Claus to the second coming of Christ. Man, you are something else."

Juriann shook his head. "I don't need your money, Kepler. But this being must exist, with the ability to manipulate the greatest power in the universe. You know it has to be true."

"The 'greatest power?' What's that? A star?"

Juriann shook his head. "No, no, no. You know the answer, as you mentioned it in the 'Groovy Gravity' episode of *Science Squad*. A star gives off great power, for sure. But what holds it together?"

"I don't remember what the hell I said yesterday, let alone over thirty years ago. What?"

"Gravity, of course. Despite it being considered the 'weakest' of the four fundamental physical forces, in large amounts, gravity 'kicks ass,' as you would've said on the show if it hadn't been for children."

He nodded. "Yeah, I sure would've said that, but that doesn't prove anything."

"The unknown being, whom I will call 'Santa' for lack of a better term, possesses the power of dark energy, which is even greater than that: the power to repel gravity."

Kepler sat back down. This guy was here for the duration, so he might as well get comfortable in his own damn chair. "Go on, you are somewhat entertaining, at that."

Juriann gestured to the other photos on the wall. "In this room are the photos representing many others of great importance—the gallery of heroes."

This dude could go to Washington, Mount Rushmore, the Pro Football Hall of Fame, or lots of other places, but he chose this place to find his first American "gallery of heroes." Damn. He never saw *that* coming.

Juriann then pointed to the massive blonde powerlifter in the center of the largest photo, who was holding a real barbell over her head. Two hundred fifty pounds in red and white spandex, with a "cleavage window" in her top partially showing off that truly impressive 52-inch chest, a God-given asset achieved without the aid of plastic surgery. There was also no Photoshop in those days—an Olympic bar with three 20-kg plates on each side. 315 pounds.

He slapped himself in the face. "Do you even know who that

is? Good Lord."

"What? Of course, she was the titular character in what we have been discussing, the massively undervalued show *Dr. Wendy's Science Squad.*"

"What? *'Titular?'* You tryin' to be funny, man? Have some damn respect for the President of the United States now that you're in my country. She wasn't always my cup of tea, but don't talk that way about the Prez's mammary glands, you're creepin' me out."

"Huh? No, I'm not trying to be funny." He looked at her photo carefully. "We do somewhat resemble each other, obviously except for the, uh, oh, *titular—tit,* a slang term for *teat,* a vulgar term for a breast in America. I get it now. I am so sorry. I meant no offense to your nation's Chief Executive."

"Boy, that's good. Most powerful person in the world, literally and figuratively, and you crack wise. Anyway, that cheap-ass golf ball was analyzed and was an Eagleton X-Out. One bonnie a dozen at Super-Mart." That was the truth, actually. He figured this guy would find that out eventually, anyway.

Juriann reached into his pocket and removed two brass bonnie coins, worth five dollars each, and smiled at the likeness of the famous scientist. "I am debating what this fact means. The Great Eagle? Symbol of this great country? Sold as that great symbol of capitalism, which has made your country great?"

He shook his head. "No, Hultaar, figure it out with that big brain of yours. If God or Santa Claus or whoever was going to play golf, don't you think they would've used a Titleist?"

"Point well taken." Juriann extended his hand. "Thank you, Dr. Kepler. I must go on the next journey of my quest. I'm sure our paths will cross again soon, as we both seek knowledge."

"Where you goin' now, Juriann?"

Juriann looked out the window. "West. To Indiana."

"Great. Go west, young man, and have a hell of a good time, if one is to be had in the Hoosier State. Don't call me, I'll call you."

"Thank you, Kepler. Goodbye for now. I'm certain I'll see you again soon. I'll give your regards to Dr. Stannous." Juriann shook hands with him and closed the door as he left.

• • •

The oddball man departed, off to enroll in his Master of Santology degree, he hoped; but he clearly was going to Aurora City in pursuit of greater knowledge. He hoped some of the more famous residents there wouldn't regret that visit. Maybe he should warn *Tinman?* He hesitated, then realized that no one deserved Juriann to drop in on them unexpectedly, so he would send Nick Stannous a text message.

He then looked through several old Princeton yearbooks until he found the senior baccalaureate photo of William Conrad Darkkin, who later went on to MIT to earn his Ph.D. in nuclear physics. And the golf ball wasn't a prank—that was just something the feds cooked up for the media. *Tinman* had him confirm the preliminary analysis, and as far as he could tell, the molecular alterations of the cheap golf ball were as if it had been thrown with incredible force and struck the forty-foot statue of Aurora Darkkin in Miracle Park.

Another one struck Rad Darkkin's tombstone in Oak Ridge. The third was embedded in concrete at the base of Vince Lombardi's statue at Lambeau Field in Green Bay. But no one else knew that except *Tinman* and maybe M-Square Junior on his trading card. Not even their famous in-law, the President. She had way more important things to do than worry about crappy golf balls.

Ah, right, as if he believed *that*. She was always good at playing the dumb blonde, likely knew everything in excruciating detail, and certainly had a big role in covering it up. Underestimating her would be a fatal mistake.

And this big guy, despite his weirdness and youth, knew some pretty esoteric things, like dark energy, for instance. Also, information he had gathered that demonstrated subtle alterations in Earth's gravity near North Pole, which couldn't be explained by random variation. How could he have known about that? He was the only one to his knowledge with the instrumentation sensitive enough to detect something like that. And what did this idiot know about dark energy? He was right, though. If someone could master and control this mysterious substance, he or she could rule the world. He called out to his secretary, as this deserved more than a crappy text message to Indiana.

"Paula, can you get my daughter's friend Nicholas Stannous on the phone? I was just out there recently."

She walked into his office and crossed her arms. "Huh, I don't get it. You said earlier you didn't want to talk to him ever again."

"Well, I do now. A man of my great intellectual stature has the right to change his mind."

"Sure, whatever. You want the Mendoza Multinational toll-free number, customer service, or financial services, Johnny?"

"No, I don't want to go through that BS, and I don't want the operator. I'm the famous Johnny Kepler, not some poor sap who can't pay my freaking light bill. I need the *Tinman* himself on his cell. Call Hanna if you have to."

"That may be a challenge, but I'll try." Paula was his assistant for a reason. She was darned good at cutting through the red tape and getting what he wanted.

He really wasn't sure what he wanted; that was the problem. That had been the story of his interesting life, which seemed to be getting more interesting by the minute. He couldn't wait to see what was coming next.

Chapter Twenty-Three

Mendoza Multinational
225 N. Bonnie Mendoza Blvd.
Aurora City, Indiana

The forty-seventh President of the United States walked with her entourage of very large men in black (the minimum height for males on her detail was six-four, and two were six-six) and Detail Chief Jackie Levickis past the thirty-foot bronze *Mendoza Milagrosa* statue, through the front lobby of Mendoza Tower. She enjoyed being the shortest person (besides Jackie) for a change, especially around guys. People gasped as they saw what might be mistaken for a pro basketball squad moving quickly towards the elevator as a security guard gaped. As usual, she stopped and waved at everyone but declined her typical practice to stop and talk as she was a woman on a mission today.

They went to the front desk as she looked at the receptionist.

"Please get Dr. Stannous, for me, Miss. I'll be waiting in his office."

The diminutive, gum-chewing woman, who had been on the job all of two weeks, continued to read her magazine as she raised her hand. "Dr. S is in conference with his Board of Directors. And your name is what, sweetie?"

The tall blonde stared at her and smiled (while her Secret Service detail scowled), as she was, fortunately, in a very good mood, and this was a comedic opportunity not to be missed.

"Do you really think I need an introduction, or do you live in a cave? And don't address me as 'sweetie.' That is not very respectful, do you not agree?"

The woman looked up at Wendy, who was dressed in a gorgeous red skirted suit. "Oh, my. You're the best one yet."

She laughed. "Excuse me? Best what?"

"Aww, c'mon. Mrs. Bella plays this joke all the time on us, with various famous people, since she knows a lot of celebrity doubles. You've almost got the accent down right this time. You're a little smaller around the chest than the real one, though."

Jackie laughed. "You—you don't believe this is the President? You think this is an actor? Are you a freaking nut case?" She pulled out her Secret Service badge and stuck it in her face.

"Hey, my little boy has a hunk of tin like that; he got it at the Muncie army surplus store on South Walnut Street, that's probably where you got yours. Tin? *Tinman*? Hee hee hee."

"Why, you dumb, idiotic—" Jackie said angrily, shaking her fist in the air.

She brushed Jackie aside gently. "Come now, Detail Chief Levickis, the nice young lady here is just doing her job; there is no need for violence. Protecting her boss, as you would do. Surely you must admire such dedication to duty."

"Dang right," the receptionist said. "I don't need any more jokers around here."

"Hmmm. A joker I have surely been, and can certainly be—perhaps I could give a stirring Sinatra-esque rendition of Stephen Sondheim's 'Send in the Clowns,' but not today." She hummed a few bars of that tune and looked at the Reti-Scan device on the counter, a necessity for classified areas. "Hey, I assume all visitors to sensitive areas are cleared with that doohickey, correct? It looks mighty fancy."

"You got it, lady. Some important stuff goes on here. Can't be too careful with who goes in and out."

"Secret stuff, eh?" She bent over and stared in the woman's face with her big aquamarine eyes. "I betcha I'm in the database; what do ya think?"

"Huh? Are you kidding? You have to be put in there first. Don't think you're on the important folks' list."

"Oh, let's see, since we're having fun." Wendy grabbed the device, put it up to her right eye, and handed it back to the secretary after the scanner made a loud "bip" noise after three seconds.

"Hey, be careful with that! It's only for VIPs."

"No problem. Here ya go, honey," she said as she handed it back. "I guess I was in there, what are the odds?"

"Let me see." The woman looked at it for a minute. "Huh. How about that. You *are* the President, go figure."

"Can I go through now, or do you want to scan my other eye?"

The young woman stared at Jackie briefly, then looked at the President and burst into laughter, as Jackie joined them.

Jackie smiled. "Did you really think we wouldn't know this was all a set-up? Your mercurial sense of humor isn't funny, Ma'am."

"Oh, come on, it is too. Some people just can't take a joke," Wendy said. "I thought it might make you laugh, which it finally did. Time to lighten up, Jacqueline."

• • •

Leah Ann Seagrape entered the M2 boardroom hurriedly and tapped Nick on the shoulder.

"Nick, sorry to interrupt you, but—" she whispered.

"I'm in a senior exec meeting now, Leah. What is it?" He was normally patient, but he didn't like to be interrupted during a business meeting by his longtime friend and assistant.

"There's an, uh, important lady waiting in your office," she whispered again, her voice shaking.

He whispered back. "I said no visitors; I'm busy. I need you to manage these sorts of things for me. That's what I pay you to do, isn't it, Leah?"

"Yeah, uh, but that's the thing, Nick—her entourage sort of took over the place."

"What the heck? On whose authority did that happen? The president of Thioco's appointment isn't until eleven AM. Have her wait. Jeez, I'm a hundred times richer than their whole company, and I'll kick her butt out."

"No, sir, that's probably not a good idea, just saying." Leah shook her head nervously. "It's *not* Ruth Esterhall of Thioco, Nick. It's *the* President."

"Um, president of what, again?"

She got in his face and stared. "There's only one President, *Tinman*. You know her pretty well. And she doesn't look like she wants to wait. I'm not kidding. Retinal scan confirms her identity."

"Here? Now? Why? Retinal scan?" He thought for a minute. "Oh, crap, not today. You dummies actually had *her* do a retinal scan? Are you idiots? Wait a minute, I know the answer to that."

"I'm sorry, Nick, we had received notification from Miranda she was on her way, but somehow she didn't end up on your calendar. I take full blame for it."

"Great to know." He stood up and addressed the group. "Sorry, ladies and gentlemen, but our Commander-in-Chief needs me. I'm probably in enough trouble already by now. Have my lawyer on standby in case I need bail money."

"I think she was just joking around, Nick; you know how she is, and our people wouldn't really do that."

"Whew," he mopped his brow with his handkerchief. "At least she's in a good mood."

The puzzled executive team exchanged glances as their boss rapidly scurried out the door, running to his office.

• • •

Nick nervously came to his office door after flying out of the elevator. The ornate mahogany entrance was blocked by four massive Secret Service agents, each one easily having eighty pounds on his 170-pound frame.

"You may go inside, sir," a tall Black Special Agent said politely in a deep voice, barely cracking a smile.

"Gee, that's great, thanks, fella, I sure appreciate it." He was glad they let him inside his own office. Which was good, as that's why it was called "his office." Not today, though, it seemed. Why today? He had experienced enough strange visitors for one week. This one was pretty strange, too, albeit one he would have a tough time dismissing.

"Jackie, how ya doin'?" he said as he gave her a high-five. "Nice suit, you and the pituitary cases outside."

"Great, *Tinman*. Good to see you. Appreciate the dry humor and all. You are always so complimentary of me and my staff."

"Really?" He looked around and grimaced. "What's with all the funereal demeanor around here? You'd think someone died. Man, if someone did, make sure it doesn't stink up the place, it ain't good for my public image."

"I think she's worried about the opposite."

"Huh? Come again, Levickis?"

"People rising from the dead. Some, we might want to still be dead. Well, you can't have everything."

"Wow. That's pretty profound from you. I can even sense a vestigial sense of humor in there somewhere." Surprise was an emotion he didn't hide well, and now he really *was* curious.

He went up to the large mahogany desk, now occupied by a late-fiftyish visitor who had spread his papers all around looking for something to write on. How rude! Didn't the big dudes carry crayons and coloring books for her? Guess not; it was like she owned the place or something. He could legally kick her big butt out now, as she wasn't a part-owner any longer, but Levickis and the big scary dudes outside probably wouldn't like that, and cotton jumpsuits weren't his favorite clothing. At least the nearest federal prison was in Terre Haute, so people could visit conveniently.

"Ahem," he said as she glanced up at him, peering over her reading glasses. "You know, you could make an appointment like everybody else, but then you would lose the random spontaneity that makes you unique."

"Excuse me, Senator." She looked at the shorter man angrily as she slurped some espresso and leaned back in his plush leather chair as she muted the headset on her wireless phone. "Please, Nick, I'm on the phone. I will be with you in a moment, okay?"

"Oh, sure, you can use my office. No problem. Glad you came all the way here just for that." He twirled around, plopped onto his overstuffed sofa, and stretched out.

"Thank you kindly." The President then blithely ignored him as she munched on some peanuts and resumed her vidcall.

• • •

She hung up the phone twelve minutes later and stared at her deceased brother's best friend's nephew.

He rose up from the sofa. "So whaddaya need, Madam President-for-Life? Or is it Doctor Vice Admiral Darkkin? Dame Commander Gallinsworth? It's very hard to keep track of your titles and name changes; there probably is a protocol officer for that with his or her own office building and expense account—"

"Nick." She stared up at him from the desk, annoyed, as she took off her reading glasses, deep aqua eyes staring at him. "Don't be juvenile. You *know* I don't use the title 'Dame Commander' any longer. I relinquished my British citizenship and title of chivalry in 2021 when I took office because a sitting U.S. President clearly cannot be a subject of a foreign monarchy. When I'm out of office, I will reinstate my British citizenship and use the title again—"

"It was a joke. Jeez. I really don't care what the hell you call yourself these days. You could just make The United Kingdom another state; then it would be okay." He looked at the strange-looking diver watch with the white face, blue bezel, and blue natural rubber strap (which smelled faintly of vanilla), and looked closer as he grabbed her right wrist. "Glycine Combat? Commemorating the simple elegance of an amino acid going off to war? What the heck kind of fricking stupid-ass watch is that?"

"One of my dad's old watches," she said, immediately dropping her voice two octaves to a loud baritone and pulling her wrist away. That vocal change usually meant she was getting peeved by his chatter.

"So sorry." He patted the watch crystal gently. "Didn't mean to insult one of the Radster's fine Swiss timepieces. My bad."

She snarled at him and ate a mouthful of snack mix from the desk bowl as she stared. "You're a barrel of laughs, aren't you?"

"Yep, I sure am, because I learned it from the master—you." He watched her large white teeth gnaw on some nuts. "Oh, darn. Better watch that diet. Those aren't the low-fat peanuts. The Overeaters Anonymous hotline is available 24/7, and maybe you should call a friend for an intervention—"

"It's serious, Nick. Stop the happy crappy, I mean it."

"Sorry, force of habit." He shook his head. "It's the trading insults with Bella every day, it keeps my wits sharp. A man must evolve to survive in a hostile environment or perish."

"You know," she said as she smiled sardonically and leaned back in his chair as it creaked under her large frame. "you remind me of your uncle more and more every time I see you."

"Glad he influenced me in such a positive fashion."

"No, that isn't necessarily a good thing, let me tell you."

"Really? That's sad." He put his head over his heart as if he had just been stabbed. "And *that* really hurt me—I guess you really *have* changed."

"Not certain I follow, but that's nothing new."

"I mean, there's no more fun and games for Goofy Gwendolyn. I miss the old jolly round blonde wearing the Santa suit at Christmas, bursting with mirth."

She pointed at him. "Yes, I have changed, genius, you're not the only one who's evolved. Maybe I'm better, maybe worse, but I am what I am."

He lifted his right arm and flexed his unimpressive biceps, clearly smaller in circumference than that of his guest. "'I yam what I yam?' A quote from Popeye the Sailor Man? How profound. Can I have Leah get you a can of spinach? It's much healthier for you than those snacks."

She frowned. "Yes, profound—I wish I had time for fun in my life like I once did, but I don't, and neither do you."

"I don't?" He stood there, perplexed. "That's a damn shame. All work and no play makes Wendy a dull girl. I am sorry I missed the memo from Washington."

"If you can't see that very clearly, then you're not the smart guy I thought you were. Life changes people." She frowned and turned the dark-haired woman's photo on his desk around to face him. "You know what I mean, right? Remember?"

He scowled angrily at the President of the United States as he picked up Marcy's photo from his desk and looked at it. "Thanks for bringing it up, Doc. You, of all folks, should know the danger of opening up old wounds."

She frowned. "We all have them, some more visible than others. It's our pain that keeps us going, you know, and we both have it in spades. Without that, we have no goals, no ambitions. Can't change the past, so might as well go forward."

"Well said, as usual." He sat the photo of his deceased wife down. "You have me curious now, Ma'am."

She stood up and started walking around. "I know we all have our secrets. I may not have the right to ask this, but I hope you would tell me anything you know as a friend. Other than my husband, Will, and Jackie, I truly trust about three people in this world. One of them is you."

He took a half-hearted bow. "I am honored, of course, by your grand presence and surprising confidence in me. Shoot."

"This may sound crazy, but what are they doing, and why are you sending them money? I need to know. Time has run out."

"Uh, where's who? What money? For the bookie? Bella doesn't gamble; she didn't inherit those special genes."

"What? How obvious do I need to be? Bonnie. Aurora. Your Uncle Jim."

He laughed and stared at the ceiling. "Yeah, that's funny. I'm sending them a few bucks here and there, sure. I do that on my weekends off from the psych hospital I stay at, where I talk to the funny green men. Sometimes they're blue men, actually. It depends on the weather outside."

"How about fifty million dollars? Do I look like I'm kidding? I've tried to stay out of your business, but I'll find out myself, in time, with the resources I have at my disposal—is that productive for any of us?"

"I have resources too, Wendy. You being threatening is so unbecoming for someone of your immense natural beauty."

She shook her head and smiled. "Not my intention."

"Well, as I recall, that plane Alex and Bonnie were in, along with Aurora, Stan, Jake, Cassie, Mike, Jose, Marcy, Teresa, Elisa, Carlos, and your mom, was pretty much vaporized by the piss-poor piece of protoplasm called *Santaman*. How could anyone have survived?"

She got in his face and stared down at his five-eleven frame. "The damn North Koreans did it, not one of Bonnie's stupid villains. Kristoff van Sant was a bad dude, but still a scapegoat."

He nodded. "Yes, and you certainly made them pay for it. The fifty-fifth state is surely my next vacation destination. We're lucky Taraq is still on the map after they kidnapped Thomasson."

"Yeah, well—keep my politics out of it, dammit. I'm here because Jay keeps seeing visions of Aurora. If we don't all get on the same page here, then things will not turn out optimally. We have a unique opportunity now."

"You mean *you* have a unique opportunity. Jay sees visions of lots of things, just like his sister did, you know that. And your language seems to have taken a turn for the worse lately since you've been Prez. Why doesn't that surprise me? Maybe we should call you Connie. Or Rada, or Radie—darn, what's the feminine derivative of Rad?"

She slammed her fist down and sat down again. "Don't make fun of my dad. He was a great man."

He crossed his eyes. "*Huh?* Did we just get transported to some alternate universe? You hated the dude's guts for, like, forever, and now you tell me how great he was. You didn't speak to him for years, Jim said." He choked on his coffee, spewing brown liquid everywhere. "Yeah, he was great at getting everybody into trouble, including you, as I recall. His fantastic legacy lingers on."

She took a sip of coffee. "Sorry, this damn job does it to you. But she could've hidden, you know."

"Why would she do that if she's still alive? It's not theoretically possible by any means we know for her to still be living."

"Jim wasn't on that plane, yet he disappeared shortly afterward. You didn't answer my question about him."

"Two weeks later. Does that surprise you? When was Jim ever responsible?" He paused. "And why would I know if he was alive?"

"That doesn't answer my question. And Bonnie, although we had drifted apart in later years, was once my best friend and one of the world's greatest poker players, as you've mentioned. But you, my friend, have a terrible poker face. I know when you're lying."

He shrugged. "I have one condition: Jackie leaves. No offense, Levickis, it's nothing personal, but Super-Chief and I need to have some private words and mix it up a little. Fortunately, we have on-site medical facilities to take care of the many broken bones I shall likely suffer during our discussion."

"Sure thing." Wendy gestured towards her detail chief. "Jackie, please excuse us if you don't mind."

"Yes, Ma'am." She left and closed the door.

He pointed at her and turned hesitantly towards the penthouse window. "This can never be shared with anyone. You say anything, even to Jackie, I'll deny it. I will tell you things only as a friend, not the President."

She stood and stared at the ceiling. "Okay. You have my word."

He got in her face and stared up. "I mean it, dammit, look me in the eye. You and I both know you wouldn't be in the White House without Bella and me, so act like you mean it, Wendy. I'm trying to be nice to you for old times' sake, but your little entrance has now become very annoying."

She stared down at him. "What did you say? *Annoying?* How *dare* you speak to me like a common peasant, Nicholas Stannous? Do you fully realize whom you are addressing?"

He smiled. "Huh? Are you kidding, lady? *I* dare. You got something to say about that?"

"Yeah, I might generate a few choice words."

There were only a few people who could stare down the mighty

President, a master of media and manipulation, and emerge in one piece. Nick Stannous and his wife were two of them. He suspected that a third was the wiry, pistol-packing Secret Service detail chief.

"Well?" he asked. "I'm waiting."

She sneered. "I will *not* be talked to that way."

"Yeah? Really? That's all you've got?" He waved his arms toward his body and laughed. "Then bring it on, Madam President, I give as good as I get. I've withstood way worse than you, and I'm still around, so I welcome it. I didn't get here by being some pansy-ass either, and I've been through some bad shit, just like you. My PAC contributions helped stack your Congress. We're alike, you know."

She laughed. "Funny, Nick. In what possible way are the two of us similar, other than we are both diploid, breathe oxygen, and have forty-six chromosomes?"

"It's obvious—we're both opportunists. Victims of terrorism who used our bad fortune to advance our careers to the stratosphere, to gain an advantage over those who might oppose us, to vanquish our enemies. So we're equals and kindred spirits, get that straight, you big bozo."

"*Bozo?* That tears it. You feel you are my equal?" The voice dropped again to a medium baritone. "Are you on something?"

He laughed heartily as she scowled. "You got it —I'll take you on any day of the week and twice on Sunday. And you don't need to talk in the deep scary voice, either; it's actually more comical than intimidating, just so you know."

She stood silent for about two minutes, then broke eye contact, just as he knew she would. She might be the President, but she was still only human, and he didn't become one of the world's richest and most powerful men by being Caspar Milquetoast, either. They were, as he had declared, more alike than different. And he knew she knew it, too.

Twenty years apart in age, but almost twenty years' history between them allowed one to easily predict the other's actions.

She finally looked away, out the window.

"I'm sorry, I shouldn't have acted so mean."

"No problem, Wendy, I'm a big boy, I can take care of myself. I deal with a lot of assholes around here."

"Okay. No more posturing from either of us. A bad habit from the rotten world I have to work in." She extended her large right hand, and he shook it.

"You mean that?"

She nodded. "Yes. I'm a person of my word."

"Deal." He walked around the room. His old friend Wendy was a lot of things—often loud, domineering, and opinionated—but *not* a liar. "I'm sorry, but as far as I know, Alex died on *Darkkday*. No other info. Promise."

"Yes, I was pretty sure of that."

"And Jim *is* alive somewhere, in the Fairbanks, Alaska area."

She nodded. "That matches up with my intel."

"He said he needed money for things. Money I got. I owe him a lot, Wendy. So do you, as I recall, from some of his stories. Bonnie, I swear I don't know about, but somehow I know she's alive, too."

"He wasn't supposed to tell you about that stuff."

"Well, he did. He needed something else also, besides money."

"Massive amounts of electrical power, and computers and other classified electronics, I imagine."

He nodded. "Yes, that's true, but how did you know?"

"I know most things, son. Anyway, why did he leave Jackie and us? He broke her heart. He always was so self-centered and immature. He could've found another way. Figures."

"You judge him prematurely. He said it was time for him to grow up and take responsibility to God and country. To hide for our own good. Because one day you would find out, and that would be the day of wonders."

"*God*? The guy was an atheist. He and Bonnie went round and round about that. And he cared little about the country. He was a registered Democrat, of all things. That's only one step from Communism." She smiled and winked at him.

"So am I, despite my, uh, helping fund your political action committees. You should know better about that. Bella is, of course, a Republican. Mixed marriage, you know. It's hard, they said it couldn't be done, but here we are."

She stuck her tongue out and smiled sardonically. "Ugh. I guess I try to forget that."

"People change. But that's what he said."

"I agree with what you've said, but why do this in this manner? It's bizarre."

"What did you expect from Jim and the Bonster?"

She stood up and put her hand on her hip, peering down at

him. "What did he need money for, Nick? Building a church and buying bibles? I would like to think positively, but those two were crazy."

"What's the old saying? 'It takes one to know one?'"

She grabbed him by the shoulders. "Duh! Yes, I get it, Nick. They, along with my dad, almost started World War III by threatening to shoot nukes off a Russian submarine. Why did they do what they did when we could've helped them?"

"They have their own agenda, obviously, which they clearly don't want you to be part of. Imagine that."

"Understandable. So, what's the deal?"

"Okay. His living expenses are very large, it seems. Over the last five years, I've given him maybe thirty million dollars. Wired to the Grand Caymans, the phone calls come from all over the world. I don't know for sure where he is, what he's doing with it, or anything. Never asked. All I know is that I trust him. He says it's to serve humanity. That it was for something wondrous beyond belief that would someday be shared with the world—with you in particular."

"Yeah, right. 'Wondrous' for him might be an endless supply of beer and barbecued ribs. The three of them are in North Pole, Alaska."

"North Pole? Santa?" He smirked.

"North Pole the town, not the geographic or magnetic North Pole. The former is a suburb of Fairbanks, where you said."

"Good to know. I thought it was there somewhere; I figured it out, vaguely."

"You mean Bella figured it out. You aren't the greatest detective, as I recall from your teen years."

"Not by myself, but we function as one symbiotic intelligence if you must know. I don't keep track of her detective work, as I don't have time. He isn't spending in on brew and ribs. And, as I said, he doesn't exist."

"Don't know. Another thing—Johnny Kepler has been seen around here lately. Remember Johnny?"

"Sure, the *Gravi-Golfer*—heard he was back on the Seniors Tour with his new bionic leg. Cool dude. He and Hanna make for the greatest father-daughter golf duo yet."

"He's also been working with you on your big dark energy project."

"My what?"

"Don't kid me. A big guy, maybe twenty, came to see him asking about the golf ball burned up in space, I heard. He thought the guy looked kind of like me."

"Those were a hoax, from what I understand."

"Come on, Nick, don't try and con me. You know the golf balls from space are no joke."

He guessed the President had access to all kinds of information, even what happened at Princeton with Juriann and Johnny Kepler.

"Okay, I'll bite. There were three. One landed here, by the lake, which is the one you heard about. Another in Green Bay; the third one, which you invariably have, thrown right by your dearly departed dad's tombstone. Kepler was here and confirmed it. And he also confirmed that the big fella went up there to see him."

"What?"

He slapped himself in the face. "Oh, no. Don't ask me to cover up any skeletons in your closet. If you have any illegitimate children, that's your problem. At least you're gonna be in your last term when you start showing, so there's not much anyone can do about it."

"No, dummy, not that." She pulled out a manila folder. "I know all about it. The guy took a drink of water at Princeton a week or so ago and left saliva on the glass. DSD had his DNA run."

"How did you get that info?"

"Come on, they're the DSD; need I say more?"

"Got it. But who is it? Anyone we know?"

"Yes, ironically. All evidence points to him being my brother."

"The great Alexander Dirk Darkkin lives? We just agreed that he was dead. That would be great; he was a cool dude."

She shook her head. "No, not Alex. My other brother."

He looked around curiously, twirling an engineering pencil in his hand. "Um, I guess I must've missed that one, and I swear I'm being honest about that. You had some other bro nobody knew about? Jesus."

She nodded. "Yes, a half-brother. His name was Travis Argon; he was an illegitimate son of my dad and a woman he had an affair with in Monte Carlo in the early seventies. He was a bad dude, and Bonnie killed him after Travis killed my dad."

He slapped his face with his right hand. "Your long-lost brother killed your pop? Man, that kind of sucks and brings up all kinds of Freudian dilemmas I don't even wanna go into. Then Bonnie kicked his ass? Man. That's enough pathos for a movie franchise."

"Yes. I thought you might've realized that by now."

He shook his head, puzzled. "So *why* would you want to find any reincarnation of him, then? Just saying."

"I didn't say I wanted to, but he's out there, so *you* tell me."

He shrugged. "Your information is correct, and your spooks are spot on. *Golfer* did talk about some dude who came by, said he eerily resembled a younger version of your dad, maybe twenty, Johnny said. Spoke in a thick Dutch accent." He paused for a minute. "Huh? What am I saying? Dutch Bro? How the hell?"

"When Bonnie was head of the CIA's Directorate of Science & Technology, it's possible, even probable, that she did something with my dad's DNA."

"What? Cloned him? No offense, but your frickin' dad created a lot of trouble when he was alive. I know he saved your life, but he was the cause of all of it in the first place, I heard."

"And I helped. I have as much guilt here as anyone." She stared out the window. "Has he been around here?"

"Who?"

"My brother, who else would I mean?" She looked around the office. "Are you hiding him around here somewhere?"

"Of course not, I just know he went to see Johnny, although he called me and said something curious."

"What?"

"That the guy might show up here. But I swear he hasn't yet. Anyway, why would you want to find another bad bro? Was the Bonster really that reckless?"

"A simple answer? Are you serious?" She formed an "O" with her mouth.

"Of course." He nodded.

"Yeah. Hell, yes, she was worse than my dad. About him, Jim also said he injected himself with the Ontario Lacus organism."

Nick shrugged. "I don't know anything about that, as I was only about fifteen years old at the time. I wasn't worried about such world-shaking things, I hadn't even met Bella yet, whose mouth can shake worlds."

"Ain't that the truth."

"But another thing Kepler said—he hasn't told anyone else, but he said that the Earth's revolutionary period and transit time about the sun have slowed by picoseconds."

"Maybe, Dexter Slabb said the same thing. It could be real or just a measurement error. Not much precedent for this."

He shook his head. "Uh-uh. This is real, Johnny says, and he has the world-class equipment to prove it. It's episodic and appears to somehow coincide with especially bright auroral displays at the North Pole."

"The aurora, what irony, don't you think?"

"Yeah, sure. He thinks someone or something is altering gravitational forces on a microscopic scale. Not enough to be perceptible, but it's there. But what does Rad Junior have to do with that?"

"Don't know."

"You and the spooks going after the guy?"

"What would I do when I found him, *Tinman?* Do I really want to know, even though I suspect he's somewhere in the country? One of my dearly departed sister-in-law's crazy experiments? A clone of my brother? A second damn *Orthoman*?"

"Maybe *this* Ortho is a good guy."

"Yeah. That remains to be seen."

"But you surely can imagine what Bonnie, Alton Lohrbach, and his nephew Dexter Slabb cooked up. From what I've heard, Alton's like your dad, but skinnier and with a New England instead of a Tennessee accent."

"Sure, Nick, I see Dexter almost every day. About the power, though, I imagine it has something to do with this." She threw down some fuzzy photographs on the massive mahogany desk.

"Wow, real photos, how quaint. What's that? A UFO?"

"Perhaps. The spectroscopic images indicate a high density of hyperdense carbon in the skeleton."

"Organic?" He thought for a moment. "Fullerenes?"

She nodded. "Yes. All evidence points to it being an advanced exoskeleton made of aggregated diamond nanorods."

"Huh. How do you know so much about the thing? You ain't no physicist or chemist."

"How? My dad and his friend, a drunken Russian bionics expert, stole a prototype from the Soviets back in the late 80s. The approximate mass and chemical composition indicate that it's the *Mendoza Milagrosa Mark I* battle armor."

"The what?"

"It's a cybernetic Soviet suit of armor which was adapted to allow Bonnie to rescue me from Malachi Argon's island in 2010."

"You're saying you actually saw this Russian suit of armor almost twenty years ago? Like I could believe *that.*"

She nodded. "Yes. Jackie has, too, if you want to ask her. Bonnie is, to my knowledge, the only human to ever have worn that in combat. Alton Lohrbach says it's missing. Along with a hell of a lot of other stuff. Not that he cares."

"I guess I have to believe you. So, you think a fifty-something autistic woman is out there flying around in a Russian battle suit from the 1980s? Are you kidding me? And you believe Lohrbach? How is that even possible?"

"No, of course not. But Aurora would be eighteen years old now. I know it's her. There are eigenface matches with a blind girl in Alaska named Paige Marshall that fits the description of an older Aurora. They must need the money and power to run some type of surveillance complex."

He nodded. "Correct. Looks like you've got it all figured out, then, so whaddaya want with me?"

"I vowed I would never interfere with whatever they're doing, but I can't stand still any longer. If there's something out there that can help this country, an ally, I must try to help."

He choked on his coffee and laughed. "And you mean help yourself, that's what this is about, as always."

She shook her head. "No, it isn't about me, Nick. I'll be entering my last term soon, but if I can use my influence to help her, make her a valued partner rather than something to be experimented on, then that's what I need to do."

"The world thinks Aurora's dead. Hence, this city."

"We both know better." She pulled out her TekPhone. "Look at this. Security cam footage of some blind girl who foiled and disarmed a robbery in Anchorage. She was just a blur on the camera. Witnesses said she was shot, but no blood was found anywhere."

"Yeah, so? I know about all that."

"Of course you do, but it's the same girl who shoots nearly 100% from the free throw line."

"Then run a facial check. Your cyber team can get on it. Oh, hell, I'll do it myself." He uploaded the video and used his own software on the virtual desktop. "It's some girl named Cheryl Paige Marshall. Who cares?"

"Listen up: I've always been somewhat self-deprecating and made fun of my dumb hillbilly blonde image. I took advantage of it, even. But I'm no dummy. That girl is Aurora Darkkin. My and Jay's niece, Bella's cousin, and Will's double cousin. I had all the cyber files changed ten years ago. I did it myself. No one else knows besides Jackie. So, yes, of course, they're the same person."

"My God." He thought for a moment. "So, you're finally admitting you've known about this all the time?"

She shrugged. "Yes, certainly I did, vaguely. I tried not to mess with their lives. If they wanted to go on thinking they are hiding, then, by God, I was going to help them."

"Help them? By letting them live in Alaska when they could have been rich?"

"Who the heck cares about their money, *Tinman?* This wasn't about that, it was about protecting them, at any cost. I may have to answer for keeping people out of their hair, but not today. Do you know what some opportunistic people might do?"

"Yeah, I get the idea. But how much of this did you know before *Darkkday?*"

She nodded. "A little bit. Aurora displayed some signs of limited invulnerability as a young child. Minimal augmented strength."

"Being really strong and not getting bumps and bruises is far different than surviving a nuke blowing up in your face."

"So you say. But they're out there, Nick. And don't play dumb. I know Bella has known for years."

"Agreed. So, what is it you want me to do?"

"I want you to help if somehow you are involved."

"How do you know I am?"

She peered at him. "I know, believe me."

"You didn't know about all the golf balls."

"Are you kidding? Of course I did. What you perceive I am ignoring, I am doing on purpose. What other stuff are you and Johnny hiding from me?"

"Nothing tangible. You have to believe that. Only theories that some dark energy field is out there manipulating energy. It comes and goes. There was some tiny amount of gravitational perturbation around the time of the golf balls, which centers around Alaska, which is where you say they're at."

"What is it you want from me, then?"

"If you hear anything, will you let me know?"

"Sure, when lost bro shows up, I'll send Jackie to bring you for the welcome party I'm gonna throw. But I have no idea what I'll hear about this or why."

"It's called Aurora City. She might come back here."

"Let's say this does actually happen—what if she doesn't want me to contact you? Maybe she doesn't want to be your friend."

"I'm her aunt and I care about her."

He laughed. "Sure you do. After yourself. That's who you care about most."

"Yes, but look who's talking." She rose from his chair and walked out briskly. "Let's go, folks. Lots to do. See you, *Tinman*."

"Hopefully not for a while."

"Probably sooner than you think."

They walked out the front door as Jackie waved politely at the crowd.

"Where are we going now, Ma'am?"

"We're going back to Tennessee."

"Why are we going back there? You just had a holiday."

"Business. To see someone I think lives out there whom time has forgotten. You remember Dexter's uncle?"

"Alton Lohrbach?" Jackie asked. "Your dad's old buddy."

"Yeah. Let's go pay my dad's old friend a little visit."

Chapter Twenty-Four

The President's Bedroom
The White House

Wendy looked at Jay in a forlorn manner, bringing up the question she would have of herself over and over. No matter how successful she became, she would confide in that one person about her insecurities. Most would think it impossible that she could have any at all, but she was only human, a person who at times had to fight low self-esteem.

"What's bothering you?" he asked.

"You should know." She looked up at the ceiling as they lay in bed together.

"Why do you keep fretting about it?"

"Because it's important. Don't downplay it. Would I have won in 2020 had it not been for the assassination attempt, *Darkkday,* and people feeling sorry for me?"

He stood up. "No one, repeat, no one, felt sorry for you. They admired you, and you earned everything you have. You were the Surgeon General, then Governor of California for two terms. You're an American hero, an Olympian. I know how hard you worked."

She looked down sadly at her blue nightgown. "A flawed one. Why am I deserving? I am so far from perfection it's ridiculous."

"A lot of people thought I didn't deserve to be in the Pro Football Hall of Fame. I had the Super Bowl MVP, but less than ten good seasons, because of the knee injury."

"Dang it, Jay, don't make this about you and compare being

President to having a bust in Canton. Not hardly the same thing."

"Perhaps, but damn right you're a flawed lady, and that's why people love you. You took four bullets for a President when his Secret Service agents couldn't. The other day you saved a little boy from drowning, putting yourself at risk. That's just you. You might be a world ass-kicker, but you're still Wendy inside."

"Am I, Jay? Would I have won? Did I win because I saved the President and we lost our family in 2016 in the attack? Because women admired me for having a child at age forty-five? Did I steal away all Garcia's Hispanic votes because you were my husband? You probably were more popular than me."

"I don't know about that, certainly not from women voters who had dated me. That would have been at least a hundred electoral votes for the other side. No, you kicked Garcia's ass in the debates and on the campaign trail; it had nothing to do with me."

"Yeah, but Nick got mad at me and said I wouldn't be in the White House without him and Bella. I wasn't happy about that statement, but was he right? Did I buy my way in?"

He shook his head. "Listen, no one gets to the Presidency alone. You sold your interests in Mendoza Multinational and Dirk T. Darkkin & Sons you inherited from Alex and your dad, so you were a multi-millionaire—that is, after you stopped spending money on stupid stuff like the *Science Squad*. So you haven't done anything more than anyone else who threw money at the election. Tell *Tinman* to shut his stupid ass up."

"Maybe. I just think he's right, at least partially." It was like her to doubt herself at times, in private. To most people, she was supremely confident, but she had her moments when she needed reassurance that she was on the right track. She knew this was what his greatest value was to her: to be the man behind the woman. "Mendozium technology had a lot to do with it, I'm sure."

He paused. "I know better. Without some of those things, you still would've been a player. People wanted something different, more conservative after that all happened and the dismal four years of Dick Trammell. But they would have seen your value anyway, without *Darkkday*."

Right now, she needed to get some answers about things that happened before Bonnie died. The person who was most likely to have those answers was rumored, for some reason, to live back in Appalachian Tennessee, of all places. Dexter Slabb's uncle. He was an old friend of her dad's, despite them seemingly having nothing in common. Friendship with her dad was liable to get folks in all sorts of trouble; or dead. Alton Lohrbach had experienced enough of the government during his interesting career, and he obviously needed some peace and quiet. That was going to end.

She wasn't his favorite person, she knew. That would just be too damn bad. Like her father, she would go wherever she pleased.

• • •

Wendy and Jackie walked up to the door of the cabin in rural eastern Tennessee, about five miles south of Solway, as the rest of the detail waited back at the vehicle. She knew Alton had been out in this part of the country with her dad many times in the past, and it was only natural that he might retire here. Plus, Dexter told her, after some discussion, that he was here. It was time for retirement to end.

She pounded on the door after wiping the snow from her boots.

"Come out of there, Lohrbach, you old son of a bitch. I know you're in there. Dexter told me where you were."

A high-pitched male voice came back. "Alton Lohrbach is dead. Get off my property. You, in particular, aren't welcome. That goddamn nephew of mine, in particular, isn't either, the traitor."

"I had hoped you would want to see me, having given a life of service to your country."

"My life is over, and I don't need whatever trouble you and your minions have brought here, so get lost."

Jackie came up to the door and put herself between Wendy and the door. "We can't go in there, Ma'am. Without a warrant—"

"Oh, hell, shut up, Jackie. I'm not an idiot." She banged on the door again. "I'll bust it down, Alton, so open the dammed door!"

A few minutes later the door opened as she spied the eighty-year-old man, wearing faded jeans, an old Iron Maiden T-shirt, and a faded blue denim jacket.

"Are you deaf, lady? I told you to get out."

"Cut the bullshit, Alton. You don't answer my calls or e-mails, so what did you expect me to do?"

"Leave me alone, that's what! I'm off the grid. Old Rad the Dad had the right idea, living that way for years up here in the hills. I wish I would've taken his advice sooner."

She laughed as they walked into the small living room. "If you really wanted that, I wouldn't have found you so easily. Listen up, I have some problems."

"You sure do, lady, that's putting it mildly. But you want help from me? You must be desperate. I'm no shrink like Dr. Elsevier."

"I do and I am. It's serious."

"What a laugh, funny girl. Well, now that you're here, have a seat. Can I get you something?" He pulled out a fifth of D.T. Darkkin & Sons Astatine Label, poured three glasses from the gleaming hexagonal bottle, and handed them each one. "Maybe some of the family brew will hit the spot for you beautiful ladies."

She took the glass of dark amber liquid (this variety named after the rarest naturally occurring element on Earth—a radioactive halogen) and sat it down angrily on the coffee table. "I'll stand, thanks. To be blunt—what do you know about my brother?"

The bony six-three man looked down at her. "Your bro, the swinging doctor playboy, the one who married my greatest protege, *Mendoza the Miraculous*? I heard somewhere they were both dead. You remember that day? *Darkkday?* It was a real corker."

She shook her head and smiled. He wasn't going to make her angry that easily. "Sure. But I meant my other brother, Alton. You know who I mean."

"Oh, yeah." He scratched his head. "Dearly departed Travis? Let's see—looked kind of like Rad, about the same height, deep voice, was a deadly human killing machine just like your army has become, and—"

"I swore to save lives. I've never killed anyone, although I may start in just a minute."

"Aww, gee. Scares me."

"Shut up, Alton. Did Bonnie and the rest of you damn CIA bastards clone him? The Ortho-Man?"

"I see you've been studying your dad's vocabulary builder tapes. It's good to have such an articulate Chief Executive. But me, clone Travis Argon? Are you nuts? One was bad enough. Maybe you'd better ask your sister-in-law."

"Bonnie's dead, you old idiot, you just said so. Are you crazy?"

The tall, ectomorphic Alton Lohrbach, former Secretary of Defense under President Reardon, laughed. "You sure about that? Enough to bet your life on?"

"The plane was disintegrated in a thermonuclear blast. Dozens of witnesses saw she and Aurora board that plane, along with the others."

"Oh, come on. You know she's alive somewhere, don't pretend you don't, even you can't be that dumb. She's got more lives than ten cats."

"Maybe." She got in his face and stared eye-to-eye with him. "But I don't care about Bonnie, or Petra, or whatever that eccentric hermit gal calls herself right now. What kind of Frankenstein's monster did she create before *Darkkday*, Alton? Wasn't one *Ortho-Man* bad enough?"

"What, you're asking me, lady? You helped with his rebirth, using the embryonic stem cells of your own child. How touching."

"What?" the President took a step back. *"My child?* How *dare* you bring that up, you bottom-feeder?"

"Yeah, I am a bottom-feeder, and you'd better be glad I was. I did the dirty crap no one else wanted to do. Your Vice President is one of those too, but you aren't too haughty to use him to do the shitty tasks you can't be bothered with, I know how you like to keep your beautiful nails clean."

"Leave Robby out of it; this doesn't concern him."

"How quickly we conveniently forget things, but I guess you have a lot on your mind these days, working with your fellow fat cats in Washington. You're the fattest cat of them all, *Professor Ubiquitoid*. Those junkets to Armstrong City must cost a bundle."

"What are you blabbering about?"

"Cassandra's bone marrow, don't you remember? You harvested it yourself, and I watched you do it. It's full of the rare genes that enabled that Malachi Argon abomination *Ortho-Man* to be created in the first place. Throw in some mutated genes from the extremophiles growing in Ontario Lacus, and you have some mighty cool stuff. You donated it to help us to experiments on your nice big brother, so it was really your idea, you being the soft-hearted benefactor of humanity and all—what the hell happened there? But don't blame me for what Bonnie did with it after that. She left the CIA before discovering mendozium and becoming world-famous. She purged all records of it. But you were there then—so don't you tell me about experimentation, you goddamn hypocrite."

"I don't consider that abomination of humanity named Travis Argon to be my kin. And that wasn't my intent. I was trying to advance science."

"Oh, yes, you sure are the great benefactor of humanity, and 'advance science' you surely did, but perhaps not in the way you had hoped. But he was your kin, or the 'dark kin,' so to speak. Ha, that's funny."

"I don't think so. Do you see me laughing?"

"The DNA was so similar. Mendoza got a lot of mileage out of that. I knew she was the right person for the job—you think your grizzly old pop was a mad scientist? He was bush league, milady. She had ideas about ten orders of magnitude beyond anything his drunken brain could concoct, even when he was taking LSD. That's why he took drugs, you know, so he could invent things; sometimes it worked, sometimes not. Mostly the latter.

"But Bonnie didn't need recreational drugs to see wild visions; she could do it all on her own. You don't know the wild shit she thought up. The greatest synthetic mind I've ever known, and also one of the most reckless, what a singular combo. I wish we could relive those times."

She laughed. "And *you* picked her for that job. Congratulations: government at its finest."

"Wow, look who's talking. No man ever got anywhere without taking some risks, and you've taken more than a few, Ma'am. In the end, she left after only four years, but she created some cool stuff while she was there. I wish she'd discovered element 119 then, though, then the government would be rich instead of M2. We thought of claiming it as a matter of national security, but then *Darkkday* happened, America had greater priorities, and I decided to get the hell out of Dodge while I was still alive. Glad I did."

"Right." She laughed. "They resurrected *Ortho-Man* with DNA from Travis Argon and Cassie?" She finally sat down and took a swig of whiskey, the first time she had taken a drink in over thirty years and, ironically, the first time she'd ever tasted Dirk Thaddeus (D.T.) Darkkin & Sons Tennessee whiskey. God, she sure needed a belt of the famous booze named after her grandfather. She swirled the pungent amber liquid around in her mouth and swallowed it, the fumes irritating her nostrils.

He nodded. "I think so. We never found out for sure. After *Santaman* and *Red Skeleton* nuked the plane, all those records mysteriously disappeared."

"We won't debate why I believe the North Koreans did it."

He laughed. "Oh, give me a break. You know the Tosians did

it, given that their dictator was found decapitated in his bejeweled palace months later with the number 119 burned into his chest with a hot poker. As in element 119? Guess who was surely responsible, with the strength to rip the dude's head off? Your North Korean and *Santaman* story is getting mighty old. Might be time to think up a new one."

"How the hell do you know about that?"

"I know lots of good shit, don't treat me like a dummy."

She sighed. "So where's my new, reborn bro been all this time?"

"Who the hell knows, Madam President? He might be dead, like Travis. More likely, though, she dumped him off on some other continent, where he'd never be found. She was a lot sneakier than you ever gave her credit for."

"Maybe. I seriously doubt her ability to accomplish that alone."

"Believe it, blondie. A human clone grows at the same rate as a normal human; him, maybe a bit faster. So he would be maybe twenty or a little bit older now."

"Let's move on to a more timely topic. The old armor—what do you know about that?"

"Huh? What armor?"

"Don't play dumb with me. Viktor Vladimirov's fullerene battle suit. Spectroscopy has possibly identified an object flying over the Pacific Northwest composed of exotic carbon allotropes and ruthenium. There can't be more than one."

"Well, there could always be more than one, Wendy, but not to my knowledge. But that sucker's older than the hills; it was built in the late 1980s, no less. You saw it up close better than anyone. It couldn't fly, in case you didn't know."

"Don't be so pejorative, Alton. Of course I know that."

"And it's doubtful the power supplies still even work."

"This one can, as the electronics were powered by plutonium-238, which lasts a while."

"Perhaps. But if one suit was of use to her, then she has another one squirreled away somewhere, she would've had the resources to have them built back in the day."

She nodded. "Yeah, I know. Probably close to here, under the distillery, mind you."

"If you know that, why haven't you gone looking for them?"

"I don't see what possible use those items would be to me right now, and that would just create more questions."

"But something else has to be propelling it. Ask your weird friends *Golfer* and *Tinman;* they can tell you. They do more than supply energy and play in charity golf tournaments, you know. Stannous has other interests, too, one of them dark energy. And if you think Travis Argon, Jr. is the end of the line, you really must be crazy." He started clapping.

"What the hell are you doing? Congratulating yourself? You need a refill on your dementia meds, pal?"

He shook his head. "Hardly, dear. Don't you think it's ironic, though? This whole mind-boggling haphazard chain of events is because of *you.*"

"Excuse me?"

"Your expensive 'spin doctors' sure did a marvelous job after the attempted Reardon assassination, but remember how this all got started?"

She put her left hand over her chest. "Hey, I wasn't even born yet when my dad had an affair with Katrina Argon in Monte Carlo, which ended up producing Travis. I don't think I had much control over that epic event."

"No, but your little manic episode a while back almost set off World War III. Bonnie, Rad, and Krakowski were in that Russian sub, getting ready to shoot nukes at that Caribbean island, all to rescue you."

She wiped tears from her deep blue eyes. "I can't go back in time. What would you have me do now, Alton? Wallow in my many failures and live in obscurity like you?" She pointed at him angrily. "Or go forward, as I had a country to run."

"Perhaps you should have a little humility yourself instead of being such a badass, Wendy."

"I *do* have humility, and you fail to see the paradox of *why* this world needs a badass like me, who does what no one else dares."

"Maybe at one time, but this world is changing. What little part I had to play in this drama, I would do all over again, you know."

She backed away. "Sorry, but what do you suggest I do, then?"

"Talk to Dexter, Wendy. He'll be there to help you if you need him. He can be rather acerb, but he respects you a lot."

"I know and I will." She walked out the door. "I was never here, by the way, Alton."

"Right. I'm sure going to try and forget it."

She left with Jackie, not certain what she had actually accomplished visiting Lohrbach, except confirming that, ultimately, a combination of events initiated by her and her dead father was responsible for many of these things, with some help from her deceased sister-in-law. Some of them were good. But if her "new" brother was anything like the last one, maybe not.

Chapter Twenty-Five

The Caffeine Bean
237 N. Santa Claus Lane
North Pole, Alaska

Russ looked at his watch as he sat at the only coffee shop in North Pole. He had offered to pick Paige up at her home, but she said it was hard to find and suggested they just meet up here. She was an odd duck, to be sure, but something about this girl intrigued him. His fellow officers would undoubtedly ridicule him if they knew he was going out with a high school senior. He couldn't quite put his finger on it—she seemed both very mature and immature at the same time.

And, he remembered when they had kissed at the high school career fair; he had never been kissed like that before. He asked one of his friends at Eielson what he thought of him going out with a high school senior and was seriously derided for his seemingly childish behavior, even though the girl was eighteen and there was nothing anyone could do about it. And he was sure his conservative parents would make their dissatisfaction known if they knew about it, which they didn't. Not yet, anyway.

To hell with what other people thought.

He watched the door for several more minutes as she finally walked through the front door.

"Hey, Paige, how's it going?" the male barista said.

"Good, Eddie. Another day that it is good to be alive." She pretended to look around. "Is my friend here?"

"The good-looking guy? He's in the back." Eddie took her by the arm and escorted her to the back table as he brought them coffee and two doughnuts. "Here you go, girlie. Behave yourself, as this is a family establishment."

"I will try my best, although I will likely not succeed."

He took her hand and shook it. "Paige, are you sure I couldn't have just picked you up at your home? It wouldn't have been any trouble."

She sat down after touching him on the face. "Yeah, it is a little bit off the beaten path, and you might have run off screaming after meeting my mom. So it might have been some trouble, at that."

"Really? That's hard to believe. Is she pretty tough?"

"Yes, she is very wiry and somewhat scary to most uninitiated folk. Mainly just weird, though. She does not mean to be; it is merely her way. I will introduce you soon, as she can be kind of a goon."

"Huh. What about you? Are you weird?"

She nodded, smiling slyly. "Of course. You should know that after being with me for about two minutes. I make no apologies."

She heard the clink of his coffee cup as he sat it down. "How long have you lived here?"

"We have lived in North Pole my entire existence; that is all I remember. It is a small place, but it is home. Anchorage is not that far away."

"*What?* It's 360 miles away on a state highway, so it's at least a six-hour drive."

"Relatively speaking, but that is not so distant, I guess, for we Alaskans. Especially for me."

"I bet. What do you like to do for fun, Paige?"

"Besides basketball?"

"Yeah."

"Stand-up comedy, for one thing. I am going to make a career of it, once I get my big break."

"Really?"

"No, not really." She pointed at him. "Come on —I do not think I am especially funny, it would not be a good way to make a living. I would be thrown out at my first performance." She took a bite of her frosted cake doughnut.

"You have a gift for sarcasm. A very dry sense of humor, so you might make it to the big time."

"Correct, I do what I like, without a care for others' opinions."

"That is plainly obvious."

"But what do I *really* like? Playing music on a keyboard or guitar, although I am not especially musically talented. Learning about history. Mostly, I like to listen to heavy metal bands."

"What era?"

"Are you kidding? Seventies heavy metal, of course, as nothing else compares. Led Zeppelin, Aerosmith, The Osmonds, Deep Purple, Black Sabbath, Edgar Winter Group, and others. I have all the songs from the major groups."

"I used to listen to those guys, not many people do anymore."

"Well, they should, sir. We seem to share the same good taste in music. Not like the garbage of today, they cannot play."

"Fantastic. So, what do you want to be when you grow up?"

She sat up in her seat proudly. "Going from rock bands to career choices? I *am* grown up, Lieutenant. Get with the program."

"High school seniors aren't grown-up. Grown-up to me is about thirty."

"Yeah, well, I mature quickly, and *you* have got a few years till thirty, sonny. I probably will not make the pro basketball league or get a college scholarship, and science and math ain't my thing. My father—my adoptive father, actually, as my real dad died, I do not remember him—told me that my mouth was my best weapon, that it shall be the salvation of mankind."

"Your mouth is a weapon? How's that?"

"Uh-huh." She slurped her coffee after stirring in a generous portion of cream and half a jar of sugar. "I have a pretty darn good one. I like to argue and woe betide the one who attempts that with me, a futile attempt it will be."

"I can only imagine."

"He said to fight with my mouth rather than my fists."

He took her right hand, which she balled up into a fist. "Doesn't look very threatening to me, so that's good advice. I think I could take you."

"Promises, promises. We can try wrestling later, and I guarantee you will win."

"Right." He thought and paused for a few seconds. "Your dad is the girls' basketball coach at your school, right?"

"Yes, but that is not his main job. He is the minister at North Pole Methodist Church."

"A minister? Say what?"

She paused for fifteen seconds. "Do not turn all white on me, Lieutenant, although that might be hard for you. You got a problem dating a pastor's daughter? It is not like I have leprosy. Well, almost as bad, maybe."

"Well, no, I just never thought about it."

"Hey, do not get heebie-jeebies about it, Russ. He is decidedly non-violent and is a pretty cool guy; he does not carry a shotgun or spout fire and brimstone all the time. Only some of the time."

"You're not going to be a nun or something, are you?"

"What?" She began laughing so hard she almost choked on her coffee. "A *nun*? You are a riot."

"I am? Why?"

She wiped coffee from her face with a napkin. "Yeah, I about died from coffee aspiration, so hopefully you will understand soon why that is not a very good vocation for me."

"I will? How's that?"

"Huh. It will be obvious, I hope, do not be such a dope."

This was one very interesting young lady. "Tell me more about your mom, since you haven't said much about her."

"Well, she is hard to describe, but she is rather different. She is a very bright science and math teacher, although I have little aptitude for those subjects." She touched his hand. "Listen up, I do what I want, not what my mom or dad want, that is how it is."

"It is? That sounds like a very good arrangement, one I sure wish I had when I was a kid. Do they know about it too?"

She nodded. "Of course, it has been so for years after I boldly declared it."

"And they agreed to that?"

"Of course not, but that is irrelevant. I told you that I have my own weapon of unimaginable power, an irresistible force." She opened her mouth wide and pointed inside.

"Your teeth? You bite your folks when you disagree? Vampire movies were so 2000's."

"No, silly, down further, I told you already. My loud larynx, down deep in my pharynx, which makes people go into hysterics."

"Yes, you told me already, but I don't get it. So what are you going to do with your big mouth to change the world?"

She shook her head. "I do not know yet, as the proper use of such a tantalizing talent requires careful contemplation. I tend to be on the irritating side, so being a salesperson or recruiter probably is not in the cards."

"Really? I would never have guessed that."

"*Now*, who is being sarcastic? Can you imagine me as a telemarketer or appliance salesgirl? 'Hey, mister, can I show you our newest crappy model of coffeemaker or can opener that sucks? Can I sell you some overpriced life insurance you don't need? You want to buy this piece of crap used car that we cannot wait to get off our lot? How are you today, Ma'am—would you like to contribute to our worthless charitable foundation?' Surely I would be fired on my first day for pissing someone off. I could not sell a loaf of bread to a starving man for five cents, do not be dense."

"I agree; I sure wouldn't buy anything you were selling. But what else could you do, then? How are you going to pay the bills?"

"What else? Are you kidding?"

"Uh, no. I am not grasping the concept."

"Duh! There is a fantastic career tailor-made for me." She held her arms out wide and moved them around rapidly. "What group of people excels at being irritating, argues all the time, and makes good money at it while simultaneously changing the world?"

A few seconds' pause. "I give up. Who?"

She laughed. "Aww, come on, use your big officer's brain, Russ. *Attorneys*."

"You want to be a lawyer? Why? Nobody likes lawyers."

"Huh? Do I look like I care who likes me or not? I must become one before I run for Congress and then President; yet, as you say, I have to pay the rent before any of that happens."

He laughed. "Right."

She frowned and got in his face. "Do I look like I am kidding to you, Lt. Russell Stanton? While I am young, my mouth is mighty, as I aspire to be no Aphrodite."

"No offense, Paige, don't take this the wrong way—but do you really think you can get elected to Congress? That's a long shot for someone still in high school."

"Yes." She nodded and pointed her finger to the ceiling. "I have no doubt in my mind, although it may take a while. You have no idea what I can do once I decide to do something."

"Are you really serious? That could take a very long time. As in, forever."

"I will get older anyway, and what else does an irritating blind girl have to do with her time?" She tried to take a sip of coffee but noticed it was gone, and she frowned and raised her hand. "Bartender. A refill, please," she said, pretending to slur her speech. "Make it a double." She felt Eddie bring them a refill on their coffee. "Thanks, barkeep."

"This is it, Paige," Eddie said. "I'm cutting you off after this one. You're getting more buzzed up than the law will allow."

"Meanie." She chugged the sixteen-ounce mug of liquid in a couple of gulps after again stirring in ample amounts of cream and sugar.

"Oww, that's hot," he said. "How did you do that?"

"Huh?" She drained the last remaining drops. "Do what?"

"Drink your coffee like that? It's boiling hot. He gave me the same coffee just now, it's scalding, but you drank the whole thing at once like a glass of iced tea."

She smiled. "Oh, well—you see what I mean? I *do* have the proper constitution for working in the legal field or in Washington. Not much bothers me. I can take anything that would be toxic to mere mortals and come back for more." She wiped the coffee from her chin with a napkin. "Well, I am waiting for it."

"Waiting for what?"

"*Constitution? Washington?* Get it?" She laughed.

"You're a barrel of laughs. You have *no* future as a comedian. Why don't we save the profound career discussion for later, since you seem caffeinated enough?"

She shook her head. "No way. That could never happen." She slurped the hot coffee. "You said before at the career fair you are from western Pennsylvania."

"Yes, that's right. I'm from Edinboro, near Lake Erie."

"I thought so. I am very good at dialects. I study them since I cannot see things. You speak Pittsburghese, typical of those in western Pennsylvania."

"Wow. That's amazing and kind of creepy."

"Thank you for both compliments. What do your parents do?"

"My mom used to be an accountant, she's retired. My dad's an aeronautical engineer for Faon but does most of his work remotely. My older brother Robert is trying to make it as a stockbroker in New York."

"Is he succeeding?"

"It's a tough life, but thankfully the economy's good. Makes great money, but works eighteen hours a day."

"And *you* are an Air Force officer, a graduate of the Air Force Academy, no doubt. Your folks must be very proud."

"Yes."

"And you had hopes and dreams when you were little. Did anyone tell you that you could not do that? Go to the Academy?"

"A few. That didn't discourage me."

"So, what is different between your situation and mine?"

"Well, for one thing, there are 1,200 positions per year in the Academy, and other service academies if I didn't get into Air Force. I could've also done ROTC at most universities and gotten a commission that way. There are only 616 members of Congress—506 Representatives and 110 Senators—and only one President. You'd need to be able to deal with a lot of rejection."

She smiled. "I shall take those odds. Know that I will figure out how to do anything I set my mind upon, given sufficient time."

"Time is something most of us never have enough of. But what if you don't succeed?"

She shook her head. "I cannot worry about that. I probably shall not succeed the first time, the second, the third, or the twentieth, yet that is nothing new to me. Understand I am a blind person and deal with rejection every day on a scale you cannot imagine. You knock me down the stairs, and I will be back up there for more before you can believe it. And I will win out in the end. Maybe not today or tomorrow, but someday."

"I'm sorry, Paige."

She shook her head and smiled. "You do not need to be sorry, because I am not. Things are the way they are, Russ, and my life is great. Even in this supposed age of enlightenment, people still consider the blind invisible and incompetent. I am neither and am used to being independent, to living my life like anyone else. For the most part, I do. That takes perseverance, although it presents challenges. We all have them. So I will get there, in my own time. No worries about me; that is how it shall be."

"Huh." She heard him slurp his coffee. "So what do you want to do now? Before you run for Congress and President, I mean?"

"Bowling," she said instantly.

"Really?"

She leaned towards him and put her hand on her hip. "You are one gullible sort. Do I seem as if I would be good at bowling?"

"I don't know; it's hard to figure you out. It might be similar to shooting free throws, so maybe."

"That is a thought, with some practice. But let us go to the movies in Fairbanks. I do not get to go a whole lot these days, with my busy schedule."

"Don't you want to know what's playing?"

She shook her head. "That concerns me not."

"Okay, let's go, I guess."

• • •

They walked into the small movie theater after the three-minute drive from the coffee shop, as she carried a large tub of popcorn and a soda.

"You really okay with going to the movies?" he said as they took their seats in the rear, the previews just starting.

She nodded. "Sure, I like action movies. Any movie with a lot of noise, explosions, etc., is good, knock on wood."

"Most girls prefer romantic storylines to shoot-em-ups."

She puffed out her 42-inch size D chest. "*Most girls?* That remark implies you are quite experienced with courting the fair sex."

"By that, I didn't necessarily mean dating. Those preferences appear to be female traits."

"You should have figured out by now I am not like most females. I have many male-brain traits. My preference in movies, activities, and sense of humor are examples. A 'girly girl' I am not."

"No kidding. But I would think movies might be boring."

"Because I am blind? You proceed from a false assumption."

"I don't understand."

She grinned. "Silly, naïve boy, you sure will in a minute."

"Okay, but I don't get you."

"No? Does red blood course through your virile veins, masculine military male?" She munched on some popcorn, turned her head, and opened her eyes wide at him. "Yes, I am simulating staring at you."

"Huh? I suppose so, like all people, why?"

"That is good, my fellow hemoglobin-harboring *Homo sapiens*." Maybe I like to get my action somewhere else, didja ever think of that? My concept of fun is where it is at."

He didn't understand the alliterative, rhyming speech and avoidance of contractions; it seemed to be natural and not an affectation, given its spontaneity and randomness. "What does that mean? You are very cryptic."

"Oh, come on. It means *this*." She grabbed him and kissed him for about two minutes, sticking her tongue into his mouth.

"Whoa, Paige!" he whispered, breaking free and catching his breath, as other patrons turned around and looked at them.

"So, was that less cryptic for you?"

"That never happened to me before, except—"

"What? Kissing a girl? Come on."

"Not like that. It was—an incredible sensation that I can't fully describe. It happened one other time."

"Huh?" She frowned. "What was the other time?"

"When you kissed me at the career fair at your school."

"No kidding. Was it a good sensation?"

"Yes, it was amazingly pleasant but simultaneously very unnerving—almost a sense of being overwhelmed by an incredible amount of energy, which is impossible."

"That is weird." She smiled.

"You're the one who's weird," he whispered. "What the heck's gotten into you, girl?"

"A bunch of hormones got into me, that is what. Mom says those hormones start out as lowly cholesterol before they undergo conversion to sex steroids, so eat some more popcorn. You should read about it, since they apparently did not teach you that at the Air Force Academy. It really does not matter if I see the movie or not, if you get my drift." She felt his groin and smiled. "*Homo sapiens* has now devolved into *Homo erectus.* Oh, my. I am flattered."

"Paige, for God's sake, people are looking at us."

She laughed. "I did not notice."

"Well, I did."

"And I also do not care, and you should not be such a square."

"It's good we're in the back row, so we don't get thrown out."

She nodded. "Correct. That would not look very good on your service record. My rap sheet is already beyond repair."

"I must say that I've never met anyone like you before."

"You most certainly have not. Would you like another kiss?"

"That's a stupid question."

After the movie, they went out to his car as he looked into her unusual eyes and noticed the multiple freckles radiating out from her face, her strawberry blonde hair, and smiled as he brushed her hair.

"You're a special young lady, Paige. I don't know what it is."

She smiled at him. "Thanks, Russ. I have not been told that much in my brief life. People tend to ignore me."

"I could never ignore you." He grabbed her hand. "I don't know what it is, but when I touch or kiss you, I feel something I haven't ever experienced before."

"I do not kiss my principal, but he tells me I am like no one he has ever experienced either. It was not a compliment."

He laughed. "I don't understand the feeling."

"Does it bother you?"

"What?"

"That you are an Air Force officer, and I am a high school senior. Some might think it odd, although you have a hot bod."

"We're not that far apart in age."

"Well, I am fine with it."

"I don't know you very well—but you make me feel different than anyone ever has. I know that sounds like a corny line, but I don't know how else to put it."

"Yeesh. People have been trying to figure that out for thousands of years. It is called the birds and the bees, this opportunity you should seize."

"No, it's different. My heart rate accelerates, I feel energetic, it's not really the same at all."

"Well, I have been told I have a lot of energy." She laughed. "When can I see you again?"

"I have a couple of away trips at work, so it would be at least two or three weeks."

She laughed. "You do not have to make excuses."

"I'm not, Paige—I legitimately am not going to be available for a while. I'm not making it up, it's my job. I can't tell you what."

"I guess I can understand that."

"Can I at least drive you home?"

"Well, okay, but let me out in the driveway. You are not up to meeting my mother yet; trust me on that one, son."

• • •

The next day, Paige finished her business class at 10:55 AM, gathered her books, and walked off to her locker to get her 11:00

AM class books.

"Paige, you need to report to the gym, pronto," Bill Targen, her English literature teacher said, stopping her at her locker door.

She turned around and tapped her cane against the wall, blowing a bubble. "What is up, Mr. Targen? I am not in any trouble again, am I? Going to bust me for my bubble gum?" She hadn't done anything very obnoxious in several days, which was a rarity. "That would be pretty harsh, even for you."

"Well, I really don't know, but it's hard to know when it concerns you. Usually, Eggserby says what it is when it's bad. I haven't seen any police officers carrying their little plastic handcuffs looking for you either, another plus. Some big deal in there, I guess."

"In where?"

"I told you. The gym."

"Huh? That is what I thought you said." She chewed her gum and blew another bubble. "Is the women's pro basketball league here to make an offer? Do the Harlem Globetrotters need some comedy relief? I did not even have time to call my agent."

"All I know is, it's a fan. An athlete, apparently. Somebody pretty darn famous. There's some big black Government cars out front, Dora said. Only she and Eggs know for sure."

"Huh. Go figure that. Didn't know I had any fans. They must require some token disabled person for a news show or something, or they flew up the whole Anchorage blind school for a pep talk. Curious."

"You need some help getting there?"

"Are you kidding? I am good; you should know that." She took her cane and made her way to the gym as she listened outside the door; she didn't hear many people in there.

She heard the heavy footsteps and big feet slapping the floor outside the main entrance where the small trophy display case was. There was only one anthropomorphic being walking the Alaskan Frontier who sounded like that.

No, not the Sasquatch, but a colossal lifeform almost as massive. Principal Ned Eggserby and his 370-pound frame, no doubt.

"Hey, Mr. Eggs. What's up, sir?"

A pause as she heard his enormous feet shuffle. "How did you know it was me?"

"The sounds of your shoes and gait are rather distinctive and difficult to replicate."

"Really? You can tell who people are that way?"

She shrugged. "Sometimes, if there are not many in the room, and if I can separate the sounds. You are pretty easy, though. You always wear the same type of shoe, an oxford with a leather sole. And you hit the floor pretty loudly. No offense."

"No comment, Paige," he said, laughing. "But let's change the subject. There's someone here who came all the way from Washington to meet you."

She put her right hand over her heart. "Washington? Seattle? Tacoma?"

"No," Eggserby said. "The nation's capital."

"What? No way." She laughed. "The *President* came here to see me? What in the world for? She either wants my vote or an autograph, or she wants to learn to shoot free throws. I heard she is a southpaw, like me. Guess that gives us *one* thing in common."

He laughed. "No, not the President, but you're *really* close."

She opened her mouth wide in surprise. "What do you mean? I was joking, Mr. Eggs, Who do you—"

"Go in and find out for yourself."

She stood in front of him for several seconds. "Wait, now. You and Mr. Targen are not putting me on, are you?"

"No. As you know, I don't joke around, unlike some students I have. This is serious, Paige."

"Well—I will therefore do so. You have me actually excited about something." She put her hand on the door handle as she felt his beefy hand touch hers.

"Paige, a minute, please. Don't go in yet."

"Yes, esteemed administrator? More words of wisdom?"

"I'm just a small-town principal and don't know much, but I do know you have high aspirations. More than any student I've ever had, and I've been here a while."

"Really?" She tapped her left cheek with her index finger, curious. "And I thought I was merely a disruptive annoyance to you."

He laughed. "You've certainly been that, to be sure, as well as a break in my monotonous existence here, but you have drive. Ambition. Energy. Fearlessness. Nerve. You don't care *what* people think of you, yet you say what you believe is right. That takes guts, especially for a teenager, where peer pressure rules."

"Thank you for the kind comments, but I am not sure they are deserved, as much intense irritation as I have caused everyone."

"I meant them."

"And, yes, I possess all those things, and inside me resides more energy than you can imagine, but—again, no offense, this is a Podunk high school, and the stakes are not very high. I do not follow you."

"I get that. Most of our students just want to get a decent job, buy a car, maybe go to community college."

She shook her head. "Waitaminnit. I have *no* plans to own a car. I was just planning on starting off with a motorcycle."

"No joking, Paige. Those other kids have no real plans for the future, but not you. You reach for the stars."

"The irony in that statement is overwhelming," she muttered to herself.

"What? I didn't understand you."

She laughed. "Never mind. But I am surely not the first student you have known who wanted to be a Congresswoman, Senator, or even President. Talk is very cheap, and I do a lot of it."

"All true."

"So how do you know I am more than who I appear to be, and not just another wannabe, then? That I possess verisimilitude in my actions?"

"Easy. Maybe you're not the first to brag about that, but you're the first student I've ever seen who was serious and might actually have a shot at pulling it off. I'm just a hick teacher at heart, but I think I know a thing or two. You're kind of a diamond in the rough, but you're the real deal, Paige."

"A blind girl in Alaska who has literally been a pain in your butt 24/7? Why would you possibly believe I could become anything worthwhile and of substantial value to the populace?"

"You have made me grow in many ways. We've never had a blind student here before, and you never wanted special treatment or accommodations. Your parents insisted on that, too."

"That is because I must live in a big world where such shelters do not exist. For that, they are wise. For other things—oh, never mind. In any case, no one will protect me when I am out on my own. But none of that is relevant to why I could ever be a good Senator or President."

"Wrong. You have big ideas, and they're good ones, for the most part. Maybe not everyone buys into them, and you're rather impatient, but they will, give them a chance. You have the passion, the ability to motivate, to be the voice of reason when others are going down the wrong path."

She shrugged. "I thank you for those charitable comments, but people think me ridiculous and laugh at me behind my back."

"Perhaps, but no great leader got anywhere without adversity. People laughed at many other great leaders—Lincoln was criticized by many. FDR was crippled and in a wheelchair, yet brought America out of poverty after the Great Depression. And, remember that, in her earlier days, no President was laughed at more than Wendy Mendoza. Look at what she's done."

She nodded. "I *do* know what Mendoza has done. Only foolish, short-sighted people—apparently, most of America, by the way—think it is all good. The repercussions of her actions will be felt long after she has left office."

"Maybe. That's one of the things I admire about you. Your honesty and ability to stand up against the *status quo*."

She shook her head. "And she *wanted* to be laughed at in her youth, as an over-the-top caricature and comedienne in her spare time, but she was a well-respected doctor in her day job, a leader of many. But *Darkkday* changed all that."

"Sure. But not everybody laughs at you. They sometimesdo because they think that's what you expect, that you're being a clown with that sarcastic sense of humor and all."

Yeah, like she could be another Abe Lincoln. She wasn't sure she wanted to be the second person, one who probably would be tough to be around.

"That is great, but why are you telling me all this now when I am desperately needed inside, as you claim? Can the two be connected in some fashion?"

"Possibly, because through that door may be one first step on that long journey. Maybe you'll get to the White House sooner than expected." She felt him place the pebbled composite leather sphere in her hands. "Hold on; you might need this."

"Huh, that is, like, profound, thanks. A basketball will be my ticket to Washington—a riddle for the ages." She had no idea what that meant as she walked through the door and to the east bleachers. She heard footsteps, smelled a faint odor of sweat and musk aftershave as she felt the large hand grab hers as the steps got closer.

"Paige, I'm Will Mendoza. I'm very pleased to finally meet you." She knew the First Son was almost twelve, and she expected him to be much shorter, not a man-child. He seemed at least six feet tall, from the location of his high voice, which placed him at the appropriate prepubertal age. She usually didn't picture people in terms of their physical appearances, as that had little meaning to her. Well, his parents were both over six feet, so his tall stature at an early age made sense. He seemed very polite for a famous boy who had everything. But what the heck was he doing slumming out here? On some goodwill tour for his mom? Why would he know who she was?

"Oh, wow, this is a surprise. Why would you be here in this God-forsaken place, thousands of miles from home and 450 miles from Nome?"

"To see you. We have something in common."

She took a step back. "We do? What could that possibly be, other than that we are both human beings?"

"Basketball. I hear you're really good. I'm an admirer."

She shrugged. "*Me?* You have heard of me? How? I may be the team captain, but I am hardly the go-to person when the game is on the line. Do not bet on me in Vegas when you are old enough."

"I'm kind of a nut about odd sports statistics, and you're quite unusual. You have one thing I'm interested in: foul shooting."

"Foul shooting? Why?"

"Because I can do better, and you're the best."

"You are an all-District player, as I understand it, and colleges are already offering you scholarships in multiple sports at age eleven. How much better do you need to be?"

"Paige—this may sound weird, but while I like sports stats, I don't really care that much about being better at basketball or any other sport. I wanted to meet you because of what you've accomplished, so I can be better as a person. I really don't care that much about foul shooting itself; it's you I admire."

"Of all the famous athletes you would have access to, you want to talk to *me*?" She shrugged. "I do not wish to disappoint you, Will, but I am merely a one-trick pony. I cannot navigate obstacles very well, you know, which makes driving to the basket kind of tough. You are a superstar as an eleven-year-old freshman, dominating against boys six or seven years older than you. We, therefore, have different games. I do not even get in most of mine."

"I don't care about that; I just wanted to meet you. You seem to transcend sports. Even I can see that you're special."

"Well, I am very flattered, but I do not know how 'special' I am, though."

"How do you do that, if you don't mind my asking?"

"Huh? Do what?"

"Come on. Shoot free throws that way."

She dribbled the ball four times and walked down the north sideline. "Just lucky, I guess, I must confess."

"No way, you'll have to do better than that."

"Well, I suppose not being able to see is an advantage in some cases. I just do it the same way every time, underhanded. Once in a great while I miss, though, but only if I get distracted by a loud noise. You should try shooting them by closing your eyes sometimes."

"How?" He took the ball from her.

She craned her head around as if looking into the stands. "Are we alone presently, or is your ever-vigilant Secret Service detail here? If they are here, they are very quiet."

"No, they're outside, per my instructions. No media as this was to be a private meeting. But they are stealthy—if they were here, I guarantee you wouldn't know it."

"Okay, I believe you. Let us go to the three-point line and I shall show you."

"Is your technique a secret or something?"

She laughed. "Not hardly. If you believe you can do what I can then go for it. I am merely going to show you some things I do not show most people." She dribbled the men's size ball to the three-point stripe at the center. "Am I there?"

"Incredible, right on the line. How'd you do that?"

"Aww, I knew I was at the line, I am just messing with you. It is called absolute muscle memory, which is the main reason I can shoot the way I can and navigate pretty well for a blind girl. Once I have been somewhere, I can somehow retrace my steps; if I know where I was, I can usually get to where I am going."

"Okay, I can get that you might be able to estimate distance, but what about direction?"

"Easy. I know exactly how many degrees my body has rotated, so I can figure it out instantly."

"That would demand not only precise muscle control but also real-time calculation of angles and such, using trigonometry. Are you good at math?"

"I am merely average. Enough about the disgusting topic of mathematics. Watch." She let the ball fly with her left hand and heard it rattle in. "Dang. Got some rim on that one."

He laughed. "Hate to tell you, but it didn't go in, Paige."

"What? Yes, it did, do not kid." She shook her left index finger at him. "Do not play jokes on the poor little blind girl, I know better. I heard it go through the net, and it would have bounced farther away had it not gone in. Rather, it bounced with the same sound, right under the basket, which meant it went in."

He laughed again. "You're right; there's no fooling you."

"That is a fact you should *always* remember." She felt him place the men's basketball back in her hands. She let the next one fly as she heard the net swish, her left hand extended in the air.

"I don't believe it."

"Believe it, boy." She then retrieved the ball and returned to the foul line. "Right place?"

"Yeah."

She let the foul shot go with perfect underhand form and heard it go through the net. "My secret is doing it exactly the same way each time, so there is no variation."

"That's amazing. Are you *sure* you can't see?"

She nodded. "Absolutely. They call it a 'splinter skill,' which is kind of like an autistic 'savant skill,' but not as great. My mom has some problems with a form of high-functioning autism."

"Weird, I supposedly had an aunt like that, but she died before I was born. Like what kinds of problems?"

"I guess 'problem' is a little harsh. It just means she's different." She flipped onto her hands and walked about thirty feet. "Bet you cannot do this." Then she hopped onto one hand. "Or this. Try holding this for several minutes."

"I can't walk that far on my hands, but I can a little bit. I can't stand on one hand, for sure. But how do you do that?"

"Just genetics, I guess. My mom can do it too."

"They could just stand you out on the three-point line and let you shoot."

"I suppose. It would not be very exciting, though, and they would have to get the ball to me somehow. Luckily, I have a good vertical jump, about thirty-two inches."

"*Thirty-two?* No way. Very few guys and no girl I've ever seen can jump *that* high. Mine's forty-two."

"Really?" She took the ball, walked towards the basket, jumped up, and stuffed it emphatically with her right hand. "I can dunk, too, as you can see, although my dad does not like me doing it because the school cannot afford to replace shattered backboards."

He snickered. "Shattered backboards, right, like you could really do that."

"You never know. Anyway, he says it is vain and a waste of my talent. I know he is right, as I do not need to be such a sight."

"But you're only, what, about five-eight? You dunking is an amazing feat. I dunked for the first time in a game this year. It helps if you can palm the ball, so you might have a little problem with that, being a girl and all."

"Yeah? And what did this mere girl do just now, Mendoza?" She retrieved the ball and palmed it first with her left hand, then the right. "Palming, huh? Like this?" She held it out at arm's length with her right hand and moved it around rapidly.

"Wow, yeah, like that, you're pretty good." She felt him try to remove it from her grip. "It's like your hand's a suction cup or something. What the heck?"

She laughed as she let the ball go and heard him stumble backward onto the wood floor. "Easy peasy, even for a tiny girl."

She felt him take her left wrist and put his hand up to hers. "I don't get it. Your hands are above average size for a girl but lots smaller than mine."

"Well, I am special, and size does not matter, except for some things you would not know about yet, I would bet."

"Huh? Like what things?"

She shook her head. "Never mind, Will, you have a few years before you figure *that* out. But a lot of good these basketball skills will do me in life."

They walked down the center of the court. "I sometimes think my life's tough, but I can't imagine what yours is like."

"What do you mean by that?" They sat down on one of the bleachers in the small gym. "Is there something you perceive to be amiss with my life, having known me for all of fifteen minutes?"

"I'm sorry, Paige. I didn't mean to offend you. I meant only that it must be hard, not being able to see."

She laughed. "I am not sure why people say that. My life is what it is, and each of us has his or her unique problems, our own secret sorrows."

"Even me?"

She nodded. "Even you, this much I know. Vast privilege and wealth surely do not exempt one from such issues."

"You must be able to read minds."

She laughed. "No, but—while most surely believe your life is the cat's meow, I can only imagine how hard your life is, all the expectations thrust upon you by your famous parents. It cannot be easy."

"At times it's difficult, others it's not so bad. Most have it worse than me."

"But as for me, I get by fine, but I suppose it has its challenges. I do not know any other way to be. I guess if I knew that, it would be tougher. I do anything I want, pretty much, but it can take me a little longer to get from point A to B. And less time, on occasion."

"How did it happen? Were you born that way?"

She shook her head. "No. Mom said we were in an accident when I was little. There was an explosion in a car, and after that, I could not see, she said. My father was killed. I do not remember anything else."

"You weren't otherwise hurt? You don't look like you were burned or anything."

"I guess I was lucky." She turned to him. "To put it into proper perspective: I know a girl who broke her neck after a skiing accident. She is now a quadriplegic and was on a ventilator but has a diaphragmatic pacemaker now and is off the ventilator and she navigates with a computerized wheelchair, but there is nothing more they can do. We talk about stem cell research and cures for diseases, but most of our government's money goes into the military, while medical advances progress at a snail's pace, ace."

"I don't know, Paige. Things aren't as simple as they may seem, that much I've learned in my brief existence."

"Maybe not. No offense, but all this is from your President mom, who was a pediatric rehabilitation specialist. Most people do not have the financial resources you do. What minor inconveniences I have pale compared to that."

"That was way before I was born; I guess I wondered that about my mom also. What I do know after talking to people is that she is a vastly different person today. I wish I had known the old one."

"And a little girl I knew just died of leukemia, that is all she ever knew—a life of suffering. Another friend has cerebral palsy and walks with a limp. So be grateful for what you have, as it can all be taken away in an instant, William. *Your f*amily, above all, should know that after all they have been through."

"I guess so, and I suppose I need to learn more about those things. But you're very wise. Living a sheltered life like mine is not all it's cracked up to be."

She snickered. "Other than high expectations, your life is better than most. Your photo is on half the girls' lockers in our school."

"Is it in *your* locker?"

She laughed. "Hardly. I meant the middle school section; you are a bit too young for me, lad. And why would a blind girl have a photo in her locker? Duh!"

"I guess that was a stupid comment."

"No kidding. And being popular is hard? I would not know. At times I would like to experience that terrible situation."

"Are you messing with me? Being in my family? We have football trophies, pro football championship rings, and my Mom's Olympic gold medal and Medal of Honor all over the place. Here, touch my hand."

She could feel he was holding up three fingers on his right hand. "Three fingers. So what?"

"Well, my family has not one Nobel Prize, but *three*."

"Yes, three—impressive. I believe that would put your family in second place, after the Curies, who had five."

"You really know your history. Anyway, my mom's is around the Oval Office somewhere, next to her Olympic gold medal and some cheap trophy she won before I was born for eating over fifty hot dogs in less than twenty minutes."

"Hot dogs? She won a trophy for eating fifty wieners?"

"Absolutely, she can almost inhale them. Eating is one of her greatest talents, yet one sparsely used these days."

"What a grand accomplishment, satisfying those visceral urges. But why would she keep that in the Oval Office?"

"It has some kind of symbolism to her because she never ate any meat after that day and went on a health kick and lost like sixty pounds, I think. Dad said she changed after that, although they weren't married then. Sometimes I wonder if the change was for the better, and, as I said before, I wish for nothing else but to have my funny hot dog mom back again, the one I never knew."

"Surely she surfaces from time to time."

"Not really; she is laser-focused on things, I'm not always sure what. I suppose I get it, though, as her life is pretty stressful. She was injured pretty badly in the assassination attempt she stopped. Mom says she has to eat properly and stay in shape just to keep up. I don't know where she gets the energy."

"But about awards, she won the Nobel Peace Prize: the fifth President to have done so, despite amassing more military firepower than any country in history. Yet, there have been no wars or significant conflicts since she took office, so I will stop there and opine no more."

"Yeah, I get you, Paige. We have kings, queens, Governors, Senators, Congressmen, the greatest world athletes, and all other kinds of important people at my house all the time. Most of the famous stars on TV or in the movies—I have met them. But, that's nothing compared to *this*." She felt him hand her a coin measuring approximately forty millimeters in diameter. "Do you know what that is?"

She felt the familiar currency with her right hand and smiled.

"Of course, this is an American five-dollar coin, colloquially called a 'bonnie.'"

"Yeah. My deceased aunt is revered as a famed scientific deity for having created the element mendozium. She won a Nobel Prize in physics for that. So my family is everywhere, even on United States coinage."

She nodded. "Yes, I know that—and, I also know she never received her Nobel Prize because she died on the way to Sweden in December 2016."

"Sure, but just wait. There's my cousin Bella, who's won a Best Actress Academy Award and was nominated for another, but she acts in movies as a hobby because she won a Nobel Prize in chemistry for inventing a unique separation process of helium-3 from lunar regolith on the far side of the Moon, something that the greatest minds in the world couldn't figure out, and it made her rich. They built a city in Indiana named after another cousin who also died, which is the headquarters of their energy company."

She smiled. "I would think you should be very proud of your famous relatives and what they have accomplished, but the tone of your voice suggests otherwise. Most folks, at first glance, would be extremely envious, but I suppose I understand."

"I am, Paige, but, as you mentioned, it's hard to hear about them all the time. I feel guilty for feeling like I do, but do you know what it's like, living in the White House? I can't go anywhere without my Secret Service protection, come on. I'm like some rock star."

She shook her head. "I do not know, no one cares where I go or what I do, so I am without perspective. Maybe I shall go there sometime while I am still in my prime."

"You can come anytime you want. I don't have any real friends, you know. Everybody wants to be my buddy, but all of them just want something from me or my parents."

She stroked his smooth cheek. "You have one now, so rest assured there is nothing I desire from you except friendship. When you are blind, you learn to appreciate the little things. Money cannot buy that."

"Thanks, Paige. Maybe you can be my big sister. I never got to know mine. Cassie died before I was born. She and my big brother Jake."

"I know." She gave him a hug. "I am sorry. We both have that in common, I guess. Losing those close to us, like me losing my dad. So, we are not all that different. People are basically all the same, Will, no matter where they come from."

"I guess we do have that common denominator." He paused for a few seconds. "You know, speaking of you being a big sister, we really do look alike. That's weird."

"We do? I have no idea what I look like other than feeling my own face. Let me feel yours, though."

"Feel?"

"Yeah." She felt her own face for about two minutes, reaching for every bump and crevice. "I can visualize what people would look like from tactile sensation."

"Not skin color, come on."

"No, of course not, but you can usually tell race from the person's features." She then went over his smooth face for about two more minutes. "We do, quite a bit. You have a chin cleft like my mom but which I do not have, and a widow's peak, just like me. That is rather strange, I guess. We are also both left-handed." She stroked his face again and sniffed his hair. "By the way, handsome lad, why do you choose to marinate in aftershave?"

"Huh? All the guys wear it after they shave. It's a man thing. You wouldn't know about that."

"Man?" She laughed and shook her head. *"Someday* you may

become a man, but that day is not today. Your face is as soft as mine, with the same amount of peach fuzz or less. No way are you shaving yet, William; you just want the girls to think you do. Give it a few years and do it right, or you will not look very bright."

"Yeah, well, all the other guys do."

"The other guys." She shook her head in disdain. "You were promoted what, three years in school because of your intellect?"

"That's the word on the street, but it's obviously because of my athletic abilities. I do okay in school, though."

"Then wise up, pup. Enjoy your life, as you seem like your own fellow. I would prefer a guy who did what he wanted to do, rather than one who just followed the crowd. Who gives a crap what the older guys do?"

"You never followed the crowd?"

She nodded. "I did when I was just a kid, when I smoked and drank booze and did other stupid stuff. I am an adult now, above juvenile jesting, jubilations, and jail. So learn from my mistakes."

He howled with laughter. "You crack me up, Paige, with that dry sense of humor."

"Huh. Being humorous was not my intent, as all those things are absolutely true. I hoped to offer the voice of experience, not mirth, for what it is worth."

"Well, the credibility is a bit lacking, and I've had enough of the philosophy lesson, Paige, I get enough of that at home. I'm hungry. Are there any places to eat around here?"

She snickered. "A few. A diner, a coffee shop, a Chinese place, Mexican, pizza; nothing fancy, unless we drive to Fairbanks, which has a few more choices. This ain't Washington, son."

"The diner sounds fine to me. We eat very little meat, with my mom's weight issues and obsession with her health and all, and some comfort food would be a treat."

"Let us go, then. I have no such dietary restrictions. Full-fat is where it is at."

They went out to lunch at Gilroy's Diner, the principal excluding her from classes for the rest of the day. Then he was a special guest at not the boys'—but the girls—practice. She would be a celebrity for a little while, at least, while the most popular teen boy in the world was likely being admired by the gawking girls.

She had no interest in him, though—he was just a little kid to her. Her thoughts were of an older man. Five or six years older, to be exact—one who wore a crisp blue uniform and flew supersonic planes. Would she ever see him again?

She stood alone with Will as the gym cleared.

"Gotta get back home, Paige. I had a really good visit."

"Me, too. Thanks for coming up." She gave him a sisterly hug.

"Please come see us at the White House. Open invitation. I'll send a plane for you."

"Oh, I'll just fly up there myself."

"Huh?"

She smiled. "Just a joke. But I'll take you up on that, coming to your place, I promise. But tell me one thing."

"Shoot."

"What's your mom really like?"

"Wow, that's a tough one. Let's see—she's big, loud, talks really fast *all* the time, and can drive you nuts. Then she'll shut down and not say much at all and stare into space. There's no 'medium' setting on her. When she's relaxed, she can be the funniest human being you've ever seen. She is also really nice unless she's pissed, then watch out. She doesn't have a lot of time to relax, though. I wish my dad and I could help her with that."

"I will look forward to meeting her."

• • •

Later, Will looked at the photo he had taken of them with his phone on the plane ride back to Washington. He decided to do something fun on his handheld device.

"I stayed away, just like you wanted," his father said. "Thought I might be a distraction."

He nodded. "And you would have been right."

"What is this Paige girl like? I felt like I wanted to meet her, somehow."

"Why would that be?"

"No special reason, other than you have an interest in her athletic talents."

"Well, she's very nice, actually. Kind of reminds me of what Cassie might have looked like today."

"Cassie? Really?" Jay said somewhat nervously. "Why would you say that?"

"Yeah. Hair kind of a dark red, about five-eight, but her skin is about the same color as mine, which is odd. That's kind of unusual for an Alaskan."

"You can't have determined that just from meeting her once. There are other ethnicities that result in darker skin color."

"I'm rather observant, Dad. Cassie would be taller, though."

"Yeah. Are we going to tell your mom we went to Alaska?"

Will scowled at his father. "You don't think she knows? Duh, Dad, how stupid."

"Maybe."

"But why should she care about that anyway? Don't you know *why* I wanted to exclude her? And *you?* Everything's a stage for you both, and everywhere you go, you both dominate everything. I get so sick of it, Dad; you're both so egotistical."

"Hey, now wait a minute—"

He punched his dad in the right shoulder with his left arm. "No, *you* wait a minute. You're both so full of yourselves. She'll probably find out where we went, anyway."

He nodded. "Maybe we have been. I'm sorry, Will. Being in the spotlight is hard. But it won't be like that forever."

"Well, it's sure like that now. We likely have four more years in the White House—great. I wish I was eighteen so I could vote for Senator Saleh, so we can move somewhere else. Not that one vote would matter anyway in the District of Columbia." He rose from his seat. "Excuse me, Dad. I need some space."

"Okay, sure."

He went to the large, empty rear cabin, closed the door, and turned his tablet on to communicate with Miranda, the artificial intelligence computer his aunt Bonnie had created back in 2016, two years before he was born. Even today it was the most advanced AI computer known, he had heard, although sometimes he had doubts about that.

He turned on his portable microcomputer. "Miranda: comparison of photos for genetic relation. please."

The holographic image of the young blonde woman appeared on the small computer's digi-projector and smiled at him. "Relation known, William? It will aid me in my prediction."

"No, Miranda. If I knew, I wouldn't be asking, would I? Duh."

She frowned. "Sorry, William, no offense intended. Please wait one moment." She paused for about twenty seconds. "Comparison suggests no match, no more than variation that could be found in the general population between random individuals."

"I don't believe that. Are you sure?"

The pretty holographic British female shook her head. "Miranda is incapable of mistakes, this you should know."

"Yes you do, you're an idiot. Go away."

She smiled. "As you wish, although I am more infinitely more intelligent than you." She faded away, pointing at him.

Stupid computer, programmed to make smart-aleck remarks like that. Well, what did he expect? Like he would have anything genetically in common with some random girl thousands of miles away. What was he thinking, wasting time like that?

Paige did teach him that he had much to be thankful for. She had remarkable physical abilities, and he had the odd feeling that he had just scratched the surface. He knew that he had to work on the things he was not good at to succeed. As Dad had said, the ride wouldn't last forever, and he would have to make it on his own. But would he ever see her again? Maybe at the White House.

• • •

Jay took the call on his Tekphone as his son was now in the back cabin of Air Force One, napping.

"Well?" the deep female voice asked.

"Well, what?"

"Did he go meet this high school girl he wanted to see?"

"Yeah. He was really excited."

"What did he say about her?"

"That she was about five-eight, had dark reddish hair, had different colored eyes, and that she looked a bit like Cassie might've looked today, except her skin was darker, of course."

"Sounds about right."

"He thought she was mixed Caucasian and Hispanic like him, and he remarked how much they looked alike."

"That's what I thought he would say."

"He was accessing Miranda just now to see if they're related. He's a pretty smart kid."

"Clever and cunning just like you. I assume he obtained no useful information. Did you see her?"

"No, what are you thinking? I thought we agreed I needed to stay away. The closer I get, I can sense her presence, it's bizarre.

Making direct physical contact with her might not be the best thing right now, you know how that is."

"She can't see you; therefore, you could've seen her without making any contact."

"Well, Will sure can, and that was against his wishes. Maybe we should start respecting some of the things he wants and treat him like the young man he is becoming, rather than always doing what *you* want."

"Hey, it was his idea to go out there, not yours. You think an eleven-year-old knows what's right for him, do you?"

"Possibly, because maybe what we want isn't what he wants. He is my son, you know. He may have been subconsciously drawn there and wasn't aware of it."

"That'll be a discussion for another day."

"There won't be a discussion; I'm sick of your wanting to be right all the time."

"It has nothing to do with me being 'right.' It has to do with the future and you-know-what. But are we doing the right thing, Jay? Staying away from her?"

"Yes. If what we believe is true, she will be seeing us soon enough. And we can always invite her to the White House."

"I both look forward to and dread that moment."

• • •

Petra looked up at her husband at the kitchen table angrily, pointing to the empty seat usually occupied by a hungry teenager.

"How the hell did this happen, Jack?"

He reached into a bag of potato chips and put a handful into his mouth. "How could I have known? I think I was probably the last person in the school to know about it, and I only found out when Paige walked into the library with Will and the Secret Service, and I almost had a damn stroke. What are the odds?"

She thought for a few seconds. "Given multiple variables, it is hard to know for certain, but approximately 1 in 97 odds that William would show up here this year."

"That's more probable than I thought, but I didn't want an exact number."

"You shouldn't have asked such a dumb question, then."

"Maybe if you hadn't been on one of your crazy trips to God

knows where yesterday, you would've sensed they were here."

"Humph. Those outings are necessary, this you know."

"Why do we think Will wanted to go out there, anyway?"

"My guess is that he is fond of obscure sports statistics and is enamored of Paige and her free throw prowess; I can see no other connection. Paige does not sense anything odd, I feel."

"You feel, or you know?"

She shook her head. "I'm not sure. I can sense little since she lost her sight, and it gets harder all the time. The ability for me to use my limited psionic abilities apparently depends on the ability of someone to see me—just as my ability to have them depends on native hearing. And, as strong as my will is—hers is far greater. In a battle of sheer determination, I would surely lose."

"Do you really believe that? You're no pushover."

She nodded. "I don't believe—I *know*. I am a tough customer, but no match for her."

"Talk about dumb statements."

"No, I don't mean the obvious. Even if you took her physical gifts away, she would be a most formidable opponent, capable of decimating any adversary in a debate. That is part of the reason she is so exasperating to me; she is far faster on the draw with words than I could ever be."

"That isn't saying much. But doing that requires an intrinsic amount of viciousness, the capacity to destroy an opponent. That quality seems to contradict the Paige I know, despite her big mouth."

She nodded. "Yes. Not physically, of course, which none of us would want, or survive—but she is absolutely capable of taking on anyone with her mouth. And we didn't need this to happen. Why didn't you say anything?"

"No need to cause a commotion about something I can't control, is there? Jay was in the vicinity, for God's sakes; I saw him from a distance. I didn't need him seeing me."

"Humph. Do you think he doesn't know we're here? My brother is no Einstein, but he's not as stupid as people always thought. He was just the world's laziest boy."

"Maybe I've underestimated him, as I have his oversized spouse. But why in the world would he have come here?"

She shook her head. "I don't know. I suppose she is a minor curiosity, given her free throw abilities, at that. Will is quite an athlete, yet I feel he cares little about such matters. But I would never have predicted this."

"Do you think they know?"

She smiled. "About Aurora? Will, I don't think so; Jaime and Wendy, of course, they have known for years. How could you think otherwise? Despite what I say of my sister-in-law, she is quite intelligent."

"Glad to hear you admit it for a change."

She nodded. "It is hard."

Chapter Twenty-Six

Mendoza Multinational
225 N. Bonnie Mendoza Blvd.
Aurora City, Indiana

Juriann walked into the main lobby of Indiana's fourth-tallest building, the forty-eight-story limestone Mendoza Tower. It was a simply designed building created for a purpose and drew little attention to itself, other than its height. While the person it was named after liked the limelight, he wondered what *she* would think of all this if she was still alive.

He walked around for several minutes, looking at the exhibits and watching videos at the interactive kiosks in the lobby. He had put on a shirt, tie, and slacks he had purchased at a big man's store earlier in the day, and he noticed that several well-dressed female employees smiled at him. He returned their gestures with pleasure.

The thirty-foot bronze statue depicting the superhero of energy, as well as magic, escapology, particle physics, and autism spectrum disorders was at the center of the atrium. He noticed the number of small children congregating around it, parents taking their picture next to the gargantuan figure. She always was a child at heart, he had heard.

The muscular likeness, broken shackles hanging from her wrists, was wearing the action costume which made her a minor local celebrity on stage and television, with the large stylized "M^2"

logo emblazoned on her chest, the company's current name seemingly a fitting homage to the dead scientist. He stared for a few minutes before he went up to the front desk, where he saw the receptionist. He waited for three minutes and watched her read a digi-magazine before he tapped the desk to get her attention.

The mid-twentyish woman looked up, obviously irritated.

"Oh, no. What is it you're selling, big kiddo? I really fail to see the humor in this stuff."

"I am not trying to be humorous, Miss. I would like to see Dr. Stannous, please."

She sneered at him. "You would, would you?"

"Yes, it is quite important."

"Huh. Well, I've learned in my three years at M2 that odd people sometimes come in here, but you don't look like Dr. Stannous' usual buttoned-up corporate visitors."

"I imagine not, although I did wear a suit, which has buttons."

"Is that supposed to be a joke? Just who are you, buddy? Do you have an appointment?" She slapped herself in the face. "Yeesh, that was a dumb question."

"An appointment?" He looked up at the ceiling and pondered her question for about thirty seconds. "Yes, I most certainly do."

"Well, my digi-appointment book says differently."

He shook his head. "No, you clearly don't understand, I have an urgent appointment with that most important entity known simply as—destiny."

"Izzat right?" She snarled and looked at her coffee as she twirled her pen and shook her head. "I get tired of all the comedians around this place. Who the heck are you? What's your name?"

"Juriann. Juriann Hultaar."

"Who? That's a mouthful. Where the heck are you from?"

"The Netherlands."

"Huh, I sure don't doubt that. Look, Mr. energy-groupie, autograph-seeker, or whoever you are, you can't just walk up and see Dr. S —are you kidding me? He's one of the busiest executives on the planet. I might get you in to see his assistant's assistant's assistant in a few hours."

He held his arms up. "But my meeting with him is imperative! The future of the world is at stake. I don't have time to explain to a mere assistant; you wouldn't understand."

"Whatever that means. I'm sorry, dude, but the answer is no,

I guess the world will have to wait." She looked back at her desk, chewing her gum.

He waved his hands around vigorously. "The world cannot wait, Miss, lest it be destroyed forever. There are complex physical science issues in play here that few understand."

"Wow, that was, like, profound. But, sorree." She looked back at her digi-fashion magazine as the phone rang thirty seconds later. "Yes? Leah? You *what?* Dr. S really wants to see this guy? No way." She paused for a moment and looked at him suspiciously. "Alrighty, Leah, you want him, you sure got him. I'll send him up with one of the guys on the express elevator. Good riddance."

He crossed his arms. "It seems I am expected. I deduced as much, given the brilliance of Dr. Stannous."

"I guess so, but it was his assistant who's getting you in there, not him. You must have some connections somewhere, fella."

"Yes, his name is *Gravi-Golfer.*" Juriann was escorted to the express elevator to the penthouse suite on the forty-eighth story of the city's second-tallest building. Leah Seagrape, Nick's executive assistant (and another of his old high school friends), ushered him into the large office.

"Can I bring you something, sir?"

"Coffee, black, if it isn't too much trouble, Ma'am, thank you." He looked around at the many fine paintings in the opulent office with two Rembrandts on the wall, he observed, as the five-eleven young CEO walked into the room.

"Hi, mister, uh, Hultaar, is it? I'm Nick Stannous."

"Hello, sir." They shook hands. "You are the famous *Tinman.* I was admiring your taste in the traditional Dutch masters."

"Well, I don't know how famous the *Tinman* is, but that moniker seems to have stuck after all these years. But my wife is the art connoisseur, not me, so you can thank her for the artful decorating. Left up to me, it would be an eyesore."

"She must be talented, as I enjoy fine pieces of art. Rembrandt, van Gogh—I am familiar with them all, of course."

"I'm fortunate to be able to have them to enjoy." He ushered Juriann to sit down in one of his large leather chairs, the mammoth man dwarfing his five-eleven frame, as Leah returned with the coffee. "You didn't come here to discuss my paintings, though, did you, Mr. Hultaar? I assume you could see all those you want back home."

"Back home?" he said, taking a sip of coffee.

"Your name is Dutch and you speak with a Dutch accent, so I must assume you're from the Netherlands. There are many fine museums in Amsterdam; I have been to several."

"Correct, you are obviously very educated and appreciate the arts. But, no, I didn't come for that."

Nick smiled. "I didn't think so."

"And thank you for seeing me; I am of neither great importance nor fame, yet you immediately have welcomed me to your magnificent office, despite your busy schedule as a global executive. I am your humble guest. However, I must assume my appearance was not unexpected."

"I've seen just about everything, so, yeah, you could say that. I understand that you went out to see my friend Johnny Kepler."

"I did. You're good friends with the greatest golfer of all time, aren't you?"

He nodded slightly. "Well, not with Johnny so much, but with Hanna."

"Hanna?" He looked at Nick curiously.

"Johanna Kepler, his daughter. I met her back in high school, since Johnny's ex-wife lived in Phoenix for a few years. She's the top-ranked LPGA golfer on Tour now. We used to hang out, dated a bit—nothing serious, but we've remained friends. She plays in my celebrity pro-am every year."

"Golf, how ironic. Yes, one of the golf balls landed here. Another in Green Bay, and the third at the base of the President's father's tombstone on the outskirts of Oak Ridge."

He frowned and pointed at his guest. Juriann was about three times his size, but he and his wife were the world's richest couple, so he wasn't used to messing around with people throwing out cryptic statements like that.

"Look, son, let's get down to brass tacks. I don't like playing games and don't know what you're after."

"I am 'after' nothing more than the truth, which I would assume you would also desire, being an accomplished scientist."

"Well—you know a lot, yes. There sure were three golf balls that somehow ended up in ol' Vince's statue, the Angel Aurora at the front of Miracle Park, and at Rad Darkkin's gravesite."

"William Conrad Darkkin—one of the Princeton greats, as is Professor Kepler. The second, a legendary yet vociferous football coach of yesteryear. But I seek the third person, depicted here, of course."

"I'm not really sure I follow." Nick looked at the readout in his glasses, immensely expensive "borrowed" government technology from his wife's deceased aunt. He had many such devices not officially sanctioned by the U.S. government. He didn't need corrective lenses, but he found the cybernetic information useful at times. The hidden computers in his office could record through various sensors heart rate, perspiration content, and other values that helped him determine if someone was telling the truth or not. Having patents on the most remarkable technology on Earth, one didn't rise to this level without garnering some advantage over others and stepping over a few as well.

But the biometrics seemed to indicate this weird fellow was telling the truth, unless he was a trained spy skilled at circumventing such instrumentation; this seemed unlikely. The wide-eyed youth really looked and acted like he had just stepped off a plane from the Netherlands and was there to discuss Johnny Kepler and alien golf balls. It was so bizarre it was probably all true.

"So, answer the riddle: why me? Why here? There are dozens of people as smart as me or smarter. All I do is run an energy company. But clarify what you mean by finding the 'third person.'"

"I have visited you because I seek the one known as Aurora the Angel. I have a feeling I'll find her here."

He shook his head. "Well, guy, as *Golfer* and a dozen other folks probably told you, Aurora is really a symbol of hope, not a real entity; there *was* a girl named Aurora, but she's dead—as in no longer alive. So you won't find any flying angels here other than the ones depicted in statues."

"No, that can't be." Juriann frowned and shook his head. "I believe otherwise, Stannous. Kepler surely told you my theories of the Santa and how she flies to and from the North Pole by virtue of the manipulation of dark energy."

Kepler did tell him that, and as insane as it sounded, he wanted to hear more. "That is certainly something I want to learn more about someday, but I don't believe in Santa Claus, and you just said you were looking for Aurora. The connection between the two isn't intuitively obvious to me, but please go on."

Juriann shook his head in confusion. "Why did you create this city, then, of not as a monument, a prelude of wonders to come?"

He frowned and shook his head. "As I said, it's merely a symbol, Juriann—one this country needed desperately after *Darkkday*. My wife and I worked night and day to build this company, to create something with the technology. The ownership of the adaptation of mendozium technology is legally shared by us, but she created almost all of it by determining how to economically extract the helium-3 from lunar soil on the far side."

Juriann nodded. "Yes, this is common knowledge, I am well versed in current cold fusion technology."

"Come on. You can't be older than your early twenties, so how can that be possible?"

"I am well educated, with the equivalent of a masters' level education in physics and chemistry. So don't let my age deceive you."

"O-kay. Well, anyway—I was also born in Indianapolis, and the flat, largely rural areas here, relatively mild climate, availability of land, and abundance of natural water made this an ideal site for the first plants. Some parks and things were built along the way, as this area became one of the most prosperous economic areas in the United States, and the Indianapolis-Aurora City-New Castle metro area is the twelfth-most populous in the nation now. Not just for fusion engineering, but for all the support services necessary. There were many factories left over from the defunct automotive boom of the mid-20th century that were used."

"And you have an interest in non-baryonic matter, as do I."

"Of course. This is a huge company, Juriann. We've got many research interests and like to think ahead. Some pan out, most of them don't. But while Bonnie Mendoza had incredible ideas, she was kind of an airhead. It took real practical application for them to be realized. What you see before you is hard work, not ideas from space."

"Yes, I know of the amazing Bonnie Mendoza. There are several depictions in this very building." He pulled out the *Mendoza Milagrosa* character trading card from the *Science Squad* movie.

He looked at the souvenir card displaying the buxom woman in the royal blue costume and couldn't help laughing at the photo of the person who had given him "personal" shows of an "adult" nature while wearing that costume—and also while *not* wearing the costume. He liked the latter better.

"That's not really her. You *do* know who that is, don't you, big buddy?"

"Of course, I know this is merely a fictional depiction, as this person is in all the celebrity media constantly. It must be wonderful being married to such a lovely and intelligent woman. I'm not here for an autograph, though."

"Pal, she's more than just lovely. Like I said before, she's the one who solved ninety-five percent of the technical problems the other engineers couldn't. Hence, why we're rich." He raised his right eyebrow. "What is it you want, guy? You've piqued my curiosity, but get to the point."

"I am a unique person. I need someone to help me realize my singular potential."

"I have no doubts that you're unique, yeah, but lots of people think they are. Many of them need a shrink. Don't take this the wrong way, Juriann, but you might be one of them."

He shook his head and tilted it slightly. "Shrink? I don't think I follow."

"A psychiatrist." The guy seemed intelligent yet somewhat unaccustomed to American idioms. "No offense, many of us need them sometimes, as the stress gets to you. It's starting to get to me right now, in fact, I'm ready to give mine a ring."

"Why is a physician who treats mental illness called a shrink?"

"It's just an idiom; they used to 'shrink your head' and were called 'headshrinkers.' Never mind."

"Very strange, that makes no sense. But I assure you, I don't need one of those." He stood up and looked around warily. "We must go somewhere private."

"This is pretty private. No one will interrupt us."

"I mean out somewhere, away from here. Do you have a testing facility?"

"Huh? I guess so, but I'm also pretty busy. I can't just drop everything because some weirdo comes in here and knows a few things about Bonnie Mendoza, the element mendozium, and dark energy. There's a dozen places you could've gotten that information. There are ten different Bonnie Mendoza museums in the country, not including the Smithsonian."

"Yes, you can, and you must. Whatever business you have, it pales in importance compared to this, as the world is at stake. I think you need to see what I have to show you. It may be a piece of the puzzle that we both seek."

"I don't seek anything; you came to see me. I was doing just fine today until you walked in. Why'd you have to mess my day up, Juriann?"

He stood up and shook his head. "I disagree. You wouldn't have seen me today were there not something you were seeking as well, so let us find it together."

Nick looked up at him and frowned. "All right, Juriann, I'll take a leap of faith, and we'll go to my house. I assure you no one will bother us there." He pressed a button on his watch. "Leah, cancel my appointments for this afternoon."

"All of them, *Tinman*? That's three hours' worth."

"Yes, all. I probably won't be back until much later."

"Where are you going?"

"Home. Don't ask why. And you have no idea where I went, should anybody ask. And that includes you know who."

Leah nodded. "Gotcha. Ghost Protocol initiated."

They went down the back elevator attached to his office and went to his vintage Cadillac in his private parking spot and drove off towards his home.

"This is an amazing car. I've seen them in old movies, but never in person."

"Great. How the hell did you get here, Juriann?" Nick asked as they drove through the gate and west towards his home.

"I flew from Rotterdam to Newark International, after I visited *Gravi-Golfer* at Princeton, then I flew directly to Aurora City International Airport and took the shuttle here."

He nodded. "Yes, I figured that, but I mean, where did you get the dough for your travel?"

Juriann looked at him curiously. "Dough?"

"Money. Cashola. You don't even have a job. I can get you one on a construction crew if you want, they'd hire you on the spot. Or maybe even the engineering section. Your choice."

"Oh. The stranger who left me said I would be taken care of. A trust fund was left to take care of my family and me."

"Stranger? A trust fund?" He laughed. "Dude! Didn't you ever worry about where that came from?"

"Are you kidding? Of course, I wondered if it was legitimate or stolen, who the heck the lady was who left it, etc."

"Yeah, I can only imagine. But your folks took it anyway, from, hey, let me guess—an oddball deaf Russian woman."

"Yes." Juriann nodded. "But how did you know that?"

"Just lucky conjecture."

"Anyway, it was necessary to achieve my goals and to take care of my family. My father, Hans, passed away years ago, so it has just been Mom and me. Would you have not done the same?"

"I probably would've, at that. So, you don't have any brothers or sisters?"

Juriann shook his head. "No, Mother couldn't have children, so I'm all she has. And I don't think there are any more like me."

"Huh, that's for damn sure."

Juriann looked out the window. "How far do you live away from the city?"

"Right on the edge, about eight miles away, almost there. What is it you want to do there?"

"I assume you have a personal gym at your estate. What I have to show you would be best demonstrated there. I needed to get away from all those people."

"Well, you'll get your opportunity in a minute."

They pulled up to the mansion, the largest home in Aurora City and the tenth-largest in Indiana.

"It's impressive, Nick."

"It gets us by. A monument to hard work and capitalism. *And* good fortune."

"One must always have that last factor as well, in order to be successful."

He pulled into the garage, and he parked as they exited and went through the door and into the private gym in the basement. "Why are we going to the gym? We have a fine fitness center at M2 if you wanted to do that, including a private area adjacent to my office. This seems a bit over the top."

"Yes, but I couldn't show you this there; I needed to be away from prying eyes."

He yawned. "So, what fantastic thing are you going to show me that you couldn't show me in the office?"

"Watch and see." Juriann loaded the Olympic barbell with six 20-kg plates. 315 pounds.

He smiled sardonically. "Look, pal, that's not so much if you want to impress me with your lifting skills. While it's way out of my league, which wouldn't take much, the President could lift that over her head in her twenties. I've got a poster of her doing it."

"That's true, and Kepler has a copy of that hanging in his office, but this isn't quite the same at all."

"What does that mean?"

"When I said there was no one else like me, I meant it."

He watched in astonishment as the dark-haired, bearded young Dutchman curled the barbell, then lifted it over his head with his left hand, while seemingly expending minimal effort. "I doubt she could do this in her prime."

He almost fell over. "Ohmigod. How the hell can you possibly be doing that?"

"I don't know, just that I've always been much stronger than normal people. This is nothing; I can lift four times this weight easily with one arm. My left is a little stronger, as I am left-handed."

"But *how?* You just curled over three hundred pounds with one hand. And controlling the inertia of that massive barbell is another matter. It's not just the strength."

"Don't really know." He switched it to his right hand and repeated the feat, then sat it down gently. "My parents—not my real parents, of course, since I don't resemble them—told me that the woman who gave me to them said I would be one of immense strength."

"You mentioned her before. This 'woman,' was she your real mother?"

Juriann shook his head. "I don't think so. She was Russian, they said, and didn't resemble me, either, although they said her skin was a little darker than Russians they'd known. She was also deaf, interestingly, as you previously guessed. How did you know?"

"I would need several hours to explain that."

"All I know is that I was born of the ashes of someone else, she had said, but that I would need to be a protector, a guide for someone of greatness. That my power would pale when compared to this one of power, the verbose deaf one decreed."

"Who is he? This 'one of power'? An enemy?"

Juriann shook his head. "I don't know, but I somehow think the one of power, the 'Santa,' for lack of a better word, is a female, maybe my age or a little younger. And that someday, our meeting in Aurora City is inevitable, as some sort of destiny."

"What is it you're saying, Juriann?"

"My intuition tells me that soon we will witness the coming of Aurora the Angel. When I was a child, I thought the being of power was really the Sinterklaas, or Santa Claus in America. But that is ridiculous, even though the slight gravitational energy perturbations come from North Pole."

"Santa Claus? The North Pole?" Was this guy missing a few marbles, or was he incredibly brilliant? His wife's aunt, surely the "deaf Russian" of record, had a knack for having both qualities, so he listened intently, as it would take a while to figure out this mystery.

"No, not *the* actual North Pole. North Pole is a small town east and slightly south of Fairbanks."

"Right, I know, but—" He heard high-heeled shoes click on the hardwood floor. "Juriann, we've got some 'splainin' to do."

"We do?"

"Yeah. Get ready."

The five-five, dark-haired woman entered the gym. "Hey, what's going on in here? What are you doing home from work?" Bella asked loudly. "No goofing off. Gotta keep the money rolling in, so don't make me fire you."

"Well, it will take some time to explain," he said.

"Yeah?" She tapped her foot on the floor. "I'm listening. What kind of shenanigans are you and your buddy up to?"

"I'm trying to figure out how to discuss this coherently."

"Good luck with that." She walked up to Juriann and stared up at him. "Who's the big dude? Didja go out and hire another personal trainer again, *Tinman?* The last one was just a waste of money, with your physique, hon." She walked up to him, put her arms around him, and kissed him on the lips.

"Your wife calls you *Tinman?*" Juriann asked curiously. "I get the connection regarding the divalent cation of tin and all."

"Well, it's better than some things she's called me." He smiled at her. "No, this is, uh—Juriann Hultaar, from the Netherlands. Juriann, my wife, Isabel." Her hand seemed like a child's as he grasped it, shaking it.

"Yes, I have heard much about you, the famous one. Part of the reason I'm here."

"Why do you want to see me? I would be very disappointed if you just want an autograph."

"I already have one. No, I am instead interested in your other, less celebrated, ability. The one I consider the most amazing of all."

"What is that, pray tell?"

"Your ability to see through extraneous information and come to the simplest, most logical conclusion possible. The unique power of parsimony."

"Huh?" she asked, her smile turning to a scowl. "Who the heck is this big dude, TM? He looks like a twenty-year-old lumberjack, yet he talks like some esoteric Dutch professor. What's the deal?" She looked up at him and squinted.

"He's a guy Kepler met and sent down here. I'll tell you later. He also has super-strength, by the way."

"What?" She looked at him, sizing him up. "He's a big guy, and I could see that he would be strong, but—"

He patted her on the shoulder. "Quiet. He'll show you."

She watched him repeat his 315-pound barbell feat with the other hand as she stared, gaping.

"Wow. I guess you do, at that. How is that possible?"

"I don't really know; as I told Dr. Stannous, I have always been stronger than others."

"Well, I have several theories that'll take some time to sort out. But what are we going to do with you, Juriann? Got a place to live?"

"The guy just did that, and you immediately move on to where he's going to live?" he asked, exasperated.

"There must be some explanation, and admiration for his accomplishment won't do anything constructive, TM. We don't want him to leave until we can figure it out, as my gray matter needs some time to digest it."

Juriann put the barbell down. "I just arrived, so, no, I have not had an opportunity to attend to such things."

"We do have several properties for corporate guests and so forth. You're welcome to live in one of our condo suites."

"I have no funds to pay you on my person, but I will procure some."

Bella shook her head. "Well, dude, something tells me that you'll find a way to make a living somehow. Don't worry about it, it's on the house." Bella looked at the odd reddish metallic necklace and felt it with her right hand. "What is this symbol? Zero-man? Such self-confidence."

He laughed. "No, it's an 'O,' not a zero. The Russian woman brought this when I was an infant, apparently. Said the arrow going diagonally through the letter signified straightness or correctness. It stands for *Orthoman*."

"Huh?" Nick muttered. "I'm Greek Orthodox Christian, and

we used to have some kind of kids' character on the Greek TV channel named 'Orthoman.' I'm guessing you're not him."

"I can't imagine any similarity, as I don't believe I have anything to do with religion."

• • •

"So, who is this *Orthoman* guy, *Tinman?*" Bella asked after they obtained an extra car and left Juriann at the Cassandra Towers, about two miles from downtown. "He kind of reminds me of a bigger, heavier Alex Darkkin or something."

"Yeah, he kind of does, at that. He went to see Kepler at Princeton and ended up here. Johnny remarked that he looked like Rad Darkkin when he was younger."

"That's what I was just thinking. No wonder he reminded me of Alex."

"He is strange, but he's also some kind of genius."

"You really think so? He wasn't a guy who just memorized a bunch of stuff?"

He shook his head. "No, I think he's for real; he couldn't have memorized all that. Johnny said the same thing. And he's left-handed, too, a quality that is partially genetic. The probability of two left-handed people who look very much alike being unrelated isn't all that high."

"So, what're you saying, *Tinman?* That this guy is Rad's son? I guess I could believe that, as the guy got around, Bonnie said."

He shook his head. "No, dear—I was *thinking*, given his apparent age of around twenty, that he might be the illegitimate offspring of someone else who's left-handed, very tall, strong, and looks kinda like Rad. Duh."

"Alex? I guess he kind of got around, too."

"Ohmigod. You're as naïve as your aunt sometimes. Alex was right-handed, and he took more after his mom than Rad." He waited for several seconds and gave her a fist bump. "Come on, you can do it, Isabel. Parsimony powers, activate!"

Bella thought for a minute, then opened her mouth wide. "Oh, no. Listen, no way could she have covered *that* up. Talk about scandalous."

"Why the hell not? It's possible. She's got the connections, the spin doctors—politicians do it all the time. Even *she* wouldn't have survived that one."

She laughed hysterically. "No, that gender of politician cannot just 'make it go away,' *Tinman*. Sheesh, you are too much sometimes. She's a big enough gal *without* a bun in the oven. She was enormous with Will and waddled like a duck her last two months when she was in Sacramento. So, forget it. She wasn't the magician in the family with sleight-of-hand mastery. Even David Silverfield couldn't do that."

"Oh, yeah, I get you. Maybe that was a dumb idea."

She nodded. "That's an understatement."

"I don't know what to think, though. A strange woman who speaks Russian, guess who that is? And Rad Darkkin? There was a lot of secret crap that went on after the Ontario Lacus incident, Uncle Jim said, but he only knew fragments of it. If Juriann's not a child of one of them, then maybe he's a clone."

"Huh?" She choked. "What did you say?"

"You heard me. Wendy already told me that, if she's being truthful, that is."

"Wendy is a lot of things, but not a liar, so there must be some truth to it. *Why* she told you is another reason."

"The dude may be a clone of her freaking brother, she claims. Maybe it's true, maybe not, but it could make sense."

"Another thing, *Tinman*. That necklace he was wearing, there isn't anything else like it on Earth, except for one thing."

"What?"

"I can't tell for sure with the naked eye, but that alloy looks suspiciously like the rare-earth ruthenium alloy Aurora's bracelet was made from."

"What? Are you sure?"

She nodded. "Pretty sure. Nothing else reflects light like that does, and we know who liked rare-earth metallurgy."

"I don't even want to think about it."

"Ol' M-Square had a lot of secrets from everyone, it seems."

• • •

Nick canceled all his meetings for the rest of the week as he and Bella went with Juriann to the Sulphur Springs complex, at the former site of the defunct Malvin catsup factory. Not much was going on out there, and no one would bother them. He and Bella, of course, were both engineers, but they might need some other folks who had a wide variety of skills in other scientific disciplines.

To do that, they needed the help of some of the most out-of-the-box thinkers in science. He had a few smart folks like that around in his research center, of course, but he needed some eclectic people who were used to being around strange stuff, and who, more importantly, would keep things quiet.

Consequently, the motley crew of probably the worst group of TV superheroes ever assembled came to mind; it was conveniently appropriate since Juriann seemed to have such fascination with them. One thing was sure, though: they were genuinely intelligent and most of them were probably available if he and Bella could locate them, other than Kepler, of course, with whom he had a decent relationship.

Luckily, they had many expensive resources at their disposal. Being rich meant they had investments in many ancillary businesses, with access to many financial records. Some of them might not have the best credit, he predicted, as *Dr. Wendy's Science Squad* had been a financial disaster. But he could help with stuff like that. Whether they would want his help was another thing.

He thought about this group and grinned. There were many accounts of the *Science Squad* that were published, given the later fame of two of its members (Kepler was more famous before than after the show); and, of course, there was the campy movie, two years before the very serious, three-hour *Mendoza the Miraculous* movie that earned his wife a nice gold-plated bronze statue. They actually put a plot into the team movie to send the group on a mission. But the original show was, while a good idea in concept, pretty lousy in execution, as Wendy struggled to find sponsors and keep the show afloat for its slightly less than three-year run on crummy local cable television.

Providence favors the prepared mind, and Bella, to that end, had kept archives of all the shows she'd taped as a kid (the stations had thrown them out), and made a healthy profit selling them back to media companies for digital remastering when Wendy became relevant again. Nothing wrong with a little youthful capitalism.

It was certainly no secret that young Bonnie Mendoza and Wendy Gallinsworth were once the best of friends, going back to when they were teenagers themselves in San Diego. Wendy was always trying to get on television—partially because she wanted attention and was self-promoting, but she also was genuinely a kind person who wanted to raise people's awareness of disabilities, since Bonnie was, of course, the poster child for deafness and the lesser-known autism spectrum disorders (the latter often at that time misunderstood).

Bonnie was also an excellent amateur magician (escape artist in particular) and mentalist, with uncanny mathematical computational abilities that defied description. So she would be the focal point of this strange group, as she was also an excellent athlete. It was a noble cause that was far more difficult in achieving than in concept, but Wendy always did think big.

Her grandiose idea was to gather a group of talented young scientists (most of whom she already knew, as she was a social butterfly with a huge network of contacts), each either a minority or with some type of disability, to be on the show, to demonstrate diversity; the goal was to teach the wonders of science to children in various skits, while showing that everyone, despite his/her limitations, can contribute. With the low-budget special effects available in the 1990s, it never made it to any status above that of a crummy local cable show.

Wendy had tried to promote it as something far more than it actually was, creating a line of lunch boxes, coloring books, etc., with her own money—but after two and a half years, the "actors" got tired of working for next to nothing and moved on. He'd heard about the tens of thousands of dollars she spent on that merchandise and that most of it now sat gathering dust in a storage unit, ironically now worth a small fortune. Wendy's husband Stan Williams finally got fed up with her obsessive harebrained schemes and moved on a little over ten years later, marrying up-and-coming Washington attorney Janaki Kapoor, who could provide a less hectic, albeit much less interesting lifestyle.

However, when someone becomes really famous, their lesser-known works become much more interesting. In the mid-2010s, during Wendy's first term as Governor of California, several enterprising people brought the series out on DVD, thanks to Bella's archives: the beginning of Bella's financial empire.

Although he didn't have much time for golf any longer, he'd always liked *Gravi-Golfer,* the alter ego of Johnny Kepler, a doctoral student in astrophysics at Caltech at the time. *Golfer* had the ability to warp gravity (with advanced technology) and make golf balls go wherever he wanted to fight the various evils that threatened the *Squad*. In the movie, he had special golf balls—explosive balls, radio balls, spy balls, etc. that could function as weapons, perform espionage, expel knockout gas, etc. A pretty worthless hero compared to the ones from the major comic companies.

But he remembered the young, pre-*Squad* Kepler was a brilliant player who won thirteen majors (five U.S. Opens, three Masters, two British Opens, and three PGA Championships), when his right femur snapped in half on the sixteenth green of the Clystarr Classic in San Diego. The diagnosis was grim: osteogenic sarcoma, an aggressive form of bone cancer. Kepler would lose the leg above the knee, although the doctors thought the cancer was localized and surgery would be curative. Of course, he had to quit the PGA Tour; they wouldn't allow him to ride in a cart, and he couldn't play at a high level any longer after losing most of his right leg. So, he moved on to something else. Whether or not it was "bigger and better" was a matter of perspective.

Kepler's type of cancer was predominantly one of children, not adults, so he spent time at the children's oncology unit, where he, by chance, met an engaging, enterprising, hyperenergetic young pediatrics resident who wanted to put a show together to help kids. He had also met Bonnie a couple of times and was impressed by her weirdness and intellect, so he said, "Why not? Might be good for a few laughs." Yeah, people laughed at them, for sure.

After the show, Kepler had acquired a variety of different prostheses until breakthroughs in robotics and bionics had allowed a permanent limb to be attached in the mid-2020s. While this might have allowed him to return to the Tour, by that time he had long since earned his doctorate in astrophysics from Caltech (where he again had worked with Bonnie, who at that time (2010) had given up forensics and magic and was an assistant professor in the theoretical physics department) and eventually obtained a distinguished faculty appointment at Princeton in 2018. Some complained that he only got that because he was pals with The Great Dame. Others claimed it was because he was Black (albeit one who was allegedly a direct descendant of Johannes Kepler). But he truly was a brilliant, albeit oddball, astrophysicist, one who had become one of the foremost experts on the mysterious entity known as dark energy, as he became more eccentric and reclusive, Hanna had said.

The other *Science Squad* members were far less famous and had mostly been forgotten by society. Wolfram K. Steele was a native of Bedford, Indiana, and was now a chemistry professor at the University of Akron in Polymer City. Wolf was in a wheelchair due to a skiing accident he suffered in Colorado in the 1990s that left him paraplegic. His specialty was polymer science, and, when he received a full professorship at San Diego State, he agreed to join the Squad as a character he wrote about in his college days, The Limestone Cowboy—named after the world-renowned rock found in his hometown's quarries. Limestone, of course, was a somewhat reactive chemical compound (calcium carbonate) in its own right. It was decided to change his name to *Chemical Cowboy*, and Steele received limited fame and speaking engagements because of his role; he now lived in the Akron, Ohio area. *Cowboy* had the ability to manipulate chemical reactions.

Todd DeOhmman was an electrical engineer who walked with a limp due to a nerve injury suffered while playing football in high school. While not nearly as disabled as the others, he represented another minority: he was gay. An avid fisherman, he wanted to become *Admiral Angler*, a hero not unlike *Golfer* in that he had gimmicked fishing poles, lures, etc., but even that was too way-out for Wendy. They settled on an electrical alter ego which complemented his technical expertise—*Admiral Ampere*—who was a well-intended super-science expert for the gay community.

He needed a physician, other than Wendy herself, for obvious reasons—someone who could examine this guy to find out what made him tick. Fortunately, a later addition to the *Squad* was such a person, although one whom he had heard was rather obnoxious to deal with. Dr. Royce Garrison Bivereaux III was a rather irritating medical school classmate of Wendy's at UC San Diego who had Tourette syndrome. His role was to discourage stereotyping of this disorder, just as Bonnie, who, in addition to being deaf, had an autism spectrum disorder. Royce G. Bivereaux, whose shortened name was, ironically, a play on the famous acronym "ROY G. BIV" (denoting the spectrum of visible light red, orange, yellow, green, blue, indigo, violet), became the intrepid *Photraman*, the master of the electromagnetic spectrum. Bivereaux ended up becoming a neuro-ophthalmologist—not a general physician or physiologist, like he really needed right now—but the closest he could get on the Squad. He lived in Chicago now, so he wasn't too far away.

The leader—Wendy—was, of course, the narrator and balladeer for the show, given her vocal talents and enthusiasm; being very tall, intelligent, blonde, freckled, blue-eyed, and one of the whitest people on the planet, she didn't really represent any minority or disability—unless, of course, you included obesity.

She was at the peak of her physical strength then; after medical school, she was encouraged to put her pediatric rehabilitation residency on hold to make a run for the Olympics but decided that was less important than helping people.

The boisterous six-one shotputter and powerlifter in her mid-twenties often exceeded 240 pounds and filled out that crimson bodysuit pretty well in the chest department. He still had the autographed "glamour" poster of her in the 1990s, which was now worth hundreds of thousands of dollars since her PR department had bought up and destroyed all remaining copies before the 2014 California gubernatorial election. His brother had bought it for him as a joke when he was a teenager; it was in his safe now, although a copy hung on the wall of his home rec room.

He didn't want Wendy to know about any of his plan; although they spoke with some regularity, it was tough to determine sometimes how much she knew about anything. She was great at playing the self-deprecating bucolic blonde, but he knew better. No one rose to that status without being highly intelligent and good at playing others. A part of him knew that, if she was staying out of his business, it was for some reason that benefited her.

He hadn't quite determined her game yet, or how *Orthoman* fit into all this, but one thing was clear:

The solution was obvious: how to get the crummy band back together without regretting it. That was going to be challenging.

Chapter Twenty-Seven

Dexter Slabb's Office
Department of Scientific Developments
2 Constitution Avenue NE
Washington, DC

Dexter Slabb looked out the window of his large office on Constitution Avenue towards the United States Capitol as his second-in-command rushed into the room, as he then turned his attention to the computer monitor. His was an old building, which used to be the Russell Senate Office Building, vacated several years ago when the needs of the U.S. Senate necessitated a newer building than one built in 1908. When you became director of a new super-intelligence agency, you pretty much took what you were given. Whether or not the DSD would be present in future administrations was uncertain, but he was pretty sure he had at least four more years of an almost unlimited government technology budget.

"You said you wanted to see anything weird, Dexter, this is it," Barbara Loretta Baxter said excitedly as she entered. Lori was a Ph.D. physical chemist and the daughter of Dr. Vaughn Baxter, one of the CIA's and the DSD's most respected electronics engineers, and functioned as Deputy Director of DSD, an elite science agency that the President created five years ago to deal with scientific intelligence breakthroughs, some applying to espionage, others not. Unlike the head of the FBI, CIA, etc., they reported directly to the White House, not the SecDef. Lori had taken the initiative in trying to find out more about this "development," although other nongovernmental scientists probably were involved, too.

"It had better be." He took a sip of his black coffee. "Well, Lori? Spare me the suspense. I don't want to hear about flying aliens or buckyballs again; those topics irritate the Chief something awful."

"Okay, I know that. But wait until you see what I have here." She pointed to the 45-inch computer monitor. "A large bank in Atlanta just had twenty million dollars drained from various accounts to some offshore account they can't trace."

"Computer hacking?" He yawned and put his hand over his mouth. "Big deal. That's so old hat, and I'm disappointed in you for bringing me something this mundane to the mighty DSD."

She shook her head. "No, Dex, that's the thing. This wasn't some hack job by some crypto-guy thousands of miles away. The chief financial officer, Maya Kelsey, went in to work with her ID, and was authenticated to the workstation by retinal scanning; everybody let her pass through. She knew all the passwords, which is authenticated by 2,048-bit encryption, so not even one of the new quantum laptops we have could've hacked that in a couple of hours. It would've taken two weeks with our best, and they assuredly don't have tech equal to ours."

"So, how did they do it then? Other than that, it must be—"

"Correct. All evidence points to it being the real person, except the cops found her incoherent at home when they broke into her house an hour later, with an empty vodka bottle next to her in bed."

"So Kelsey stole a bunch of dough and got smashed afterward. Not the smartest move, I admit, but criminals aren't always known for their great intellects. I would've made it to South America before I got wasted, but that's just me."

Lori shook her head and pointed at him. "Stop interrupting me, Dex; that isn't it at all. They thought she might just be drunk, but it turns out she was drugged, so there was no way she could've been there at all at the time this occurred. The real crooks set her up to look intoxicated. This is the kind of stuff the DSD was made for."

The tall forty-seven-year-old raised his eyebrows. "Maybe—but how the heck did they do that?"

She shook her head. "Don't know, it's the damndest thing. The security cameras show a woman going in who looks like the real person. The other stuff like the fingerprints, even a retinal imaging contact lens, could be faked, but *not* the passwords. This lady knew all the important stuff the original did. Pretty weird."

He got up and walked around the room. "What have we stumbled upon here, Lori? This surely represents concepts far beyond what we know of. The ability to read minds? To manipulate them into thinking or seeing anything?"

She shook her head. "No credible technology exists which could allow that, Dex, despite your high aspirations for such things."

"No, not that we know of, we never got anywhere with our ESP experiments. But my uncle Alton always told me about something he saw once. I don't know if it's true, though."

"What, Dex?"

"A ghost."

She shook her head. "I don't understand what that means."

"Alton had a lot of strange buddies, Rad Darkkin for one. There's a crapload we still don't know about Darkkin, and he won't talk much about it."

"Why?"

He shook his head. "Don't know, heard the guy exaggerated a lot and was generally an asshole, but he was involved in some dangerous stuff. I know he had something to do with the fullerene Russian battle suit which is similar to the one we believe is out there flying, but all the files have conveniently been lost or destroyed, as Ashburn said."

"Don't I know it? But isn't it a coincidence that these events are occurring simultaneously with the emergence of *Stella Scura?* Two unbelievable events occurring at once?"

"There's only one logical explanation."

She nodded. "Yeah. The ability to manipulate minds and steal secrets, to appear, with a little help from makeup and prosthetics, to be anyone. Stuff right up our alley."

"Who would have the money and technological resources do to that?"

"Besides us?" he asked.

"Well, yes."

"Kristoff van Sant is out of prison now; we know that. He has the money, but not the technical sophistication or finesse to do something of that magnitude by himself. Neither does Reuben J. Skelton." She took a sip of coffee. "What about Ashburn? How much do we want to involve him?"

"Shit. Tom's a loose cannon. Stay away from him; he's going to do something stupid as there's something wrong with him."

"At least he's not your boss."

He nodded. "He thinks he is sometimes, but DSD was set up to report directly to POTUS. Which is the way I want it."

"Got it. Sounds good to me too, Dex."

• • •

Secretary of Defense Thomas Ashburn walked into his well-furnished office at the Pentagon to see a strange woman sitting in his office chair, sipping an espresso.

Alice, his assistant, was in big trouble. No one was to be shown in until he had gone in first, and he didn't know this person.

"Excuse me, but who let you in here, Ma'am?" he asked the fortyish brunette woman, who was wearing a tan business suit and matching pumps. "This is a private office."

"Your assistant did, Secretary Ashburn, after I told her to."

He shook his head. "That's impossible. Alice knows I don't have time right now. Please excuse me, but I'm quite busy."

"I don't think you're too busy for me, sir. Give me just a minute of your time." She extended her hand, which he took reluctantly.

"I still don't understand why I should talk to you—"

She smiled. "Are you sure? Look deeply into my eyes and re-think that last statement, Tommy."

He tried to let go of the woman's hand, but somehow he couldn't release his grip. He also tried to avoid contact, but couldn't resist any longer.

This is the most beautiful woman I have ever seen.

I feel like someone is inside my mind. What trickery is this? Did some-one slip me a drug?

No, I am completely alert. Yet, I somehow feel compelled to do any-thing she tells me to.

I want to pull away so badly, but for some reason I can't.

I won't remember any of this after we're done.

Somehow I know I'm going to be wealthy beyond the dreams of ava-rice. For this, I'll need to bring down the most important person in the world.

My boss.

It will be a pleasure to bring down your sorry oversized ass.

And I know exactly how to do it.

Chapter Twenty-Eight

November 7, 2028
North Pole Public Library
656 NPHS Blvd.
North Pole, Alaska

Paige eagerly hiked the two miles to the library after school on this, the Tuesday after the first Monday in November: Election Day in the USA. She had been eighteen for about three weeks, but that was enough to become a registered voter and vote for the President of her choosing. It might or might not be the one that over ninety percent of the other voters were choosing, but she cared not about such things. No way was she going to miss out on this. Somehow she knew that Alaska's three electoral votes were not in jeopardy.

She made her way through the front door and bumped into a table in the front lobby, which wasn't normally there.

"Are you here to vote, young lady?" an older man said.

What the heck did he think? No, she was there to read the encyclopedia. Well, she didn't want to get kicked out by being impolite.

"Yes, sir." She showed her official ID to the clerk at the table out front and signed the register. She felt another clerk take her arm.

"Hi, Cheryl, I'm Brenda. I'll help you today," a woman said.

"Thanks, but I go by my middle name, Paige."

"Okay, Paige. Let's go over here." The woman handed her ID back, took her by the arm, and guided her over to the voter's booth.

"I've never done this before, so I'm a little nervous. I don't want to push the wrong button and vote for the wrong party."

"That's okay, honey. This booth is set up for the visually impaired. Can you read Braille? If not, there are audio prompts."

"Yes, of course."

The woman guided her to the console. "The candidates are here. You can vote straight party or singular candidates. I can help you, or you can do it yourself."

"No worries, I can do it. I have done harder stuff than this."

"Okay, here, this will help." The woman put a pair of earbuds in her ears. "This will tell you the choices you've made before you finalize your selection since you can't see the screen, so others can't hear who you voted for."

"Thanks." The whole world could hear who she was going to vote for, it was certainly no secret.

"Good luck, Paige. Let me know if you need help."

Right. Her candidate was sure the one who needed help; no, more like a miracle. She closed the curtain and ran her fingers over the candidate list. One Senate race was up, their one U.S. Representative, the various state and local offices, and, of course, the one most important to her:

President of the United States. As if Alaska and its three electoral votes would make a big difference in the outcome.

There were the obligatory five or so independent candidates, none of whom really stood any significant chance. And the other two. One of those didn't stand much of a chance, either.

Wendy Mendoza, incumbent. Republican.

Fahnaz Saleh. Senator, New Persia. Democrat. It was the first time the candidates from both major parties were women.

She thought for about five minutes before making her decision. Not that it mattered a whole lot, as Dr. Mendoza was likely to get all of the country's electoral votes, and her single vote in a highly Republican state would not matter. But, to her, it was a symbol of what she had become now.

An adult.

Cheryl Paige Marshall, proud adult, cast her vote, pressed the "confirm" button, and jogged back to the school to get to basketball practice. She would be excited to hear the election returns later on when she got home. Not that there was much doubt to the outcome. But it gave her a sense of satisfaction to have contributed in some small fashion.

• • •

Paige and Jack returned home from basketball practice at about seven PM as she took her coat off and walked into the small living room. She could hear the television, her mom no doubt alternately watching it and staring off into space. It sounded like old cartoons from the 80s, not the current events she was interested in.

"What are you doing, Mom? Anything unusual going on?"

"Huh," Jack said. "She's drawing equations on scraps of notebook paper with crayons."

"So, I guess nothing unusual is happening." She heard the stupid cartoon voices and sighed in exasperation. "Why aren't you watching the election, Mom?"

"Humph. Do not depress me, child; the result surely will not be to my liking. My mathematical models of the election have been shown to be correct, unfortunately."

"You really need to waste your brain's precious computational cycles on that?" No surprise there. She walked over, found the remote on the coffee table, felt for the numeric keypad, and changed it to channel 306, one of the major news channels.

Jack put the pizza he had bought on the small dining room table. "Let's talk about it later. I'm hungry."

"I am as well," she said.

They sat down, ate the pepperoni and mushroom pizza, and consumed copious amounts of diet soda as they listened to the results come in as her mother continuously whined and complained.

"Has Senator Saleh conceded the election yet?" Jack asked.

"She has a fighting chance! How can you say that?" she asked, standing up angrily. "This is America! All will have a chance to be President."

"She has about as much chance as I do of becoming President," Mom said. "The odds are astronomical."

"Oh, my, that sounds scary," she said. "I am surely moving to another country if that happens."

"Yes, I agree, that would be dangerous." Mom said. "But, the things Oogly and I could accomplish with our higher order intelligence, the fantastic benefits to mankind . . ."

"It doesn't matter; Mendoza passed the 309 she needed to win hours ago."

"The polls closed in New Persia several hours ago, and Mendoza had lost the twenty-five electoral votes there, as well as the twelve for Arizona, a small victory for us; so, for a brief time,

Sen. Saleh was winning the election. The only ones not in yet are in North Korea, where the President is enormously popular, but the path to 309 is already lost."

"Well, get used to it," Mom said sarcastically. "Another four years of wonderment from the truly wondrous one."

"I guess we agree on something for once, Mom. That probably will not happen again for decades."

Chapter Twenty-Nine

Todd DeOhmman's Home
1396 W. Herndon Ave.
Fresno, California

The brown-haired, fortyish man answered the door of the modest ranch house, where a vaguely familiar figure from twenty years ago stood in the early morning sunlight.

"Yes? Can I help you, Miss?"

"You must be Adam," Bella said.

The tall, handsome man looked at his visitor curiously. "That's right. What can I do for you? Didn't you read the 'No Soliciting' sign out front?"

"Sir, I'm not selling anything, and I'm looking for Todd." She removed her sunglasses and hat. "I'd like to speak to him if he's home, please."

"Who are you? What do you want?" The man crossed his arms.

"I'm *not* a creditor, if that's what you think. He was a good friend of my aunt back in the nineties." She looked at him intensely. "I'm sorry, I'm not trying to be rude or arrogant, but I assumed you'd know who I am, although I haven't seen you for about twenty years, Adam."

"What?" Adam Kirkpatrick looked at her curiously as he took a bite of an apple. "Oh, yeah, I didn't recognize you at first, but I guess you don't look all that different. Why are you here, again?"

"I said, to see Todd. I'm sorry for the intrusion, but it really is important. It seemed more appropriate for me to come myself rather than to send someone."

"Okay, come in, I guess." He went to the stairs. "Todd, there's, uh, someone here to see you. You'd better come down now."

"Adam, I'm busy working on the bills," the second man said from upstairs. "Who is it?"

"I took a double-take at first, but she sure seems to be—Isabel Mendoza."

"No, it's not; come on, Adam. It must be some celebrity look-alike, some joke somebody is playing. Why would she come here?"

"Really, Todd, it isn't a joke. She's standing right down here."

The six-one athletic blond man came to the top of the stairs and looked down. "Bella? What the heck? It is you, at that. Why would you be here?"

"You knew Bonnie pretty well." He came down the stairs, and she extended her hand as he took it slowly. "I know I haven't seen you since I was a little kid, and you probably don't remember me from back then, but I need your help, Todd."

He shook her hand hesitantly. "Of course I remember you; you're pretty hard to forget. And I suppose it's nice to see you again, too, but what do you need me for? Don't you have enough money to buy anything you want back at M2? I don't have any, just so you know."

She shook her head. "I don't need that, and we have a problem that requires other expertise. We're trying to get the old *Science Squad* back together to work on some issues of immense importance, of a magnitude you cannot even begin to understand."

"The *Squad?* Why should I help you, and why do you want me? I don't want to do any more Comic Cons, and I thought you'd be above this stupid shit. I heard you were only interested in intellectual female roles and had pretty much given up acting and the *Squad*, given you've won an Oscar and all."

She shook her head. "It's not dumb; I swear it's for something vitally important, and it has nothing to do with me or acting or anything else that's trivial. If you have some bone to pick with my family and me, I'm sorry, but this is information essential to our country, maybe for the future of civilization."

He shrugged. "I'm sorry, Bella, I don't mean to be an asshole, but I'm not following. So you have money, big deal. What's that got to do with national security and the future of mankind?"

She nodded. "I am dead serious, and I can't tell you here."

"Adam is my husband, you can tell him."

She shook her head. "It has nothing to do with not trusting Adam or anyone else. It's just not something I can discuss here or in any 'regular' place."

"I don't get the joke, Bella, and I'm not in a great mood."

She shook her head angrily. "No joke, son. Of all the *Squad* members, Bonnie liked and trusted you most of all, because you were her friend and never made fun of her because she was different, unlike some of the others, such as Kepler."

"Now that's certainly true about that pompous ass."

"Anyway, do what you want, it's a free country. From what she always said of you, I expected better." She handed him a manila envelope. "This is for you, by the way. I wanted to give it to you in person rather than mail it, I thought that only appropriate."

He took the large envelope and looked at it. "What is this?"

"The title to your and Adam's house."

"What did you say?" He took the small parcel from her and opened it angrily.

"Paid in full."

He looked at the deed. "I don't understand. Why would you do this? We haven't seen each other in years."

She shrugged. "Look, I'm not stupid. I know you were behind in your payments and were nearing default on the loan."

His face turned red as he threw the papers down. "Why, you nosy little jerk! How dare you mess around in my financial affairs? I don't care who you are—get the hell out of my house!" He pointed to the door.

"Yes, Todd and Adam, it is yours, now. If you want me to leave, I will, but hear me out first."

He snarled for about twenty seconds. "Okay, Bella. You have five minutes, for old times' sake."

She shook her head in disdain as she sat on a chair in the living room as Todd and Adam sat on the sofa.

"Listen to me, pal, I didn't mess around with anything; if you knew me you'd know I'm not like that, despite how the media may portray me. My dad was a policeman, not a wealthy, glamorous playboy athlete like Jay or an esoteric scientist like Bonnie—I'm a blue-collar person at heart and always will be. And I *don't* play games. This is damn serious, so you better pay attention."

"I don't know, but it looks like you were snooping around in my business. Most would come to that conclusion."

"That's why I came in person, so please listen. I realized, three months ago, after going over stuff with my attorney and accountant at a regular meeting, that I *owned* United Bank Services, the bank that has your mortgage, and the loan defaults came up, so it *was* my business. I told them to try and work something out for the people in default when your name caught my attention, as it's unusual. They told me I was crazy, but I have paid off dozens of them. Would you and Adam rather be out on the street? You were a good friend to Bonnie, you know. It's a token of gratitude, nothing more. I did it for a number of others or helped them refinance, too."

"I don't take charity. Not from little rich girls."

She pointed at him. "Hey, *Admiral Angler*, or *Ampere*, or whatever the hell you used to call yourself, shut up. Every penny I have, I've earned through the sweat of my brow by taking tremendous risks. But I do owe Bonnie. I can't repay her, but I can help you."

"Yeah, right." He laughed.

She stood up and pointed at him with her right hand. "I'm the one who had most of my family blown to smithereens, so go to hell, you arrogant ass. I came out here because I really do need your help. How disappointing." She knocked the envelope out of his hand. "You don't answer your phone or e-mail. Neither does Wolfram Steele or Royce G. Bivereaux III. Kepler is the only one on the radar, and he's rather high-maintenance. We need you."

"*Kepler?* You just mentioned him for the second time; that just dropped you about ten points." He shrugged. "Anyway—sorry, Bella. When you have creditors after you, you tend to ignore that stuff. I don't know about those other guys. I know Wolf had some problems with abusing prescription drugs, you probably know that. Biv does okay, but he's never managed his money well either, he's been divorced twice. We're all losers, except for Wendy and that arrogant SOB Kepler, who, of course, was rich and famous before he joined the *Squad*. And Bonnie, of course, but she's dead. Why the hell would I want to work with those idiots again?"

"I'm sorry your situation hasn't been what you wanted, Todd, but I am offering you a once-in-a-lifetime chance to become great again. My life hasn't been perfect, either, but I've made the best of it. I'm not passing judgment on anyone, but put your personal issues aside for a moment here. There are no strings attached. The loan's been paid. I just wanted to say thanks."

He paused. "Were I to help you, what is it you want from me?"

"*Golfer* is on his way, but I need you to help me get *Cowboy* and *Photraman* out there."

"Kepler is going? Where is 'there?'"

"Sulphur Springs, Indiana. This is finally a real mission for the *Science Squad,* Todd, not something dumb of Wendy's."

"Thank goodness. I would think she'd have higher priorities."

"Again, I'm not joking around here, and if she knew about any of this, she'd make it a priority. You have an opportunity you can't possibly imagine."

"Why? You're being very cryptic, so what is this about?"

"Something bigger than all of us. I can't talk about it here. *Tinman* and I need your unique expertise. The M2 jet is waiting to take us back to Aurora City."

"Sounds like a pretty awesome offer; sorry that my exuberance isn't showing."

"That's okay. I would be pretty creeped out if I was you and I showed up on your doorstep without warning."

"I hate to dwell on this, but speaking of Wendy—are you sure she doesn't know anything about this?"

She shook her head. "I don't know; it's extremely likely, but you never know with her. She comes around once in a while to talk to the *Tinman,* but I don't see much of her, we were never best buds. Usually, that's a good thing. This isn't the type of caper I would want her involved in, anyway. She learned a bit about playing poker from the world's greatest—Bonnie—and she doesn't often show her hand."

Todd looked at the floor. "I'm not promising anything, Bella, but I'll listen and go with you to Sulphur Springs, wherever the hell that is. I am sure it is quite opulent."

She shook her head. "Wrong, *Amp*. It's an old catsup factory that's been re-tooled for think-tank experimentation, to be under the radar. You can let your imagination fill in the rest."

"Fantastic. I can't wait."

Continued in:
Book Three
Science Squad Unite

www.ingramcontent.com/pod-product-compliance
Lightning Source LLC
Chambersburg PA
CBHW070642310726
48982CB00001B/385
9781734937206